Crystal stared at her diamond-studded Cartier. Four-fifteen. She was only a quarter of an hour late. And considering the fact that she had sailed out of the Beverly Wilshire ten minutes ago, it was a minor miracle. Across the room, a pair of eyes bore down on Crystal. She turned to find them staring right through her. *Lauren Conrad.* After so many months of nerve wracking competition and dread, the two women were finally face to face.

"*You* must be Crystal Cooper," Lauren began as she languidly extended an immaculately groomed hand. "You know, actually, you look far different on tape. Much . . . *younger*. . ."

The words hit Crystal with the force of a blockbuster. She had seen it coming, but somehow couldn't believe that even Lauren Conrad could be that vicious. Or that it could hurt so much. She felt the composure shatter inside her and the thin facade of self-confidence she had mustered crumble.

The score was *Conrad 1* round,*Cooper 0.* And the real match hadn't even begun. . . .

CATCH A RISING STAR!

ROBIN ST. THOMAS

FORTUNE'S SISTERS   (2616, $3.95)
It was Pia's destiny to be a Hollywood star. She had complete self-confidence, breathtaking beauty, and the help of her domineering mother. But her younger sister Jeanne began to steal the spotlight meant for Pia, diverting attention away from the ruthlessly ambitious star. When her mother Mathilde started to return the advances of dashing director Wes Guest, Pia's jealousy surfaced. Her passion for Guest and desire to be the brightest star in Hollywood pitted Pia against her own family—sister against sister, mother against daughter. Pia was determined to be the only survivor in the arenas of love and fame. But neither Mathilde nor Jeanne would surrender without a fight. . . .

LOVER'S MASQUERADE   (2886, $4.50)
New Orleans. A city of secrets, shrouded in mystery and magic. A city where dreams become obsessions and memories once again become reality. A city where even one trip, like a stop on Claudia Gage's book promotion tour, can lead to a perilous fall. For New Orleans is also the home of Armand Dantine, who knows the secrets that Claudia would conceal and the past she cannot remember. And he will stop at nothing to make her love him, and will not let her go again . . .

SENSATION   (3228, $4.95)
They'd dreamed of stardom, and their dreams came true. Now they had fame and the power that comes with it. In Hollywood, in New York, and around the world, the names of Aurora Styles, Rachel Allenby, and Pia Decameron commanded immediate attention—and lust and envy as well. They were stars, idols on pedestals. And there was always someone waiting in the wings to bring them crashing down . . .

Available wherever paperbacks are sold, or order direct from the Publisher. Send cover price plus 50¢ per copy for mailing and handling to Zebra Books, Dept. 3711, 475 Park Avenue South, New York, N.Y. 10016. Residents of New York and Tennessee must include sales tax. DO NOT SEND CASH. For a free Zebra/Pinnacle catalog please write to the above address.

Number One Sunset Blvd.

By Teddi Sanford & Mickie Silverstein

ZEBRA BOOKS
KENSINGTON PUBLISHING CORP.

To Don and Ray — for living through it with us.

The characters in this story are fictional, and any resemblance to persons living or dead is purely coincidental.

ZEBRA BOOKS

are published by

Kensington Publishing Corp.
475 Park Avenue South
New York, NY 10016

Second printing: February, 1992

Printed in the United States of America

One

Lauren Conrad drummed five blood-red fingernails restlessly on the monogrammed silver surface of her cigarette case.

The pilot reached over and double-checked her seat belt, lingering too long as he brushed against her black angora sweater and casually checked out her small, firm breasts.

"Everything okay, Captain?" she chided coolly.

"Couldn't be more perfect, Miss Conrad," he smiled as his downturned eyes locked on the controls and his right hand firmly grasped the air stick. A millisecond later, he was busy staring at the space directly to the right of his slightly trembling fingers, no doubt calculating the trajectory from the air stick to her exposed left knee.

Lauren frowned and edged closer to the cockpit wall. With only twenty minutes to make it to Kennedy, it was just her luck to get saddled with a helicopter pilot intent on playing explorer.

He painstakingly went through the pre-flight and ground clearance, and when there was no more reason to delay, he brought the chopper blades to a grinding, whirring crescendo. Slowly, the helicopter swayed to the left, then the right, then forward and up.

Below her window, Lauren stared out at the slowly shrinking island of Manhattan. In all directions now, tiny specks of humans headed home to their husbands or wives, children or parents. Endless rows of tail- and headlights pushed stubbornly forward, homeward, away.

To the north, the 59th Street Bridge was already jammed, and Second Avenue was turning into a disaster area. To the south, the BQE was now backed up for hours at a dead standstill.

It had been five years since her last Traffic Copter report, but the situation really hadn't changed. She could almost hear herself screaming over the drone of the blades, "Well, Art, the traffic picture down there is pretty usual for a Friday afternoon. The Holland Tunnel is backed up for five miles, and traffic is at a standstill. Motorists are urged to take the George Washington Bridge to New Jersey. East River Drive is clogged, and traffic on the Triborough Bridge is heavy, but moving . . ."

In those days, she had had to go through the ritual seatbelt check once a night. Twice a night when the pilot was a real tiger. And whenever she refused to play the game, the helicopter would just sort of slow down to a drifting hover, just like this one was doing. The pilot hadn't gone through 2500 hours of combat flying in Viet Nam for nothing.

Changing tactics, Lauren flashed on her best studio smile and stretched languorously. Just for good measure, she arched her back and leaned toward the pilot.

In the dim cockpit light she could see his lips break into a schoolboy grin. He turned to stare at her, unconsciously revving the blades. The airspeed was up five miles per hour.

Time to switch into Phase Two. "Why look at those cars down there," she laughed breathily. "They look just like little crawling insects. We must really be zooming."

"Naw," he answered, stroking the airstick proudly. "Lady, you ain't seen nothin' yet." The whine of the blades dropped down a register to a protesting groan. Manhattan disappeared behind them as the helicopter sped forward.

Lauren consulted the wafer-thin Piaget watch on her left wrist. At this rate, it would still be cutting it a bit tight.

She placed her hand lightly over his on the control. "Is this the thing that speeds it up?" she beamed. "Do you think I could try it?"

"Sure thing, Miss Conrad. But listen, be real gentle. And don't tell anyone back at the news desk that I let you fly 'er, okay?" He yanked his right arm off the airstick and made room for her. "Promise?"

"It's between you and me, Captain," she swore, pushing the control to within a hair's breadth of the red line. A second later, the helicopter lurched forward and shot off toward the airport.

Wearily, Lauren brought another perfumed Sobranie up to her lips. Fumbling on the vacant seat beside her for the little gold Tiffany lighter, she hesitated. Smoking wasn't getting her to LA any quicker. And if her lungs looked at all like the ashtray at her side, maybe it was time to lay off for a few minutes.

Six miles below the westbound jetliner endless waves of grain and millions of sturdy Iowa hogs were slowly slipping into night, until at last not even the grain silos were discernible from Lauren's porthole. The cocktail cart had come and gone, depositing a Courvoisier—compliments of Captain Gerhardt and the crew. One neon smile and six autographed cocktail napkins later, Lauren was once again alone.

Lauren Conrad detested waiting. And at the moment, she hated herself for letting it get the best of her, making her lose self-control.

Her reflection in the tiny window gave no indication of the turmoil which was pushing her toward the edge. In fact, the more she was driven, the less it seemed to surface.

Heading out to Hollywood for the most important weekend of her life, Lauren's features had never seemed more beautiful, nor more perfect. Framed in the immaculate mane of shoulder-length honey-blond hair, her amber eyes were irresistible. Eight years of broiling klieg lights and camera makeup had done nothing to spoil Lauren's flawless complexion. At thirty-two, the insidious crow's feet and brow furrows which every close-up highlights and magnifies were miraculously absent from her face.

Lauren's smooth alabaster skin not only was a cameraman's dream; it was also the dream material of a quarter of a million men who sat glued before their television sets every night drinking in her carefully restrained smile, and the fiery, almost mocking amber eyes set between her exaggerated cheekbones.

Beneath the perfectly modulated anchorwoman's voice, almost concealed behind the severe suits and the sparse jewelry, lay another woman entirely. Behind her impenetrable surface, the currents of emotion ran just close enough to Lauren's surface to be continually on the verge of exploding.

It was that underlying tension, stretched taut like a bowstring through every inch of her tall, rangy body which had gradually established Lauren Conrad as the reigning queen of prime time local news on Network Row in Manhattan. And it was controlling it which kept her there.

No one understood control better than Lauren Conrad. She conducted her every motion with the precision of a Beethoven symphony, fine-tuning each gesture beyond perfect pitch.

Sipping on a lightly iced Pernod, she gazed around the dimly lit cabin. Two rows ahead, a decidedly Parisian woman with tightly pursed lips nursed a plastic cup of Perrier, a look of annoyed disdain on her face.

Behind her was an item of slightly more interest. Lauren recognized the faces of the couple at once. Instinctively, her mind began zipping through the memory banks, looking for a name or names to fit the image. She had definitely seen the woman's face recently. Wasn't she the heiress who had just scandalized Beverly Hills—which is to say, as much as anything *possibly* could—by . . . by what?

No matter. All in good time, Lauren would have the Hollywood A group pouring out of her ears. Smiling to herself, she peeled off her gray boatneck sweater and prepared to get down to business.

Directly across from her, Sid Gold watched her movements intently. He liked what he saw. Like a greengrocer appraising a new shipment of plums, he gave her elegant, arching torso a proprietary nod. As she stretched over to grab her attaché case, his eyes became riveted to the sleek contour of her long, tan legs. She was even better in the flesh than he had expected.

For Sid Gold, life held remarkably few mysteries. He never once stopped to wonder what made a talent big, or even what made for talent. But ogling the leggy newscaster across the aisle, he grew uncharacteristically philosophical.

Why, he wondered, did God give such a voluptuous derrière to an *anchorwoman*? Firmly ensconced behind her studio desk, it was about as appreciated as a rare filet mignon in India.

His eyes passed over her one last time, giving her a

more professional appraisal. He stared at the Jourdan heels, the Italian glove leather attaché case. She was a class act in the grand tradition of a Katherine Hepburn, or a Leslie Stahl, but with a kicker. Beyond the impassive beauty mask, she was generating the kind of voltage, sheer animal magnetism, which couldn't be ignored.

Apparently, today would be Sid Gold's lucky day. He had just signed up a bouncy, street-tough Brooklyn comedienne who was a real comer. Now fate had led Lauren Conrad to his row.

" 'Scuse me," he called, making his way toward the aisle.

Instinctively, Lauren flashed her best smile and reached for her pen.

"Mind if I join you for a cocktail?" he urged, hovering expectantly.

Lauren took an instant to size up the intruder. He was singularly broad-shouldered, combing his hair over a bald spot. His magnificently tailored Brioni tweed suit barely revealed the substantial rubber tire which wobbled beneath his red Qiana shirt. One gold chain glittered upon a field of thick black chest hair. Below his cuffs, the motif was echoed in a hammered gold bracelet, a chunky Rolex watch, and no less than three rings. Just for effect, he also sported a pair of diamond-studded cuff links, and a Gucci belt buckle which must have weighed in at twenty ounces.

"Sid Gold," he announced, annoyed at the blank which continued to register in Lauren's eyes.

"Lauren Conrad," she icily replied, throwing out her right hand, while the left prepared to deliver a pre-autographed cocktail napkin. "WNRP. It's been a real pleasure. Would you like an extra autograph for your sister? How about your mother?"

Jaws gaping, Sid Gold stared from the once-again

10

engrossed anchorwoman to the napkin in his hand. A moment later, he threw himself back into the window seat and fumed. Lord how he hated uppity blonds. Particularly those of the stuffy WASP persuasion.

He hated that asshole mechanic of his whose slip with a wrench had led to grounding the Lear jet, and the indelible insult he had just received at the slender hands of little Miss WNRP.

But most of all, he hated the East Coast. All of it, from Long Island Sound to Chicago. Where no one knew the difference between a Silver Cloud and a Silver Streak.

And where insignificant little pieces of ass could dare to insult the likes of Sid Gold, Hollywood's most sought-after agent.

Tomorrow, Paramount, ABC and Red Rock would pay for the damages.

Two

The shrill ring of the night table phone pounded in Crystal Cooper's ears until she could no longer bear it.

Drowsily, she felt for the dial and then inched her fingers up toward the receiver. A moment later, it was cradled between her ear and the pillow.

"Crystal," he groaned. "Crystal, is that you?"

"Mmmhmmm," she nodded.

"Oh, yes," he exclaimed, "it is you. Ah jest had to talk to you . . . Are you . . . nekked?"

Her eyes shot open like snapped window shades. "*Who* is this?"

"Crystal," he breathed. "Ah jest wanted . . . you . . . to know . . . that . . ."

"Why don't y'all dry up?" she screamed into the receiver, slamming it down so hard that her hand hurt.

A moment later she reconsidered, and left the receiver dangling into space.

Blearily, she stared at the digital alarm clock until the orange lines of light slid into formation: 7:45. "Oh, shit," she mumbled, gazing at the gray morning sky. "That's all I need to wake up to."

At least she had answered it, and not Marcie, her precocious pre-adolescent daughter. Then again, Marcie probably would have known the score right off, and hung up at once.

Heavy-breathing perverts, and eleven-going-on-seventeen-year-old daughters. Somehow, this wasn't like the good old South she had always imagined.

The sound of gravel crunching in the driveway brought Crystal over to the bay windows. Drawing back the turquoise damask drapes, she caught a glimpse of her daughter's big-limbed form wrapped in a school jacket and plaid skirt, bouncing into the back seat of the Bentley. A stoop-shouldered, mahogany skinned Jeffers then shut the door and sauntered around to the front. A moment later, her husband's car disappeared around the corner, en route to drop Marcie off at the Lovett School.

For a moment, Crystal surveyed the overcast sky. Below it, the tops of the dogwoods were still thin and scraggly. Throughout the Atlanta suburb the stretches of manicured lawn and the hedges lining the road looked naked and withered this year.

Wearily, Crystal threw off her form-fitting green satin robe, and plodded toward the shower. Steam billowed into her blue tiled bathroom for what seemed like hours, but at last the fog lifted from her thoughts.

Maybe a trip to Phipps Plaza would cheer her up. She hadn't been to Saks in months now, and there was also that new designer boutique which she had never had time to explore, and . . .

Bad idea. Crystal knew that she would never be able to resist the allure of just the tiniest little Hermes scarf, or a pair of Gucci or Delman shoes. But by the end of the month, even a Louis Vuitton key case would be out of her price range.

Besides, shopping at a time like this would be demoralizing. Crystal Cooper was an anchor-woman—one who had just been fired and viciously discredited—but an anchorwoman nonetheless. If she was ever going to hold her head up in this town, she needed to break back into star status, and fast.

Abruptly, she threw off the shower and grappled with one hand for a towel. Still dripping wet, she draped the bath sheet around her and stepped back into the bedroom.

The dripping white gold curls encircling her finely chiselled features only highlighted the sense of delicacy which her tiny hands fostered. For a woman who stood five-foot-eight without heels, Crystal Cooper had remarkably little trouble looking dainty, almost frail. Particularly this morning, when the emerald eyes which were continually darting back and forth seemed to have lost their unlimited curiosity. Instead of bursting with vitality, they looked weary and scared, sunken into her otherwise flawless features.

Sadly, Crystal stared down at her full, high cleavage, then turned to examine her profile in the mirror hanging on the closet door. At thirty-five, her figure was still pin-up perfect. But was she still desirable?

At least on that score, she couldn't take her self-doubt too seriously. Remembering the endless stream of admiring stares, flirtations and propositions which had plagued her since first arriving in Atlanta, Crystal had to laugh. When the plumber stopped by to fix a leaky sink, he was always sure to arrive before she was out of bed. At work, the cameramen were forever focusing on her — much to her male cohort's displeasure. Whether she was reporting on the Mideast arms race or the grain embargo, the focal point of interest somehow or another always ended up being Crystal's bosom.

Maybe losing a bit of her sex appeal wouldn't be such a bad idea. Lately, in addition to the endless stream of heads turned downtown, the paperboy was now getting into the act. And he was only twelve.

Somehow, her orgone waves seemed to attract them from miles away, like guided missiles. Year after year, as the propositions were tossed at her downtown on Peachtree Street, at the Club—even in the Capitol—one man alone had consistently resisted her charms.

Her husband.

Through all those years of trying desperately to please him, Stephen Benjamin had denied her until she could no longer plead for his love. And now that she was at last free, Crystal's estranged husband of thirteen years was just waiting for her to make a slip. So much as one heavy breath in a man's ear would give Stephen all he needed to make a bid for custody of Marcie.

Crystal stared out the back window, past the postage stamp of a yard, toward the fringe of pine trees marking the property line. She was more than just washed up at WATL—she was finished in Atlanta, and she knew it. She was one uppity woman whom the Georgia statehouse would be only too glad to escort out of state.

She was miserable at the prospect of tearing Marcie away from Atlanta, and discouraged by the thought that after a dozen years here, she would have to pick up and establish roots all over again. At the moment, she was already walking a tightrope between nervous exhaustion and a total breakdown. The thought of leaving home suddenly seemed unbearable.

Then again, "home" in Atlanta would never be Sandy Springs, or Peachtree Street or Tenth Street. Home was the white columned, red brick Georgian mansion on West Paces Ferry Rd., NW. The one which spewed forth a chauffeur twice a day, to pick up and deliver Stephen Benjamin's only heir.

Across town, an impeccably suited Stephen would just be stepping behind the wheel of the Lincoln, headed for Five Points. In the kitchen, Mary would be polishing the silver while nursing a cup of tea, a Thursday morning tradition which had begun long before Stephen was born in that house.

Her thoughts wandered to the formal garden, where hollies and azalea lined the cobblestone paths in a maze, parting only to frame the peak of Kenneson Mountain in the far distance. There was the gazebo huddled in the rosewood grove, and the luxuriantly cool and secluded reading porch filled with the scent of roses, gardenias and the every-present honeysuckle.

If she let her thoughts go on a moment longer, Crystal knew that her depression would go beyond nostalgia — to regret. And that was the last thing in the world she needed.

As long as she could remember, her life had always been a roller coaster. But suddenly, it was all diving downhill, out of control. Like sitting ducks in a carnival firing range, the last supports in her life had suddenly been blasted away. First the house, then the husband, and now her career. Without a doubt, she was finished in Atlanta society. What would it be like, she wondered, when her old friends and acquaintances refused to answer her calls, stared right through her at the club? She might find out soon enough.

Just a week before, Crystal Cooper had been the belle of WATL, and co-anchor of its prime time news show. Now it had just been blown apart, and she right along with it. Whatever hopes she might have had of finding a network anchorwoman spot at thirty-five had vanished as well. Crystal surveyed the next few weeks ahead. With luck, they would only be a *little* nightmarish.

But in the meantime, she had her work cut out for her. There were cassettes to mail to her agent, several hundred fan letters to answer, and a million more pedestrian household chores to attend to.

During the last few weeks, between research, the daily broadcast, and weekend trips to Los Angeles—interviewing for the anchorwoman spot at the new "Satellite" Network—the structure of her life with Marcie had slowly eroded into chaos. Following the broadcast which had cost her her career, that chaos had erupted into a volcano.

But now it was time to get things together—and in a hurry. Crystal glanced into the full-length mirror, flashing her best camera smile. At least that hadn't vanished. If only she could get up the courage to set foot out the front door . . .

The shrill ring of her private line jolted her out of her reverie. She bit her lower lip, debating whether or not to answer it. Already, the other phone had been pulled off the hook. Any beautiful woman in the media is accustomed to an endless stream of obscene and crazy telephone calls. But ever since the broadcast, the tone of those calls had changed. Suddenly they were both terrifyingly threatening, and real.

Paralyzed, she stared at the phone as it rang again atop her night table, then leapt across the room to answer it.

"Crystal?" The voice on the other end sounded distant, and echoed faintly. "Hello. Is this the answering . . ."

"No. It's me, alright." She recognized the voice of Dale Stevens at once. For a split second, she found herself knocking on wood, praying that somehow he hadn't got wind of the scandal in Atlanta, or the fact that Crystal had been fired.

Fat chance, in an industry where everyone knows what you've had for breakfast before you can order it.

17

There was nothing to do but grit her teeth and wait for the bombshell. The anchoring slot in the Satellite Broadcasting Network's Hollywood headquarters which she had fought so hard for was about to slip through her fingers.

"Oh. You *are* there. Y'know, I've been through so many damned services and answering machines lately that I don't know if I can manage a real person."

"Well, try me." Crystal's laugh sounded too nervous and forced to her. Dale's preliminaries were driving her up the wall.

"I just came out of a marathon breakfast meeting at the Polo Lounge with the big guns. Rob Steinholtz, C.J. Redfield himself, plus the new network president, and a dozen dossiers an inch thick. Did you ever stop to realize that . . ."

Crystal's stomach was already beyond the knotting and despair stage. She could imagine Redfield, the network's stern CEO, and his reaction to her firing. Right now, all she wanted was to get it over with. One more clay pigeon couldn't hurt that much—even if it was her last chance at a big break. "Just spit it out, Dale Stevens," she chided, as laughingly as possible. "I know you didn't call me up this early just to chat. C'mon and get it over with." She braced herself for the impact.

There was a dead silence at the other end of the phone, then the sound of Dale sighing. "I'm sorry," he mumbled, "but Clay wants you to come out for one last session before making his decision."

Dale's voice crashed down around her like a tidal wave. But a moment after impact, she was still standing. Speechless, but still breathing.

"I know what you must be thinking," Dale continued. "But I promise it won't be like last time. The field has been substantially narrowed."

So far, the only thought registering in Crystal's brain was, *I'm alive.*

18

More than that, she was still in the running. When her new agent had entered Crystal Cooper into the running at SBN, it seemed about as likely as winning the Irish Sweepstakes. The first callback had narrowed it down to two dozen. Next round it was down to ten.

Suddenly, it was almost within Crystal's grasp. She felt as though she had reappeared at the far end of a black tunnel, and was almost blinded by the light. Now, Crystal thought there was a chance she could win and she was prepared to fight to the death for it.

She stared at her beautiful profile in the mirror across the room. Apparently, Crystal Cooper, formerly of WATL was not over the hill yet. "Okay, Dale," she laughed. "So far, so good. Now tell me what I'm up against."

"Lauren Conrad of WNRP. Hate to put you through the mill one last time. But if you could possibly manage to fly out on the Red Eye tomorrow night . . ."

"You know I have to. Let's see. I think that Eastern has a flight which . . ."

"Number 785. Leaving Atlanta 12:00 midnight. I figured that would give you time to tuck Marcie in . A limo will be waiting for you at the gate. Better figure on 1:00 am, Pacific Time. You'll be staying at the Beverly Wilshire. I took the liberty of having everything confirmed. So unless there are any last minute problems — which *none* of us need — I'll see you at RedRock around four pm. How's that?"

"Not as good as a call from Deena with final terms on the contract. But thanks, Dale. For everything. You're a sweetheart."

"True. All true," he chuckled. "But after last Friday's broadcast, you've turned into a bit of a celebrity in the biz. You should have heard Clay cheering when we watched it. The first thing he had me do was get the ball rolling, before your price went up. At any rate, I'll see you Saturday. And *stop worrying.*"

Crystal hung up the phone and immediately thought of Lauren Conrad.

She was tall—probably the same height as Crystal. Her thick mane of tawny hair would make Crystal's flaxen curls look like a kewpie doll's hairdo. Every inch of Lauren Conrad looked impeccably groomed, like a page out of Vogue.

Crystal remembered a broadcast she had caught in New York, and her heart sank. Lauren's delivery was so cool, so one hundred-plus percent professional and deliberated. Flawless class—and expensive.

Lauren Conrad would be a hard act to match, an impossible one to follow. Clearly, Crystal would have to get her trim, over-thirty ass in gear, and quickly. There were a million things to do before she left town, and no more secretary to do them for her. Call up Stephen's office and arrange to have Marcie picked up and brought to West Paces Ferry for the weekend. Rush to the drycleaner, her dressmaker, the bank. Find someone to talk to the plants and water the cat. Call up Dusty Fleming or Aida Grey and beg for a Saturday morning haircutting appointment.

The bills could wait another week. The laundry could be damned. There was the Standard Club Lunch. Cindy Greenspoon would have to understand. But the High Art Society would probably kill her for missing the Sunday opening—unless she had already been knocked off their roster.

Most of all, Crystal had to borrow some money, *fast*. If it was Lauren Conrad whom she was up against, the emergency clothing budget would have to be at least two thousand dollars. If Crystal couldn't outclass that bitch, she could certainly outshine her. Between her showgirl figure and platinum blonde curls, *no one* could out-dazzle Crystal Cooper once she turned on her charms.

First she dialed Marietta Rondell, to let her know the good news. Marietta was always good for a quick loan in a pinch. Two thousand dollars really wouldn't cover very much ground on Rodeo Drive. But stretched out thin, it might make it through Giorgio's, Right Bank, then maybe over to Gucci's downstairs.

With any luck, she would still have enough change left for the parking valets, with maybe a cup of coffee to spare.

Five minutes later, Crystal dialed her agent. On the other end, the familiar answering machine message closed with, " . . . Please leave your name, number and a brief message, and I'll get back to you soon. Wait until you hear the beep." *Beep.*

"Deena," Crystal beamed, "we're off and running. I'll check in with you as time permits. But right now as it stands, my itinerary is as follows: Leave tomorrow evening at . . . Oh *damn.*" Once again, the machine had cut her off mid-message.

Cradling the receiver against her neck, Crystal then dug through her wallet in search of a business card. Finally, she pulled out a stained and dog-eared scrap of pseudo-parchment, the name JOEL HANLIN engraved in gothic letters, his Malibu Beach phone number directly below.

"What in hell am I *doing?*" she groaned, starting to hang up as she dialed. Joel was 41, sexy and arrogant. Besides, for all she knew, he would turn out to be one more flaky California writer.

Actually, Crystal had interviewed him two weeks earlier. He had impressed her with his wit, his deep cerulean eyes, and the greatest ass she had eyed in a while. Something had sparked between them, and now she had the chance to find out more about him.

But what would people say if she got involved with him? What would her *mother* say?

Then again, how in hell could Rachael Coopersmith find out? Tucked away safe and sound in her St. Petersburg condo, the little Jewish mother who still sent Crystal twenty-five dollars every birthday would be three thousand miles from the scene of the crime . . . But somehow, she would manage to.

Rachael Coopersmith *always* found out.

But what if she did? Was there anything wrong with a separated woman getting together with an up-and-coming writer with a nice body? Considering that Crystal had had the pleasure of a husband who only got it up for bank holidays for thirteen blissful years, and a news director who mauled her in the dressing room for the past two, maybe a real man was in order for a . . .

"Hullo," came a groggy bass greeting on the other end of the line.

"*Joel,*" she exclaimed in her best honeyed drawl, "This is . . ."

"I know who it is, Crystal. My God, you sound great. What can I do to be of service . . . at nine-thirty in the morning?"

"It's just that . . . I'm coming out to LA this weekend, and I was wondering . . Do you know what time Giorgio's opens?"

Three

"Hey! Miss Conrad! You Lauren Conrad?" yelled a voice to her right.

Lauren turned and found herself eye-to-eye with a shaven head. Below it, a pair of thick black-rimmed sunglasses and a turquoise earring dripping from the man's right lobe were only slightly more startling. But if his coiffure was right out of *The King and I,* the rest of his costume was straight out of the Indy 500. Bulging out of his coverall as he was, Lauren could immediately discern two things at a glance. First of all, he was built like a gorilla.

Secondly, he was hung like one. And from the look of things, he liked her.

"Calm," Lauren said to herself as he advanced another step closer. "Just keep your cool. If he takes one more step, you can either scream or aim for his groin . . . it's an easy enough target."

She quickly surveyed the corner of the baggage carousel area. With any luck, there were enough passersby to discourage him from immediately doing anything they would both regret. But with one glance at his straining groin, it became pretty obvious that he wouldn't settle for just a cocktail napkin.

Buried under the Satellite Broadcasting Network dossiers in her attaché case were three particularly risqué photographs which she had brought along for publicity. A bit of flesh on an autographed 8 by 10 glossy seemed like a small sacrifice to make if it would buy her half a minute.

As she reached down for her case, fear like an electric current raced down her spine. Out of the corner of her eye, she saw him lunging forward, closing in on her. She clenched her hands, and prepared for the worst.

"I'm Thomas," he gently whispered. "CJ Redfield's personal mechanic." He grabbed her suitcase from the terrazzo-tiled floor and turned around to face her again. "He just found out that you were taking an earlier flight. Unfortunately, the chauffeur was over on the other side of town. Oh yeah, Mr. Stevens also apologized for not being able to make it here and give you a more formal welcome. . . ."

Lauren stared once more at his overfilled coverall, and suddenly felt a little shaky. *Just in case,* she thought, *better not take any chances.* Once again, his hand was thrust in her direction, taking hold of her attaché case.

"I'll get this one," she countered, dubiously.

"RedRock's a madhouse right now," he shrugged, leading Lauren to an impeccably spit-and-polished Rolls Royce Silver Cloud, painted a deep Cordovan. He held the door open for her, then deposited her single Louis Vuitton suitcase.

"You'll have to forgive my appearance, Miss," he mumbled, removing a ten-inch wrench from his front pocket. "Goddamn fan belt's kicking up again. Been squealing like a greased pig." As Lauren made her way into the back of the limousine, Thomas struggled out of his grease-soaked coverall to reveal a pristinely cleaned and pressed chauffeur's outfit.

"Now that's the ticket," he laughed, as the Rolls Royce purred out onto the access road.

As the touring car made its way out of the airport and onto the San Diego Freeway, Lauren studied its impeccable interior. Sinking back into the rear seat she luxuriated in the natural finish glove leather upholstery inhaling the clean aroma of saddle soap, reminiscent of a classy horse tack room rather than a garage.

The wood trim was a rich burled walnut, hand rubbed and lacquered. Even the most fastidious of Rolls connoisseurs could never fail to be moved by its time-worn patina, diffusing a warm golden light. In addition to the window and dashboard trim, there was also a mirrored walnut bar protruding back into the passenger compartment. Its contents — like everything else in the limousine — showed the owner's compatibility with the fruits of affluence. Beside the Armagnac 14 and the Pernod, the Islay Malt whiskey and the Dubonnet, vintage monogrammed silver shot glasses and shaker were set quietly off to the side.

In fact, the only concession to the 1980s was the small control panel to Lauren's left. She glanced from the labelled buttons to the miniature screens mounted in either corner of the Rolls' rear compartment. Not just a telephone intercom and a miniature set. From the back of his car, CJ Redfield could hook right in to RedRock's microwave receiver, and monitor all of the local cable broadcasts. The other screen was a computer readout — undoutedly from the Satellite Broadcasting Network's quarter-billion dollar installation.

Accustomed as she was to Rolls Royces and Bentleys — and to men who fashioned themselves as captains of industry or governmental giants — Lauren was impressed. Not just by the show of opulence, but by the way in which Clay Redfield showed restraint and subtlety in his decor. The man had class.

And in Hollywood, maintaining it was no mean achievement.

As the limousine swung onto Santa Monica Boulevard, Lauren's attention was suddenly jolted back into the world beyond the tinted glass windows of Redfield's coach. Off in the distance, she caught a glimpse of the triangular Century Towers which marked the edge of Beverly Hills.

All at once, her professionally trained senses were going full-tilt. Many times before, Lauren had driven through this oasis of the blessed, cruising down Rodeo Drive and staring at the rows of boutiques and salons. Once or twice, she had even ventured into Sassoon to match his skill against Jean-Louis David, the reigning genius at New York's Bendel's.

Now Lauren stared with fascination at the multi-million-dollar bungalows, the endless stream of designer fashions and vanity license plates, for the first time approaching it all from a new angle: if things went well, this was the world she would be plunged into.

No longer with the eyes of a condescending Easterner, but with the feeling of being a willing—and hungry—disciple, Lauren took in the passing Mercedes and rented mile-long Cadillacs, the designer-stamped derrières and the artfully draped silk scarves with a sudden feeling of elation.

Let the New Yorkers sneer and call it *nouveau riche* or decadent. Let them assail it for its "phoniness," its glitter and hype. To the residents of Beverly Hills and the industry known as Hollywood, the accusations were laughable. Sour grapes, from a part of the world which did not enjoy perfect climate and untold wealth. If there was one word to describe it, it was simply *opulence*.

Off to the right lay the famed 20th Century Fox studio lots. As Lauren stared out at a facade straight out of the Lower East Side in the depression, the driver quietly detoured around the sets. One turn, and Lauren found herself staring at a colonial New England village. A moment later, she was staring at a London cobblestone street straight out of Dr. Jekyll and Mr. Hyde.

To the world at large—the uninitiated who had not grown up in the midst of Sunset Strip and Rodeo Drive, mile-long red carpets and parking valets waiting in attendance at every door—there was something magical about seeing the mythical names in the flesh. Like arriving at Atlantic City, and seeing the Monopoly board spring to life.

Lauren lowered her window and breathed in her surroundings. The air was somehow as different as the desert sunshine and the royal palms with their leaves limply suspended atop towering trunks. Ultra-modern blended right in with English tudor style, brick colonial with Spanish.

Compared with even the striking colors-about-town in New York, the LA Basin looked like a Jackson Pollock canvas done in dayglo. Smiling, she recalled the landing at LAX, and the millions of electric blue and indigo splotches which eventually resolved themselves into backyard swimming pools in a thousand sizes and shapes.

It was almost as if she were in the midst of one great dream factory, spitting out colors and textures in every conceivable form. Quietly acknowledging the maroon Rolls with an effortless nod, an endless stream of Mercedes and Porsches, Jaguars and Maseratis—the ever-present Cadillacs and Rolls Royces—breezed continually by. But for once, it was not Lauren Conrad that they recognized. It was the initials "CJR" emblazoned on the license plate which made her stand out from the crowd.

Lauren leaned over to the window, and began to read their vanity plates as they approached. *YENTA*,

RENTED, DUNPHY— that had to be the L.A. newscaster's Rolls, CBS I; every message was like a private joke or a password. A name tag at a convention of the most affluent society in the nation.

On the right, up ahead, glittered the renowned, now faded Brown Derby restaurant. A moment later, as the car was looping around Rodeo Drive. Lauren struggled to focus her attention on the ambience of the enclave, the feeling of its streets, and shops and inhabitants.

Success seemed to ooze out of the million-dollar-an-acre earth. The women—to a one—were too damned good-looking. Gorgeous and impeccably groomed. They were tan, and slim, and decked out to kill. Whether they were draped in mink, jeans, or silk jacquard, designer labels sprouted from every conceivable place.

The men were no different. Fashion was everybody's sport here. With a gasp which bordered on exasperation, Lauren gazed at a tawny poodle tugging at the end of an elegantly slim rhinestoned leash. Around his neck was clasped a collar which she instantly recognized as Louis Vuitton.

The boutiques were not much less striking. Wedged in along with the Spanish Colonial and Art Deco store fronts was a potpourri of Streamline Modern facades, or occasional fantasy shapes by architects with names like Frank Lloyd Wright. Stretching out along Rodeo Drive, Hermes, Giorgio's, Gucci and dozens of other exclusive boutiques lined the sidewalk.

As the chauffeur continued heading north, the landscape quickly changed. North of Santa Monica Boulevard, there were cozy little mansions or humble million-dollar bungalows. Tucked away on pristine manicured lawns, they peeked out from immaculate rows of cypress trees and imported palms. Then, as the Rolls crossed Sunset Boulevard and swung up a climbing semi-circular drive. Lauren found herself face-to-face with a sprawling, glittering, cotton-candy pink dinosaur of a building.

In the midst of this splendiferous oasis of the blessed, only one commercial establishment would *dare* to dominate the stage.

The Rolls slowly glided to a halt, falling into place behind a fire engine-red Maserati, and a massive white Cadillac convertible with matching bleached blond driver, and a license plate which announced: SHICKSA.

They had just arrived at the Beverly Hills Hotel.

Under the Kelly green canopy, a steady parade of fashion plates were helped onto the runway carpet. One by one, they smiled and strutted for the papparazzi who gathered in clumps surrounding the hotel entry.

Each passing guest elicited a steady buzz of running commentary. Once or twice, a rumble of excitement rippled through the observers. Even Lauren watched raptly as a breathtaking redhead emerged from the driver's seat of a vintage Porsche to strut before the crowd. Every inch of her exuded star quality, from her outrageous Kenzo bloomers to the luxuriant flame-colored mane flowing down to her waist.

But despite the woman's perfect hourglass figure, and an array of fabrics and jewelry which would have stopped a cavalry charge, the crowd stared right through her. Lauren watched in amazement as one or two of the unofficial greeters shook their heads in seeming disgust. Was it possible that *that* luscious a package didn't make the grade here?

Out of the limousine across from CJ Redfield's car stepped a radiant and buxom blond who was immediately swarmed with admirers. The ranks of her entourage seemed to swell with arrivals from all directions. As the woman pressed through the entryway,

29

Lauren caught a glimpse of her familiar face. It was only a few years before that Lauren Conrad had interviewed Zsa Zsa Gabor. But seeing her in the flesh once more, the newscaster suddenly felt afraid of being snubbed by her in this setting.

The thrill of stalking Hollywood vanished from Lauren's senses. In its place, a million fears began to surface. Waiting for the valet to open her door and escort her to the runway, Lauren suddenly felt the Rolls Royce closing in on her. Outside, the eternal California sun seemed relentless.

It was more than a new town Lauren was entering: it was a new world. Everywhere she turned, there was another beautiful, leggy blond just like her. And the clothing and jewelry! All of a sudden, her gold Tiffany hoop earrings looked like grade B brass. Instead of feeling supremely subdued in her conservatively cut Adolfo jacket, she was struck with the feeling of being boring, pale, washed out.

"Get off it, Conrad," she mumbled to herself, trying to rally her flagging spirits. "You've got it all: a co-op on Central Park West, a chauffeur-driven limousine to escort you to the studio and wherever you're covering stories. You have a hundred thousand dollar a year salary, with a ten thousand dollar wardrobe budget. You've got all the men you could ever want, and all the perks."

Yes, Lauren sighed, as she watched a green jacket with brass buttons approach the car window. By New York standards, she had everything.

And by Hollywood standards, everything wasn't enough.

In the new game Lauren was entering, she would just be one more beautiful star in a sky already overcrowded with them. Suddenly, the mere act of entering the Beverly Hills Hotel was transformed into a major event. Not only did Lauren have no idea of the rules in this town, she was just about to arrive on the playing field — and her name wasn't even on the scorecard.

She sank back into the rich leather upholstery, grateful for the solace of its opulence. However much it might hurt to have the crowd give her the thumbs down — or even to ignore her — Lauren realized just how much greater the hurt would be to a Hollywood star to the manner bred. And scattered through the Santa Monica Mountains, staring down from the Hollywood Hills, there had to be a thousand fallen stars, remembering what it used to be like each time they attempted to make a grand entrance and encountered only blank, hostile stares.

A massive hand gently turned the door knob, then offered Lauren assistance out of the Rolls. With all of the graciousness of a footman in attendance to the Queen of England, he escorted her toward the runway.

Smitty, the broad-shouldered, big-handed and warm-hearted official greeter for the Beverly Hills, easily had the rugged, handsome looks to be another John Wayne. Instead of playing the lead in westerns, he had spent the past few decades drawing his disarming smile in this semi-circular drive. Welcoming the likes of Presidents Reagan, Roosevelt, Truman and Nixon, Jack, and the rest of the Kennedy clan, Henry Kissinger, the Duke and Duchess of Windsor, and virtually every other head of state whose path had ever crossed the Pacific Coast.

Of course, there were also the thousands of Hollywood figures he was constantly greeting. Ones with names like Liz Taylor and Cary Grant, Lana Turner, Barbra Streisand. He joked as easily with Johnny Carson as he had in the Golden Age of movies with Clark Gable. Sooner or later, he would welcome anyone who ever dreamed of being anyone in Hollywood.

Included in the last group was a steady stream of Ladies-Who-Lunch, tourists, young network execs, and electronic persuaders like Lauren Conrad. Each in turn, Smitty ushered them into the exclusive enclave of the Beverly Hills, offering to one and all the same democratic grin of welcome.

With a grateful smile, Lauren retrieved her attaché case from Smitty, and remembering her first opening night jitters so many years ago, she took a deep breath. A second later, she strode forward with long aggressive steps. With every stride, she gave them ample opportunity to absorb her long, sensuous legs and appreciate the sleek, panther-like body New Yorkers had come to worship.

Once again, the haunting, almost mocking smile graced her perfectly arched lips. Her eyes were on fire, challenging the least of them to dare a comment, or even a shrug in her direction. As all eyes pored over the unknown features, Lauren strode with an air of imperiousness straight through them and into the foyer, surrounded by dead silence.

A moment later, the crowd was once again staring and being stared at as the next arrivals sprinkled forth. Lauren Conrad—an unknown name attached to one more stunning package—had passed beyond, back into obscurity. Until she was discovered by Jody Jacobs, and mentioned in her *L.A. Times* column, it was as if the likes of Lauren Conrad had never really appeared.

But somehow, standing before the rose marble reception desk, Lauren felt as if she had just won a minor battle.

Now it was time to turn her attention to the real contest. The only thing standing between her and RedRock was the competition of a newscaster named Crystal Cooper.

Smiling, she remembered her recent interview with the black powderkeg who had just taken the heavyweight boxing crown. In a decidedly off-the-record moment, late at night in her apartment, he had laid out the hard cold facts for her. "Baby," he laughed, wrapping his massive arms around her, "the easiest way to win a fight is to fix it."

That was exactly what Lauren Conrad was about to do, reserving the crown for herself.

Four

CJ Redfield dropped the gear shift down into fifth gear, and the Jaguar roared as it hit a long straightaway on Sunset Blvd.

As a shimmering red sun cut through the dawn mist, his thoughts turned again to two blonds and vague misgivings.

For any other chief operating executive, making a choice between the rapid-fire blond bombshell approach of Crystal Cooper and the calibrated explosive quality of a Lauren Conrad would have been nerve wracking. But CJ Redfield had always carved his career in television by making the hard decision, one way: the right way.

In talent, as in all areas of life, he had no trouble distinguishing brass from gold. He had the natural affinity for quality which only years of upper class breeding can ever truly distill in an individual. As naturally as selecting silk over polyester, or his classic black XKE over a Datsun 280Z, CJ Redfield invariably chose the top candidate in every field.

And he knew it. He reasoned with an impassioned, connoisseur's subjectivity, then selected. The choice made, Redfield carried on, without looking back.

When it came to thoroughbred horses, his arrogance and singlemindedness had won him a minor fortune — and a reputation which far outweighed it. In Hollywood, it resulted in the creation of the Satellite Broadcasting Network.

Rarely did CJ Redfield make major mistakes. But even when he did, he never felt the need—or even the inclination—to review them.

But this morning, as the Jaguar tore through the early morning haze along the Blvd., something kept bringing him back to Now News.

In just three months, SBN would be on the air. By that time, the programming for its first eighteen months would be more or less set. Already, he was looking ahead to the 1984 Olympics, and beginning to put together the financing package necessary to outbid the major networks for coverage rights. In the meantime, there were still a handful of variety shows to fill, a few more pilots to develop or cancel. But most of all, there was the Hollywood-based prime time news team.

What was the problem floating in the back of his mind? It was a choice between Lauren Conrad and David Kirschener or Crystal Cooper and David Kirschener. Either way you went, how much was there really to lose?

An image of the senior anchorman whom he had just stolen from ABC, came into his mind: Kirschener, with his long, thin face, the slight affected British lilt in his voice, the perennial tweed jacket with the arm patches. Beside him, the strong lines of Lauren Conrad's face would be slightly softened, although the angularity of her shoulders would seem enhanced. Her long, slim neck always looked dynamite on the videos. And her amber eyes with their almost violet edge contrasted nicely with his soft brown eyes.

Conrad could outcool him word for word, while playing counterpoint with her aggressive, challenging smile.

On the other hand, Crystal Cooper might offset his reserve altogether. From the moment the red light came on, she was all there, bursting onto the scene like a skyrocket. In contrast to the faint trace of a Southern accent seeping through her Standard American delivery,

Crystal's pace was rapid-fire and concise from the time the red light cued her until the last story was over. She was emotional, personable. And for all of her imposing height—and the centerfold figure *no one* was likely to overlook—there was something so absolutely un-threatening about her she was impossible to dislike.

The bottom line was this: he could be sure of Lauren. He could also be sure of Crystal. But there was something about the pairing that was hanging him up, and preventing him from making the decision.

Thursday mornings, Redfield always appeared at RedRock headquarters around seven a.m. But no matter what time he arrived, Barbara, his fiercely loyal personal secretary, was always there ahead of him. On his desk was the customary breakfast of protein toast, a three-minute egg, and Columbian coffee with a hint of chicory.

This morning, one additional element would be present: the long-awaited contracts for David Kirschener. After months of haggling with Sid Gold, the agent had finally given in, and agreed to the quarter-of-a-million dollar price tag—plus a list of perks a mile long. Two months ago, Redfield would have jumped at the opportunity to sign the deal. Now, all of the sudden, he was hesitating. Something was missing.

"The spark," he mumbled unconsciously, downshifting as he left the Santa Monica Freeway, and headed on-to the San Diego Freeway. "He hasn't got the spark."

The spark.

Suddenly, like Archimedes in the bath tub, he had found it. Eureka! There was nothing more to say.

When Lauren Conrad and Crystal Cooper were selected, it was only after viewing upwards of five hundred contestants' videotapes. Redfield and his staff had looked at reporters, anchorwomen, models, actresses—anyone who could scrape up a minicam or an agent—submissions that ran the gamut from tapes of live broadcasts, to edited and overdubbed promotional extravaganzas.

But no matter how much glitter the act had, either the undefinable spark leapt out of the screen and grabbed you, or it didn't. If she had the spark, a fading model could be singled out in a supermarket promotion and make her way to the top of the news world. Without it, an anchor might still achieve a meteoric rise with the right agent. But the success would be shortlived, and the plunge which inevitably followed it was always in sight.

Conrad had spark. Cooper had it.

And David Kirschener, the man one of them would be selected to anchor with, had nothing. Just a two-hundred-and-fifty thousand dollar agreement, awaiting final signature.

That, and Hollywood's most powerful agent to make sure Redfield didn't back down.

It was no coincidence that David Kirschener's agent was Sid Gold. Only Sid could have dressed Kirschener in enough hype, glitter and bullshit to dazzle him to the top. Like the two major networks before them, the Satellite Network had just been screwed with Kirschener. For months now, Sid had kept his client just close enough to excite, just distant enough to be unapproachable.

Suddenly, the method in his madness became clear. A classic case of Rolling Thunder. Like an avalanche gathering speed, the hype surrounding Kirschener just kept getting pushed and pushed. Eventually, his reputation had picked up momentum from *its* momentum, and had just taken off. With all the roar it made, no one would ever have a chance to stop and examine the anchorman.

In one way, it was a good sign: Sid Gold never bothered to rob the two-bit operations. They would pay through the nose like everyone else in town, but they

37

would get what they paid for. First of all, because Sid was always looking for cheap markets for second-rate talent and girlfriends. Secondly, because there was no challenge in robbing them blind.

Like battle scars, the number of times a network or studio was ripped off by Gold became a mark of distinction. Now that RedRock had been screwed royally, they rated a distinction shared only at the top.

But unless something was done, and fast, it would end up costing a lot more than a quarter of a million—in ratings and audience share. Nothing was signed yet, so there was still a chance to break free. But somehow, it would have to come from Gold.

In Hollywood, the verbal agreement is inviolable. That unwritten law was established when the first dollar of mob money was funneled into the Coast. Establishing names and numbers in ink was dangerous business. Even notes on a deal could mean trouble with the feds. So early on, big media agreements were finalized with a gentleman's handshake. As long as everyone kept up their end of the bargain, there was no problem.

When they didn't people got hurt. If they were lucky.

These days, with the FCC monitoring every cent they could track down, agreements were always strictly codified in legalese. But the perks, bonuses and kickbacks were always carefully omitted. Later on, they took the form of tens of thousands of dollars of "general expenses."

But the handshake and the verbal okay remained the bulwark of the industry. That determined the sale, and the rest was just formality. Of course, CJ Redfield could always try not signing the contracts. Legally, Kirschener had nothing more than a breach of promise to stand on.

Nonetheless, Sid Gold would never damage his client's image by publicly displaying him as second-hand goods. Nor would he have Redfield's Rolls tommy-gunned or his legs broken. There was no need for that.

Instead, the agent would attack his jugular—and his groin. Overnight, he would arrange for half of the Satellite Network's talent to vanish or quit. Their contracts would disappear. The stubborn ones would be strong-armed into quitting. With fifteen hundred subscriber stations on line and probably twice that many pirate stations using RedRock material broadcast via satellite, Redfield could never back down on his big name talent commitments.

He slowed to a stop on Santa Monica Boulevard and ran his fingers through his thinning sandy hair. Now Redfield saw the battle lines being drawn. A quarter-of-a-million dollar contract would never be worth jeopardizing the RedRock lineup. The only way out was to outflank Sid Gold—no easy task.

For all of his public visibility, Gold was an enigmatic man. He was shrewd to an extreme, and his mind was like an IBM computer when it came to the machinations of a scam. By the time a Sid gold movie deal was completed, not only the studio owed him—so did the producer, the director, and the upper two-thirds of the cast. And all the time he was spreading around the favors, he was raking in the chips. At twenty per cent commission, there wasn't a grade B sci-fi movie worth less than half a mil to him.

Despite Sid's wheelings and dealings, his ethics were strong and rigid. They consisted entirely of getting the most for every one of his clients, then holding onto it come hell or high water. Redfield knew that it would be easier to wrest a T-bone steak from a great white shark's maw than to wrest an agent's commission out of Gold's grasp.

Greed was as much a part of his trade as sunglasses. But his ego was also tremendous, his image all-important. That made anything resembling bribing his way out of the Kirschener deal out of the question.

39

Then again, perhaps a series of sweetheart deals with a "bonus incentive" kicker wouldn't be.

As RedRock loomed into sight, CJ inspected himself briefly in the rearview mirror. His pale blue eyes smiled back at him with patient confidence. And although his craggy face was too weathered to be considered Hollywood handsome at fifty-five, his long aquiline nose and rough-hewn features were at once captivating and solidly aristocratic.

In an industry where appearances become realities, he had it made. His features never failed to look impressive and relaxed. One look at CJ Redfield was enough to convince you that he was totally in control, and always had been. The more the pressures mounted at his infant network, the more he smiled, determined to overcome them.

The truth of the matter was that he thrived on it. On the gut-wrenching pace of the industry, the smoothly polished facades disguising back-biting and desperate climbs to the top. Redfield was a man who liked life best at the edge, sailing into the wind and taunting anything which threatened to overturn him.

It was a dangerous game for a gentleman with a billion-dollar network hanging in the balance. But then again, one thing separated him from the crowd of thrill-seeking sportsmen, wild game hunters and duellists: gentlemen fought for honor.

CJ Redfield fought only to win.

So being conned, even when it was done with the flamboyance of an artist like Sid Gold, meant nothing short of a declaration of war. All at once, CJ's mind plunged into the battle of wits ahead. Like an infallible chess computer, his brain would follow every strand of logic, every conceivable maneuver. Sooner or later he would find the chink in Gold's armor, and lead the agent into an ambush.

With any luck, within a month or two, both men would sit and laugh about the incident over a drink at the Polo Lounge.

In the meantime. Redfield knew this maneuver would end up costing him as much as a million dollars—depending upon how much Gold's ego was tarnished.

At Sunset, Redfield dropped the shift down to third gear. As the roar of the engine faded into a well-modulated hum, a determined smile crept over his taut lips. This morning, he would outwit Sid Gold, fire Dave Kirschener before he was hired, and sign on either Crystal or Lauren.

As the massive red-glass complex loomed before him. CJ zipped past the astonished valet, and headed into the VIP parking garage. Two minutes later, he emerged from his private elevator, and passed through the massive fruitwood doors to his outer office.

As always, Barbara had arrived first. "Good morning," she greeted him in a crisp, emotionless voice. "I'll have breakfast brought in."

"Thank you," he called over his shoulder, tossing off his navy St. Laurent pin-stripe jacket and attacking the pile of papers awaiting his signature. A moment later, he was buzzing Barbara on the intercom. "Get a hold of Rob. Any way you have to. Tell him to meet me over in the D conference room at ten a.m. sharp. We'll want to go over the Cooper tapes, and the Conrad tapes, plus all of those damned promo throwaways. Tell Dale Stevens I want him in here as well. We need to make that decision fast, so we can have enough time to replace Kirschener."

"You mean David's *out?*" Barbara asked, a bit incredulously. She alone was privy to all of CJ's dealings. Television, real estate, and "other." She had sat through days of anxious negotiations with him, and realized how much of a coup getting the anchorman represented.

41

"How could Sid possibly let him back out at a time like
. . ."

"He didn't," laughed Redfield. "He was just fired. But
listen, Sid and Kirschener haven't heard the news yet. So
no one is to know. Not even Sloan or Moe Alexander. I'll
tell Rob and Dale myself this morning."

CJ clicked off, and began sifting through piles of
papers. A minute later he came up with two glossy
photographs.

In the short, powerful and impeccably manicured
fingers of his right hand, Lauren Conrad smiled provocatively over her left shoulder, her honey blond hair
setting off her strong, handsome features like a gilt
frame, then flowing away from her long, slim neck.

Beyond a doubt, Lauren Conrad was a grade A fox.
An independent woman — and certainly a talented
news reporter. She had the imperious style of a woman
who knew she was beautiful — and got as much
mileage as possible out of that fact.

And as CJ had seen on all too many occasions,
Hollywood was a rough place for beautiful women.
They flocked there from lesser places all over the
globe, drawn by the challenge of the crème de la
crème, using their looks and their talents and bank
rolls as an entree.

Within a year, they always discovered the inevitable: at the top of the industry scene, every woman
was breathtakingly beautiful, or incredibly talented,
or a celebrity.

In that crowd, Lauren Conrad would have to fight
just to keep from being buried in anonymity. Suddenly she would be just one more of the beautiful
people — and starting at the bottom of the heap, to
boot.

If CJ's guess was right, she would at least hold her
own against the local news anchors like Connie

Chung, and Christine Lund and Kelley Lang. And oddly enough, he was confident that she would give Barbara Walters a run for her money in the national ratings.

At the same time, she could be broadcasting into millions of televison sets at five p.m. every night, but still have trouble getting a seat at the Polo Lounge. To many people in Beverly Hills, her two-hundred-and-fifty thousand dollar salary was peanuts. Perhaps five decent soirees. Just under three minimally appointed Rolls Corniches.

But a quarter-of-a-million dollars annually was just enough to get a beautiful woman with a lust for the glamorous life in over her head in Los Angeles. Especially a woman like Lauren, who had all of the trappings of her family's wealth—despite the fact that she was unable to actually tap it.

In Redfield's left hand, Crystal Cooper smiled broadly. She was wearing a stunning red silk chiffon blouse, that enhanced her perfect breasts. But behind the gleam of her emerald eyes, there was a hint of desperation that gave the lie to all of her bubbly chatter and endless neon smiles.

From the start, Crystal had let SBN know just how much she wanted the job. And now Redfield realized how few choices she must have left. For a woman at the pinnacle of her career, the fall from grace in Atlanta must have hurt deeply. At thirty-five, she was a far cry from the peppy little wonder girls on the air. Sequestered, but hardly invisible, was her teenage daughter, and Crystal's rather unglamorous burden of parenthood.

If she was offered the spot at RedRock, she would certainly work her ass off. She obviously enjoyed the reputation of a newsmaker and a scrapper—an honest working anchorwoman, not just a reading actress.

But once already, her dedication and zeal had gone too far. Her investigation into in-fighting between the Atlanta local government and the FBI had hit them where it hurt. Public confidence had been eroded, and someone had to be scapegoated. Sure, Crystal had the scoop and the backup material and affidavits when she went on the air. But so far, being right had cost her her job and her reputation.

As much as Redfield admired guts, he had no interest in martyrs. Crystal would have to learn in a hurry what to leave alone, and when to kowtow.

Ruffling peacock's feathers was a forbidden sport in Hollywood. The media had their favorites, the public had its idols, and the ruling powers had their sweethearts to protect. All of them were sacred, untouchable.

If Crystal didn't learn that in a hurry, all of the irresistible charm of her hourglass figure and golden Shirley Temple curls wouldn't save her. In Vegas, she might be killed. In Chicago, merely injured.

But in Hollywood, she would be shunned. Overnight, she would discover that her society friends had never heard of her, her station had no office for her. Anyone in the industry would just stare right through her. And as for jobs, from that day on, she could forget about *any* of the networks. As much as they warred with one another, no one would tolerate a traitor. The same went for their affiliate stations, and even their advertisers.

With any luck, there would always be some mom-and-pop station out of Boise looking for a newscaster. And every time she walked into the studio, every little crack in the cement block walls would remind her that she was a has-been.

As a rule, people ousted from the top soon discover that they can't survive without the recognition. When newsanchors like Shel Blanford were removed, their names disappeared from the industry white lists. Which meant that they were not "approved for hiring." In short, Blanford couldn't even find a job taking tickets in front of a Hollywood theater.

In the end, he took the coward's way out: he cracked. From time to time, his widow was spotted wandering in and out of Rodeo Drive boutiques like a lost sheep.

Hollywood could break your heart. But with luck, it was something Lauren or Crystal would never have to learn.

Now Redfield looked from Crystal to Lauren, then back again. For two blonds over thirty and over five foot seven, they had remarkably little in common. Their tastes, temperaments, even their reporting styles seemed 180 degrees apart. But they both had the spark, and in a funny way, seemed almost complementary. If only he could dress one of them in drag, his problem would be solved, and kissing Kirschener goodbye would be that much simpler.

The unfortunate thing was that the Satellite Network needed a man and a woman for their news team. It was the formula pioneered with the Eyewitness ABC teams, and now it was the industry standard. Already, in choosing women in their mid-thirties, Redfield was gambling with the ratings.

Still, gazing at the women he held in his fingers, CJ Redfield realized that he really didn't want Lauren Conrad _or_ Crystal Cooper.

He wanted them both.

With a start, he read the time on the clock. Any moment now, and the rest of the staff would be flooding the gates of RedRock. His call was already late.

At once Redfield's mood grew dark again, as he braced himself one more time for the Thursday morning ritual. His fingers carefully pushed the familiar tone-pattern, and drummed anxiously on the elaborately-carved mahogany table-top as he waited.

"Hullo," came a gruff greeting with an unmistakable Down East intonation.

"Mel? It's me."

"CJ! For a moment I thought . . ."

"Forgive me, Mel. But everyone is about to come busting in on me. Can I speak with her?"

"Sure. Just hold on here a moment."

After a moment of confused shrieks and a muffled scream, Mel's voice came back on the line. "Okay, Clay. Go ahead."

"Kikki?" He paused for a few seconds, hoping for a response, or at least a sign of recognition. "Darling, do you know who this is? . . . Kikki, I . . ."

Five

Crystal closed her eyes and leaned back against the thickly padded backrest of her booth seat.

Scattered throughout the club, half a dozen couples and a few lone stragglers quietly nursed brandy or Irish coffee as they listened to the melody flowing out of the corner of the room.

The pianist's voice was subdued, almost melancholy as she wrapped up the set with Jacques Brel's *"Ne Me Quittez Pas."* The stale nightclub air mixed with a gentle sea breeze flowing in from the beach beyond the cafe's terrace. Slowly, a chill washed over Crystal, and the pale skin on her arms began to shiver.

Instinctively, she leaned over against the sheltering warmth of Joel Hanlin's chest.

Somewhere, sounding like it was a thousand miles away, Joel's voice was busily engaged in discussing his favorite topic of conversation: himself. "Then,"—he paused for a moment, twirling the Remy Martin around in its brandy snifter before sipping it once again—"when the show was entering its last month on Broadway, I suddenly decided to say *'yes'* for a change. Since Universal had underwritten the New York run of the play anyway, it made sense to come out here and do the screenplay."

"You mean: you came out here six years ago for two months, and just never left?"

Joel threw a comforting arm around her shoulder. "Isn't that how *everyone* goes Hollywood? There you are, a big fish in a smaller pond. One day, the offers start to float in. For five years, you've been making $15,000 a year cranking out the plays and reviews. Then all of a sudden, you hit off-off Broadway, and Hollywood picks up interest. Next thing you know, some cat in a Rolls is flying you out to have dinner at Chasen's. You laugh, and call it absurd. But you go anyway. Next, there's a deal. *Nothing* by Hollywood standards: just a forty page screen treatment. And in two weeks and twenty-five breakfasts and lunches, you've just made so much money it's obscene.

"That's when you decide to hang around long enough to really make up your mind about . . ."

Yes, thought Crystal, *that's when you really have to make up your mind*. It was two-thirty in the morning, and she had spent half of the night on a long tiring flight.

Once again, she had found herself staring at the bleak lightscape of Los Angeles International Airport in the wee hours of the morning. During the past few months, as the interviews at RedRock grew more frequent, the anodized aluminum control tower and the suspended restaurant—like a long-legged spider's belly—had become familiar landmarks to Crystal, a sort of second home.

Downstairs, the RedRock chauffeur would be waiting and two freeways later, she would be bearing down on Wilshire Boulevard, headed for the Beverly Wilshire Hotel. With any luck, that would leave her with about five hours to sleep before the Rodeo Drive Campaign started with a nine o'clock wake-up call.

"God, I hate being catapulted into early morning shopping," she had sighed to herself, as she headed out of the arrival terminal.

"Welcome!" shouted a voice which immediately muffled itself with a firmly and passionately planted kiss on her lips. Throwing his arms around her, Joel Hanlin swept her high into the air, pressing her tight against

him like a long lost love. "You look even more delectable than in Atlanta," he had laughed, keeping his right arm wrapped around her tiny waist.

"You must be kidding," Crystal had replied, freeing her ribcage from Joel's palm with a friendly but insistent hand. "You mean I looked even more washed out than *this?* But never mind that. What, if I may be so bold, brings you here at one in the morning? Let alone in such high style."

"Oh, you mean the tux? I'm afraid that wasn't for you, per se. There was a screening party for a friend's movie. A wild pack of dogs on a deserted island, running amok. I tell you, California has changed Peter Randall. Back in New York, he was what we used to call an *artiste.* And $150,000 for the screenplay! My God. When I stop to think about . . . Oh, shit, you just got off of the plane and here I am raving about my *boring* night. At any rate, the joint was loaded with the regular bullshit Hollywood crowd. I thought to myself, Crystal must feel so lonely arriving in this decidedly hostile town in the dead of night . . ."

"So you just came on down to meet me? Now *that* is what I call a perfect gentleman." She had leaned over and planted another kiss on his lips.

"Well, shall we?" Joel had inquired, offering her an escorting arm as he slung her travelling bag over his shoulder. She had hesitated, taking a moment to look him over once again. Back in Atlanta, she had never really permitted herself to examine Joel. He was somehow taller and far more muscular than she had remembered. Beneath the perfectly-tailored tuxedo, his angular body looked lean and athletic. Amused as she was with the consciously provocative posture the writer was affecting, she had to admit that it was having its effect on her, as well.

"So," she had smiled, accepting his arm and deciding to cut off their rendezvous as soon as possible, "why don't we head somewhere in the airport for a nightcap? I'd love to sit and chat with you, but tomorrow morning I'll be up and running at the stroke of dawn—practically."

"You mean before ten a.m.?"

"Precisely, so let's make this a quick one. I feel so terrible after you came all this way just to see me, but . . ."

"Oh, don't worry, Crystal," Joel had answered at once, leading her to his awaiting MG convertible.

Don't worry, indeed, Crystal laughed, draining the last of her brandy. Two hours later, the sky out above the Pacific was already transformed from black to a hazy electric blue.

She brought her ear closer to Joel's heart, pressing against his thickly forested chest. Although she had been going for almost twenty-four hours straight, Crystal's senses were still alert and her limbs were feeling wonderfully tired and relaxed.

To her utter surprise, she felt totally at home with this stranger in the middle of the night. Ever since she had met Stephen, Crystal had been constantly thrown in with attractive, interesting men. Unfortunately, the moment they got alone with her—or out of eyeshot of her husband—they would inevitably fixate on one topic: Crystal's voluptuous body.

Sipping brandy with Joel in the pre-dawn hours, Crystal was grateful for his conversation. It had been so long since she could just lean back and relax with a man, have him talk with her as if she were a human being, not a sex object.

More than that, Joel could stare into her eyes without immediately dropping his sights to encompass the fullness of her breasts. He could place his hand on hers without treating it as required foreplay. And when she opened her mouth, he listened, as if her words somehow mattered.

It had been many months since she had allowed herself to open up to loneliness. But suddenly, she was overwhelmed by the dreadful feeling of *being alone*. For some things, a nagging mother on the phone and a loving but testy daughter were useless.

But as an anchorwoman for Atlanta's top local news program, what was Crystal supposed to do? Head out to singles bars after her broadcasts were over? Tell Marcie to eat at her father's house, or tell her that she needed to make her own dinner, so Mother could go out and get laid? Maybe she was supposed to be discreet, and take up skiing so she could head off to Vail for the weekend and hang around in the warming hut in designer après-ski clothing. Or was it après-screw?

Crystal didn't know, but she was tired of holding herself in check, denying how she missed the aroma of a man filling her nostrils, the warmth of his body against hers.

Tomorrow morning, the onslaught would begin. Deep down in her heart, Crystal had never once imagined that she could ever win at RedRock. With painful disaster behind her, and more of the same staring her in the face in the days ahead, more than anything else, she needed reassurance now.

". . . so, quite frankly, Crystal," Joel concluded, "I'm not really sure what I think about the offer. It would be a great opportunity . . . clearing out my head for a year, teaching in London. But maybe I should stick it out for one more year here, and see how far I can develop the screenplay before heading out. What do you think?"

She looked at him with puzzlement, from the halo of fine brown curls on his forehead to the earnest light blue eyes, to his thick, sensuous lips.

"I think I want to make love with you," she blurted out.

Affecting perfect calm, Joel pulled her lips to his and murmured, "I'd like that too. Been thinking about it ever since you called. Wondering what you would look like naked . . ."

"Well, you can't find out by sitting here talking," Crystal laughed, while inside she was suddenly flooded with astonishment at her own courage. "Will you take me to that little beach cottage of yours?"

"I don't know, Crystal. It's really sort of a mess. Besides, there's Malibu Beach houses, and Malibu shacks. I'm afraid that mine falls into the latter category."

"All the better," she smiled, allowing her hand to press his tensed thigh.

As they drove along in silence, Crystal breathed in the Pacific at dawn, and the tiny cottages and ocean bluff houses of Venice Beach, still veiled in shade. With careful movements, she allowed her hands to wander over Joel's groin, caressing his stomach, his arms and thighs.

Her fingers moved carefully, like a blind woman's. After so many months, the sensation of a man's body was overpowering. The most basic solace in life had been denied to her for so long.

But tonight, three thousand miles from home, Crystal had broken through. She knew herself well enough to know that tomorrow morning, she would be filled with guilt. Making love on the first date? To a man she hardly knew. Once again, she remembered the ugly, cruel raised eyebrows with which Stephen Benjamin had met her shy attempts to seduce him.

But tonight, she had matters firmly in hand. Beneath her probing fingers, Joel's cock swelled and slowly grew hard. She coaxed him, teased him, pressed hard against the stiffening shaft, then abruptly stopped — only to let her fingers trace the outline of his penis against his straining pants.

However many women Joel had made love to before, Crystal hoped that tonight every inch of him was hers. After so many years of emptiness, the appreciation which Joel's touch expressed was echoing throughout her every nerve ending. She knew that he would be slow, lingering, greedy in his lovemaking.

Already, the old familiar thrill was making her breath come in short gasps. The warmth was pouring down from her belly, until the moist lips of her vagina were trembling for the pleasure Joel would give her.

Tonight, she thought, *the old life dies.* It was high time to cremate all of those wasted years, then bury the ashes. Then her thoughts turned to the desire overtaking her.

By the time they had passed through Palisades Beach Road and pulled to a halt before an undistinguished-looking cottage in the midst of a row stretching out for miles in either direction, Crystal was so anxious for Joel that she was ready to burst.

She gazed at his profile in the pink early morning light and saw the outline of his cock straining at the fabric midway down his thigh. Coolly, Joel wrestled with the lock and immediately threw down her Gucci bag and his tuxedo jacket.

Turning back to her, he stood still for a moment, drinking in the curves of her body. Then, he moved forward, and pressing up against her, his tongue began exploring the tips of her lips, then gradually inside her teeth while his fingers sought her breasts.

Then his mouth seemed to be all over her at once, exploring her neck and shoulders, breathing softly into her ears, then gently encircling her tensed nipples.

Leading Crystal to the deck, Joel gently spread out a blanket on the redwood planks. With aching slowness, he carefully pulled the white silk blouse down along her shoulders, pressing tight against her as he unbuttoned it. Now with the same deliberate attention, his right hand moved between her trembling thighs while he cradled her ass with the other hand. She felt the moisture flowing between her legs, and the hypnotic movements which

53

began with her swaying hips and gyrating pelvis.

The more Crystal wanted Joel, the more he was determined to give her. His mouth trailed greedily over the mounds of her breasts, then traced a lazy, undulating path along her ribcage.

With a shudder, Crystal took his head in her hands and guided his tongue toward her aching clitoris. Softly, then with increasing pressure, his mouth pressed against her until she thought she would scream.

As her body began contracting with uncontrollable fury, his tongue swept faster and faster over her. Greedily, Crystal brought Joel's face up to her own. Then she reached for his cock. Long accustomed to the slim, semi-erect shaft of her husband, she was startled to feel the massive tip of his penis filling her hand.

Shifting his weight, Joel cupped Crystal's ass as he allowed her to bring him into her, spreading her lips and arching her back. Joel gently pushed forward, then hesitated, then thrust a little harder.

Now Crystal's hands clasped his buttocks frantically as she sought to open up more and pull him further into her. With a gentle rocking motion he pressed harder, until at last she could feel him fully within her.

Pelvis racing furiously now, his lips sought out hers in a frenzy. With a gasp, Crystal gave in to the contractions which were bubbling from deep within her. She dug her fingernails into the powerful shoulders and pulled against him with all of her might, coming in a shattering series of spasms, crying out, "my God, Joel, my God—it's fantastic. I've waited for you so long!"

A moment later, she felt Joel's body give way to a shudder, then slowly dissolve into hers.

Six

Sloan Schwartz awoke with a gasp.

As her eyes shot open and blearily assessed the gold embroidered fringe dangling above her, she felt something pressing down against her diaphragm, forcing the air out of her lungs.

The table. She was under the dining room table. Pinned down by a massive forearm. Like a streamroller, it had slowly pressed across the rise of her ribcage, but hit a roadblock at her tiny, child-like breasts.

"Jeez," she muttered, slowly inching out from under the stubborn appendage. She rolled out onto the Oriental rug and staggered onto her feet. The room was swaying, and the blood rushing to her temples pounded like a piledriver.

"That's the last time," she swore out loud.

Every inch of her petite little boyish body ached this morning. She checked out the parts she could see: the skinny bow-legs with the knobby knees, the flat, small-hipped waist, the conical breasts with their large, violet nipples. At least there was no visible damage.

"I gotta give up champagne," she whimpered.

It was either that, or coke. The combination was killing her.

That together with the animal snoring under the table, now curled around one of its claw feet. Blurrily she examined the mass of golden locks and rippling muscles, broken only by his upraised lily-white bottom. "My God," she exclaimed, "he even *looks* like Tarzan."

There were bits and pieces of clothing strewn all over the place. Off in the corner, there were three empty bottles. The chilling stand had been kicked over at some point, drenching the Oriental, the wood parquet floor and God knew what else. In the midst of the carnage, she spotted a familiar sheer blue peignoir.

As Sloan donned the garment and struggled over to the intercom, thoughts slowly began filtering down into her brain. This afternoon, CJ would be screening those two blonds. While her vote as RedRock's vice president for programming wasn't required, Rob Steinholtz's was. There would be nothing worse than to get in someone she and Rob couldn't trust.

Step one was tracking down Rob. And the way he hopped around made George Washington look like a recluse. She could just imagine little signs bearing the words "Jackrabbit Rob Slept Here" plastered all over Hollywood. He hit hardest on the starry-eyed cheerleader types. Maybe all she needed to do was run down to the lot where they were casting "Gidget Goes to Moscow" and poke underneath the cattlecall bench with a broomstick. The bastard was such a lech he would probably even get off on that. She laughed in a low, throaty chuckle.

Beneath the Queen Anne table, Tarzan groaned and showed signs of life. Reaching back behind the couch, she fumbled with the intercom until she located the switch. "Marge?" she whimpered hoarsely. "Marge?" No answer from the outer office. She turned up the volume and tried the pool area.

Tarzan slowly went from moaning to stirring. In a panic, Sloan hit the PA switch and tried again. She hugged her arms across her tiny chest, and examined her matted waist-length black hair as she waited, hearing her voice echo from a dozen different corners of the mansion.

"Sloan?" Marge's voice had an angry, dead-even tone this morning.

"Marge, I've been calling and calling. I *need* you. Where in hell have you been?"

"Confirming your weekend schedule . . . That is, now that Friday night has finally come to a climax."

Sloan decided to ignore the barb. "Did you settle the date with Sid Gold?"

"Polo Lounge. Five o'clock cocktails. Anything else, Ms. Schwartz?"

"Cut the shit, darling. Puh-lease. It's the last thing in the world I need right now . . ."

"What's goin' on?" bellowed a voice beneath the table.

In a flash, Sloan turned down the PA, and continued in a whisper. "My God. He's awake. Marge, you gotta get him outta here. *Please*. Where in hell did you find this animal?"

"*Find* him? You had him delivered!"

"*What?*"

"Don't you remember?"

With a shudder, Sloan remembered the lines which seemed to have permanently numbed her nose and palate. Vaguely, she could picture his outline in the hallway. He was wearing nothing by a denim overall, and carrying a folding rule and some Florentine tile. "Oh *God*," she moaned, "he never even finished the hearth."

"Finished? I don't think he even got the measurements. Last *I* knew, he was following you into the game room as you jerked along the measuring stick and giggled like a teenager."

"Well listen. I was gonna have a little soiree tonight for our anchor candidates. A sort of sounding out. Nothing special. Catered Middle Eastern, maybe a Greek band."

"How about jasmine then? And some wild poppy arrangements?"

"Marge, darling, you always have just the right touch."

57

"How would *you* remember?"

"Not now, honey, I'll make it up to you. But listen. Have this stud finish the tile job, then put him out to pasture."

"You don't want him on the 'A' list, I take it?"

"No way. He's hung like a horse, and his stamina is great. An hour and twenty-three minutes to the Big O. I timed him. But he's got the sensitivity of a bronco. I've got saddle sores all the way down to my knees. When's the last time you saw someone bang away 'til you were blue in the face and *still* not get it right?"

"Only in *your* gameroom, sweetheart."

"*Please,* Marge," There was an imperious tone in her voice now. "I just can't handle it right now. A *stone mason*, that's all I needed. Listen, don't let him pull any of the union overtime bullshit. If he gets weird, just have George show him the door. I'm heading into the dressing room, to barricade it before he gets aroused again. Tell Ginna to bring up some OJ, will you?"

"Anything else?" asked the disembodied voice.

"Yeah. Have Sarah send out the carpet, *tout suite.*"

Lauren gazed out restlessly past the shimmering blue water, absent-mindedly scanning the scattered bronzed bodies.

Across the pool, a petite brunette tossed her newly permed curls defiantly back from her face, arching her back and waiting for the moment when all eyes would be focused on her. A second later she dove over the water with flawless form.

Lauren took in the performance with a bemused smile. At that precise moment, as the white woven triangle of the diver's Brazilian bikini bottom swung up over the scanty top, a good ninety-nine per cent of the girl's charms were placed on public display—including five hammered gold bracelets, a brilliant cut diamond large enough to use as a mirror, and a string of pearls provocatively encircling her exquisitely rounded hips.

Spread-eagled upon their chaise longues or strolling with exaggerated languor, a dozen other women were warming up to their bids for attention. Stripped of the double chins and sagging stomachs of middle age, uniformly bronzed and polished, shaped and trimmed, it seemed impossible to guess their ages. Was the skinny bleached blond fawning under the umbrella to Lauren's right twenty-seven or forty-five?

Nowhere in her life had Lauren ever seen such aggressive youthfulness. It was easy enough to make fun of these women. To make jibes about their fanny lifts and eyelid tucks, their silicon injections and cellulite treatments. But like E.S.T., their five-hundred dollar Elizabeth Arden sessions and their exercise classes, their plastic surgeons and their designer fashions *worked*.

To a woman hoping to break in from the sidelines, it was so terrifying that it almost paralyzed. The Western look might come and go, the hems could rise and fall and collars could grow thin and then fat again a hundred times. But at the Beverly Hills, youth and success would always be a way of life.

Walter Cronkite could grow gray and Dan Rather could have bags under his eyes. But with the first hint of middle age settling, an anchorwoman had had it. Like the women scattered all around her, Lauren knew only too well what the tightrope was all about.

When you're a born winner, there's nowhere else to go but higher. Each new goal brings the thrill of the hunt to your nostrils, and excitement courses through your veins as you execute every act with the deliberation of a war campaign. For as long as she could remember now, Lauren had been caught up in that cycle, feeling the victory within her grasp, then just squeezed as hard as she could. Eugene, Oregon, Boston and New York—one by one she had stalked them day and night until she won them over.

59

With men it was no different. The more elusive they were, the more indifferent at first, the more she burned for them. *Vidi, vici, veni.* She saw, she conquered, she came. And ten minutes later, lying in the arms of her latest conquest, the old feeling of emptiness would begin to creep back.

A hundred times before, Lauren asked herself why she had ever bothered to try for the top slot at RedRock. Now, staring out at one perfect face after another, Lauren, for a different reason, asked herself what she was doing in Hollywood. Was this why *she* had flown across the country one more time, come back for Redfield's cattle call again and again.

Suddenly, the question was *"Why me?"* She had striking features and a sleek, dazzling figure. A sharp mind and a solid track record. But what of it? There were probably a dozen women scattered around the pool right now who could meet half of her qualifications. And what they didn't have, they could probably buy.

But what was the elusive quality that RedRock was after? For weeks now that mystery had plagued Lauren. And coming down to the wire, she still had no clear answer. She had planned this campaign as she always did — as precisely as a full armed forces invasion. Facts, figures, profiles and projections.

Wearily, she raised her lounge chair into a sitting position, pushed the shimmering sunglass frames up into the golden knot of hair on her head, and picked up the folder at her side.

REDFIELD, CLAYTON JENNINGS. *Ht.* 6'4. *Wt.* 190 lbs. Substantial holdings in real estate, money market and diversified tax-exempt bonds, estimated in excess of 700 million dollars, according to . . . Invalid wife . . . One daughter, Kiki, dead . . . apparent suicide . . . Interest include horse racing, sailing . . . Numerous allegations ranging from stock manipulation to fraud . . . federal probes never mounted sufficient evidence to hand down an

indictment . . . Legendary for rigid moral conduct
. . . public stances anti-abortion, anti- . . .
SLOAN SCHWART . . . DALE STEVENS . . .
MOE ALEXANDER . . .

Lauren leafed through the bios and photographs,
then tossed them all aside. For months she had been
adding to them, following the trade press, rifling the
WNRP data banks. And up until this morning,
nothing had clicked. Redfield remained distant and
beyond approach. Moe Alexander was too dangerous
and capricious. Whatever Sloan Schwartz was in the
market for, Lauren wasn't sure she wanted to sell.

That left Dale Stevens, who as News Director really
had no influence over the highest-level decisions. He
looked like he could use more love and money. But he
was far too forthright to go in for the casting couch
scene.

All in all, Lauren's overtures were striking out
everywhere she turned. She had failed to find a way to
leverage her bid for the co-anchoring spot. As the
hour for the RedRock meeting grew closer, she was
beginning to have a sinking feeling in her stomach.
She was no closer to the job than she had been two
weeks before. And while she was busy being ignored in
her stunning skin-tight black maillot beside the pool
of the Beverly Hills, Crystal Cooper was undoutedly
ingratiating her sickly sweet charms on anyone who
noticed them—as if anyone could *avoid* it, the way she
decked herself out like a Christmas tree.

Angrily, Lauren snapped off her sunglasses and,
throwing caution and her Dusty Fleming hairstyle to
the winds, dove into the lukewarm pool with one brisk
motion. Hands knifing through the water, she swam
lap after lap, until the last bit of tension had been
released, and the only sensation left was the exhilara-
tion of her own perfect form.

Five minutes later, she was toweling herself dry

under the late morning sun. *"Lauren Conrad,"* called an amplified voice from the wet bar, "telephone call for Lauren Conrad."

As a dozen onlookers turned to her at last, poring over her features with vague nods of recognition, Lauren threw on a light turquoise *crêpe de chine* jacket and strode into the shade.

"Lauren?" asked the unfamiliar voice on the other end.

"Speaking."

"This is Rob Steinholtz. Following yesterday afternoon's board meeting, I have been elected as President of the Satellite Broadcasting Network. Under the circumstances, I thought that perhaps we might get together before this afternoon's meetings. Perhaps at your bungalow?"

"Why certainly," Lauren replied automatically.

"I know that this is awfully short notice, but I thought that if I dropped by at about one-thirty, we might chat for half an hour or so. I have a lunch at the Polo Lounge anyway. Does that upset your plans at all? If so, then . . ."

"Not at all. I'd be delighted."

"One-thirty then. I look forward to seeing you . . . again. Ciao."

For a moment, Lauren stared in puzzlement at the receiver, wondering if she had heard him right. *Again?* She never forgot a name, whether it was a handshake at a convention or a quick cocktail at a reception. And Rob Steinholtz just didn't ring any bells.

Yet there was something in his deep, Eastern-accented voice that rang a disturbingly familiar note. The rich, almost theatrical tone could have belonged to a dozen men she knew.

But it didn't. And Lauren's instincts told her that at last she had found her entree into RedRock, or run into a roadblock. Either way, she would have to fly back to the bungalow and prepare for this unexpected turn of events.

As she slammed the door behind her and threw her papers back into the attaché case, Lauren's gaze suddenly dropped to a small vase beside one of the white straw arm chairs.

In her absence, someone had dropped two dozen long-stemmed roses, unsigned, into the cut-glass holder. She leaned over and breathed in the perfume of wild roses, rather than the pale scent of a florist's bouquet.

Laughing, she remembered the horticulturist who had bombarded her with flowers for half a year in New York. If only he hadn't gone from posies to panties — crotchless ones from Fredericks' — their postal romance might have gone on forever. But at the moment, Lauren had no time for playing post office or lingering over the identity of her phantom admirer.

She threw on the shower massage and let stinging needles of hot water pound her skin. Softening the pulsating spray, she grabbed the massage head and played the shower over her feet, then languorously up her legs. As the sensual warmth spread over her body, Lauren found herself thinking of the voice on the other side of the phone.

Beneath the businesslike, self-assured tones of Rob Steinholtz's voice, he had seemed almost too eager to get together with her. Not just a man with a mutually beneficial proposition, but something far more personal. Was it possible that *he* had sent her the roses?

Nothing could be more ridiculous. And yet something in his words seemed to anticipate . . . Lauren closed her eyes and tried to imagine the man who would go with that voice. His eyes and his lips, then his back and buttocks and calves. Why did she imagine that his hands would be slightly rough, the fingers long and thick?

If she let herself go a minute longer, she might even swoon all alone in the shower stall.

Smiling, Lauren replaced the shower head and braced herself for the final phase of her morning routine—the one she always delayed as long as possible.

Biting her lower lip, she threw the shower control all the way over to COLD, then clenched her fists in anticipation. Slowly, the icy stream cascaded down her drenched blond hair, only to fall onto her tightening shoulders a moment later. Then, as the rest of her body was subjected to the same excruciating pore-tightening treatment, Lauren froze in paralyzed agony.

Suddenly, a chill of another kind gripped Lauren's spine, and sent goosebumps travelling up the backs of her arms.

For a moment she found herself looking not at the pale blue tile of her shower stall, but at the dimly lit ceiling of a Boston apartment.

It was the Christmas of her twenty-second year, and Lauren was screaming hysterically. Trying to break free from the grasp of Skip Collin, her fiancee, as he wrestled off her clothing in the faint glow of the hearth embers.

Then all at once there were bursts of light like gun-blasts all around her. Somewhere between laughing and crying, the girl clutched desperately at the one thing before her eyes. The massive cock of the tall, slim, bearded man kneeling in front of her . . .

With a start, Lauren jammed off the shower and made a break for the bedroom, struggling into the open air.

A moment later she lay sprawled out on the bed. Slowly she brought her knees up to her chest, and held them pressed tight there as the sobs sent a shudder rippling through her body.

Without a doubt, that bearded man had been Rob Steinholtz.

Seven

The Lord omnipotent reigneth . . .

The overpowering strains of the "Hallelujah Chorus" poured out of the speakers and filled the tiny radio studio as it was being broadcast.

"Ohhh, that's sen . . .sational, Lauren," her fiancee groaned. "Hold it right . . . *there!*"

Hallelujah! Hallelujah!

"Okay love. Now just a little bit higher . . ."

Kneeling before the music director of WKRX, twenty-two-year-old Lauren Conrad felt overpowered by emotions she could scarcely understand. Eyes closed, she lingered over the image of his long, lean athlete's body. Perennially tan, as devoid of hair as a teenage boy. From every angle, his body looked young and well-muscled.

At forty-five, Skip was twice her age. But no one would ever have guessed it from the way he kept up with her, playing tennis at dawn in the secluded private court of his Brimmer Street carriage house. During the week he kept residence there, at the foot of Boston's patrician Beacon Hill. Every weekend found him sailing on his thirty foot sloop out of Marblehead, or skiing in Vermont, depending on the season.

Skip Collin was beautiful, alright. Beneath his incredibly long lashes, his deceptively soft brown eyes shone with incredible intensity. His forcefulness had been the first thing she noticed the first time she entered the radio station two years before.

Hallelujah. Halllujah.

There wasn't a woman listener within forty miles who hadn't sighed just a bit the day his deep, theatrical voice delivered a prime time message, announcing his official engagement to Lauren Anne Conrad, hostess of "Afternoon Repertoire."

Lauren did love him, without a doubt. But slowly their model romance was souring. It hurt to admit it, but at times Skip was so demanding that it seemed like he was indifferent to her and her needs. And the more outrageously he behaved, the more obediently she found herself responding to his every whim.

"*Dar*ling," Skip languorously moaned. "see if you can't move your tongue just a little bit faster."

"Hhhhhmmmm?"

"Yes. *Yes*. Please don't stop . . . puh-lease . . ."

Cupping his balls tenderly, she brought her hands together around his tapered shaft and slowly began moving them up and down, hungrily devouring the tip.

And He shall reign forever and ever. For ever. And ever. *For* ever . . . And ever.

Halle*lu*jah Halle*lu*jah. Haleeeeeeee-luuuuuu-

"Yahhh!!!" With a series of wrenching spasms, Skip almost toppled off the grey stool. He clamped Lauren's head between his hands and forced himself fully into her mouth until she was gagging.

The tears forming in her eyes, Skip held her firmly in position as he threw his head back and shuddered.

Out of the corner of her eye, Lauren could just make out the blue warning light flashing on the control panel. *Thirty seconds to broadcast* when she would have to cut it live once more. At the same time, she was choking. Her stomach was threatening to give out at any second.

Grimacing, she stumbled to the panel and reached for her program notes. The Hallelujah Chorus ended, and she switched on the studio mike. "For our next selection . . . we'll . . . be listening to 'The Art of the Recorder by David Munroe.' Together with the 'Munroe Recorder Consort' and 'Members of the Early Music Consort of London.' Angel Recording Number SB-3861. We will begin with a Britten Scherzo, then follow it with a trio by Hindemith."

As the first note sounded, her stomach had finally given out. Lauren hastily threw off the microphone and vomited into the wastebasket. Feeling utterly humiliated, she slowly turned around to face her fiance.

Skip had already assembled his belt buckle, and was just zipping up his forest green corduroys. Anxiously, she observed him reaching over to the counter for his brown Harris tweed jacket. He was already wearing his post-coital business smile, the one Lauren knew all too well.

"You're not . . . *leaving*, are you?" she asked, incredulously.

"Afraid so. The Fine Arts is having a party, and I promised that I would . . ."

"But I'm off in half an hour. I thought that we were going to . . ."

"I know, sweetheart," he grinned, stroking her head solicitously.

"You made a promise to me, too. You said that as long as I left you free to . . ."

"*Damn it,* Lauren. Not now. Stop acting like a spoiled little bitch. I apologized. And you *know* I'd rather stay in the studio than go off to some half-assed society bore. But this is business, and it's important."

"You mean, now that you stopped by to get your

67

cock sucked!" she screamed, as he reached for the door of the sound-proof chamber.

"I'll call you later," he snorted, storming indignantly out into the dim corridor.

The door swung silently shut. Once again, Lauren was alone in the hermetically-sealed booth where she had spent so much of the past two years. Through blurry eyes, she tried to make out the rest of her program notes. Three selections from J.S. Bach's Anna Magdalena Notebooks, followed by a Deutsche Grammophon recording of Handel's "Water Music." First performed for George I on July 17, 1717, the first movement . . .

Just past midnight, Lauren's Porsche 911 hobbled over the rough cobblestones of Brimmer Street. Grimly, she surveyed the block for a parking spot sufficiently removed from Skip's door to avoid arousing suspicions, and painfully maneuvered as the snow spun under her tires.

For once, she resented the fact that she could never say no to Skip. No matter how much of a bastard he was, *she* was the one who always came crawling back. If he wanted to see other women, it was "of *course, darling.*" When he announced that he was falling in love with another man, feeling that his passions needed to be explored, it was, "I love you and I understand what you have to do."

When Skip's crazy ex-wife took up residence with him for three months, Lauren had continued to see him, at the Bradford Hotel, with its dingy curtains and aroma of faded elegance and mildew. Lauren had long ago stopped asking herself what hold Skip had on her. Sexual, oedipal, masochisic . . . she couldn't explain it. All she knew was that she needed him and would have him—no matter what it cost in self-esteem.

Arctic winds whipped across the frozen surface of the Charles, hitting Lauren with a stinging blast as she stepped out of the Porsche. Carefully, she made her way up the granite stairs, huddling out of sight at the top as she fished in her leather shoulder bag and produced his keys.

Tonight, she didn't care if his ex-wife's private eye *was* staked out on Beacon Hill. After all, it was Christmas Eve, and she was *not* about to use the servants' entrance across the way. It always made her feel like a call girl.

"Come up, come up wherever you are," Skip yelled down the stairs. From the way he was leaning against the bannister, he was a good nine-tenths crocked. That generally meant a fight was brewing.

Hesitating, she removed her down coat and woolen scarf. "I don't really know if I should," Lauren countered. "After the way you treated me this afternoon. Honestly, Skip. How do you think I feel when you just—"

"Love, it's Christmas Eve and I'm shivering. So take pity and come on up." Frowning, she made her way up the two stories.

Roaring with laughter, Skip swept Lauren up into his arms, then threw her over his shoulder. A moment later he brought her into the loft-like living room and then dumped her unceremoniously into a frail Queen Anne love seat beside the Christmas tree.

After a series of oaths from the kitchen, he returned laden with gifts. "Here's your egg nog. And *here* is some of the best Columbian weed you ever tasted. Four hundred dollars an ounce." He lit the joint and summarily pressed it between her lips. "Now toke up, lassie. There's a good girl."

Skip poured himself a double scotch, gulped down half of it, then took a long drag of the grass. "Ambrosia," he chuckled.

Halfway through the joint, Lauren was already very stoned. In the corner of the room, Mick Jagger was singing "Wild Horses" in the loudspeaker. With a shudder, she watched the snow outlining gale force winds as they tore through the deserted alleyway below.

She stared dumbfounded at her fiance. In the flickering firelight he looked very old and vicious, his mouth locked in a demonic, toothy grin. Suddenly, he was a stranger, and his urgency as he pulled her to him and greedily devoured her lips was terrifying.

Abruptly, Skip knocked back the rest of his Johnnie Walker Black and mumbled, "How very selfish of me . . . *Rob, do you want some grass?*"

As if on cue, a man dressed in a bathrobe appeared out of the guest bedroom.

Lauren straightened out her blouse and stared at the stranger who grinned back at her apologetically.

"Robbie, this is my incredibly luscious fiancee. Darling, meet Rob Steinholtz. Since his Mum is out west and his girlfriend is down in St. Maarten, I suggested that he share Christmas with us."

"Well, that's cozy," Lauren frowned, retreating to a corner of the couch.

Fifteen minutes later, Skip was absent-mindedly fondling her breast and passing around another joint. "Lauren," he whispered, "tonight I want you to drive me wild. I want you to just strip off your clothes and . . ."

"Well, what about what *I* want? Do you *ever* stop to think about *that?*"

"That, my love, is exactly what I was thinking about. I thought about giving you diamonds or roses.

But that's *so* passe. So I thought to myself, how about an *original* present. Here we are in the Swinging Seventies. Sooo . . . I thought I'd give you Robbie."

The roach clip dropped from her lips. *"Whaaat?"*

"That's right. I know you really want him. And don't think I haven't noticed the way you're cockteasing him to death with all of those little looks and languorous stretches."

Lauren was stunned. She gazed from Skip's drunken mask-like features to a suddenly embarrassed Robbie. "If this is your idea of a joke, I don't think it's very funny."

"No joke at all. Face it Lauren, you've already got the hots for Robbie. Admit it! You want to get into his incredibly tight and sexy pants. So I decided to not be selfish. I know how much you want to stuff his humongous cock into those little pouting lips. Now *admit* it."

"This is the craziest thing I've ever heard of, Skip. You're *drunk.*"

"Of course I am. It's *Christmas.*" Abruptly, he grabbed her around the waist and pulled her to him, sliding a hand into her jeans. "I know you want him, Lauren. And *I want to watch.* I want to see just how expertly you can give him head."

By now, Lauren was impossibly stoned. She felt as if she were in a glass bowl, watching the scenario unfold. Skip, her lover of two years, was grabbing Rob, dragging him over to the sofa. Suddenly, she burst out into hysterical laughter.

"That's better," Skip grinned, the image of his Chesire Cat teeth burning into her consciousness as he ripped open Rob's robe to reveal a ten inch erection in full readiness. "Come on, sweetheart. Let's see what that woman of mine can do."

The tears streamed down her face as she continued

to laugh uncontrollably. She felt somehow fascinated, as if she were across the room now, watching the bizarre tableau unfold.

Lauren Conrad was opening her lips as Rob Steinholtz straddled her. His massive cock slowly pushed between the sensuous folds of her mouth. *Flash.* Her fiancee, Skip Collins of the Beacon Hill Collins, was taking photographs. *Flash.* Her mouth began to move with a hypnotic rhythm. *Flash.* His cock moved in, then out. *Flash.* Her head slipped down into the cushions.

Flash.

Flash.

Flashflashflash. An electric blue afterimage burned in Lauren's eyes, swelling until her thoughts were swallowed up and she sank into oblivion.

A sharp rap on the door threw Lauren back into the present.

Startled, she looked herself over quickly in the full-length mirror. Her freshly dried shoulder-length hair set the tone: Every strand in place, it high-lighted her cheekbones exquisitely, but with a severity which repelled attempts to touch it.

Turning around, she surveyed the effect of her Chanel suit. The black with gold piping looked glamorous, but discreet. Together with the underlying ivory silk crepe blouse and pale cameo brooch, her image was complete.

"Coming," Lauren called out, pasting the patrician smile firmly onto her glistening lips, struggling to remember just how much she might need Rob Steinholtz. Pausing once more at the door, her knees started to give out on her.

It was one thing facing up to a ghost from her past. It was entirely another to need him.

"So glad you could come," she announced, throwing open the door. The sight on the other side startled her. In place of the tall, slim bearded young man of a dozen years ago, Rob Steinholtz was balding now, with a broad, stooping set of shoulders and several chins.

"Ah, Lauren, you're even more beautiful than I remembered," he leered, running his eyes lustily over her body and nodding. He stared at her slowly, with the obvious air of a man who has had a woman, and consequently considers her his.

Lauren stared at the man in the doorway and knew:

Somewhere, Rob Steinholtz was sitting on the pictures which would destroy her for life. Given a reason, he would use them.

At that instant, she wished he were dead.

Eight

Crystal arrived at Giorgio's.

Screeching to a sudden halt in her rent-a-Ford, she took a deep breath and prepared to once more enter the fray.

With only six hours left until the RedRock interview, she should have been in a panic. Instead, she was flying along on automatic pilot.

Just after sunrise, she had awakened to a shivering dampness beneath her back, and the aroma of fresh roasted coffee permeating the air. Like a love-struck puppy, Joel was up and about, preparing to get her back to the Beverly Wilshire, so she could check in and pick up a car.

Crystal was touched by his concern, but her career was at stake, and she wanted to be on her way—alone.

"We'll see each other tonight," she promised an ardent Joel, as she called a cab for the long trip from Malibu to Wilshire Blvd.

At the moment, there *was* something desperate about Crystal. Like Cinderella at the Royal Cotillion, any moment the clock might strike twelve, and put an end to her shopping spree. She planned to "Go Hollywood"—and in record time. Which meant, in short, that she was going to blow every last cent she had on clothing.

And Crystal was damned if she wouldn't enjoy it to the bitter end.

Time and again, the magic spell was cast. She stared in bewilderment at the melange of boutiques and salons beyond the windshield of her car. It seemed as though economy cars and family station wagons had been swept off the face of the earth—or at least banished from this exclusive district.

A moment later, she was once again escorted into never-never land. Flying on a plastic carpet charge plate, she passed through the entrance and into Giorgio's.

Within a matter of seconds, owner Fred Hayman was toasting her with Perrier in a Baccarat goblet. When he left her several minutes later, Crystal glanced around at a magnificent hardwood bar, the massive scimitar hanging up on the wall behind it.

A *clothing* store? It was more like the setting for a party.

Over early morning Bloody Marys, a pair of sleepy husbands distractedly racked up the balls for a game of pool, as browsers loafed all around the beautifully restored walnut pool table which was illumined by a massive chandelier.

From somewhere above a mahogany-panelled den with overstuffed easy chairs circling a fireplace, a voice with a distinctly European lilt called out, "Igor darling, what do you really think? Honestly now?"

The reply came from one of the pool players, a portly man in his fifties with an almost balding cranium, and a slightly sour turn of the mouth, as if he had drunk too much champagne. In his heavily Swiss-German accent, he called, "Francesca, my pet, as always your taste is impeccable. Like an arrow, you shoot straight for *de creme de la creme*. Buy one or buy ten of those Galanos dresses, my dear. I don't care. But if we don't get going right away, we will miss the starting race. And that I *do* care about."

A moment later, a dark-haired woman with an aquiline nose, badly applied make-up and a slightly blowsy figure, came prancing down the stairs. Behind Francesca Van Rensalaer, a troop of attendants carried several armloads of designer fashions.

As Crystal watched wide-eyed, the Beverly Hills doyenne bent over a display case, exhibiting a freshly ripped seam in her latest $5,000 acquisition.

Her eyes passed over Mrs. Van Rensalaer, taking in the Maude Frisson heels, the textured Dior stockings, the purple Galanos dress, the David Webb earrings and the faded turquoise antique silk scarf. Individually each piece was beautiful, but it was apparent that the woman had neither the taste nor the eye to put them together correctly.

Somehow, Francesca looked more like a clothes rack than a fashion plate. The expensive designer labels dominated rather than enhanced her.

"Damnit, Francesca. Get into the car," roared her husband from the door, as half a dozen onlookers attempted to avert their attention from the mortified woman.

Crystal wandered into the main gallery and paused here to examine a pleated skirt, or there just to stare at a five hundred dollar feather boa, or shake her head at a pair of gold lame harem pants.

From the second floor, a deeply tanned Lolita displayed her perfect form to advantage as she leaned over a brass rail and admired the scroll work on her ostrich boots. "How do they look?" she called down.

"Fabulous," answered her escort as he stood transfixed, ogling her exposed budding cleavage. "Where's my Nikon when I need it?"

"I meant the *boots*," she pouted.

"I'll buy them too."

Wearily, Lolita turned once more, examining her

profile in the boots, inspecting her flattened tummy and tight young derriere thoughtfully in one of a dozen mirrors intermingled with the shoe etagères.

Inch by inch she explored her image, searching for the first warning signs of cellulite, of creeping middle age.

A moment later she was gone, but that last image of her remained in Crystal's thoughts. What was it about Hollywood that could do that to a young girl? What kind of industry marked you as over the hill at twenty-five? She ran her hands over the voluptuous Venus curve of her own stomach and wondered if the stamp of motherhood was visible?

With a pang of guilt, she thought of Marcie passing over adolescence, going directly from her training bra to full-grown anxieties, like the Lolita who had just left.

Everywhere she went, the star consciousness was like radioactive fallout. Invisible, but constant. That above all else set Hollywood apart from the rest of the world. Instead of promotional calendars of the Greek islands, tailors boasted autographed photos of Telly Savalas. Instead of Bar Mitzvah announcements, the local deli would plaster its walls with photos of Barbra Streisand or Ed Asner.

Like the legendary neon-decked Schwab's Pharmacy which had made its indelible mark on Sunset, every little soda fountain or drugstore seemed to have its own cachet, its own clientele of the great and near-great. Everywhere Crystal turned in LA, she was greeted by the same timeless photographs. Inevitable carefree grins frozen solid on Perma-pressed faces without so much as a hint of a wrinkle.

Her eyes suddenly lit on a series of photographs mounted on the wall of the "den" at Giorgio's. The pictures might have been daughters in their wedding photos, or sons who had just made captain in the army. But the dazzling Burt Reynolds or Goldie Hawn smiles, the sparkling highlights in the flawless hair, the row after row of pock- and pimple-free complexions made their celebrity status obvious.

She silently stared at the dozens of intimate inscriptions to Gale and Fred Hayman. In a way, they *were* family portraits. In a very Hollywood way.

Like favorite sons and *enfants terribles,* the people you watched on television and in the movies could become a part of your life. Everything they did seemed to be public knowledge, subject to approval or reprimand. How Burt Reynolds treated his bed partners was as important to his gardener as it was to Sally Fields.

A never-clouding fishbowl was part of the arrangement. John Travolta and Brooke Shields could be "observed about town" as they wheeled a shopping cart burgeoning with groceries. Dean Martin would make the society columns by dropping in at the local Haagen Daz. Or else a twenty-four-hour dry cleaner would find the establishment Standing Room Only at three a.m., the night after Rod Stewart was sighted there.

Watching and being watched. For every star at the top, there were five hundred hopefuls. And perhaps five thousand secretaries, store clerks, waiters, bank tellers, and people somehow caught up in cogs and wires of the media machine.

Waiting in the aisles in Hollywood, perhaps tomorrow *they* would be discovered, make that meteoric rise to the top. In the meantime, they would continue to watch those who had. To see and make the scene, struggling to beat the odds by making it into a science.

This year, the Bistro was the right spot in Beverly Hills, as Crystal had quickly learned. Louis Vuitton and *le must de Cartier* were the proper look for making an appearance.

Next year, no one could say. But they would all keep their eyes peeled waiting for the next fashion message to be decoded . . . with the help of Rodeo Drive. If the clothing on the street had you confused, one look at the mannequins in boutique windows would set you straight. Setting a Stetson on the heads of a half dozen mannequins made it certain: the western look would be making a comeback.

But every bit as important as the message was the massage. The strokes which eased the pain of ego bruises was the other part of what Rodeo Drive was all about. If money was no object, then you could get "the works" at Elizabeth Arden—for a price upwards of five hundred dollars a day.

Otherwise, there would always be some young Sassoon protegée waiting to style your hair for a fraction of that.

If you couldn't afford the sapphire-crowned tiara in the window of Van Cleef, or the rose coral strands at Fred Joallier, you could nonetheless run your fingers over them, or practice adorning yourself with antique jade before settling for a pair of microscopic fourteen point earrings.

Of course, Crystal had also heard of the upstairs at Gucci's, where only keyholders were invited to examine the finest exclusive designs. One or two other boutiques on Rodeo had followed suit, establishing a policy of opening by appointment only.

But for the rest, there was always an open door, and *something* in there you could afford to buy. Whether the label was Balenciaga or Izod. Outside on the street, you might be no one. But once inside you could be pampered and flattered at every turn.

Now more than ever, Crystal needed that

reassurance. As she stepped over to the mirror, she was startled to find herself modelling for a handful of onlookers—and loving it. Feeling the soft silk of the Halston evening dress reassuringly delicate against her skin was almost an aphrodisiac. With every approving glance and nod, the current running through her seemed to spark a little more, until she was glowing.

Like radioactivity. Too much exposure would do you in in no time. But being seen just enough to create excitement, to bolster flagging self-esteem. In Atlanta, they would call it exhibitionism.

But in Hollywood, it was just a matter of survival.

Crystal felt half a dozen pairs of eyes riveted on her as she exited with her latest acquisition—a designer bikini which weighed in at two-and-a-half ounces of material—half of which was strap. Back home, she might have smiled an acknowledgment. On Rodeo Drive, it was just part of the game. Watching and being watched.

As she tipped the valet and threw her packages into the backseat, Crystal began to suffer an attack of panic. Somewhere across town, she recalled, a gold-plated bitch named Lauren Conrad would be girding her loins for battle. There was no doubt in her mind that Lauren could keep up the appearance of confident success forever.

The question was: how long could *she?*

With a self-mocking shrug she gazed at the pile of boxes and shopping bags in the rear seat. It consisted of about ninety per cent air, another five or six per cent cardboard, tissue paper and bag.

The remaining five per cent accounted for the three thousand dollars she had just spent on clothing.

Cursing herself for not having the sense to mutilate her credit cards, Crystal enthusiastically examined her purchases. She now had one status Gucci bag—a filmy beige silk chiffon blouse; one pair of red silk pants with matching top; one pair of bronze ankle strap sandals; one Hermes scarf; a bikini worth its weight in gold; an elegant coral raw silk suit and another delicate gold bracelet to add to the dozen she already wore on both wrists.

And a three thousand dollar hole in her pocketbook.

Suddenly the plug of her buoyant mood was pulled—she was sinking once again. And for good reason.

Like the stereotyped Hollywood millionaire who drove a Rolls but couldn't afford a tip for his coffee, Crystal Cooper was in a bad way.

Of course, she had *needed them*, Crystal told herself, staring at the brightly wrapped bundles. And they were gorgeous, without a doubt.

But Crystal's life had revolved from one side of the Cinderella coin to the other too many times for her to ignore what she had just done.

As a little girl, she had learned to hide her feelings behind all of her pretty dresses, take refuge in them whenever her house exploded. Her mother had taught her how to smile in all occasions, and how to keep up appearances.

Crystal had learned that lesson well. By now, hiding behind a facade of exquisite beauty was an old trick of hers. Putting on bright colors when she was depressed; dressing to kill when what she wanted to do was commit suicide.

Ignoring the debts piling impossibly higher, the broken marriage and severed career, the adolescent daughter who disdained her, Crystal had kept right on keeping on. Wearing the mantle of success and happiness. It was always so much easier, so comforting.

For thirty-five years now Crystal had tried to barricade herself in beauty, refusing to confront the world beyond it. Gradually, the mantle had become so heavy that now she was being crushed underneath it.

The masquerade was coming to a close. When the clock struck, Crystal would once again be forced to be herself. There was no way to pretend that a Prince Charming would somehow come to her rescue.

And at that moment she would have to face the armor-plated Lauren Conrad.

Alone.

Nine

Nervously creeping on tiptoes, Crystal's tiny hands clenched the hem of her flannel nightgown as she headed downstairs to the kitchen.

She was petrified of what she would find downstairs this morning, but too scared to just lie in bed and wait for Nanny to bring her breakfast.

Most of all, she was afraid that she would let her nightgown hem drag across the floor and get dirty. Of all of the offenses she could commit, that was always the worst one. Particularly after a night, like last night.

Sometime in the dark, she had woken up to scuffling down the hall.

"It's my right, Goddamn it!" screamed out her Daddy's voice.

"You . . . you pig," Mommy had screamed back. "You goddamn . . . filthy . . . animal . . . get your hands off of me!"

Crawling out of the nursery, Crystal kneeled down at the bannister and pressed her face between the railings. Sam was disappearing into the kitchen below. Rachael, her torn nightgown billowing out like a sail, raced down the stairs after him.

By the time the little girl with the golden Shirley Temple curls arrived downstairs, they were wrestling on the kitchen floor. Screaming hysterically, Rachael drove her fingernails into his neck, strangling him with all of her might.

His face turned pink, then scarlet as the veins bulged from Sam's temples.

She stared down at him in horror and released her grip. But a second later Rachael was screaming at the top of her lungs, slapping him with all of her might.

For a minute, the only sound in Crystal's ears was the continuous *whap! whap!* as her mother's hands whipped across her father's head, delivering blows that bounced him from side to side.

It was a scene Crystal had witnessed several times before. She felt so sorry for Daddy, lying there so quiet as Mommy hurt him. He always had such a sad expression in his eyes, like the little fawn in the Walt Disney movie.

But suddenly, Sam's expression changed from passive misery to rage. With a roar, he threw over the slender form of his wife, sending her head slamming into the stove. Blood began gushing from a cut on her forehead, all over her pretty face and down her shoulders, dripping over her breasts and down onto her thighs.

Never before had Mommy been hit, and the new change of events only made this fight even scarier than all of the others. Sam had finally reached his limit.

"*You vixen,*" he screamed, punching the side of her head. "You frigid, ungrateful bitch . . . I hate your guts." He punched her again. Then rolled her over onto her back.

Crystal saw Mommy doubled up on the floor, screaming and clutching her body.

"*Noooo!*" the little girl screamed out. "Daddy, *No!* Please. Mommy didn't mean it. Honest. Don't hurt her. She . . ."

In a moment, Sam's fury was forgotten as he spun

and rushed over to comfort the little girl. "It's okay, Princess," he whispered hoarsely, sweeping her up into his arms and carrying her out into his card room. "Now stop crying. Daddy will read you a story. Would you like that? What do you want to hear? . . . How about *The Water Babies?*"

Soon he was gently rocking her, his deep and gentle voice lulling her to sleep. The last thing she remembered seeing was Mommy clutching her nightgown to her breast as she retreated upstairs to her bedroom.

As Crystal stole around the corner into the kitchen in the morning, she imagined the worst possible. Pools of blood all over the floor, broken dishes, the dinette furniture smashed beyond recognition. Holding her breath, she opened her eyes . . . only to find everything just as it had been before the fight.

On the breakfast table, a pale blue vase held a handful of daisies and baby's breath. The floor, the walls, everything was spotless. For a minute, the child wondered if she had dreamed it all.

But there was something too normal about the house this morning. Crystal could see that Daddy's Nash convertible was already gone. Daddy *never* left the house before noon. As Mommy hummed cheerfully to the tune on the Victrola, she bent over a place on the mahjong table just long enough for Crystal to see the cut on her forehead, almost hidden by hours of painstaking make up.

But for the rest, she seemed gay and carefree as she wandered around the living room wearing one of her fancy yellow organdy dresses.

An hour later, Crystal was all spotless in polka-dot crinoline, just the way Mommy liked her to be. She had carefully washed her face and cleaned beneath her fingernails, meticulously brushed her teeth and her hair. And now she was sitting at the piano and practicing, because she wanted to please Mommy.

As her tiny fingers struggled over the keys, Rachael came and sat down beside her. The smile was still pasted firmly on her perfect cupid bow lips. But her eyes were moving in that funny, nervous way that meant she wasn't so happy after all.

With a sinking feeling, Crystal put on her own best smile and tried to play her very best. She missed one note. Then another.

"You didn't practice yesterday," snapped her mother.

"Oh, yes. Yes I did." Crystal nodded emphatically as her hands lost their place on the keyboard. "Honest. I promise."

"*Liar!*" Rachael screamed, as her palm shot across the girl's face. "You're a no-good filthy liar, just like your father." And then Rachael was straddling the little girl on the floor, pulling her golden curls as she drove her fingernails into Crystal's arm.

"You filthy . . . vile . . . ugly wretch. *I'll* show you to talk back to your mother."

As the tiny child's screams of agony filled the air, a terrified neighbor called the police. As the sirens drew near, Rachael fled in despair to the shelter of her bedroom.

By the time the police officer arrived at the door, Rachael's luminous smile was once again pasted firmly on her face. She was masterful with that smile, using it to coax, ingratiate and charm every man in the world.

Eventually, her daughter and husband, plus a few relatives and neighbors came to see through it. But to the policeman arriving cold at the doorstep, the notion that such a beautiful and charming woman could harm a fly was unthinkable.

Besides, for a man in Sam Coopersmith's sensitive

position, even the smallest rumors took on disastrous proportions. In addition, he had not been oiling the Baltimore political machine all of these years without effect.

The situation was always handled with utmost discretion.

Without a doubt, Crystal Sarah Coopersmith was a War Baby—though not in the usual sense.

Her father had remained at home—and blissfully single—throughout the years of the Great War.

In fact, in his spacious and well-appointed Pikesville home, the times had never been better. Although making cardboard boxes was hardly a glamor industry, it was as essential to the war effort as fighting in the trenches. The factory which Sam had inherited from his father was in full production around the clock, providing packing materials for everything from dive bomber parts to K-rations.

Sam Coopersmith was a patriot to the core. But particularly when it came to helping defeat the mustachioed monster who was sending his people off to concentration camps in Germany, he did everything he could to help. He offered government purchasing agents packing materials for a fraction of their market cost. The sheer volume of his patriotic production more than insured his already secure family fortune. Even with wartime inflation raging at thirty per cent, it couldn't begin to eat into the profits that United Box was posting.

Sam was a good-hearted, sensuous man, armed with a knack for pleasure and a small fortune. Settling into his thirty-fifth year—with American victory approaching and sure prosperity ahead—he was suddenly greatly in demand socially.

Once merely an eligible bachelor, he now felt like

the prime mark on the Most Wanted List.

Sam Coopersmith was not unusually handsome by any stretch of the imagination. He was short, with large, meaty hands and a pot belly to match. His face was attractive enough though, and his financial position was positively irresistible.

But more than that, Sam loved women in a way which turned on even the most unapproachable ones. He loved to charm them and to please them, and took endless delight in doing both. Even when charming her pants literally off was out of the question, Sam thrived on making a woman feel special, beautiful and glamorous.

For years now, he had been the inevitable target of the matrimonial attempts of virtually every young and marriageable woman—or her mother—in the Jewish communities of the Baltimore-Washington axis until he couldn't attend a High Holy Days service or a Bar Mitzvah without at least one "prospect" leaping into the fray: making his acquaintance, then attempting to bag him with all of the subtlety of a big game hunter poising an elephant gun, while protecting her new turf with the ferocity of a lioness.

But Sam's tastes always seemed to run in other directions. Instead of wasting his money on expensive theater dates, he donated generously to the Art Museum. He shunned tea dances and cocktail parties in favor of civic club meetings, or hours spent alone with his violin, trying to master the formidable Mendelssohn.

His remaining passions ran to gambling, the horse races, and *schicksas*. Above all, the latter. The charms of gentile girls which he had first sampled as a teenager, between slugs of bootleg whiskey in the back of his father's Pierce Arrow, had left their indelible mark. For the rest of his life, the matronly appeals of

88

"nice girls"—*Jewish* girls—would leave him cold and limp.

Or so he thought. When business brought him to Little Rock, Arkansas, he was greeted in the front office by a secretary named Rachael Kammen.

"May I help you, sir?" she inquired while his eyes swept over her waist-length flaxen hair and fiery blue eyes.

"Joe Goldberg's expecting me," he said, as his senses were fired with her seductive willowy curves. Her neck was so delicate that it was all he could do to keep from nibbling it as she leaned over to consult the appointment calendar. "Sam's the name, Sam Coopersmith, Miss . . . uh . . ."

"Kammen. Rachael Kammen. I'll call in to double check, but just for the record, I don't see any mention of your appointment in . . ."

But at that moment, she might as well have spoken Swahili. There were only two words in his mind: "*Rachael*" . . . Was it possible? . . . and "*Kammen.*"

Suspiciously he eyed her delicately veined skin, her tall, slender form.

Smoothing down his slick black hair and buttoning the straining tweed jacket to hide the perennial stain on his silk tie, Sam eyed her long, finely-chiselled nose with elation.

Rachael looked like a shicksa. She acted like a shicksa.

She even *smelled* like a shicksa. But best of all, she was Jewish. For once, he could have his cupcake and eat her, too. His years of prayer had at last brought deliverance. Here was a gorgeous, sparkling, and seductive woman he could show off all over town—even at the synagogue. Destiny had led him to his lifelong dream: a fairy princess wife who looked like a shicksa.

A hastily extended lunch invitation led to more revelations. Rachael Kammen was the eldest daughter of a doting tailor, and the original creation she was wearing was the fruit of his labors, after his small cluttered storefront closed for the night. While she struggled to help support her Russian immigrant family, the small-town beauty with simple tastes still managed to dream of better things.

Somewhere in the corner of her blue eyes, he could sense a hint of lust for the good life. *So much for the better.*

That afternoon, as he motored back to Baltimore, Sam Coopersmith counted his blessings and began planning his wedding. Already he could picture her in the kitchen, at the canasta table, poised for action on his king-sized bed.

If he had looked for a lady in the parlor, Sam was not disappointed. Rachael embraced Baltimore society as if she were to the manor born. Her poise and her iron determination to go beyond her humble origins aided her self-improvement program unflaggingly. It was only a matter of months before the transformation was complete.

When Rachael Coopersmith emerged from her cocoon, it was as a distant and untouchable butterfly. Her pretensions quickly got out of hand as the last traces of her past were swept aside. Receiving an endless stream of merchants, tradesmen and people of the service class as she sought to upgrade the substantial brick homestead, Rachael was at once disdainful and imperious. As though her parents had never deigned to shop for bargains, or soil their hands with the likes of a sewing needle and thread.

When the second bedroom was remodelled, Rachael officially established quarters there. But the groundwork had been laid out clearly on their wedding night. She understood Sam's needs and was willing to submit to them: once a week, on the Sabbath. That was a mitzvah—a good deed.

But Sunday through Friday was out of the question. As if it were a commandment written indelibly in the Bible.

It was during their seventh religious observance, the Saturday night following Sam's Birthday that their only daughter was conceived.

The announcement following Rachael Coopersmith's confirming trip to the doctor meant two things: Sam would at last be a father. And Rachael could be free of the oppression of sex for at least nine months.

When the daughter was born, Sam could not have been more delighted. His mother had died just a few months before, and he wanted a little girl to carry on her spirit and her name, *Sarah*.

But Rachael had deeper ambitions for that daughter. She was going to grow up and marry *really* well, not just to some slob like Sam who cared little about grooming or clothes. It had not taken long before her husband's grossness became unbearably apparent.

In public, it seemed that all he talked about were the finer things in life. But at night his lower class tastes came out, and transformed their little suburban castle into hell. But at least those gross, sensuous lips and probing hands would not infect the next generation. Her daughter would mix only with the *crème de la crème*. And Rachael was determined to name her appropriately.

When he gazed at the birth certificate, Sam silently raged at the name "*Crystal* Sarah Coppersmith" and knew that he would have to fight for a place in his daughter's life.

That evening in a drunken fit he smashed every piece in Rachael's Waterford collection.

In the battle for the baby's affections, Sam had a healthy advantage. Unlike his wife, he was driven only toward pleasure. He kept up his drinking and gambling, but also developed a new string of interests to include his young princess. He bought a cabin cruiser so they could spend long summer afternoons together. He erected a miniature train set which ran halfway through the second floor of the house, and spent hours laughing with baby Crystal as she sent the tiny locomotive careening off the tracks. He bought her a perambulator which was only slightly less ostentatious than a gilded coach and four, and showed her off throughout the neighborhood at every opportunity. His gorgeous princess with the Shirley Temple curls and the bright green eyes.

Rachael moved about in a constant rage. The dainty crinoline petticoats she selected with such care inevitably came back from the park caked with mud or sand whenever Sam took Crystal to the playground. When she walked around with her curls in tangles and her shoes untied, Sam found her charming. But Rachael's response was to reach for the strap.

She had long ago had it with Sam. It was all very well that he had brought operations at the factory to the point where they ran smoothly without his help. But how could she explain to her friends a man who had no ambition, and no normal work-ethic? A man who stayed up to all hours of the night and slept until noon? It seemed that he was always finding excuses for staying in the house—to teach Crystal how to ice-skate, to add on to the train set.

The bottom line was that she was a sternly ambitious young woman. And she had married a *putzer*.

When she had her mah jong luncheons, his presence was so mortifying that she literally had to throw him out of the house.

Even then, he didn't spend that one day a week by cleaning up things at the factory. He knew that his plant manager was dipping into the till. Had been for years. But fire him? *Never.* That would mean giving up some of his *own* freedom.

The arguments kept getting worse—about Sam's lack of manners, his undignified hours, his sloppiness, and the bad habits he was giving his daughter. Unspoken was the fact that his animal lust sent waves of revulsion pouring through Rachael.

Late at night, Sam's sexual frustration would be vented in bouts of drunkenness. But usually the noise subsided after a few moments of yelling and banging and scuffling down the hall.

But tonight, Daddy was gone altogether. He was "running with the shicksas." Whatever that was.

All Crystal knew was that Nanny had fed her dinner tonight, and Daddy was gone and Mommy was locked up in her bedroom again.

"Tomorrow," she swore, "I'm gonna wear my itchy white dress with the long sleeves. I'm gonna practice *forever.*" Then Mommy wouldn't be so angry, and Daddy would come home at night.

But all alone in her room, Crystal's bruises were quickly forgotten. Surrounded by bunny rabbit brothers and teddy bear sisters, she slipped into her secret fantasy world once again.

In their happy little nest, the daddy always dressed respectably. When he left on the morning train the mommy just smiled and never beat the children or screamed at them. Just because they got their clothes dirty or slouched in their chairs.

Mommy never beat up Daddy either. But even if she did, Crystal could take a little bandaid and place it over the wound. Then the pain was all gone. Everything was okay and happy again.

Nonetheless, as the little girl turned out the light and waited to fall asleep, a choking feeling tickled at the back of her throat. Tears burned in her eyes, until she gave in and let the salty tears stream down her cheeks.

The next day, Rachael took her all the way downtown. They bought a beautiful new dress that itched her only a little, and a pair of patent leather shoes with big old brass buckles.

Ten

By the time Redfield arrived at his parking area, the gate guard had already radioed ahead to the awaiting valet.

"Damn waste of money," Redfield mumbled, waving aside the valet with a friendly grin as he veered into the first of a dozen bays bearing his initials in red Gothic letters. As a concession to Hollywood lifestyle, the RedRock chief had hired a massive parking crew. Nonetheless, Redfield made it a point to politely shun the valets, and continually looked for signs of staff members following in his frugal shoes.

So far, he had had no success.

With an exasperated frown, he noted the empty space reserved for Rob Steinholtz. Apparently, his appointment as president of the Satellite Broadcasting Network had done nothing to make him more punctual.

Then again, at least Rob's Mercedes had finally left the lot. During recent weeks, as Rob's pursuit of MarieAnne, or Maryjane—whatever his latest secretary was named—reached a climax, he was clocking in at least eighteen hours a day.

In spite of his own disgust for Rob's extramarital calisthenics, Redfield had been willing to tolerantly overlook them. But the former vice president didn't help matters. Discretion was hardly his modus operandi.

In fact, Steinholtz's lechery was the stuff of legends. If his 450 SL bore a halfway discreet vanity plate like "PLEASER" it was only because the State of California refused to issue him a retired surfer's license plate—one which read "HUNG 10."

Rob was brilliant enough, as fifteen years of media experience documented. He had a vision somewhere between art and pure commercialism, and the know-how to put it together. More than that, Rob knew how to get it done. Not just how to put together the package and develop it—but which palms to grease and which egos to stroke.

The "massage"—as it's known in the biz—is a somewhat exacting science. Too much by way of perqs, incentives and bonuses, and your talent begins to move a little too freely. If they don't just get too sloppy, then they fly off the handle altogether. But without sufficient encouragement, the project or talent just sort of freezes, then slowly starts to fall back on the treadmill.

Rob Steinholtz was a prime mover when it came to development. He knew when to hype things and when to lay low. He always kissed the right cheek, and paid out precisely the right amount of kickback to offset a show of respect with a demand for one. He knew just how far to push the unions—and that alone was an invaluable trait.

But for all of that, Rob Steinholtz possessed a distinctly unhealthy flamboyance. The only hand he was interested in biting was the one which fed him. Twenty years of rising to the top from the obscure reaches of the Valley had taken their toll. Rob Steinholtz was streetwise, but he was taking chances.

The recognition he wanted could come only from the top. And to get it, Rob was continually challenging his betters. Thus far, the skirmishes had been almost beneath Redfield's notice: a parking space taken, a meeting delayed without notice, a personal secretary seduced.

The signs were all there. Someday, Rob Steinholtz was going to make life very miserable for the wrong person.

In the meantime, he was doing a good enough job with Moe Alexander. As chairman of the board of Alexander Enterprises, Moe personally controlled as much media money as any other figure in Hollywood. Moreover, when he retired from the movie end of the media industry, it had done little to temper his tyrannical bent.

As a financial partner, Moe Alexander's resources made him second to none. And when it came to using his unlimited influence, Moe stopped at nothing. When a waitress had the audacity to say no to the gnarled old lecher, she suddenly found herself out of work. Actresses who failed to accept the withered hand exploring their asses might wake up to find themselves cast off the casting couch . . . permanently.

And that was when Moe was being a gentleman. He had far less patience for *lésé majesté* when it came from an upstart like his son-in-law.

For all of his obvious genius, Rob Steinholtz owed the presidency at RedRock to one person: his wife, Maria. She was the only virtue that Moe had ever possessed, and he would stop at nothing to keep her from getting hurt. These days, Rob was testing Moe's patience—and his limits. As the son-in-law's exploits grew more brazen, so did his father-in-law's threats.

"Keep it up, Mr. Bigshot," the old buzzard had screamed at Rob the week before—in full earshot of Redfield—"one of these days, I'm gonna cut off our schwanz and feed it to your schnauser. I'm *warning* you. Sooner of later, Maria's gonna *have* it with you. That's the day you're gonna dig your own grave, looking for a hole to hide your disgusting *punem.*"

Personally, Redfield would have been happy to settle for less erratic brilliance, in return for steady, plodding diligence and a touch of loyalty. The second he got the right signal from Moe, the axe would fall.

In fact, the blade was already waiting.

"Whatssa matter, CJ? You got insomnia or something?" The raspy voice on the other end of the line belonged to a slightly sleepy and extremely hungover whale of a man. An agent named Sid Gold.

"You told me you always wanted to hear it from me first, and get it straight. So before the rumors start hitting town, I thought you would want to know . . ."

"At eleven in the morning? After a night like last night? Did you buy out CBS, or what?"

"It's about Now News." CJ heard the eyes spring open on the other end of the wire. He paused for effect, then added, "I'm coming to a decision."

"Bee-*u*-tiful," replied the agent, throwing his portly body into sitting position in the center of his ten-foot diameter circular bed. "I knew you'd do it . . ." Draping the green silk robe over his bulging midsection, Sid disentangled his legs from the blond-haired girl curled up next to him under a tan satin sheet. *Too bad she can't act for shit,* he sighed.

"The decision isn't final yet, but . . ."

"I knew you'd do it, CJ. Fiona couldn't be a more perfect choice. She knows Kirschener, respects his work. The two get along like brother and sister, if you know what I mean. And on the air, she's got that . . ."

Redfield stared at the reflection of his tensing fingers in the mirror-finish tabletop of his desk. *Calm,* he told himself. Losing patience right now would be one hell of a costly error. Just let Sid keep talking on, until he's got it all of out of his system.

Agents are always more reasonable once they're hyped out.

But *Fiona McLean?*

". . . she's absolutely *tops,*" Sid rattled on. "One hundred percent professional. She doesn't get stymied by those three syllable words. Know what I mean? She's a class act . . ."

RedRock had never even seriously considered Sid's client—and suddenly CJ couldn't quite believe that Gold had, either. Fiona had been kept on the screening list in deference to the agent, to make him look good to his client. But most of all because Sid Gold was a vindictively sore loser—especially when he didn't place.

But unless Gold was so swept up in his bullshit that he was starting to believe it, he had something else up his sleeve. Redfield's mind tuned in like a radar antenna as he surveyed the far wall of his office. Hanging above the heirloom Duncan Phyfe harvest table were two portraits. Israel Roodefield and Katherine Winslow his wife peered sternly down at him.

Facing eleven generations of Redfields always reminded him of the virtue of patience. He sat perfectly still, upright, waiting.

"Fiona's one tough lady," Gold wheezed over the phone. "She says to me, 'I know Redfield's rep, but *how* can you speak about 'job security' when the Satellite Network isn't on-line yet? What if it goes down after five months of Nielsen's? What good does job security do me then? As far as I'm concerned, it's 350 plus, or I stay at ABC.' Can you imagine *her* saying that to *me?* When I found that girl, she was bending over a file in the obit room of KJRX."

On the other end, Redfield sighed in exasperation. Sid Gold was worse than a dog circling a park. Where in hell he was trying to lead the conversation was anyone's guess, but it didn't do much to ease Redfield's mind about the deal he was about to cancel . . .

". . . But don't worry, I'll deliver her. As a matter of fact, I'll do more than that: you give her the same benefits we worked out for Dave, and you can have the team for four-fifty. I'm sure I can swing it. Of course, being a woman, she will have to have a monthly allowance of ten thousand, for . . ."

Suddenly, Redfield understood the ploy. Sid Gold was sharp, alright. He *knew* Fiona would never land the spot. Fiona McLean was just a bargaining chip. By rejecting half of the auctioning package, RedRock would have to concede more for Kirschener. The old line about "breaking up a set" was about to arise.

And by pushing too hard, Sid Gold was about to screw his own client out of the running. Not Fiona McLean—but Kirschener. Now all Redfield had to do was sit back and relax as he listened to the fireworks. "Sid," he sighed in his most repentant voice, "I called to tell you that we *wouldn't* be picking up Fiona. In fact, we just found what we were looking for. Tall, blond, well-spoken. Dynamic."

Gold went on as if CJ had never said a word. "So you think Fiona's a pushover? Try pinching her ass sometime and see how long it takes you to get knocked flat out on the ground. I tell you, I been in this business almost thirty years now, and I honestly think you're crazy. She's got beauty, brains, an Ivy League education."

By all account, Fiona McLean had earned her BA the same way she had gotten her first news job, her anchoring position, and probably the better half of her jewelry. Redfield was sorely tempted to point that

100

out to Sid Gold.

But then again, it was probably also the talent which had landed her Hollywood's top agent.

"There's another thing," Sid mumbled, straining to make it sound unrehearsed. "David really had his heart set on Fiona. They were together in the good old days on Channel 9—and that's going back some. You *do* realize that he has the right of refusal."

Actually, the only right Kirschener had was the right to tear up his own contract. And Sid Gold was leading him straight into it. Hoping to get an extra hundred thousand or so, Redfield, who had been listening in dead silence, waiting for his cues from Gold, suddenly saw everything drop into place. Before his eyes, the carefully wrought Kirschener contract was dissolving faster than an Alka-Seltzer, leaving him a clear solution to his problems, with just a little bit of residue to clean up later.

The network chief gazed up again at his forebears, this time smiling triumphantly.

"At least let me know who the lucky dame is, so I can break the news to David gradually. And who's her agent?"

"I can't give you a name yet, Sid. But I promise, the moment contracts are out, I'll fill you in."

"In that case, you better just sit on the Kirschener deal for a while. I'll massage Kirschener, but you're askin' a lot. It won't be easy."

"I appreciate it. Whatever you can do to smooth things over . . ."

"Y'know, you really know how to make a guy's weekend. Lemme know something soon, okay? *Ciao.*"

Eleven

"Return it?" Regina Stevens gasped, almost choking on a sip of black coffee with sweetener. "I most certainly will not!"

Her light brown eyes were stalking the kitchen with ferocity now. She glared at the espresso machine and the Cuisinart, then seized upon their first human quarry: the housekeeper.

With a sinking feeling in the pit of his stomach, Dale realized that sagging, middle-aged Betty, who was hunched over the kitchen cabinets, dusting, was totally oblivious to the guided missiles which were being launched in her direction.

It was a scenario which was played in perhaps a thousand homes scattered throughout the San Fernando Valley at any given moment. Husband dumps on wife, wife does not dare to bite the million-dollar hand which feeds her . . . so she attacks the maid.

In some ways, it was Betty's most important job. Twice a week, for three hours in the early morning, the Stevens family would set to work. If the house wasn't vacuumed, or the beds weren't made, if there were lint or wine stains on the shag carpet, then Betty would think they were slobs. She was their cleaning woman Mondays and Thursdays, and divided the remaining days of the week between two other families, both of whom were in the industry, and on Regina

102

Stevens' party circuit.

For a few seconds Betty continued to hover over them, quietly humming to herself. Then in the blink of an eye she vanished, retreating to a safer region of the house.

This time, she had gotten off easy. Sympathizing with a distraught wife's burdens was one thing . . . *witnessing* marital discord was another. And no more permissible than watching Faye Dunaway belch.

Now, Dale Stevens realized, it was just the two of them again. And unlike the thousand other maid-bullying wives scattered across the region at this hour, Regina Stevens was *not* afraid to stand up to her husband.

Far from it. She had merely been warming up for the kill. And battle exercises had just come to an end.

As his hands clenched tight around the stoneware mug, the color drained from Dale's fingertips, and they seemed to be losing their grasp. His fighting stamina was petering out. Staring surreptitiously at the smouldering inferno across the table, Dale watched powerless as the last of his resistance was broken. Next a tidal wave seemed to break across his farmboyish features. Pounding his courage into dust, and leaving only jelly where his spine had once been.

Gazing into the sugary sludge dredged up from his coffee on the tip of his spoon, Dale felt the evil eye bearing down on him again. "Sweetheart," he picked up in a placating voice, "we just can't afford it right now and . . ."

"*We just can't afford it right now,*" she mimicked with devastating accuracy. Regina Stevens knew just how to home in on every pleading inflection in her husband's voice, how to pin him down like a worm on a dissection table. "We just *can't afford* to join the Mulholland Club. Or a decent vacation this year. Or a bigger swimming pool. No health club. No masseur and no exercise class. I have to plead like a welfare case every time I want to go to Magnin's to buy a dress."

"From the looks of our bill it looks like you spent most of your time there," he shot back.

Dale instantly regretted it. Too late.

The distance separating them across the breakfast table seemed to shrink. Her long painted fingernails were quivering, ready to shoot across and into his eye sockets. Regina was preparing to explode.

"You *would* keep track, wouldn't you?" she sneered. "Well, I suppose it wouldn't concern you that I have to dress in rags. My hems have been raised up and down so many times that they look like the rings on a sequoia. *You* have a new Brougham. But me? *I* have to drive around in that old shitbox of a stationwagon."

"That's not fair. In my position, I *have* to have that car." He gulped down a mouthful of coffee grounds and started to choke. A sharp stab of pain rose out of his protesting gut linings. The ulcers were beginning to kick up again.

"Don't the *rest* of us need anything? Or are we just here to be the laughing stock of Sherman Oaks? I have to get down on my fucking knees and crawl before Gordie and Steve can attend a decent school. I have to turn down invitations left and right because I haven't got a decent new dress to wear to a formal. Of course, we *can't afford* to have me looking half decent." She snorted in disgust and headed for the sink, blocking his escape route. "Just tell me one thing, Dale. *Whose* fault is it? Are you trying to tell me it's mine? If not for me, we would probably still be living in that dumpy ranch house in Van Nuys and our boys would still be going to school with those druggies. Is *that* what you really want? Do you want to save money by having

104

your sons in school with jailbirds and drug fiends?"

Dale sat passively, barely looking at his wife's mouth which was arched in a crooked sneer. He gazed at the pear-roundness of her bottom, outlined in the tan knit running suit. His eyes moved up her flat spine to the surprisingly long and delicate neck.

Even across the kitchen he could make out the spot on each side of her throat—about two-and-a-half inches above her shoulders. Just once. What he wouldn't give to sink in his meaty fingers and squeeze every last bit of venom out of that bitch.

"It's not as if I go to Van Cleef every day," she continued. "We barely *ever* entertain. Don't you see what the problem is? It's not this *bill* . . ."

Dale pressed the stoneware mug against his lips in an attempt to conceal the way they were trembling. Dancing around it long enough, Regina always managed to hit upon the unspoken problem, puncturing his defenses and deflating them like a popped balloon.

The nightmare of it was the fact that she was right. The problem wasn't this bill. And it wasn't RedRock, or even his wife. Instead, it was something he lived with secretly, twenty-four hours a day. He stared at her mercilessly probing eyes and wondered how much she suspected. Did she still believe that his impotence was just a question of "brewer's droop?"

Or did she know that the drinking problem was one more camouflage?

The real problem was precisely the fact that Dale Stevens *didn't* have the least desire to strangle his wife. Not even to stand up to her. Quite the contrary. The problem with the way she tortured and belittled him was that it was simply no longer enough.

What he really wanted her to do was beat the shit out of him.

105

You sick bastard, he inwardly sighed.

"You've gotta learn to stand up to Rob and CJ," she droned on, sensing that his last defenses were caving in. "They *owe* you a raise. Your salary is a disgrace to the industry. Besides," she crossed over to him and seductively threw her arms around his bulging red neck, played her palms over the plains of his broad back. "It would make things so much . . . easier."

She led her hands gently over the round of his belly, toward the miraculously stirring bulge beneath his light cotton pants. "It would make things so much better between us."

Dale sat paralyzed with humiliation as his member shrank and recoiled at her touch. Utterly unmanned, he gazed across the table, to the crumpled piece of paper which had kindled the fires of his aborted rebellion. A two-thousand dollar bill for Regina's latest acquisition: A chunky Rolex watch. Only several months earlier, it was a wafer-thin Cartier which had been *de rigueur.*

"I know you're trying darling," she continued soothingly. "Maybe I was wrong to buy it in the first place. I just thought that with the Steinholtz party coming up, you would want me to shine a little in front of the big guns. I thought that I needed something to go with the turquoise St. Laurent dress. The one with the chiffon sleeves."

"Keep the fucking watch," he surrendered, gathering up his blue linen blazer and stomping off to the garage.

"Do you *mean* it?"

He nodded angry affirmation over his shoulder.

"Thank you, darling," her saccharine voice echoed victoriously. "And Dale . . . *speak* to CJ. I'm sure that if you can just get up the courage . . . he *has* to agree. 'Now News' is essential to the network. If Conrad and

Cooper are talking a quarter of a mil for sitting on their asses an hour a day, and Kirschener is getting over three hundred thou for just as much, you've got to be worth more than *sixty-five* a year. Jesus, Uncle Steve gets *twice* that much for the *weather* report, not to mention . . ."

Dale drove pensively along Ventura Boulevard, heading for Coldwater Canyon. He cringed at the thought of how Regina had broadcast his salary like that . . . and within earshot of Betty! Not to mention the boys.

As if they—and everybody else in Hollywood —didn't know anyway . . . if they bothered to care. It was written all over Dale Stevens, and his wife, and his two snotty sons, and his car and his house and his birdbath swimming pool without jacuzzi or pool house:

Dale was a middling five-figure man.

Staring at the mansions peeping out from behind cypress and palms, the automated driveway gates sweeping off of Mulholland on either side, the Rolls Royces and Mercedes made him feel even more wretched. Dale was in hock up to his ears for the ranch house which had the distinction of being the only unimproved suburban property in the entire region.

Once again, he had been cowed and defeated by Regina. That was another reason for self-disgust . . . if he needed one.

Worst of all, it was his own fault. Every bit of it. Dale Stevens was simply not a fighter. In Hollywood he was used as a door mat and stepping stone by everyone in trampling distance. And if he hadn't been able to cling to Rob Steinholtz's coat tails, he would probably still be a third string reporter at KNRK. If not a writer lost in the sea of desks in the newsroom.

Miraculously, Dale was Director of the Satellite Network's Now News Program. Maybe once it got firmly off the ground, he would have a showdown with the RedRock brass. In the meantime, he still couldn't afford a decent restaurant without the expense account, dress his wife the way other network execs did, or cash in on the perqs that everyone else seemed to have no trouble arranging.

The fact was, Dale Stevens was a spineless jellyfish, a great cosmic washout. A *wimp*. He had gone from being the runt of his daddy's litter back in Iowa to being a senior executive kigmee at SBN. The only battle he had ever fought and won was for the hand of Regina. And Dale had been paying for that victory ever since.

He was a washout clear around the bases. Especially as a man. And if Dale was not proud of their home life, he was downright ashamed of the lengths he had gone to escape it. It was one thing to admit that *all* men need a little encouragement as they grow older. But he had long ago surpassed mere kinkiness.

First it had been young girls—dangerously young. Then it had been an insatiable desire for older women. The more they looked like the old aunt who used to tan his hide with a willow switch nightly, the better.

And then he had been introduced to a new passion: bondage.

Twelve

As the Tail-o-the-Pup rolled into sight, an uneasy smile crossed the chiseled features of Lauren Conrad's face.

Two years ago, the art deco roadside stand—a concrete wiener sunk deep within a roll—had been the most celebrated landmark in the immediate vicinity. At that time, the corner of Kings Road and Melrose had been like any other patch of suburban sprawl in the unincorporated area of Hollywood.

In the time of the Spanish Missions, Kings Road had been part of the lifeline stretching from remote Mexico City all the way to San Francisco. From their vantage point in the hills, the residents of the Angelino pueblo had anxiously monitored its endless parade of priests, conquistadores and Indians.

Much later, the area had developed a cachet all its own, housing a colony of twentieth century writers from Theodore Dreiser to Aldous Huxley. Nonetheless, it remained largely draped in obscurity. If New York had its SoHo and TriBeCa neighborhoods, then this one was clearly SoSun, BeNoBev. South of Sunset, and Beneath the Notice of Beverly Hills.

Now suddenly, the Satellite Broadcasting Network towered like a massive cut ruby over Kings Road, from Santa Monica Boulevard all the way up to Sunset. For the gawkers, the studio tourists and celebrity groupies, there was a sweeping archway and a black basaltic column to announce their arrival at Number One Sunset Boulevard. The network staff and limousines were always discreetly routed to the rear gate just off of Santa Monica.

She rolled up to the rear entrance and flashed her television smile.

"Can I, uh, help you, miss?" hedged the guard, sensing her determination to head toward the staff parking area.

"Lauren Conrad," she nodded imperiously. "Now News."

"Sorry," he mumbled apologetically with a reappraising stare. "Go right ahead."

She eased the rented Mercedes slowly up the inclined ramp. Taking in every contour of the opaque red glass monolith, and nodding. In some ways, the network headquarters was even more impressive from the back. But she was determined to get the stars out of her eyes, and concentrate on an image of perfect ease and calm.

Later on there would be time for ooohing and aaahing. After she owned the Now News co-anchoring seat, beside David Kirschener. What were a few more hours of holding back, after the seven years it had taken to get her here?

Lauren lit one last Sobranie and snapped the silver monogrammed cigarette case shut. she glanced at the Piaget watch on her left wrist and panicked. Time was closing in on her. At the same time, she was dwarfed by Number One Sunset Boulevard. By the promise of the Satellite Network, and the enormity of its vision.

What was a local newscaster like Lauren Conrad—or the ten minutes remaining before the final meeting—when it was compared to the vision of an entire fourth commercial network, and the massive structure exploding out of the earth before her?

How long had it taken to create the "superstation" in the heart of Hollywood? One decade? Two? Using half a dozen intermediary agents, a multimillionaire Beverly Hills entrepreneur named CJ Redfield had slowly acquired two running blocks of virtually undistinguished lots. Ultimately, it was *precisely* the right location for his Satellite Broadcasting Network headquarters. Within spitting distance of CBS, and just a kiss away from Rodeo Drive, the Beverly Hills Hotel and Laurel Canyon. And in a city which stretches on for months in all directions, ABC to the east and NBC to the north were mere minutes away, separated by the Hollywood Freeway.

After three years of painstaking negotiations with the owners, the last of the eighth-of-an-acre lots fell into place.

The next week, a trickle of the world's most renowned architects quietly began sketching up plans for his billion-dollar-baby.

One by one, they were flown in from Tokyo, New York or Rome, and ushered into Redfield's Beverly Hills office complex. While outsiders speculated on the latest Redfield shopping plaza or condominium development, behind closed doors the designers unrolled wall-sized sheets of vellum developing their plans for the headquarters for an as yet non-existent television network.

After months of searching, CJ Redfield had found his man—in the person of Jennifer Saltonstall Siskind. Like him, she was a fugitive from the ranks of stultified New England Brahmins. Following a dozen years of working for the right firms in New York, Siskind had found herself mired in the stifling anonymity of middling management. The architect took one glance at the hq specs and found her ladder to the stars.

Six months later, the plans for Redfield's brainchild were unveiled. Across the boards, the responses were uniformly peevish little remarks and cheap shots from the other networks. Around the clock, other architects were being interviewd by the media to decry the Satellite Network structure as an aesthetic abortion—or just the tackiest thing east of the La Brea tar pits.

"Yet another chapter opened tonight," deadpanned anchorman David Kirschener, "in the ongoing Hollywood saga of the Battle of Sunset Boulevard. In the latest of a series of surprise moves, Beverly Hills entrepreneur CJ Redfield today unveiled plans for his newly consolidated site. Following the filing of an FCC application for a license to broadcast locally, plus the installation of a controversial microwave transmitter on the Pacific Palisades, Redfield has now revealed plans for his 'superstation' headquarters.

"The architect's design has local residents up in arms, encompassing as it does over a block-and-a-half within a massive five story monolith, all sheathed in translucent red glass sitting on a base of anodized aluminum. While this challenge to CBS's RedRock does not yet have the major networks packing up and leaving town," he reported snidely, " 'RedRock' promises to develop into a full-scale war in the weeks to come. Here, filing an eyewitness report on the battle, is KJRX reporter . . ."

Two-and-a-half years later, the name RedRock had stuck. But now no one was sneering—especially David Kirschener. Not only had Redfield managed to achieve his dream, he had even convinced the city powers to give RedRock the address of One Sunset—a number which actually was miles from the prestigious Beverly Hills location.

Lauren stared out at the massive hangar-like structure, sprouting a series of towers and connecting gangplanks. Reflecting the afternoon desert sun, it looked like a cross between the world's largest ruby and the city of Oz. All around her, the reflected sun cast deep shadows on the pale white sidewalks and roadway.

From the beginning, she had followed RedRock's "birth." First with a detached sense of amusement, then with a reporter's instincts for history-in-the-making. Finally as her next conquest.

If it was notoriety that Redfield was looking for, he was not disappointed. From the first, RedRock had gotten more than its share of press—all of it bad.

During a lengthy debate on the proposed structure, a prominent local zoning board member died of a heart attack. "*RedRock Claims First Victim*" one headline screamed. Once ground was broken, the situation intensified. Ecological groups claimed that the station's microwave transmitter would ionize the stratosphere, and publicized their protest with mass lie-ins under towering construction derricks.

By far the largest protest came from the three commercial networks. Sneer as they might in public, they lost no time in filing suits to block the Satellite Network's FCC license. In the meantime, each of the three was pressuring major national advertisers not to succumb to the tempting rate packages offered by the Satellite Network's salesmen.

In addition, every hue and cry was picked up by the networks and catapulted into prime time scandal. But the more the major networks bore down on him, the more Redfield smiled into their cameras. Boldly—and with cunning.

He loved the frantic pace of the industry, the behind-the-scenes deals, the back field power plays. And it showed. But more than that, *nothing* could buy the sort of staunch underdog advertising which SBN was receiving gratis, nightly. He was smiling his way right into the major leagues.

That much Lauren had clearly seen from nightly camera footage and industry press. But in addition to the workers swarming like drones over the head-quarters' massive web of steel, Redfield had several other armies at work behind the scenes: a battalion of lawyers on each coast, blocking lawsuits and counter-suing; and hundreds of representatives, pounding the pavement as they sold the satellite concept to countless local mom-and-pop stations across the UHF spectrum.

By the time the major commercial networks were organized for a full onslaught to crush RedRock, it was already too late. The Satellite Broadcasting Net-work had already sold its made-for-television movies, variety shows, sports exclusives, star-studded specials, and Now News.

Actually, CJ Redfield seemed more like Santa Claus, giving away exclusive carrier options in return for affiliations. For tiny cable stations and inde-pendents in Dubuque or Hoboken, it was a lifeline they couldn't refuse. Five-star television and entry into the ratings game—at bargain basement prices.

The pathways from communications satellites to receivers throughout the nation had already been guaranteed. For ten cents per subscriber per month, the cable stations could have it delivered, syn-chronized. RedRock claimed five minutes of advertis-ing per hour, and scheduled in eight minutes for their own local sponsors.

Or else, for a measly hundred and fifty thousand, they could purchase their own receivers, and pluck it right out of the sky at no cost, whenever they wanted. Either way, they got five-star programming, and RedRock stole a bit more of the national audience away from the majors.

Ted Turner had tried it with CNN and his "Superstation" out of Atlanta. But only CJ Redfield had done it with full programming, turning RedRock, its microwave transmitter and comsat hookups into a complete fourth commercial network.

As the chauffeured Rolls glided up to the massive burnished steel entryway, Lauren took in Redrock in all of its immensity. At a height of three stories, the block-long red glass hangar began to sprout catwalks and moving pedestrian ramps, while transparent elevators whoosed up and down the central core. Six stories up, the structure exploded in a series of barrel vaults, connecting three towers to the central core. All in all, there were millions of square feet of surface. And every one of them was shrouded in reflective red glass.

It was now just over two years since Lauren had first reported on the announcement of the Satellite Broadcasting Network's existence. While the last of a quarter billion dollars' worth of electronic equipment was being installed, the headquarters was already going full tilt.

"Good afternoon, Ms. Conrad," smiled the valet, helping Lauren from the car without a moment's hesitation. Apparently the gate had telephoned ahead.

Lauren quietly nodded and found herself smiling broadly. She liked an operation that ran smoothly. But more than that, she thrived on recognition—any way it came.

Behind the uniformed doorman, twin doors swept silently apart, forming an entry arch. Lauren stepped through and was immediately greeted by a staff member eager to escort her to the studio. All around, in addition to the workers and technicians, were occasional glimpses of familiar celebrity features, and continual sightings of producers and directors as they bustled past. Throughout its anodized aluminum hallways, RedRock was alive and humming, despite the fact that it was a Saturday afternoon.

As the transparent elevator doors closed and Lauren was whisked upward, her thoughts turned to Kirschener. Rob Steinholtz had promised to do everything he could. But when it came down to the line, it wasn't much—*if* she didn't spark next to Kirschener.

It was going to take an Oscar performance. He was about as charismatic as a wet dishrag. She had worked with him on location once in Washington, and been singularly unimpressed. Both as an anchor and as a man, his qualifications seemed pretty scant.

How he had ever made it to the Nielsen olympics was anyone's guess. Only the pacemaker set could mistake him for a live wire. But now and for the next few years, Lauren was going to have to fake multiple orgasms every time he opened his tight-lipped mouth.

It wouldn't be easy. If Kirschener wasn't the prissiest commentator in the biz, it hardly said much for the industry. After six months in the United Kingdom, he had slid into the pseudo-British accent which was his trademark. A decade later, that act was growing about as thin as the hair painstakingly woven across his forehead.

But when it came down to the wire, Lauren could always complement his impeccable taste in white shirts. And his make up. Not only that, but for a shot at the national news spot, she could even manage it with enthusiasm.

Now that she was finally about to bag the big prize, Lauren was pulling out all the stops. From here on it was anything they want.

In the case of Rob Steinholtz, paying those

dividends was going to hurt. And keep on hurting until she could find a way out.

Compared to that, Kirschener would be a breeze.

Thirteen

"Crystal Cooper," the newswoman announced as she exploded through the zebrawood doors leading into CJ Redfield's outer office.

Directly in front of her, Redfield's personal assistant stared at the approaching skyrocket of color and motion with a look of unveiled disdain.

"I'm Barbara," she offered coolly. "CJ's assistant. We've met before. *Do* have a seat. I'm sure Dale and Rob will be joining you presently—they're generally pretty punctual."

Crystal nodded and stared at her diamond-studded Cartier. Four-fifteen. She was only a quarter of an hour late. And considering the fact that she had sailed out of the Beverly Wilshire ten minutes ago, it was a minor miracle.

Across the room, another pair of eyes bore down on Crystal. She turned to find them staring right through her.

Lauren Conrad. After so many months of nerve wracking competition and dread, the two women were finally face to face. Or at least would be—if Lauren would acknowledge her presence.

Crystal decided to try to fight fire with fire, matching Lauren's frigid disinterest in kind. Self consciously, she glanced at her reflection in a gold-tone table lamp. Make up and hair had survived the dash from

Beverly Hills intact. Everything seemed to check out.

Then a last minute burst of paranoia struck her. Trying to look as casual as possible, she ran her fingers along the back of her neck, underneath her billowing golden curls. Then feigning nonchalance, she slipped her hand down into her neckline and probed for the label. It wouldn't be the first time she had gone before the cameras with a price tag fluttering in the breeze.

This time, her fingers came up empty. Patting the curls back into place, Crystal strode across the room, crossing toward an ornately carved eighteenth century arm chair, and Lauren Conrad. The rich maroon silk brocade was so exquisite that the idea of sitting on it was almost sacrilegious. Lowering herself into the plush seat, Crystal smiled.

Beside her Lauren raised her eyes just long enough to level a nonchalant, somewhat amused stare.

Shrugging to herself, Crystal tried to move her mind in another direction. She gazed around her, enjoying the feeling of stepping back a century which always accompanied her first impression of Redfield's office. Throughout the RedRock complex, everything was streamlined chrome and glass, ultramodern. Efficient and functionally perfect to the nth degree.

But for his own personal space, Redfield had excluded high tech design in favor of Bokhara and Shiraz rugs. An intricately carved oak reception desk, a harvest table complete with heirloom Paul Revere silver service, a perfectly restored coffered mahogany ceiling from God knew where, or when.

Between the carpets and the high, arching ceiling, hung huge French Impressionist canvasses which flooded the room with color. Behind her, a Monet triptych of water lilies infused the room with the muted lavenders and aqua blues.

Her eyes trailed over the adjoining wall to a pair of

late Renoirs. Beyond them lay the real prize in Redfield's collection: an unobstructed view of Los Angeles—a panorama sweeping from Century City clear around to the Hollywood Hills.

Crystal gazed out beyond the curved mullionless glass wall at the turquoise dots of swimming pools, the fleeting glint of cars twisting through the tortuous spine of the hills. Once they had all been totally anonymous to her, foreign and intimidating.

But during the past few months of meetings and interviews, each of those towns and canyons had come to mean something to Crystal, to represent people in her life, and important experiences. By now, the twin Century Towers were like the town gates to Hollywood, greeting her every arrival from LA International Airport.

On the other side of the Pacific Palisades lay a thousand beach houses hugging the coast, including the one in which she and Joel had been making love scant hours ago. Farther to the north was Redfield's palatial residential complex.

Surrounding the RedRock towers were Mulholland Drive and the Canyons, Bel Air and Beverly Hills. Perhaps fifteen square miles of real estate where legends nodded to one another as they rubbed elbows or brushed fenders. Where it wasn't uncommon to have Rod Stewart living down the block from Gregory Peck, just a stone's throw from the old Walt Disney place.

During the past few months, Crystal had gone from detached curiosity about Hollywood to the stirrings of understanding. Gradually, it was beginning to seem like home, from Rodeo Drive to the seamy jungle of Sunset Strip. Much as she adored Atlanta, it had always been sort of like a corset—staid in all the wrong places.

In Hollywood, one thing was for sure: prudery was *not* going to be a problem. Neither was "immodest" dress, as Stephen had labelled Crystal's taste. Here, it seemed as if they *all* had it—and all flaunted it. The worst thing that could happen would be for no one to notice.

But then again, she was growing a little too comfortable with the thought of living here. Particularly in view of the immaculately turned-out copper-blond seated in the corner.

It was clear that as far as Lauren Conrad was concerned, *she* already owned the place. Reclining back into the thick silk brocade, Lauren arched her back with stiff-necked elegance, like a queen surveying her realm from the throne. That in itself was hard enough to handle.

But it was just Crystal's luck that the preppie look was in this season. Every inch of Lauren Conrad seemed to exude Miss Porter's School, Ivy League, tennis camp and LaCoste diapers.

Today she was dressed for a coronation. Her thick hair looked as though a dozen ladies in waiting had brushed it for days. The black raw silk Chanel ensemble was just as perfect. No wrinkles, no straining seams—yet it flowed over Lauren's lithe body like a second skin. She looked like she'd spent a quarter of her life at the spa or jogging—and the other three quarters holding court.

Of course, Crystal knew better. As enticing as Lauren might look, she also had a reputation as a reporter's reporter. She wrote her own copy, rode out in the eyewitness vans, and *never* gave up an inch of story to anyone. Wherever the best story was, Lauren would be covering it, or there would be hell to pay.

It had also been rumored that she wasn't above using her abundant physical charms to nab a scoop. Of course, like everything else about her, Lauren's lovers were strictly top drawer, as well as professionally useful. And seeing Lauren Conrad in the flesh, Crystal had no problem believing the rumors. If she would go to those lengths just for a good story, how much more had Lauren done to win the anchoring spot at RedRock?

Tentatively, Crystal turned to the woman who had spent weeks trying to undermine her, and extended a friendly hand. "You must be Lauren Conrad," she announced in a guarded voice.

In response, the other anchorwoman stared at her for a second, leaving Crystal's hand dangling clumsily in mid-air. Then, as she straightened her exquisite Hermes scarf, the corners of Lauren's lips lifted in a cool smile. She removed the Sobranie from her lips and stared pointedly into Crystal's emerald green eyes.

"*You* must be Crystal Cooper, then," she replied as she languidly extended an immaculately groomed hand. "You know, actually, you look far different on tape. Much . . . *younger*. . ."

Well you asked for it, Crystal chided herself. And Lauren had delivered it, alright. Hitting Crystal just where it hurt the most. She removed her hand from Lauren's grasp, stunned. How could that bitch have *said* that, without even batting an eyelash?

Lauren continued uninterrupted. "I followed the series you did on the Atlanta killings last spring. It was quite good. Really very interesting. Unfortunately the only thing people will remember about your work is that it got you fired."

The words hit Crystal with the force of a blockbuster. She had seen it coming, but somehow couldn't believe that even Lauren Conrad could be that vicious. Or that it could hurt so much. She felt the composure shatter inside her, and the thin facade of

122

self-confidence she had mustered crumble.

She felt battered, winded. The score was *Conrad 2* rounds, *Cooper 0*. And the real match hadn't even begun.

Crystal clutched the arms of her chair and waited for the sensation of teariness to pass. She gazed in her pocketbook mirror and was astonished to see that she did not look like the shambles she felt like. Her cheekbones were still high, her long fine eyebrows perfectly pencilled. Even her full lips looked sensuous and alive . . . But her eyes, looking scared and vulnerable, betrayed the mask of self-confidence.

She ran one fingertip lightly over a smudge in her eyeshadow . . . a second later, "oh shit" she muttered as a contact lens popped out of her eye and was lost somewhere on the zigzagging purple of the oriental rug.

She hesitated. But there was no way out of it. Without her contacts in on camera she'd be lucky to recognize a hand, let alone count the number of upraised fingers.

Dropping down onto her hands and knees, she began to comb the tightly knit rug inch by inch.

Across the room, Barbara took in the spectacle with a smile. She had had Crystal Cooper marked for a flake from day one. A flake and a *Southerner*—it was a bad combination. And she would be damned if she would rip *her* hose getting down on her knees for anyone.

Behind Crystal, Lauren looked down with amusement as the shapely blond crawled on all fours. She took a puff from her Sobranie and blew the smoke thoughtfully out in a ring, then watched with arms folded as it floated up toward the ceiling panels.

Simultaneously the two women heard the sound of Redfield's private elevator opening and for a brief moment their eyes met in mutual apprehension.

Fourteen

One two three four. One two three four . . .

One. Violet Duval bobbed her head down and gritted her teeth as her spine cried out for relief. Her fingers grasped feverishly at the insides of her knees.

Four. With a sigh of relief, she flopped back on the exercise mat and took a deep breath, staring up at the blazing klieg lights running in tracks along the sharply sloping roof.

A moment later, she wrapped a turban around her head, then slid into a bath sheet and headed into the privacy of her sauna.

This afternoon, the temperature was at 150. She breathed through a damp sponge, and rubbed a loofa systematically over her arms, shoulders and back as the heat seeped in and the sweat poured out.

Upstairs, in the far wing of her Benedict Canyon split-level deck house, Rick would be stretching out seductively on the suede covered sofa. She could just imagine his tousled brown hair, head cocked to one side, as he chatted on the phone.

Her secluded redwood home.

Rick Pappadopoulos was without a doubt the most seductive stud in America. And like Dr. Frankenstein after the creation of his monster, Violet had no one to blame but herself.

She leaned back and shut her eyes, surrendering

herself to the dry heat melting the tension out of her pores. Was it only a year ago that she had discovered him? Misery had made it seem like centuries.

Even in his funny red wrap around bag boy uniform, Violet could have spotted him a mile away. She had not spent the past forty years in the beauty world for nothing.

As for Rick, it was safe to say that he had not been wasting his time as a checkout boy at Gelson's, either. They had a union wage, room for advancement, an excellent pension plan. It was only a matter of time before even a sullen, lazy kid like Rick moved up to assistant produce manager.

But that was the last thing on his mind. His kind of action was up front at the register, where the fringe benefits could be . . . extraordinary. Every day opportunity knocked as a trickle of *possibilities* drifted out of range of the protected inlets of Beverly Hills or Bel Air, and wound up mooring their Cadillacs at the Gourmet Supermarket for the rich.

His father, who ran a little souvlaki stand just off Ventura, had the boy pegged as a total washout. He couldn't grill lamb on a spit to save his life. He was too weak to move an olive barrel, and too lazy to be a cook. At school, he was a miserable failure as well.

Under the circumstances, Gelson's seemed like a heavensend. And it was, in more ways than one. Rick had exactly two talents—his exquisite beauty, and an unfailing attraction to opulence.

That power was eerie, infallible. When a Silver Cloud hissed into the massive parking lot, his ears would suddenly perk up as he huddled over a half-filled double bag. He could spot an authentic Cartier watch—and denounce a phony brand X at fifty paces. As if controlled by a hand greater than his own, he was attracted to diamonds like iron filings to a magnet. Yet he was instinctively repelled by zircons; and his mouth formed an almost allergic sneer when approached by a woman dressed in knocked off designer fashions.

If fate had not intervened, his talents might have gone undiscovered forever. By some freak of nature, he could well have lived and died in the Valley, unknown. But suddenly he was stationed at the checkout counter at the crossroads leading to the *other,* exclusive LA, and he blossomed overnight.

Daily he tested his powers. Batting his Greek God eyelashes, encircling his prey, courting and sparking, breathing in their heavenly musk and swooning, then recovering just in time to load the bags into the back of the Mercedes, the custom white Cadillac, or the flaming pink Maserati.

In the case of Violet Duval, she had appeared just as he was about to punch out for the day. He helped her to her car. To her kitchen.

. . . To her bedroom door.

Actually, there was nothing unusual about that. It was not the first time Gelson's had extended Nick's services to the elite. But after sampling Violet's charms—her car, kitchen and bedroom—he signed on for a temporary berth.

His ship had come in. But it was not the QE II. Not by a long shot.

It was forty years since Violet had outgrown the term 'starlet.' She looked beautiful, but that was where it ended. And swear as she might that nothing had been nipped or tucked or bolstered, who knew for sure?

Then there was the question of security. Violet's house, her lavender Eldorado convertible, her Ralph Lauren outfits, Bottega handbags, Van Cleef earrings—they were all acceptable. Sufficient, but hardly up to the lofty standards he was determined to become accustomed to.

Likewise, Violet's income was adequate, but waning. It was getting harder and harder to keep body and soul together—and a touch of Beluga caviar in the fridge. Violet ran a sedate little modelling school in a medium rent district on the Beverly Hills/Hollywood border. She pushed enough of her fledglings up into the heights of minor stardom to keep up her reputation and her lifestyle, but there was nothing left over.

Enter Rick. Violet had not kidded herself for an instant concerning the score—at least not that much. But as an avid collector with an eye for beauty, she found him at once collectable and affordable. And at least for a short while—maybe even a long one—she could seek some solace in wrapping her tapered fingers and voluptuous thighs around star material that genuinely sparked.

Unfortunately, the spark fizzled in bed. In bygone days, Violet had gotten better from the gardener, from her lawyer—even from her biology teacher back in high school in Davenport. But nevertheless, nothing could compare with the feeling of having a hunk like that wrap his arms around your sixty-year-old body, spend hours caressing the nipples on your high and miraculously firm breasts, tell you that your legs and ass were shapelier than those of a woman half your age.

More than that, Rick was going to be *bigtime*, and they both knew it. If she didn't bring him up, then someone else was going to. And, while she waited for the big break which would bring her back from the dregs of near-obscurity, Rick would be a tremendous boost to her visibility.

Within a week after their first parking lot liaison,

Rick moved in to Violet's Benedict Canyon house. The next morning they had breakfast at Nate & Al's, then she bought him a debutante outfit at Jerry Magnin. Inch by inch and month after month, Violet went over him painstakingly. With her fingers, her tongue, and her model's eye.

She threw away his Levi's and dressed him in high-waisted pants. She taught him to order Perrier instead of beer, to wear silk instead of Qiana. She coached him in posture, in etiquette. She paid for his voice and tennis lessons.

As her Prince absorbed her training, she marvelled at his sponge-like talent. But as his marketability expanded, so did his hunger. Soon she was nursing a monster.

Within a year, Rick had twice made the pages of *Mademoiselle,* modelled fashions for the *Playboy* advisor, and was now threatening to accept an offer to share his treasures with the world—as a *Playgirl* centerfold. To say nothing of the conquests he made behind Violet's back.

Gazing at the clock with horror, Violet flew out of the sauna and dove into the kidney-shaped pool. One flawless swan dive, then a race to the little pool house room she had equipped with yoga mats, a massage table, and photographs . . . millions of photographs.

She tugged on a scarlet leotard and began another round of exercises. Facial tightening, breast supporting. She patted her firm tummy with a feeling of elated triumph. At sixty, Violet Duval really *did* look thirty-five, on a good day. And sexy and vibrant as well.

She stared at a magazine cover dated January '59. Her all-American cheerleader breasts were high and full. In '63, her then-bouffant blond graced the covers

128

of no less than 16 magazines. Her long, almost oriental almond-shaped eyes, the pert un-bobbed girl-next-door nose, the Miss Universe legs—all of them were still in prime condition—desirable, fresh-looking. Miles away from being "well-preserved."

Twenty years of Violet Duval were staring down at her with provocative, mocking eyes from the walls of the massage room. Quietly tucked away in albums, the first twenty years of her career were kept in a safe deposit box. Only once a year were they entered: at the changing of the guard.

Each year twelve months' worth of ads and publicity photos were added, and an equal number was removed. The mathematics and logic of the situation were simple and inescapable.

No one could remain twenty-one-plus forever. But as far as Violet Duval was concerned, Eternal Forty-One was a realistic goal. She had the looks to do it. And no old-timer would *dare* expose her. *Everyone* had too much to hide. It was an unwritten rule that in Hollywood, no one discussed age. Who you were lay-ing—*fine*. How broke you were, a natural topic of conversation.

But as far as age went, it was a forbidden topic—like failure. Until your shoulders sagged down and your bones shrank and the flesh started to droop so badly that *no* plastic surgeon would go near it—mentioning anything more than twenty years ago was like farting at a formal affair. You kept it in at any cost.

As long as no one asked and no one looked under your chin for the tell-tale scars—or refused to believe that you had spent the entire past season in London (instead of holed up inside the house, waiting for your face or derriere or breasts to heal)—life could go on. If everyone couldn't always be happy and wealthy and under contract, at least they could be eternally young and on the verge of stardom.

"Knock knock. Darling, you look just *scrumptious*. May I come in? Or is this some sort tryst I'm walking into."

Laughing, Violet stood up and allowed herself to be kissed on each cheek by Alex. His hand dropped briefly down and over the contours of her firm buttocks before he stepped back. In response, Violet leaned into his body a bit more, until her breasts were just pressing against his ribcage.

It was nothing so bold as a come on. Something like that would have been beside the point. But rubbing up against his tight young body just felt so *good*. And feeling good was what Alex Lanson was all about.

She stared at the sandy bangs, the broad sloping shoulders and powerful chest forming a Superman triangle with his thin waist and hips. Alex always wore white-verging-on-transparent drawstring pants which hugged his powerful thighs and buttocks. Slung over his shoulder was an unpretentious silver LeSport duffle, containing the implements of his trade — a dozen scented and lubricious oils, plus several pore tighteners and balanced pH moisturizers.

He slipped off his Japanese sandals and tightened his simple cotton *ghi*. Violet stared at him in plain admiration. Then she slowly removed her leotard. First one strap, then the other. Her fingers hesitated over her breasts, waiting until his light brown eyes were admiring her voluptuous curves. Only then did she carefully slip the leotard down to reveal her breasts. Finally, with the carefully choreographed motions of modesty, she turned around and slipped a light sheet over her shoulders as she stepped out of the leotard and lay down on her belly on the massage table.

"I was over at Francesca's yesterday," Alex

mumbled matter-of-factly. "Why to hear her rave over the birthday party she's giving for Roy, you'd think that it was the affair of the season!"

If money could only buy that, it *would* be. *Poor* Francesca. Violet sighed and felt the tension flowing out of her shoulders. It was always *poor* Francesca. Back in the days when Ronnie Reagan and Nancy were A Group leaders, it might have been different.

In those days, just about anyone could make it—provided they had the money, the connections, the visibility, and the willingness to entertain the *right* people. Then you could get by for 50 thous a year. But nowadays, the "A" crowd was tightening up the ranks, and eternally shutting the door in the face of borderline members.

Time after time, Francesca found herself on the outside, looking in. And each insult only made her more desperate to break in. *Poor* Francesca.

"Haven't seen you in . . . can it *really* be three weeks?" she sighed, changing the subject. "How's business?"

"Never been better. As a matter of fact, I was telling Wade the other day I couldn't even fit in *Mary Beth* twice, not if she *begged* me . . . Well, maybe if she really got down on her knees and . . ."

"Did for you what she's doing for her producer?"

Alex looked at her blankly.

"Oh, come on," Violet cajoled. "You'd hardly be letting onto something that half the world doesn't already know. MB has been laying Bill for half a year now. Showing up in Palm Springs with him, at those little midnight fêtes here and there. About the only one who hasn't figured it out is his wife."

Alex just shrugged and turned back to his preparations. Gossiping to Violet about the women in *her* group, and their flings with tennis instructors and

131

local lawyers and doctors was one thing: gossiping about his five *star* clients—the actresses like Mary Beth, whose latest movie was up for four oscars—that would be *disloyalty*.

He had been working for half a dozen years to make it to the top. At last he was there, and more than content to be the perfect confidant. If Alex charged outrageously high prices, it was only because of the Hollywood mentality—meaning: the more you paid, the better it *had* to be. But he still dressed in the same simple light cotton clothing, drove the same rusting MGB that he had in the beginning. And if it came down to it, he would have *paid* every last cent he had just for the privilege of serving some of the hottest names in the business.

"I hear that Victoria and John are on the outs. For the *tenth* time," he offered, as a sort of consolation. "As usual, she's flaunting it all over."

Violet laughed. "And who's her lucky victim this time? Her hairdresser, or her dietician?"

"Neither. It's Ted Manning. Mr. Real Estate himself."

"You're kidding. She must've inherited an awful lot of money."

Alex glanced at the voluptuous contours of his client. Was there just a hint of *jealousy* in her voice? Probably not. Even at sixty, Violet was one hell of a broad. Her skinny model's figure had filled out perfectly. She was still a striking woman with a good body and a terrific pair of boobs. She had been dodging the magnate's caresses for years.

Pouring some warm lilac-scented oil into his palm, he commenced to massage her back and shoulders, feeling the tension running like steel bands up into her neck. Maybe she did have reason for dissatisfaction. Forty years ago, Violet Duval—nee Shirley Farnum—was a household name. You couldn't pass a magazine stand without seeing her face and Betty Grable legs plastered all over the covers. In 1940, she was bigger news than Hitler.

"Relax," he breathed tenderly, his hands bearing down on her lower back. For ten years now, he had been massaging Violet, watching her stroking her, listening to the ebbs and flows of her life. As a successful masseur, Alex was part psychiatrist, part father confessor, with a hint of the gigolo thrown in. He had serviced dozens of women like her—faded or fading beauties clinging to tarnished old images, to exiting lovers, to self-respect.

But for all of that, Violet had always been more to him. There was still something vulnerable and innocent about her. She was impulsive, self-destructive, like the romantic heroine she had never gotten the chance to play.

If only she could have been satisfied with being a top fashion model, or some wealthy dress magnate's wife, she could have had it all. Everyone in Hollywood knew about the proposals she kept turning down. For Violet, it had to be love or nothing. And if it came down to it, even grand passion would be sacrificed for the chance to be a movie star, like the wonderful old silent movie stars who haunted her dreams as a little girl in Iowa.

After forty years in Hollywood, she still refused to give up. She had the legs and the body and the face of a star—and the acting ability of a Gong Show reject. Everyone in Hollywood knew that too, except Violet.

"Just relax honey," he said, his hands working over her calves. "You're so tight today."

Beneath his soothing fingers, he felt her flesh begin to melt. Her shoulders heaved once or twice as she fought to stifle a sob.

"Any word from ABC?" he probed, kneading the tight skin of her forearms, running his hands gently back and forth over her tensing fingers.

"Still waiting," she mumbled optimistically. Early in your career, there could be nothing more agonizing than being on hold. Every day you dreamed, prayed, lived by the telephone—even though your service would be taking the call anyway. After every ring you frantically dialed the unspeakably arrogant service operator, *just in case*.

But forty years down the pike, *no* news was good news. By the time word of the final cast selection got out, there were already three more you could string your hopes out on. And go to sleep on every night, imagining what it would be like, once the chimeric call finally appeared.

On the professional front, Alex concluded, it was status quo. Which meant that it was once again the Greek God who was casually tearing her apart. Her jealousy and suspicions, under the circumstances, was genuinely pathetic.

"Isn't Sloan throwing another of her wild parties tonight?" she muttered, confirming his suspicions. Lately, Rick had been working overtime at Sloan's, giving her everything he had and more, to insure a place at her fêtes. For a young man dedicated to cruising, Sloan's guests were the hottest rides in town. Without exception, they were always beautiful and famous. And if they weren't up in seven figures yet, it was frequently only a matter of months.

It went without saying that Violet was uninformed of his participation.

"The theme's 'Arabian Nights,' " he nodded. "Now back to the massage: Would you like the hot oil first, or . . ."

"Are there any other sirens this time? Or is it a

134

repeat of her Catherine the Great party? Just twenty-five studs, a pulley, and l'il old Sloan?"

Alex decided to drift into silence before he was forced to tell Violet something she didn't want to know. But from the sharp edge in her voice, she probably suspected something. He began kneading her calves reassuringly, as if that could somehow make up for everything else.

If Violet didn't suspect Rick, then she was a fool. Not just because Rick and Sloan Schwartz and half of the young up-and-coming starlets and starfuckers drifting up and down Sunset happened to be making it. But because he had stellar ambition written all over him, and it was obviously time for him to jettison the first stage of his career.

"Oh, Alex," she sighed, spreading her thighs and sinking down into the table. "You always know just what I need. I've got to be at my best this afternoon. There's a casting call down at Universal."

"Mh-hm," mumbled the masseur, his fingertips hypnotically soothing, as he gazed at the walls surrounding them. Fading covers of *Vogue* and *Harper's Bazaar*, two years' worth of ad campaign as Miss Alabaster Skin.

In Hollywood, to make it you needed three things: money, looks, and connections. Lacking two out of three, Violet would continue to be one more aging beauty with a voluptuous body who could pass for half her age, on a good day, and a lifestyle and dreams which sooner or later would crumble around her.

Violet Duval deserved better. They all deserved better—the tens of thousands of has-beens scattered throughout the Hollywood Hills, just waiting forever for that last stab at stardom, the last big break. But some of them—like Mary Beth—sparked. Violet simply didn't. She had come to Hollywood to break her heart, and had succeeded for almost four decades now.

Alex felt a stab of compassion and instinctively kissed the soft golden back of her neck. As he ran the fingers of one hand underneath the flowing black hair, he stroked her back softly, then absent-mindedly began caressing her rounded derriere. At once he felt her dissolving beneath his touch, as she leaned into his hand, like an abandoned kitten desperate for affection.

It was only a matter of time now. Before Rick walked out on her, before her agent made her face up to reality. How long would it last before she had to wake up one morning, stare into the mirror, and make an appointment with the plastic surgeon? It was either that or grow old at last.

She didn't have to open her mouth for Alex to know what she must be feeling—or what she needed. There was a desperation in the way she was rolling her hips, a burning which increased as his soft hands crept down between her thighs.

"He's a fool," Alex whispered, as his fingers slipped into the silky softness of her, already moist and throbbing. "Violet, your skin is so smooth . . . I think that you're even more beautiful than when we met . . ."

As his hands traced tiny circles around her clitoris, Violet began to moan. She clutched his other hand and pulled it against her breast, thrilling to the flesh pressing against her aching nipple.

Only Alex could do this. Make her feel like she had so long ago. Ripe, sensuous, irresistible. She could tell by the trembling in his hands that he wanted her, would do anything for her. Raising his fingertips to her lips, Violet covered them with soft kisses. She drew him to her and buried her face against his rock hard belly while her fingertips dug into the firm young buttocks beneath the draw string pants.

A moment later she was groping beneath the loosened waiststring, feverishly stroking his long, thick shaft.

"I want you," he groaned, and her legs spun round to receive him, wrapping around his waist as he gently separated her lips and thrust deep within her.

She pulled him against her and let her hands devour his shoulders, his hips, his tensed buttocks. She felt herself wriggling, her hips arcing wide. His lips travelled softly over the contours of her face, her neck, her breasts. His hands dropped down to clench her buttocks and pull himself deeper within as his thrusts began to grow harder, faster.

Her body heaved uncontrollably and she clawed at his back. Churning against him, she felt her contraction coming on. In a frenzy, she locked her legs around his hips and pulled him to her with all of her might.

She felt so beautiful . . . so alive . . . she was young again . . . she could feel the eyes beaming up at her. The hands that wanted to caress her. A million sets of lips, trembling. They were begging for her, crying out. The klieg lights burned down upon her and she felt her breasts heaving and her cunt throbbing and they wanted her so desperately and they rushed forward out of their seats. She stood there naked now, staring down from the movie screen. Suddenly there was one pair of hands cupped round her breasts. A set of lips was tracing the outline of her nipples. She felt the sensations as two men, and then two thousand, rushed forward and inundated her with kisses, caresses. She was beautiful . . . She was . . . irresistible . . .

The throbbing became an earthshaking roar as she arched her back and came in a series of sharp, jerking spasms.

Fifteen

"Here honey. Let me *help* you," Lauren offered patronizingly. Smiling for the benefit of Redfield, Dale and Rob, she fell to her hands and knees to help Crystal search for the lost contact lens.

Scant seconds later, Lauren held the strayed bit of pale green plastic between her scarlet fingernails. It would be so easy to just snap it in half, or absent-mindedly grind it under her heel.

Then again, Lauren didn't doubt for a minute that Crystal would milk *that* one for all it was worth. As it was, she had already managed to use the lost lens as an excuse for plunging her neckline down to ground level—just in case anyone had miraculously failed to observe it at normal elevations.

It was known in the trade as the "soft sell." Only the trade in question was the world's oldest profession. And newscasting, of all things, was supposed to be a bit above caveman instincts.

As Lauren knew all too well, sexual politics in the newsroom were filled with innuendo, leverage, and cheap thrills. But if Crystal thought she could win support by showing off her ass and playing the stacked blond in distress, she had another think coming. CJ Redfield was *not* about to yell out, "Good girl, Crystal. You get the job . . . now roll over." In fact, his features as he slowly approached the women were more noncommital than ever.

"Here it is!" Lauren exclaimed, holding up the lens, then dropping it into Crystal's outstretched palm. Out of the corner of her eye, Lauren could make out Dale's gaze as it darted over the hills and valleys of female flesh.

She turned to the approaching figure of Rob. An hour-and-half ago, he had been panting all over her, sweating rivulets and breathing like an asthmatic horse, riveting his eyes on the contours of her body as he struggled to keep his stubby little hands under control.

Now all of a sudden, he was staring right through her. If it was just an act to keep up appearances, even Lauren was convinced.

When his gaze finally did met her own, it was cold and distant.

A bad omen.

Lauren gracefully arose, smoothed her skirt and flashed her best smile as she strode across the carpet and offered them all a firm handshake. Her stomach was already balled up in knots. It felt like the butterflies that had been in there earlier had put on roller skates.

"I gather the two of you have met," Redfield smiled politely. His solid Down East baritone betrayed no emotion. But there were scarcely contained bursts of excitement bouncing back and forth between the three network executives, and occasional darting glances, as if something were unsaid, but clearly understood by all present.

Redfield escorted Lauren into his private glass-walled elevator, then held it open as each of the others filed in.

Naturally, Crystal just happened to end up beside

the RedRock head, Lauren observed, chattering and bubbling and simply overflowing with cloying honeysuckle sweetness. The stuff just came pouring out of Crystal's little old mouth at the most *amayzin'* rate. Why, it was simply pro*di*gious.

And if Lauren heard one more of those artful little "Oh mahs," she was going to puke for sure.

She had seen acts like this one before. But when it came to playing the *ingenue*, Crystal Cooper really took the cake. The tender, bruised little sparrow with the 38C bust. Lauren could practically imagine her protests as Rob cornered *her* in the Beverly Wilshire. "Wha-at? You mean y'all wanna stick that big old grown up thang in a nice L'il girl like me?"

She watched Crystal walking beside Redfield as they headed down the glowing chrome hallway. If they were lovers, then their body language was the greatest act of all time. Besides, far be it from Shirley Temple there to sully her flesh with that sort of cheap trick.

That sort of thing she would leave up to Lauren Conrad and Rob.

Instead, Crystal would casually sport a silk blouse that was so *décolleté* you could see down to her knees. Then there were the silk Kenzo pants she must have been poured into, and the strappy bronze spike heels. She was apple pie and mom and the girl-next-door all rolled into one, alright. Just like Linda Lovelace in her prime.

Topping it off—the frosting on the tart—was the jewelry. As far as Crystal was concerned, the fashion message was *the more the better*. The gold was just leaping out of her pierced ears, diving into her cleavage, springing into the limelight from three or four fingers. The glare was devastating and, if Hollywood cameramen thought Farrah Fawcett had a dazzling smile, wait until they saw Crystal blazing under the klieg light.

How could they *miss* her? If it was Crystal's intention to *go Hollywood,* she was succeeding in spades. You couldn't just pick her out in a crowd . . . you could pick her out at LAX in the fog, outflashing the runway.

There were a hundred things wrong with Crystal Cooper. Her cloying personality, her exaggerated and slightly flashy appearance. Off-camera she acted like a real flake. Scatterbrained, nervous, jabbering away a mile a minute. She was about as calm as a claustrophobic in a house of mirrors.

If she had won a Heiman award, then there was undoubtedly some broadcasting ability there. Lauren had looked over some of Crystal's work, and it was good. But the rest of the act . . . ?

If nothing else, it succeeded in doing one thing: demoralizing Lauren.

She sighed and stared down at her own tasteful black ensemble, the toney, understated elegance of her dark Jourdan heels. The conservatively tailored crème silk blouse with the high lace collar, the luxuriant Italian leather executive case—every inch of her image was deliberate, controlled, precisely executed. When it came to the world of carefully unbuttoned elegance, no woman in the world could compare with Lauren Conrad.

Which was why Crystal Cooper was getting to her. For once, it seemed almost impossible to compete with the competition. Lauren knew what she had, and how to make the most of it. But despite the fact that they were tall, varying shades of blond, and anchorwomen struggling over a job, what did the two of them possibly have in common?

141

Was Lauren supposed to giggle and *y'all* like a country schoolgirl? Was she supposed to puff up her chest and pretend that her breasts were like overripe grapefruit, instead of small and firm mounds on a slim and well-toned physique? Every day of her life, Lauren donned her jogging togs and ran a minimum of three miles. Crystal Cooper was about as likely a candidate for the Boston Marathon as Dolly Parton.

Beneath the transplanted Georgia Peach lilt in her voice, Lauren suspected that there lay another Crystal Cooper—the haunted, struggling street reporter who had left the Baltimore Tribune for Atlanta high society just a dozen years before. From those earlier years, the only remainder was a hint of desperation.

But Lauren was street-tough too. Savvy in the way only a New Yorker could be—a mixture of one part culture and intelligence to four parts survivor. It had been etched into her brain from the very beginning, out in the family compound in Salem, Oregon. *Conrads were winners. There had never been a loser among them.*

Losing out now would mean crawling back to New York in defeat. To the network affiliate station she had spent the last eight years moving up and out of. To the same stale romances and local audience she was hoping to move beyond. Gradually, every conquest and every ribbon added to her collection had turned sour. Every success just left her with a bitter aftertaste.

After fighting her way to the front of the cattle call lines at RedRock, could she possibly be nosed out by a limpid-eyed cow like Crystal? It didn't seem possible.

But something in her gut told her that Crystal already had it sewn up.

"Well, here we are," announced Dale, breaking

142

into the thick silence which had gathered around the group. "Studio C. Actually, we'll be broadcasting only local news from here. Now News will be shot in the studio down the corridor from the bullpen. But since the techies are crawling around there thicker than flies, we had to set up down here. The decor isn't much, but it'll do just fine for video."

"If you'll excuse me for a moment. . . ," interjected Redfield, walking toward the back of the studio. Lauren turned and watched the stately figure as he made his way to the production booth. Behind the glass, he was having an animated discussion with the producer, gesticulating the familiar signs for camera zooms and angles.

Beside Lauren, Dale was visibly trembling. "It's your baby, isn't it?" she sympathized, squeezing his hand.

He nodded grimly. "Every inch of it. Remember that . . . *if it flies.*"

No one had to ask what he meant by that. Until the first ratings were out, the success of Now News would be the number one concern within RedRock. With stringer correspondents in thirty cities, camera crews scattered all over the globe, ten million dollars' worth of talent and perhaps twenty times that in additional investments, Now News wasn't just big business. It was the heart of the Satellite Network's programming.

If it captured its fair share of the prime time news audience, the rest of SBN's evening programming would, too. Together, they would generate enough ad dollars to keep the Satellite Network rolling.

For Dale, it would mean the chance to be someone, after so many years of being elbowed and rabbit-punched in the scramble to the top.

If Now News flopped, it was more than a distant

possibility that confidence in Redfield's network would wane. Once the cork was pulled, baby and bath might slip down into the drain as everyone watched, helpless to stop it. The trickle eventually would turn into disaster for tens of thousands of people. It would begin with casualties in the Satellite Network's Board of Directors. If Redfield could hold onto his status as Chief Executive Officer, then those immediately below him would probably be spared.

The purge would start with middle management and their assistants, then slowly spread out to include general staff by the hundreds. Then the independent producers and everyone working on their pilots and scheduled shows. Next came countless people at the fringe of the operation: from clerks to guards to gophers and waitresses and air conditioning repairmen who catered to the trade.

For RedRock's stringers around the globe, from Cairo to Peking, it would be the most devastating natural disaster imaginable. For all of the shaky cable stations, clinging to the Satellite Broadcasting Network's communications satellite lifelines, it would be *arrivederci, baby*. For the rest of them it would simply mean perpetually teeter-tottering on the brink—and the end of their much-vaunted big-league status.

Whichever anchorwoman they went with, the RedRock brass were taking a gamble. She might hold her own against Barbara Walters and Connie Chung and Kelly Lange or she might become merely—What's Her Name with that guy Kirschener.

The day of reckoning would come after the first few months of Nielsens. Until then, Now News would sit heavily on everyone's shoulders. But for no one as much as Dale Stevens. *Remember that . . . if it flies.* Even if Now News soared in the ratings, Dale would still have to fight for recognition. As soon as the numbers were in, Redfield and Rob and everyone in the upper echelons of the management pyramid would be elbowing to the front row, looking for a piece of the credit.

From that moment on, the Now News watch would be on. Every camera angle and every sentence would be scrutinized by the entire industry. *What makes it tick? Why can't our news team spark?* To stay on top, Dale would have to keep pushing: for a bigger budget, more exclusive coverage, more glitter and prestige for the show.

Advertisers and audience would want more than superb reporting. They would want to be dazzled by a legend. If the ratings levelled off, Dale would be replaced. He would join the ranks of the thousands of one-shot movie stars and producers. The ones who were scattered throughout the Hollywood Hills, living in a world which had ended years before. Their vanity plates bearing names no one remembered, and their houses filled with publicity shots no one bothered to ask for.

If Now News flopped the stench of failure would cling to Dale wherever he went in this town. Failure was the only thing no one in Hollywood could ever forget . . . or forgive.

It was a terrifying thought for Lauren as she stood in the darkened studio where one of the two anchor-women was about to make the grade.

"Why don't you two head up there and get ready?" Rob suggested, deliberately avoiding Lauren's eyes.

She was convinced that he was hiding something. But more to the point, what was Redfield trying to prove? Was he really asking the two of them to sit on either side of David and scrap it out, upstaging and outclassing one another as the video cameras kept rolling? That went beyond viciousness, even in an industry where kindness could be back-stabbing gently.

She gazed out at the tangerine wall, the curving white formica desk before it. As a matter of fact, the studio wasn't even set up for all three of them—there were only two armchairs showing—not three. And something else was missing.

"David must've been held up," she stalled, as her eyes followed the curvaceous Crystal up to the platform.

"I'm afraid he won't be making it here today," Redfield casually answered out of the dark row of seats at her side.

Mind reeling, Lauren tried to grasp the situation. It just didn't add up. No Kirschener. Two arch-competitors side by side. The way the three men kept looking at the pair of them. As if each were more perfect than the other. As if they were a matched set, and all you had to do was smile and nod appreciation. Where in hell were the cold appraising stares that were going to get this decision made?

Or was it a *fait accompli,* and the absence of Kirschener a clear indicator? If that was the case, and Lauren wasn't in on their choice, that spelled disaster. But until she found out for sure, she had to climb those stairs with all of the strength and self-assurance of Itzhak Perlman playing Beethoven.

Shrugging, Lauren straightened her shoulders and coolly lifted her chin, walking with a brisk, measured step past the newsdesk, toward the last minute sanctuary of an awaiting dressing room.

She walked in and closed the door behind her in the darkness. Drawing deep breaths and exhaling with slow, controlled rhythm, she fought to slow down her

146

racing pulse. At the same time, she felt the familiar panic of stage fright creeping into her chest. The terror which a lifetime of performances under the lights had failed to diminish.

As she grappled for the light switch, Lauren felt herself being swallowed by the blackness. Like the nightmares which sometimes made her resort to phenobarbitol for months on end, she could feel terror struggling in the void at the center of her heart, shrieking deep within her.

Suddenly the old fears were once again welling up inside her. The fears which kept her jumping from relationship to relationship, bailing out at the first signs of emotion, continually running from herself.

Slowly the emptiness had grown. Until it was a cancer, poisoning her from within. For all of her imperious beauty and cold sarcasm, at the core Lauren had never grown beyond the loneliness and terror of the isolated six-year-old stranded in Salem, Oregon with no way home. Since that time she had remained alone, hidden within armor so thick that perhaps no one would ever break through. Or even bother to try.

Didn't anyone see how she had systematically underminded her life back in New York, until it was about to topple down all around her? Didn't they understand how much she needed to get away to Hollywood, to make a new start?

At thirty-two, the peak of her career might come any day now. So far, she had failed to build a life or a relationship which could last more than a few seasons. Even Crystal Cooper had a daughter.

Increasingly, Lauren felt the walls begin to close in around her. Suddenly it was like being in a runaway car which kept racing faster and faster out of control. It seemed that the collision would come any second.

The very flawlessness of her image had become a prison. Built to keep the rest of the world out, she now found herself suffocating within. Sometimes she dreamed of shutting off the lights—and keeping them doused forever. Knowing that each reappearance of her facade made it a little harder to break through—if she still remembered how to, at all.

She flipped on the light switch and was momentarily blinded.

But when her vision cleared, it was the familiar haunting mask which stared back at her, framed by two dozen makeup lamps. Every strand of hair, every movement of her eyebrows and her lips calculated, controlled, devastating in its perfection.

With fluid grace, she left the dressing room and strode past Crystal, already installed behind the newsdesk.

Up in the production booth, the silhouetted bald head of the producer was framed in the plate glass window as he donned his headset and huddled over the control panel. Throughout the small theater now, cameramen and technicians were scurrying madly back and forth.

Suddenly, the newsdesk was flooded with the familiar harsh blue-white light. The air was filled with the soft insistence of half a dozen humming cameras. The prompters blinked on and began scrolling out text.

The producer's fingers hesitated, then orchestrated the broadcast countdown.

Tension stretched throughout the room like an invisible web.

For Lauren now, there was nothing beyond the producer's fingers, no reality beyond the broadcast.

Underneath the burning klieg lights, the confidence

once more flowed into her veins. She stared straight into the cameras, eager for them to record every gesture of her fingertips, every attitude of her neck, every crisp and perfect syllable bursting from her lips.

The *other* Lauren was gone now, she told herself.

The red light flashed on.

Twin neon smiles lit up the studio monitors. In perfect synch, the anchorwomen beamed first over toward the empty rows of audience, then toward the far side of the studio, then toward one another.

Sitting in the front row, CJ, Rob and Dale exchanged quick glances, then silently nodded in agreement.

Sixteen

Joanne Conrad watched with scarcely concealed anger as the familiar black Bentley rolled along the long low fieldstone wall, then through the gates leading to the family compound.

As it slowly wound its way up the quarter mile semi-circular drive, she could make out a little figure standing on the front seat, blessed with an abundance of puppy fat. With that spray of unkempt strawberry blond hair tangled in one long mat, she looked like one of the little savages from downtown—a backwoodsman's daughter.

That would be Lauren.

In fact, Lauren Anne Conrad looked like anything *but* a Conrad. Every Conrad woman before her had been extraordinarily ambitious and intelligent from the toddling stage on. They grew beautiful from birth, and kept on that way.

The old woman nodded and rubbed her arms against the gathering evening chill as they arrived at her position beneath the great yawning porch of the main house.

"Lord save us," she whispered to the old man by her side, as she watched the fat and ugly little girl hopping to the back door and holding it open. "That isn't any child of our John's. I knew it all along. Phil, that woman is bringing us her bastard."

Then they both watched in silence as the child held open the Bentley door. A moment later, out stepped a voluptuous and slightly drunk woman. That would be her mother, Daphne.

With a look of sheer contempt, the older woman watched her emerge. The theatrical wide-brimmed black hat gave way to waves of reddish blond cascading down onto her thin bare shoulders. Dressed in a strapless black lace corselet and gathered silk skirt, with those long black gloves and spiked high heels, Daphne Conrad was about as likely a sight in the Conrad compound as Fanny Hill in the front pews of their tiny Methodist church.

And about as welcome at the funeral of Captain John Aiken Conrad, her husband.

"Well, you're *home!*" exclaimed Jonesy, doffing his cap at the eight-year-old girl.

Lauren Anne wrinkled her nose. She liked Jonesy, even though in the short time since their arrival at the Eugene Airfield she had already become aware of the fact that he walked bowlegged—like a real cowboy—and spoke a bit like one too.

Mama liked him, too. Lauren could tell by the way she was laughing in that deep, throaty nervous way. And she kept pulling down her tight black corselet, smoothing it over the curve of her waist. Then she would sort of breathe deep and throw out her chest . . . just like she did when she was having her picture taken.

But these days no one came to take their pictures anymore. And the only time Daphne Conrad posed was for lean and muscular young men like this chauffeur.

At any rate, Jonesy was okay. And the big old Bentley which smelled like leather polish, with the chrome glittering everywhere you turned—that was alright, too. But the three white clapboard mansions with the porches all around . . . were creepy. Like something out of a tv program, or the stage set from Mama's last play. Anything *but* home.

"Do you know *Under Milkwood?*" she asked.

"Nope." Jonesy was already focusing his attention on the shapely woman he was escorting up to meet Joanne and Phil.

"Silly," the little girl retorted, bringing up the rear. "*Under Milkwood* is a play. And *my* mother was the star. It was just Off-Off Broadway—which isn't the same as a Broadway show, really. But it doesn't matter. Mama says that it's better to start off . . ."

"Darling, that's enough now," Daphne chuckled nervously.

"Hello there, you must be *Lauren!*" declared a pasty faced woman. "Well, I'm your . . . your Aunt Joanne. And this is Uncle Phil . . ."

Lauren felt herself whisked into the air as a massive hand cupped her buttocks and a pair of scratchy lips deposited a kiss on her forehead. Next came Berenice, the house manager, and a maid named Julie.

"Oh my," said the maid, bending down as if inspecting a head of cauliflower. "Her nose is *just* like her father's."

A dead silence fell over the group, and Joanne mumbled between gritted teeth as they headed into the living room, to await the other two uncles.

When Lauren wrote postcards to her friends back in New York, she always said that Oregon was *marvelous.* The same way that Daphne would always say how simply marvelous everything was, then confide to Lauren later that it was an intolerable bore.

But Aunt Joanne only thought that her Daddy was marvelous. And *he* was dead now. Of course, his mourning wife and daughter both knew better. "Daddy was such a *terribly* nice man," Daphne would always say.

Which was another way Daphne had of saying he was a bore.

Before coming to Oregon, Lauren had worked up a small list of things which were a bore. Like taxi drivers who made passes at Mama, and very hot summer days and the opera. In Eugene, all of those boring things seemed to be a hundred miles away.

Nonetheless, Lauren's list was growing every day. Beginning with going to church school, and Aunt Joanne. She was always scolding her for something or another. Smacking her hands and telling her she'd go to hell.

Wherever that was, it couldn't be much worse than the Conrad compound. There was no other kids around, and no theater to hang out in. Mama just acted silly all the time. Dressing up in the middle of the day, laughing at nothing and then breaking into tears.

Uncle Phil just shook his head and mumbled, "She's been at it again."

And the more Daphne drank, the more Joanne would yell at Lauren. She was always calling her mother "that *slut.*" And when she spoke of "the devil's child," Lauren sensed that Joanne meant her.

But the worst part of all came every night at dinner. When all the family gathered in Phil and Joanne's house. The servants would cart in silver platters overflowing with roast beef or lamb or pork chops.

Together they would gulp down enormous portions in silence.

Only once the coffee was poured did the family permit conversation. And then they would speak about either the business or John. One night Daphne simply failed to show up at the dinner table.

And from that day on, Lauren was forced to face her grim Aunt Joanne and Uncles Phil and Don and Jack alone every night.

Under those circumstances, it wasn't very long before Lauren knew all about the family business. How Grandpapa Henry and his four brothers had come through the prairie stretching out to the east. All the way from Iowa, half a century ago. They used all of their savings to start a small furniture repair store in downtown Eugene at the turn of the century.

Conrads were hard workers, shrewd businessmen, and sure of success from the start. They had been in America for six generations, and there were no losers among them.

Soon, the brothers moved into making furniture. Next came a crude lumbering operation. It was only a matter of years then before the arrival of the first Conrad's factory, and factory showroom.

Now there were only three surviving brothers, Phil's wife, Joanne, and thirty-five stores scattered throughout the Northwest, plus more timberland than they could exhaust in ten generations. It did not take too many dinnertimes before Lauren realized that the businesses, the clapboard houses and the people in them were boring and she hated them.

She never realized that she stood to inherit all of it.

Lauren and her mother had been invited to spend the summer in Eugene for several reasons. As an act of charity, because the two of them were reduced to living on an air force widow's pension while Daphne was out of work. To see to it that Lauren Anne was not smothering in moral depravity. And to give Joanna the opportunity to prove that the girl was illegitimate, after all.

Once that had been ascertained, the family trust could be left to Joanne's struggling sisters down in Arkansas. Somehow, Joanne had become convinced that Lauren Anne's mother was responsible for her nephew's death, for deceiving him about her daughter, and for infecting the world around her with evil. Joanne was always willing to cast the first stone where sinners of Daphne's sort were concerned. And in this case, the Lord Himself couldn't stop her.

As September approached, Lauren looked forward to returning to New York. Soon Daphne would be back in the theater and she would make it to Broadway, and Lauren could hang out backstage and help run the lights . . . maybe even get a part as a walk-on. The only problem was that now Daphne seemed less and less ready to leave. She had always slept late, but now she was sleeping all day long. In the evening, she would wander around upstairs in her nightgown, as if no one else was there.

Then one evening, she didn't get up at all. Uncle Phil found her lying naked on the bed with all of the lights burning and a bottle of phenobarbitol in her hand.

For Joanne and for Lauren, the long period of waiting came to an end on a cold and damp September afternoon, as they watched the handfuls of dirt flying onto a lowered casket for the second time that summer.

Hands lovelessly clasped, they turned and walked back to the awaiting Bentley.

Lauren attended public grammar school like every other little girl in Eugene, Oregon. She brought her sandwiches in a brown paper lunch bag with her name written on it in magic marker. She went to Sunday School, and took piano and ballet lessons.

But she was always alone. Lauren was different, and there was no getting around it. She wasn't at all like all of the Conrad women were supposed to be: tall, thin, beautiful. Beneath the rolls of fat and freckles, only Lauren's waistlength mane of thick strawberry hair—which she freed from her pony tail at all possible occasions—kept her from being irredeemably plain.

Conrads were winners. But Lauren didn't fit the mold. She was a slightly morose, laconic child. And all of her obedience and politeness weren't enough to make up for that in the family's eyes.

Occasionally, Lauren Anne would be invited to birthday parties. But only when it was quietly suggested by her Aunt Joanne. The chauffeur would drop her off and the other girls would stare at the receding Bentley. Then they would eye Lauren's expensive new dress, the patent leather shoes, the fancy ribbons wrapped around her pig tails.

At least at the parties, Lauren could watch other girls play. She could run around in a nice little postage stamp backyard, or snuggle into a soft, comfortable couch, put her feet up and watch television.

Back at the Conrad compound, you couldn't even sit in the living room. Everything was too breakable, or else covered so it wouldn't get dusty. Lauren's domain was limited to the piano, the dining table, and ten bedrooms upstairs, which she shared with a succession of Nannies.

Actually, Lauren was confined to one bedroom at a

time, since Greta thought it would be impractical to clean up after a child in too many places. In the summer months, she would move to the Blue Room, with its wooden balcony and four windows over looking the Coast Range to the north. The rest of the year Lauren stayed in the Empire period bedroom, where her mother's personal effects had all been stored.

As soon as the chauffeur dropped Lauren off from school—Jonesy's departure coming on the heels of Daphne's—the little girl would bolt and head straight up to her room. Then she would do her schoolwork, or cut out paper dolls.

An hour-and-a-half later came the dreaded suppertime. That was the worst part of the whole horrible day. They rotated now: one night at Don's house, the next at Phil's, then at Larry's. But it hardly seemed to matter.

The second she sat down someone would inquire, "Lauren, how was school today. Did you bring home an A?" On Wednesday, it was, "Did you get that gold star in bible class?" On Saturday, "I hope you were brought up to the front of ballet class." "Did you do well in your piano lessons?"

The answer was always "No, sir. No, ma'am." And Lauren would just try to sink into her chair and shrink all hundred and forty pounds of her out of sight.

Before the meal was over, Phil would give her a firm pat or a pinch and say, "Look at that. Lauren Anne, you've grown again today." It was a fact that she was painfully aware of. She was now not only the loneliest girl in town and one of the fattest, she was also the tallest girl in her class, and she stuck out like a swollen thumb.

Then Lauren would sink into the oblivion of a thick ham steak or a roast chicken with baked potatoes, perversely wishing it were one of the starchy casseroles and meatloafs everyone else seemed to eat for dinner in the trim suburban ranch houses surrounding downtown.

As the adults surrounding her turned their attention to the business at various stores, Lauren would quietly ask to go to bed. Permission was granted without a break in the conversation.

Late at night, after Greta and Nanny and the rest of the Conrad households were fast asleep, Lauren would steal into the wardrobe closet where Daphne's clothes had been stored. One by one, she would pull down the window shades and shut the drapes.

Then, with the precision of a technician running lights on Broadway, she would assign cues to each of the dozen lamps she had carefully stolen from other bedrooms in the house, and stashed in her cedar closet.

Just as Lauren had seen Daphne do so many hundreds of times, she sat on a stool before her mother's vanity and began the precise work of applying her makeup.

Out of the hollowed-out diary she kept under lock and key would come the lipstick and rouge and powder and fingernail polish. That collection of contraband was the greatest achievement of Lauren's young life. One by one, she had smuggled them out of birthday parties, where she sought them out during visits to the mother's bedroom, or extended forays into the bathroom.

And the other little girls would giggle when she finally emerged. Because when you were *that* big, it had to take a long time.

Lauren would feel their stares rolling over the ripples of fat surrounding her. She would smile to herself,

158

knowing that those rolls of flesh were also concealing deep red lipstick, or an eyeliner pencil, once or twice a powder compact or eau de cologne. She was careful to never leave a trace, and only to take cosmetics which were refills and duplicates, or else tucked so far in the back that they would never be missed.

When she was awake, Greta would scream at Lauren endlessly for leaving on a lightbulb, wasting electricity. But now fifteen hundred watts bathed the curtained room in pure white brilliance.

Lauren had all the time in the world before dawn. She experimented with pancake make up, with dramatic eye shadows and mascara. She brushed her thick, beautiful mane into long, sensuous waves, or piled it atop her head the way ballerinas backstage always did.

Then, when she was finally ready, the orchestra would strike up and music would burst forth. All of the sudden, the audience would hush, and excitement would fill the air. The lights would dim to a flicker.

Drawing up her shoulders and throwing her head defiantly back, Lauren burst on to the stage. At once every light in the house swung down onto her, as the rafters shook and cheers and applause rained down deafening.

She could feel the thrill sinking down into her being. Her heart was beating faster now. The emotions were so intense she didn't know whether to laugh or cry. It was *marvelous*. Simply *marvelous*.

Of course it was. And she was Lauren Conrad, the famous actress. She was long and tall and beautiful. And quite elegant. But most of all she was a success at last. The *other* Lauren Conrad was gone, buried out of sight.

Now as the applause tapered off and the orchestra

quieted down to a soft timpani roll, she launched forward and calmly spoke, every inch of her proud and beautiful and as perfect as white alabaster,

Let us being at the begining: It is spring . . .

Seventeen

"Just think of it," Dale Stevens continued as his Cadillac Brougham cruised down Lomitas Avenue. "In the 1880's, this place was still trying to become the church capital of America—a sort of second Vatican. They were giving away free lots to anyone who would build a church. When the Beverly Hills Hotel was opened by Burton Green and the rest of the Rancho Rodeo de Las Aguas investors back in 1912, Sunset Boulevard was still very much of a bridle path . . ."

Crystal dully nodded and peered out the back window, trying to imagine the winding boulevards filled with horses discreetly cantering, occasionally passing a coach and four. But every direction she turned in, there were only tightly-packed multi-million dollar mansions.

Moreover, her brain felt as though every chamber was misfiring. After two gruelling hours under the lights, what else could anyone expect? She had showered and splashed gallons of icy water on her face, but nothing seemed to help. With difficulty she could follow Dale's train of thought, but that was about it. And until she knew about the outcome of the anchoring job, it was all she could do to seem alert.

Except for noticing every now and then that in the

front seat, Superwoman Conrad looked as fresh and carefree as a tampon ad. Crystal suspected that it was half intended for her benefit, just for spite. Or was Lauren just lording it over her, knowing that it had already been decided: Kirschener and Conrad?

As Dale's voice drifted off, she slowly focused on the Mercedes and the Jaguars, the Rolls Royces and priceless Italian sports cars, and the custom mile-long Cadillacs.

"Did you girls know that there are more Mercedes in this vicinity than in all of Germany—not to mention more Rolls Royces than in London?" he cackled in his hearty manner.

Dale's Hollywood legends might have been apocryphal. But they made his point. For hundreds of years, the drought-and coyote-ridden Rancho Rodeo de Las Aguas—where they couldn't raise sheep, strike oil, or even grow beans—remained a losing proposition.

The California land boom came and went, leaving the barren acreage here unaffected. The Morocco Junction train station came and went. It seemed like nothing would ever spark the huge expanse of land to life. The German Colony of the 1860's, called Santa Maria, the land boom town of Morocco—all of them were ambitious on paper. But they never got much farther than that.

Then in the early 1900's, Burton E. Green founded the Rodeo Land and Water Company. For an area continually plagued by drought, the name brought tremendous reassurance. And a good thing, too. The sheep herds had been decimated by rattlesnakes, the oil rigs had missed time and again. Even the Holy City approach had got them nowhere: they couldn't *give* the land away.

There was no gold to be found in those hills or

gulches. So Green decided to bring it in from outside. With its warm, dry climate, other parts of California were already bringing the winter vacationers and the retirement set. Now all he needed was a plan.

In 1904, a land speculator named Abbot Kinney had decided to build a Venice in California just southwest of the Rancho. The seashore resort featured Venetian architecture, Venetian canals—even imported gondolas and their gondoliers.

Green decided to go him one better, and found a New York architect to design a town exclusively for the well-heeled, based on the plan of Rome. It was an ambitious design, based upon roads radiating out in all directions from one focal point, just below the intersection of Beverly and Sunset. In 1907, lots of land in Beverly Hills were put on the market.

That year, someone built a house.

And that threatened to be the end of it, unless something desperate was done. So in 1910, the Rancho developers once more imported some talent in a hurry, this time to landscape the place, and plant stands of palm and acacia trees.

A year later, the population had leapt to the hardly impressive total of *five* families.

The opening of the Beverly Hills Hotel changed all of that. In grandeur it was second to none. And while it did deign in those early years to host local weddings and community events, it immediately attracted the lawyers, and the bankers and oil magnates and retired people from Down East that Green had been courting for years.

Beverly Hills exploded overnight, then kept right on exploding. The first movie people to arrive on the scene could barely have afforded an overstuffed sandwich at the resort. And they were hardly the desirable sort for so exclusive a setting. But by 1919, when Douglas Fairbanks and Mary Pickford built Pickfair in the winding hills just behind the hotel, movies had gained both respectability and extreme profitability.

Sixty years later, Venice Beach was a Bohemian hangout known for its cafes and its roller skaters. The canals were filled in for sanitation reasons, and urban renewal was moving into the picture to reclaim some decaying buildings.

Meanwhile, in Beverly Hills, one single property had just sold for almost a quarter of a *billion* dollars.

The numbers and what they represented went beyond staggering. They were inconceivable.

Here at the radius of Beverly Hills, though, people took that sort of thing in stride—or at least without having tachycardia. The monstrous cotton-candy pink Beverly Hills Hotel still lolled over acre after acre of priceless land in all of its Spanish Mission gentility.

Now the sudden blast of a horn jolted Crystal out of her reverie.

In the front seat, Dale was laughing easily with Lauren. As if they hadn't just spent two grueling hours in the studio, with *all* of their careers on the line.

As if all of them hadn't had the sweat dripping down their spines as the video cameras maintained their steady whirring clicks. Maybe for Dale, the real test would come down the pike, a few months after Now News went on the air. Maybe he already knew the score of this final round of takes.

But why in hell were the two of them so blasé about it? *No one*, she told herself, *can be that mellow*. But there were Dale and Lauren, smiling, idly chatting, while the axe prepared to fall . . . on one of them.

"What the hell" Crystal reflected, "I may as well enjoy the local color—it *does* boggle the mind."

The cars alone represented a small town's gross annual income. Then there were the people in their designer clothes and accessories. Added to that were their endless bands and strands of gold, with dangling emeralds, diamonds, sapphires, rubies and other heavy artillery.

Dale watched her nose in the rearview mirror as it once again came perilously close to pressing against the glass. "Quite a show, isn't it," he laughed. "But don't worry, Crystal. Half of the Rolls Royces and Cadillacs are rented."

"Those don't worry me a bit, darling," she rejoined. "It's the Other Half I'm thinking about."

If she craned her neck at every grand touring or sports car that passed down on Sunset, she would be dizzy in a matter of seconds. But the most terrifying part of all was the *naturalness* of it. Everyone around them—down to the children who bicycled to the Beverly Hills Hilton for breakfast, simply took it for granted.

Maybe it was the California sun. Or maybe it was the L.A. smog. But whatever it was, it was beginning to infect Crystal with the same blasé attitude. What she needed was a good hard shot of reality. A starving Appalachian child, a boatload of refugees, survivors of the Three Mile Island accident. *Anything*.

Professional considerations aside, she was ready to scream.

Then finally Lauren Conrad *did* do something. She turned around to observe Crystal stargazing. Crystal could see her own tense, animated features reflected in Lauren's amber eyes, and that the other newswoman was amused at the sight. For a moment, she kept Crystal pinned beneath her gaze.

165

Then, tossing back her burnished gold mane, Lauren smiled mockingly.

That was good hard reality, alright. It hit Crystal with the double force of a cold towel in the face and an amyl nitrate "popper."

Here they were, sitting in the car, waiting to find out the most important decision of their lifetimes, mortal enemies separated by two feet of air conditioned air. They've just come out of two hours of grueling taping. And what does Lauren Conrad do?

She grins and stretches, like a goddamn house cat waking from a nap. Suddenly, Crystal felt her teeth clenching, and the blood pounding in her temples. Once and for all, she had had it with that supercilious bitch, the coolly raised eyebrows, the condescending smirks, the holier than thou imperiousness.

Even if she lost the RedRock spot, in the end, Crystal wanted to get the better of Lauren at least once. When this roller coaster ride was over, she would probably be bumped off the track by the newscaster from New York. But she was *not* about to go back home and crumble and dissolve in a slow barbiturate fade, or slash her wrists in the bathtub.

At least, not until she had settled the score. Crystal was convinced that for months now, Lauren Conrad had been backstabbing and maneuvering to get the job. It didn't take much to figure out that there was something unsaid between her and Rob Steinholtz. But the face-to-face oneupmanship, the cold shouldering and the personal insults were too much to endure.

"Maybe she doesn't mean it," Crystal immediately told herself. "Maybe she doesn't realize it. She must want this job, too. Even more than me."

Then again, it was more likely that Lauren knew

precisely what she was doing. That there were a calculated number of casualties every time Lauren Conrad pushed her way up the line, and the emotional expense to others was merely written off.

Crystal supposed that Lauren didn't really seem to have much use at all for women. Well, if she was a misogynist, she had just hated the wrong woman. She could have just done her dirty work and been minimally civil. But not Lauren Conrad. She had to go beyond that and declare an enemy. Humiliate Crystal and toy with her. Demoralize her, as if winning itself wasn't enough.

Well, whatever Lauren's problem was, she would get what she wanted. An eye for an eye and a tooth for a tooth. She wanted a vendetta, well, now she had one. In all of her life, Crystal had never hated anyone—not even the Atlanta banker who had made her miserable all the years of their marriage. She had never learned to hate the father who walked out on her, or the mother who couldn't forgive, or forget.

But where all others had failed, Lauren had finally succeeded. Never before had Crystal felt so insulted—whether real or imaginary was not the question. Well, it was about time Lauren learned what it was like to be on the receiving end. But even as she resolved to retaliate, Crystal knew that there was not much chance of matching her rival's arrogant bitchiness.

"Welcome," came the greeting from outside her window as Smitty helped Crystal out of the Cadillac's rear seat.

Flashing her most seductive smile, Crystal threw back her shoulders and swept onto the red runway carpet.

A few paces ahead, Lauren Conrad seemed to have

167

no difficulty looking like she owned the place.

As a red-jacketed valet appeared and whisked away the Brougham, Dale watched Smitty as groups of stargazers honed in on the women. Lauren's imperious cool was unusual for a newcomer strolling into the Beverly Hills. Her black suit was calculatedly devastating, quietly suggesting every curve of her back and slender hips. It was as if she didn't have to advertise *anywhere*. And that was the sort of understatement that never failed to make the heads turn in Hollywood.

While everyone else was dying to outshine the last act, Lauren was content to parade by dressed as an elegant fashion model.

But her impressive entrance was upstaged. Directly behind her, Crystal was ready for combat. No sooner was Lauren out of the limelight than Crystal seemed to slow her pace. Her smile was radiant. Her body moved with subtle sensuality.

No one could outdazzle Crystal when she really turned on. With her prominent curves amplified by the shimmering pants and the décolletage, a loudspeaker couldn't have announced her arrival more clearly.

Smitty observed the women with a nod of appreciation. For years now, he had watched the new hopefuls arriving, exiting from their limousines and strutting their stuff before the inevitable crowd. Lauren and Crystal, he concluded, had the spark.

Dale also observed the pair. The tension between them was almost palpable as they poured their hearts into the cameras, oblivious to the fact that they were now being tested as a team. Backstage, he shuddered to think about what would go on between the two of them. But in public, it all became positive energy, like a force field surrounding them as they each struggled to project the most magnetism and allure.

From the second they had begun taping side-by-side, their chemistry had leapt from professional excellence to riveting excitement. The more the fires were fanned, the more they *each* seemed to glow.

For all of their physical and emotional contrasts—and the personal differences quickly piling up between them—there was something special about the way they fit together. Slowly, Dale was coming around to Redfield's way of thinking.

For all of the contrast between them, they were complementary, like yin and yang. And hopefully *not* like most of the marriages around town. Without a doubt, the tabloids would have a field day with *this* prime time duo. As an odd couple, they would be hard copy to pass up, particularly with good publicity photos.

SBN was going to use a female team prime time, clear across the country. It was so perfect, so obvious. So sensational!

And once again it was CJ Redfield who had come up with the bold stroke, the sort of thing that a News Director might never have dared to dream up.

It was also a sore reminder of the difference between a CJ Redfield, and a five-figure employee locked into the lowest rung of the industry's high society.

Crystal glided past the rose marble reception desk, once again amazed at the way Hollywood could continually change its appearance. One moment she had been walking into a massive Spanish Mission-style palace. Now she was suddenly standing in the midst of

169

what looked like an art deco country club foyer. The green-and-tan geometric carpet, the overstuffed floral print sofas and easy chairs, was like entering another world.

Back East, you would have expected to find heavy Mexican leather furniture throughout the palace, and maids wearing Mexican peasant dresses. The thought of building a dozen different styles into a single structure was never even considered.

But in a town with the phenomenal growth of Hollywood, it was unavoidable. Things changed quickly, everywhere you went. It was like second nature. In the studio lots, every corner you turned would bring you into another part of the globe and another era. In the studios, themselves, new stars were discovered every other week, and old ones discarded as often.

A few years ago, the look had still been rhinestone on denim. Everyone had been wearing awning-like eyelashes, and miles of gold chains, dripping with mushrooms and razor blades and Zodiac signs. Crystal remembered the fashion report showing forests of black hair erupting out of men's tailored Qiana shirts opened to the navel. This year the look was All-American, and either Western or preppie. But decidedly more Neiman-Marcus than L.L. Bean.

Six months from now, most of the women milling about this lobby would move on to something else. Their entire wardrobe would be given to charity, resale shops or the maid. Around the room, Crystal could immediately spot a dozen Rolex watches, and she instinctively slipped her Cartier back under her sleeve. Whatever had happened to the Cartiers? At last report, *they* had been the coming fashion, replacing Omega's.

170

Then again, whatever happened to Mia Farrow? Or a newscaster like Joe Benti? How many people had already forgotten his incisive news coverage? In this town they shot up like skyrockets. And many of them came down pretty hard and fast. If you blinked, it would all be changed, just like yesterday's news.

In the meantime, Lauren had made a beeline straight for the Polo Lounge. Crystal sighed, and headed off in hot pursuit. "If I ever make it back here," she promised herself, "I'm having the grand tour." But in the meantime, her job was to keep up with Lauren Conrad 'til the bitter end.

By now, Crystal had become almost familiar with the boutiques on Rodeo Drive. She had been to a few studios, and checked out network headquarters. She had been to Chasen's and the Bistro Garden, to Tony Roma's and Morton's. But somehow she had missed the fabled watering hole of the Golden Age of Movies—the Polo Lounge.

Standing with icy elegance beside the bustling maitre d', Lauren was already posing in the doorway. Slipping his arm through hers, Dale appeared and escorted her to the Polo Lounge entry. "Redfield, party of four," he announced.

"Right this way," Walter replied, giving Crystal and Lauren the once-over with new respect in his eyes. As resident greeter of the Polo Lounge, it would *not* do to snub guests of CJ Redfield.

In fact, as much as running the Polo Lounge, keeping track of the whereabouts of guests, pulling out chairs and lighting cigarettes, Walter's job consisted of knowing who each guest of importance was. At certain times, there could never be enough banquettes and tables to go around—with or without reservations. Whether they came with advance notice or just happened to be dropping by, a Richard Burton or a Johnny Carson or a Barbara Streisand and Lew Wasserman could not be kept waiting, under any circumstances.

With reservations, a minor celebrity might be kept waiting for up to fifteen minutes, a local tv anchor or hot young producer for no more than 20 Non-celebrities might be kept waiting out in the lobby for up to half an hour. Then there were the scores of local Ladies-Who-Lunch. They gravitated to the Polo Lounge in droves, hoping to see someone—*any-one*—or be recognized by a demi-celeb they could brag about bumping into.

Dale spoke as soon as they were seated around one of the tiny fake-marble tables crammed near the bar—the "right" side of the room. "CJ wouldn't miss this for the world, if he could avoid it. But since he has some urgent things to look after, he asked me to apologize."

The waiter appeared, and Dale's voice trailed off. "Either of you ever try the famous house avocado dip? No? Then you're in for a treat. And I believe that Mr. Redfield has already called up to reserve . . ."

"Everything has been arranged, sir," replied the waiter.

"I'm sure that will be fine for starters," Dale concluded, then contented himself with briefly taking stock of the Polo Lounge crowd; waving once or twice, and nodding with an almost imperceptible tilt of the head half a dozen times. "CJ wanted you both here this afternoon," he began, "as a sort of coming out for . . ."

His sentence was cut off midstream by the arrival of the bustling figure of Walter, waving through the scant aisle space and plunking a telephone down on the adjoining table.

Crystal turned and found herself almost elbowing . . . could *that* be Dustin Hoffman? The features were unmistakable. But between his worn Levi's and the scruffy beard, he looked more like a Venice Beach drifter than a screen idol. But his voice as he whispered into the telephone receiver—even in the buzz of the afternoon crowd—was unmistakable.

Now that her eyes had adjusted to the light, Crystal had no trouble making out a handful of familiar media faces, and at least twice that many sets of vaguely recognized features.

At every table there was at least one Vuitton or Gucci bag—his *and* hers. The fashions ranged from Brooks Brothers to Kenzo, and from expensive to phenomenally expensive. And if that was casual afternoon jewelry the women were wearing, she couldn't wait to see their formal attire.

A moment later, a magnum of Mumm's champagne in a silver bucket was placed at Crystal's side.

In another corner of the Polo Lounge, Sloan Schwartz and Sid Gold were practicing their own one upsmanship. ". . . so I think that we see a move away from the sit com crap, toward an upscale market," Sloan Schwartz concluded, pausing to nurse an outsized goblet filled with a Bloody Mary. So far, her hangover hadn't improved in the slightest. "What do you think?"

Sid Gold drew his lips into a lop-sided grin. He considered her skinny little body, swathed in a black Halston, with a matching turban and a red Celine scarf. When she gesticulated with those two-inch fingernails, she looked just like a black widow spider. Sloan would never be half the man her father had been, he thought to himself either in negotiations or with the starlets.

"Yeah," he said, leaning back and chewing on the stub of a freshly smuggled Havana cigar. "You'll be in tough company. I was speaking to Tom over at ABC this morning, and he says to me, 'It's the inflation. We're goin' after discretionary income. Fishin' in those deeper waters.' I say,

'If Spelling and Goldberg have been bringin' home the bacon for so many years, why change the formula?' . . . But I guess that a person can only watch 'The Love Boat' or 'Charlie's Angels' for so long . . ."

"Even you?"

"On the record or off?"

"That depends."

"You drive a hard bargain, Sloan. I got a little somethin' cookin' up over at MCA to pick up the slack. New series. Called Benson's Brownies. Gonna be tremendous . . ."

"Mr. Gold?" interrupted a waiter.

"You have to ask?" He grabbed the receiver and waited. "Oh, so it is you, CJ. Yeah, I'm sorry about it. I tell you, maybe it's all for the best. At any rate, you can't say I didn't warn you about Kirschener. Told you he'd rip it right in half, huh? Well, what're you gonna do? Maybe you're better off without 'em. You know these broadcasters . . . Yup. That's right . . . the second they don't get their way. Well, lissen. You wait a while, and give him a chance to simmer down. Maybe for four, he'll see the light. In the meantime, who's the lucky lady . . . La*dies*? . . . Mmm-hmmm. Well I'll be goddamned. . . . Yeah. Sure will. *Ciao*."

As Sloan watched in amazement, the crab-red features of Hollywood's top agent seemed to blanch for a moment. He stuck a finger in his collar and wrestled for air.

"*WAITER!*" he yelped, throwing up a hand, "Wanna give me a double Vodka Gimlet . . . nothin' for you Sloan? . . . No, wait. Better make that a *triple.*"

Gold stared down at the silent telephone and frowned. Then his eyes scanned the Polo Lounge until they focused on a familiar figure just making her appearance.

Gold stared at the bleached blond fall scattering wisps all over her face. The slightly uneven Mae West bust. The ultra suede pants and Maud Frisson boots that ill-suited her.

For the thousandth time, he sized up Deena Willis and found himself staring at a sad case. A loser. Rumor had it that she had been nipped and tucked so many times that the top ten plastic surgeons in LA wouldn't go near her.

No matter. What counted was the bottom line. And she was building up clout as an agent. How many times had Sid offered to buy her out? Three? Not only did she persist in making herself a laughing stock in the industry, as she laughed all the way to the bank, but, incredibly she had just signed up one of her clients to Fiona's job at RedRock. Humiliating Hollywood's top agent in the process.

He took a good hard swig of the Vodka gimlet, and ordered another. Then with a shrug, he watched the agent make her way across the Polo Lounge with as much fanfare as she could muster. It was a cinch she hadn't dared to show her face here for awhile.

Across the room, he could just make out the bloated features of Dale Stevens. Sitting across from him was a vaguely familiar blond, who reminded him of Little Annie Fannie. His kind of talent. Beside her sat a

175

leggy woman with honey blond hair and exquisite cheek bones. He studied the features silently, then slowly raised his glass back to his lips. This time, he drained it off entirely.

Lauren Conrad. The dame who had put on the deep freeze on the New York flight. Jesus! If that bitch had just landed the Now News spot, it would cost Redfield double to get Kirschener back. Once again he remembered his resolve to sign Lauren. From the looks of things, there wasn't a moment to lose. "C'mon, Sloan," he barked hoarsely. "Why doncha bring me over to the rest of the RedRock party for an introduction."

She stared for a moment at the table across the room, then softly shook her head no. "Listen Sid. You'll get your introduction soon enough. I promise. But let's give them a chance to let the dust settle a bit. At least on the contracts. You didn't *really* think you could meet them before we had them *signed* darling. Did you?"

Besides, she thought to herself, for once Sid Gold was not going to demand the pick of the litter. This time, that was one right that no one was going to take from her.

Lauren gazed around her reinforcing her first impression of the Polo Lounge.

It looked like an outtake from a vintage Sidney Greenstreet movie. Everything needed dusting, brightening, polishing. Actually, what it needed most of all was redecorating. And yet the rich and the famous vied for the privilege of sitting in one of the plastic upholstered booths.

Sitting next to her, Dale was busily engrossed in raising his champagne glass for a toast.

As the waiter popped the cork, Dale announced in a voice meant to be overheard by a dozen tables, "Let's fill these glasses and get on with it, girls."

"That's women," Lauren shot back, annoyed.

"All the better," replied the news director. "A toast. David Kirschener is now officially out of the Now News picture. To the new co-anchor of SBN's Now News."

Lauren raised up her glass and smiled with perfect ease. Underneath the table, her knees were wobbling so badly they were actually knocking. She braced herself and prepared for Dale's words.

"Here's to Crystal Cooper . . ."

Lauren's features froze into a lifeless smile, as she tried to catch her breath. Now more than ever, she needed the control which a lifetime career had perfected. *She had lost.* After months of preparations, thousands of dollars and hours. She had given it everything, even sacrificed her self-respect this morning to win over Rob. And everything hadn't been enough. Lauren had been prepared for the worst . . . until it came. She was crushed, and the room seemed to be closing in all around her. At the same time, tears were welling up in her eyes. For the first time in eight years.

"No," she screamed to herself. "Don't give in to them. Don't let that bitch have the satisfaction of seeing that she's won." But any second now, the flood gates were going to open.

"And here's to Lauren Conrad," Dale continued, laughing. "Our new co-anchors. A toast to our new team. Just the three of us."

It took Lauren a moment to make out his words in her confusion. When she did, they ripped through her like an earthquake shock. The look of venom she was directing toward Crystal became a bewildered stare.

She looked at the other woman's face, trying to make sense of it. In one second, they had suddenly been transformed into . . . *partners?*

Then, in a flash, her features sprang back to life once more. Out of the corner of her eye, she could make out a figure she recognized as Crystal's agent, heading for the table. Simultaneously, as if it had been choreographed and rehearsed a thousand times, the two women leapt up and threw their arms around Dale's neck.

For a moment, there was nothing in Crystal's mind but the sensation of hugging Dale and the relief of *knowing* at last. Slowly it turned into elation and then to light-headed excitement. Crystal was so thrilled by this unexpected turn of events that she began to laugh and cry simultaneously. If it wasn't for the steely presence of Lauren, Crystal would have jumped up shouting with joy, right there in the Polo Lounge. It might've all been a dream, except for the arrival of Deena, her agent, to make it official.

As Crystal watched the agent approach, she suddenly shuddered. Somehow in this setting, Deena Willis looked like last year's news. The woman who had impressed Crystal so much in Atlanta would simply never be able to carry it off in her own backyard. If Crystal was going to do it right this time, she would have to start again from scratch. And that meant finding a more respectable agent, pronto.

Two months ago, she might've been horrified by the thought of being disloyal. But in Hollywood, either you were top drawer, or you were nothing. Soon enough, Lauren would catch on and sign on with International Artists or one of the other giants. And if Crystal was stuck with a second-rate agent, she would not have the leverage that she would need in this town.

As she reached over to hug Deena, Crystal's champagne glass was knocked across the table. She closed her eyes and imagined the fury that awaited her. She didn't have to look to know that it was just her clumsy luck to pour it all over her rival. She could just imagine the expression on Lauren's face.

"Ohmigod," she cried out. "Lauren, I'm *so* sorry. I was just . . ."

"Don't worry, honey," Lauren answered cheerfully, "after all, it *is* just champagne."

"And quite a vintage year at that," Dale chimed in, watching with trepidation as Lauren's hands clenched into fists of rage beneath the table. Only champagne, indeed.

Sitting at a banquette several tables away, Adam Ward's amusement slowly crumpled and died. He had been keeping tabs on the women ever since their arrival with the SBN news director, right up to the champagne bath. But just why they were all smiles and hugs when they should have been tearing out one another's eyes, he had no idea. And as chief of KJJX, a local network affiliate, his job was to know.

What RedRock was going on-line with, who was skirmishing in the background, how the programming slots were filling up. From LA to Las Vegas . . . Washington to the Big Apple, he had reports coming in every hour, providing just that information.

He was keeping track of CJ Redfield's appointments, his phone conferences—even his waste baskets. Adam Ward knew why Sloan was having drinks with Sid, and about the studio set designer who was keeping Rob Steinholtz busy in a motel a dozen miles away.

He caught Sid Gold's eye and raised a questioning eyebrow. In return, the agent shrugged his shoulders, then angrily tilted back his glass, as he continued to stare at the rounded derrière of Crystal Cooper.

From the look of things, Sid Gold was upset. And that meant that something big was in the wind at RedRock. "Good old Redfield," Ward mused, as his eyes wandered over the two anchorwomen, and seemed to stumble and fall deep into the heart of Crystal's cleavage, "you may be a humorless and vindictive son-of-a-bitch—but CJ, my boy, you sure know how to pick them."

He tore his gaze away from Crystal at last, only to marvel at Lauren's sleek legs, outlined by her tight-fitting skirt. "My God," he thought, "compared to them, the Barbie and Ken clones we have on the air are nothing. Each of those dames has more personality in the dimples of her ass than all of the KJJX News Team's combined."

He called for a phone and continued to stare at the unfolding mystery as he dialled headquarters. They had known about the elimination of the other candidates five hours before Dale Stevens had. They had gotten a juicy rundown on Lauren Conrad's last minute rendezvous with Rob, and a sketchy report on Crystal's movements since arriving at LAX. But where in hell had they been when Dale Stevens pulled the ace out of his sleeve?

All in all, there was something distinctly unnatural about this latest turn of events. There was always something the competing network had going just to keep him off balance. And the situation would be unhealthy for him unless he found out why Lauren and Crystal were suddenly making like turtledoves. And reported back to HQ fast.

Eighteen

"Beige and burgundy have simply *always* been one of my favorite combinations," Sloan Schwartz gushed in a cloying little girl voice. "Don't you just *adore* it. Lauren?"

Lauren gazed down at the anorectic-looking woman. Then up to the graying porte cochere of the hotel. What in hell was Sloan referring to? All around them, a group of star-watchers awaited the latest arrivals. She stared at the muted pastels, the fiery reds and oranges, the occasional patch of denim heading out to the traffic island.

Suddenly the answer came rolling into view. A four-door stretch Mercedes, to be exact, painted beige, with burgundy accent panels and roof. Beaming a self-satisfied smile, Sloan proudly threw open the door for her guest.

Lauren tried to match her nonchalance as the custom interior leapt into sight. The seats were covered in natural antelope, with burgundy piping. Over and over the motif was repeated, right down to the cream-colored console housing a telephone and television set. The vanity license plate that read "SS I" wasn't kidding. It might as well have been a yacht.

Plopping down beside her, Sloan snuggled back into

the leather seat and dialed her personal secretary as the chauffeur raised the glass partition and set off for Sloan's home.

"Marge," she gushed into the receiver, "make that a celebration for *two*. We just signed on Conrad *and* Cooper. Lemme tell you, these two are really *knockouts*. I shit you not. And they look even *more* beautiful off-camera." She paused to wink at Lauren. ". . . CJ has just about run them ragged, so I'm sure they'll appreciate a night of relaxation. How's the guest list working? Yeah? *Great* . . . I'm sure this is one A Group that's dying to meet them. . . ."

Lauren thrust one hand into her purse and ran her fingertips over its contents, uncomfortably aware of Sloan's eyes slowly going over her features. She found the silver cigarette case and slowly extracted a Sobranie, trying to seem absorbed in the jumble of traffic lights and cars beyond the tinted windows of the Mercedes. Up ahead, she could make out the grotesquely painted monstrous features of the latest punk rock band, leering down at her from a billboard.

Then she heard Sloan mention the "A Group" and her heart skipped a beat. The fabled *crème de la crème* of Hollywood society, the people who imported snow from the Rockies for Christmas theme parties, or whisked groups of two thousand off to Israel for a son's Bar Mitzvah. To that crowd, ten thousand for a Galanos dress—or a hundred thousand dollars to "personalize" a limo like Sloan's, was nothing

"Okay," Sloan continued on the line, "what about Dusty? He *whaaat?* Well lissen darling, you just call back that ungrateful little prick and tell him to start wiggling his buns for another network. He is *out* at RedRock. No, better yet, *I'll* tell him. In person . . .

183

Friday morning breakfast at the Polo Lounge, when the whole goddamn world is signing contracts. You *did* keep Peter away, didn't you? One look at Lauren here and he'll be lost to me forever." She giggled into the receiver. "Okay darling, we'll be arriving in about twenty minutes. Bye bye."

"Marge just can't wait to see you," Sloan concluded, turning back to Lauren.

As Lauren sat there and listened to her companion rattling on, she tried to figure out what it was about Sloan that raised her hackles and her guard. Although she had a long, prominent nose which crowded her other facial features, there was nothing really repulsive about Sloan's appearance. Her little Twiggy body was really cute, objectively speaking. And she seemed genuinely interested in Lauren's career.

But there was something about the gushing little girl image which didn't jibe with the other side of Sloan. The side which talked endlessly about getting laid and used words which would make a truck driver blush.

It wasn't caring, womanly concern which had made Sloan Schwartz one of the most dreaded women in the industry.

And if the rumors were at all true, certainly *the* hungriest.

She gazed over at Sloan and found the other woman frowning. "Lauren," she announced—suddenly all business, "I wanted to be clear that we understand one another."

"Oh?"

"Rob told me about your little chat this morning . . . I just wanted to make sure that we all understood the lay of the land. As president of the network, Rob's technically my boss. But we work as a team . . .

184

equals. He's more ambitious than anyone imagines. And brilliant—that goes without saying. But without me, that's as far as it goes."

Lauren nodded silently. Suddenly the conversation was taking a very interesting turn. She began to realize why Sloan had been so insistent on taking a drive after the Polo Lounge celebration.

"I'll be frank with you," Sloan continued, "he's too hungry. The man has no class, and he's apt to do things which are a little, uh, impetuous. But let it suffice to say that you owe your job here to the *two* of us. We are quite willing to reward cooperation. In return for which, we'll expect loyalty, *at the appropriate time*. Think about it, darling."

Lauren quietly nodded. She recognized the carrot being held in front of her nose—it sounded suspiciously like a bribe—and the fact that the bullwhip wouldn't be lagging far behind her. The battle lines were being drawn, more quickly than she had thought possible.

Before RedRock had even begun to broadcast, Sloan and Rob were already engineering a takeover. When it came down to the final showdown, it might tip the balance. But it could go either way. She turned to Sloan and smiled noncommittally.

Never, since Dale's announcement this afternoon had Lauren doubted that it would come down to that: *outlasting* Crystal. CJ Redfield would be a fool to dream that the two of them could survive as a team. But sooner or later one of them would get an edge in the recognition ratings. Then the landslide would begin, as the other felt everything shifting out from under her, then began losing ground.

In the meantime, Redfield knew that both of them would be doing their utmost to cling to the top, upstaging and outbroadcasting every inch of the way. In the process, they would undoubtedly be producing the tightest reportage in the nation. CJ was nobody's fool.

Back East, the CEO's of Network Row could wake up one morning to the astonishing fact that SBN was now vying for their primetime audience—and winning. Lauren now fully expected it to happen. For the first time, she realized just how much everyone had underestimated the RedRock brass.

They had their faults—writ large—to be sure. But behind their facades of California ease and comfort, their brains never stopped racing, scheming, manipulating.

And behind their easy Hollywood smiles and blasé remarks was a stark ambition that would stop at nothing—if it brought success.

She puzzled over just how much Redfield knew about this brewing mutiny. Somehow, she doubted that Dale Stevens would have the balls to be in on it—or be trusted by Sloan. At the right time, this information might prove . . .

"Just one other thing, darling," Sloan urged, grasping Lauren's hand in earnest, "it's only fair to warn you that when it comes to Rob, there are no secrets . . . we share *everything*."

A second later, her features were once again soft and smiling, as she rambled on in her coy, kittenish voice. Vanished was the woman who had just outlined the upcoming corporate struggle to Lauren, offering a limited partnership she couldn't refuse.

And more than hinting at blackmail if she tried to.

Lauren thought once more of those photographs taken three thousand miles away, a decade ago. The sooner she found and destroyed them, the easier life

186

would be. But as collector's items, their value to Rob was increasing too quickly.

Perhaps the price was already too high.

All in all, Casa Schwartz spread out over a dozen acres of prime California. The central structure was a 1920's Tudor style stucco mansion, with massive turrets rising a story above it. To the right, the original paddock and stables had been incorporated into the house, as a series of duplex guest apartments, carved right into the sheer rock face of the canyon. On the other side of the house, a long, low wing swept down toward the pool.

"Darling, you look absolutely delicious," called out a voice as the taxi screeched to a halt and Crystal bounced out of the car. "Doesn't she, Alex?"

Crystal blushed. She felt the eyes of the man Sloan was crawling all over unabashedly checking her out, as he posed in his skin tight white drawstring pants and loosened *ghi*.

"Alex, allow me to introduce Crystal Cooper. Formerly of WATL, and one half of the new anchor team of SBN's Now News. Crystal, Alex is my masseur—so don't get any ideas. Besides, you *know* what's it's like when you're dealing with a professional. Like laying a taxi driver—with the meter running. Alex, why don't you be a dear and round us up some champagne, while I show Crystal around."

Crystal followed Sloan towards the greenhouse solarium. From a distance, it had looked almost like a jungle.

On closer inspection, it *was* a rainforest. And scattered throughout were orchids of every conceivable size, shape and color. Twisting around tree trunks, bursting out of the moist brown soil, climbing up the corners of the glass wall.

Impulsively, Sloan opened a door and leaned in, picking a pale violet orchid. She held it against Crystal's red jumpsuit and laughed. The next thing Crystal knew, the RedRock vice-president was pressed against her, as she fastened the orchid with a small pin.

"And what's this?" called out a man's voice in mock indignation. "You really don't waste any time, do you Sloan? Well, I demand an introduction to this *gorgeous* creature."

"I see that shyness is still one of your virtues, Rick. . . . You look devastatingly sexy. If those pants of yours were a scooch tighter, the little secret of your success in Hollywood would be out of the bag. This my dear, is Crystal Cooper, our network's latest find. Crystal, allow me to introduce you to my favorite Greek God, Rick Pappadopoulous. He'll tell you he's been in more magazines than Jackie O, and more beds than George Washington. He's a dreadful two-faced liar—and what he called eight inches the rest of the world calls six—but the rest of him *more* than makes up for it. Rick, *do* show Crystal around. That's a dear."

Twenty steps behind them, Lauren observed the scene as the handsome man escorted Crystal, obviously enchanted by her emerald eyes and full cleavage. During the past few hours, Lauren had begun to realize just how attractive Crystal was. The dainty southern charm, the vulnerability, the big eyes framed by pinwheels of golden curls were bowling them over left and right.

Not that heads weren't turning for Lauren too, but Crystal somehow made her feel that her own beautifully molded torso was unfeminine, that her sumptuous honey-blond hair was dull by comparison. When they were in the same room, Lauren actually had to fight for her share of the limelight. It was a new and disconcerting experience for Lauren to be upstaged by any other woman.

Her thoughts were broken off as a flash of golden muscle appeared and announced, "Hi. I'm Terry," offering her a gentle, massive hand and a pair of cerulean eyes.

At the same time, another bronze God appeared on her other side, shouting, "Lauren *Conrad?* WNRP. I used to watch your show alla time, back east. Gosh, you're even sexier in person. My name's Bill."

Great, she thought, taking in their matching blue and green togas, over bulging white crepe pants, *a sisters act.* Slowly, she began to realize two things: The overflowing golden muscles and the outlines of the twin muscular buttocks were having an effect on her.

The airheaded twins were also the farthest thing from A Group material imaginable, as were most of the other guests she had observed so far at the party.

Flanking her, they escorted Lauren past the chrome and glass living room, into an adjacent parlor done in authentic Louis XIV furniture. One wall blazed with the light of a dozen crystal sconces reflected in gold-veined mirrors reaching up to the ceiling. On the opposite side, maroon brocade curtains were pulled to the side to reveal French doors towering to a height of twenty feet.

Beyond their glass panes, Hawaiian torches were being lit over a vast terrazzo patio. On the far side of the pool, a massive marble poolhouse recreated the sumptuousness of an ancient roman bath. Flickering in the torchlight, she could make out a half dozen living, breathing replicas of Michaelangelo's David, pos-

189

ing like nude statues or diving into the pool.

So this was what it was like to inherit a Hollywood fiefdom from the golden age. Sloan Schwartz, like Rob's wife and a handful of other women, was heiress to a movie fortune, in the form of a chain of first-run theaters scattered throughout the country. Hadn't there been a whisper that the Schwartz empire was running in the red? To all appearances, the incredible opulence, the luxurious surroundings, and the young Gods were commonplace to Sloan. Like the jungle in the living room, they were simply one more fantasy to explore.

"So much for 'reliable' sources," Lauren mused, shrugging off the rumor of financial collapse. From the looks of things, there wasn't *anything* Sloan couldn't possess.

Even with all that she stood to inherit, Lauren had always had grandiose desires for money, power and ambition. Suddenly she felt an irrepressible urge to explore Sloan Schwartz and this incredible Walt Disney world of hers.

At the far end of the room, Lauren saw a small crowd gathering around a delicate antique etagere. She stepped forward to find out what was causing the commotion.

"You bet it's real," a husky woman's voice beside her pronounced. Lauren recognized the voice from a dozen award-winning movies, before she even spotted Patti Springfield in the crowd. Squatting down, the screen idol had her face pressed to the inch-thick glass encasing the etagere. Reflected in her eyes, the object sparkled like the crown jewels.

Lauren had seen reproductions of Fabergé eggs only in books, but it didn't take long to figure out what it was—or what it was worth. Even eighty years ago, when Peter Fabergé constructed it for one of the tsar's mistresses, it was already priceless. She stared at the gold cradle, the ribbon of rubies and diamonds surrounding the egg. Only after awhile did she turn her attention to the inside of the egg, where there was a porcelain painting of two beautiful young nymphs locked in an embrace.

Beside her, Patti Springfield stared at the scenario and gently nudged Lauren with her elbow, as she issued a low gutteral laugh. Lauren stared at the actress, with her outlandish inch-long coif, the exaggerated arching eyebrows, and the voluptuously fleshed body. It was obvious that she shared Sloan's manner and sense of humor. How much more did the two have in common?

Patti Springfield, according to all of the tabloids, swung both ways, although in her case, men were clearly a last resort. Her coke habit was rumored to be up to three or four grams a day, and her political activist lovers had given Hollywood, the women's movement, *and* the black panthers a bad name. But somehow, none of that seemed to matter here. When it came to celebrity, fame or notoriety amounted to the same thing. As long as you had the draw, you could travel in any circles.

And without any doubt, Patti attracted the men like flies. Lauren turned to find that they were surrounded by young men, scantily dressed and flashing seductive smiles. They were costumed in everything from tunics and gold embroidered Turkish vests with bare skin beneath, to transparent Indian silk shirts, and jersey tank tops.

"I should've expected as much," Sloan announced, slithering through the sea of flesh with an expression of total bliss, and a slightly glazed look in her eye.

"Lauren's in this house for five minutes, and you've already got her cornered, Patti. Well lissen, she is *my* guest tonight—so you'll have to find yourself someone else. Not only is Lauren stunning, but she is also one of our new anchorwomen at RedRock. So . . . hands off."

Sloan threw her arms amicably around both of them. The Chinese silk robe she wore was more than a little revealing, fluttering open to parade her small conical breasts and well-tufted mound for the other women. With a coy blush, she re-tied the sash. But the material was so transparent that if Sloan had been wearing her Rolex around her waist, anyone in the front row could have read the time.

At the edge of the room, Crystal suddenly reappeared, leading a small train of admirers in tow. She stared at the scene in disbelief.

Sloan led the entire group to the new wing of the mansion, where tambourines, tabla drums, high-pitched pipes and a *bouzouki* were already weaving their rhythm. A nondescript woman in a plain cotton shift introduced herself as Sloan's personal secretary, then rushed over to join her employer at the back of a huge horseshoe-shaped table. Sloan urged Crystal to sit beside Marge, and Lauren and Patti to flank her on the other side. Then, with a clap of her hands, she commanded the dozen men milling around to join them.

A moment later, as carafes of red and white wine appeared, Sloan stood on her chair and struggled to make herself heard. "Here's to friendship and success," she shouted, glancing at Crystal, then lingering, her gaze on Lauren. *"To the three of us."*

Lauren shivered as she sipped her wine. Now the only sound was a cymbal and a tambourine. All around her hash pipes filled to the brim were being passed around. She watched Crystal timidly toke on one then pass it on. Sloan watched in delight while Lauren took a long, slow pull, then felt her lungs expanding.

As the pipes continued to circulate and servants kept refilling glasses for additional rounds of toasts, Lauren suddenly became aware of a figure leaping into the center of the floor.

A golden spotlight flashed on from the ceiling, the music exploded once again. All at once the figure of a woman began to shimmy and undulate beneath a set of veils.

All eyes were riveted on the belly-dancer. She was close to forty, the ripples of flesh heaving hypnotically up and down across her broad belly. Above her naked midriff, two full breasts bobbed with mesmerizing rhythm.

Lauren gazed at the audience, every member gaping at the swaying body in their midst. She could feel the tension around the room building up, feel Sloan and Marge squirming with delight beside her.

Only Crystal seemed to avoid the trance. She was peering at the assemblage of guests with an uneasy smile.

Crystal stared at Lauren Conrad's face. It was filled with amused disbelief. She silently nodded agreement. For a fraction of a second, Lauren seemed to be caught off-guard, and her smile was conspiratorial, almost friendly.

Then again, maybe it was just the lighting. Crystal blinked her eyes and the moment had passed. Lauren's impenetrable mask had fallen back into place.

As the dance grew more frenzied, a new tension filled the air. Crystal sipped on yet another glass of wine—was it her third? Fourth? For the rest of the night, she vowed to empty her glass into the potted palm behind her. If only she had thought of that a glass or two earlier.

Although it was unlikely that anyone else would notice her condition. One and all, their bloodshot eyes were focused on the ruby held by unknown means within the belly-dancer's navel. Without a doubt, she and Lauren were the only halfway sober people there— and that was a very poor indicator.

She glanced over at Sloan just in time to see the diminutive figure leap onto the table. The startled servants rushed to clear it. In dreamy ecstasy, she kicked off her sandals, then began gyrating her hips. The music slowed down to her tempo. Beneath the golden spotlight, the sheer silk of her robe seemed to evaporate, leaving every inch of her body bared to her captive audience. The tempo once more increased. It was accompanied now by the wild arching of her back and her shimmying hips.

As if on cue, all twelve men suddenly gathered around her and began to dance. Sloan jumped down onto the floor in their midst. Next Marge sprang out of her seat. Grabbing Lauren and Patti with a surprisingly strong grip, she led them out onto the dance floor, tossing them more or less like sacred offerings.

Patti Springfield's powerful body began writhing in counterpoint to Marge's. Lauren seemed dazed for a moment, until it boiled down to dancing or being trampled.

Like an airplane propellor, her body jerked into a few false starts and sputtered to a halt. Then the music and the hashish really took hold of her, and sent her pelvis into orbit.

Still seated, Crystal watched with dismay as the entire room was transformed before her. She rubbed her eyes, wishing the scenario would vanish, and feeling like Alice in Wonderland after a particularly bad mushroom.

By now, she was beginning to feel twinges of nausea. In a panic, she bolted from the room and headed for the patio. A minute of fresh air—and distance from the maddening beat—would probably help counteract the effects of the wine.

She was still staring at her reflection in the pool when she saw something looming overhead. As she slowly turned, her eyes focused on a huge darkskinned figure.

"Sorry. Didn't mean to startle you," reassured a voice from somewhere above her. Looking up, she discovered the ebony features and 6 foot 9 inch frame of Mitch McNair. One look was all she needed to recognize the Los Angeles Mustang's center who had been making front page news every night for the past month.

"I just came out for a swim," he continued. "Kind of like a freak show in there. Just isn't my scene."

"I know what you mean," she nodded, staring in fascination at his chocolatey stomach muscles shimmering in the torch light. Feeling his gaze burning through her, Crystal felt unnerved.

Then, as she dropped her eyes, she noticed the stirring in his bulging crotch. Her body, still warm with the memory of Joel's caresses, was both repelled and undeniably attracted. She wished that Joel could be with her right now.

At the same time, she wished that she could have started her sexual rebirth a night later. How in hell could she pass up a chance like this, beneath flickering torches on a perfect California night, just to be faithful to a man she might never see again?

Maybe Joel would amount to nothing in her life. But until she knew for sure, Crystal also knew she couldn't bring herself to sleep with anyone else. At the moment, considering the lust seeping into her limbs, it seemed like a damn shame.

She closed her eyes and breathed in the night air filled with honeysuckle and the scent of burning torches. In two nights, she had met two undeniably attractive men. At the rate available guys were appearing, within a year or so anything might happen.

And with any luck, it would.

It was also good reason to rush home and get things tied up in a hurry. To get Marcie into a boarding school a safe distance from Hollywood—before *she* could get her hands on a hunk of manhood like McNair, and prove that she could perform all the acts she was already too curious about.

In the meantime, Crystal was content to stare up at the stars and fantasize about the man silhouetted beside her. Had he been following her all night, in hopes of scoring some points? Or did a superstar with statistics like Mitch's take the free throws for granted?

She observed wryly, soaking in the beautiful lines of his body as he spun and dove in the lighted pool, he must have *forgotten* to bring along his bathing suit.

Lauren stared blearily at her reflection in the mirror. A lopsided grin replaced her usually well practiced smile.

She looked stoned alright. After all of the wine and hashish, and the intoxicating music and dancing, it was natural enough.

But more than anything else, Lauren was high on the feeling of relief, of having finally won—or at least tied. In two months, she would be on the air, and the real battle would begin. But for the meantime, she had made it. Under the circumstances, it seemed only fitting to cut loose a bit.

God knew that Sloan would be the last one to object. Obviously, that was the entire point of Sloan's little party. One by one, the other women—including L'il Miss 'Lanta, the Blushing Virgin herself—had vanished. And Lauren had been left on the dance floor with half a dozen vacuous but nicely packaged muscle beach types.

Thank God she hadn't given in to Rick Pappadopoulous. He was about the most blatant gigolo she had ever come up against. Experience had told her to steer away from men who were too beautiful, in any case.

Maybe she was a little higher than she had thought. It seemed to take her forever to find the powder room. She hoped this was the one meant for guests. No matter. She could touch up her mascara and . . .

"*Aaaahhh!*" came the urgent scream which immediately was muffled. She could hear scuffling in the room next door. She considered running to get the staff, but ruled it out. Lauren slipped out of her heels and turned off the light. Silently she crept to the door and turned the knob.

In the dim candlelight of the adjoining bedroom, she could make out Patti Springfield, her dress torn into shreds. She was clutching herself and shuddering, as she curled into the foetal position.

"Sloan?" she whispered plaintively.

But Sloan's only reply was a series of gasps and moans, as she wrapped her spindly legs furiously around someone else. She ran her fingernails up and down his back, pulling his body down onto her.

Then the candle flickered and Lauren could tell that "he" was none other than Marge, a fiercely protective smile on her face as she cupped the slight woman's lips to her breast.

Lauren turned and fled, pausing only long enough to scoop up her discarded sandals.

Rob Steinholtz reached into the backseat for the bottle of champagne, then tossed the keys to the valet and made his way to the bungalow.

He paused at the door. Placing his package momentarily on the ground, he squatted down and removed the top of the small vial hanging around his neck. Fishing in his billfold, he soon produced a minuscule spoon. Half a minute later, he was ready to go. He rubbed his fingers over his upper lip and felt the tingling numbness spread over his mouth. His mind was halfway to heaven; and his fingers and thighs felt like they were well on their way.

It was the best toot he had had in months. He felt like a million. And at the price of this coke, that was the least he should feel. Now if only Lauren dug coke, too, their little tryst would be off to a good start. Ever since his arrival at RedRock, he had been following her interviews. Him and his cock.

For her part, Lauren had been decidedly cool at their meeting earlier. Then again, considering the way she had cockteased him back in Boston, that was hardly surprising. But tonight, the story would end differently.

For months now, he had been remembering those full and sensuous lips. Waiting. With any luck, she would be in the mood. If not, he would have to resort to the mogul methods. The kind he had watched his father-in-law pull a thousand times. Not by protesting or pleading or demanding. For Hollywood movers, that was decidedly out.

Instead, there was gentle persuasion. Smiles and soft caresses and promises. As an extra encouragement, he could always promise not to sell those photographs to *Hustler*. Or the *National Enquirer*. But with any luck, he would never have to resort to that. Blackmail was such an ugly term. Particularly when a liaison was going to last for months. Maybe years.

The sharp raps on the bungalow door pierced through Lauren's dream.

It was two a.m. After a night like tonight, this was the last thing in the world she needed. Who in hell could it be?

But even in her fuzzy state, Lauren couldn't kid herself for very long. It was a scenario which had been conceived back on Beacon Hill a decade ago. And finalized with Rob's leering eyes and probing fingers this afternoon.

She had wanted the job at any price. And now she was paying it.

Gritting her teeth, Lauren headed into the closet for her satin Lucie Ann gown. *"One moment,"* she called. She paused in front of the mirrror, arranging her hair. Using all of her will power, she composed her features and willed her fear to disappear.

As the door swung open, she took one look at his glazed eyes and leering smile. "Oh Rob! What a *surprise,"* she exclaimed. "What brings you to the Beverly Hills at *this* hour?"

"I tried to reach you all night, but I understand

that Sloan arranged one of her little pillowing parties. Decadent, wasn't it? Her and that ridiculous 'A Stud Group' bit . . ."

"Oh I don't know," she shrugged. "I thought it was kind of fun."

"Anyway. I thought we'd better talk, and in a hurry. I thought that under the circumstances it would be better if we . . ."

"Talked in *private?* Why *certainly*, Rob." Lauren felt the hatred flaring in her eyes and did nothing to restrain it. She felt him recoil, and inwardly smiled. Rob had her where he wanted her, and they both knew it.

But under the circumstances, there was one thing that Lauren could do. Make the bastard squirm, and assure that he would never enjoy a second of it.

"Thanks," he muttered, retreating from her onslaught of sarcasm. "Listen, I don't want you to think that I would . . ."

"Of *course* not," she spat back, closing the door behind Rob.

She trembled with helpless fury as Rob slipped the nightgown from her shoulders. As his beefy fingers traced the outlines of her breasts, she felt the nausea rising in her throat.

Nineteen

"Note for Winston," Lauren growled as she swung the wheel and screeched back onto Sunset, "full data bank background on George Silvetti. Known associates, watering spots, high school album pictures . . . the works. Mark it *'For Your Eyes Only.'* This may be the biggie. *Note: Gloria*—Where in hell is the back-up material on the . . ."

With a start, she slammed on the brakes and veered her Mercedes onto the shoulder, leaning on the horn as a Toronado with New Jersey plates spun in front of her and crossed two lanes, tying up traffic in both directions.

Its destination, as she soon confirmed, was a little roadside stand offering the latest map of "Starland Estates and Mansions." In early June, it was little more than a seasonal hazard in Hollywood—like typhoons in the Far East. But that knowledge did little to placate Lauren—or the cars piling up on both sides of the Boulevard.

"Shit," she muttered, glancing at her Rolex. At this rate, she would be fifteen minutes late for her weekly lunch at the Polo Lounge.

Tossing her thick mane of hair back over her shoulder, she fumbled inside her bag for the comfort

201

of her cigarette case. Why had she ever allowed Jackie to talk her into these two inch nails? They were so long that they made even the simplest task almost impossible to—

This time it was a blaring honk from the Cadillac beside her that made her jump. Lauren just had time to look down in dismay as the silver cigarette case clipped shut. Her Sobranie—and half of her pampered fingernail still inside. *Four hours down the drain.* That was exactly the slice that the Juliettes exacted out of her life every two weeks. Tonight there would be no time left for a nail transplant.

So much for her daily jog tomorrow morning.

The way things were going, it would take a miracle to make it through tonight's broadcast. And it was only Monday.

Another barking honk from a Cadillac shook her back into a calm, professional demeanor. It was just two harmless Beverly Hills dowagers wanting to be noticed by Lauren Conrad of Now News. She flashed her best neon smile for them, waved the hand with the broken nail and noticed that the dictaphone was busily recording her moans and mumbles. Snapping it off, she put the convertible back into first gear and settled in for the long crawl to Beverly Hills.

Note: After living in this town for almost half a year, you should have more sense than to drive on Sunset Boulevard at this time of year. Note: What does it matter? The day that Crystal Cooper makes it on time for a lunch, it'll be bigger news than a woman being elected President.

Personal Confidential Memo to Yourself: Honey, you better break it off with that prick Rob before it gets totally out of control. At this rate, it's either that or cyanide.

At last she approached the familiar drive to the hotel and swung up into the line of arrivals. It was time to try to forget all of that, gather up her strength, and plunge back into the fishbowl.

As Smitty offered Lauren a hand, Crystal's slightly dented baby blue BMW screeched to a halt on the other side of the traffic island. She leapt breathlessly out of the driver's seat, pausing to adjust her TV smile and smoothe out her jacket.

Lauren took in her partner's cerise silk ensemble and grimaced. On anyone else, the suit might have looked Hollywood conservative. But of course, Crystal had bought it fashionably tight. And she just happened to be wearing a sheer silver and cerise *crêpe de chine* shirt more devastating than a neutron bomb.

In five months, she had not missed one opportunity to upstage Lauren. She wondered if Crystal were really guileless or whether it was part of her standard operating procedure. If it wasn't her clothes, it was five strings of pearls, or a new hairstyle — or *something*.

"Now don't make a scene," Crystal pleaded. "You're late too. I had to pass by Rodeo Drive and . . . well, you know I'm a sucker for a sale."

Lauren nodded with resignation, and turned toward the entry. Pasting the automatic smile on her lips, she nodded demurely to one or two familiar faces in the crowd of onlookers, and glided effortlessly through the doors.

She felt Crystal's hand tap on her shoulder as she strutted past the brass and marble reception desk. "Gotta run to the ladies' for a sec," Crystal hissed over her shoulder. "I ran out of Dorso's so fast, I think there may be a tag left on. Just sit here in the lobby and people watch for a second."

Lauren settled into the corner of an overstuffed couch and lit a long overdue cigarette. A momentary hush settled over the foyer as Robert Redford, tanned, radiant, and wearing denims and cowboy boots, entered the lobby. Undoubtedly, Walter would usher him right to an awaiting table. Even without a reservation, Redford could never be kept waiting. On his heels trailed a pair of exquisite but anonymous starlets. A moment later, they reappeared, crestfallen. Shut out by the quiet authority of the *maitre d'*.

Lauren paced over to the Polo Lounge entry and Walter nodded in her direction with a smile. He held up his fingers, to signify, "Just a *few* minutes." Of course, being seated *without* a wait at the Polo Lounge would have catapulted her into the heights of the stratosphere. Heights reserved for Burt Reynolds, Marvin Davis, CJ Redfield or the President.

Now that Lauren Conrad's face was seen by millions of viewers every night, she had progressed to the stage known as, "Just a Few Minutes." As bizarre as the whole scene had seemed at first, Lauren had quickly grown to understand her publicist's point. In the status- and recognition-starved entertainment scene, being seen was a matter of survival. No matter who or what had to be sacrificed, Crystal and Lauren committed themselves to this Polo Lounge business lunch at least once a week.

And after half a year, they had yet to get a decent table without waiting.

During that time, she had met scores of people who waited for *no one*—industry biggies and sit-com stars, jetsetters and Washington notables, all hovering around the entrance to the darkened lounge.

204

They might have mansions and chateaus scattered here and there, custom Corniche convertibles and diamonds that would make Harry Winston and Sol Lakin drool. But if Walter failed to recognize them immediately, they sulked in a blue funk for days.

Or else got a tip-off to bad times ahead. In Hollywood, Walter knew what the Nielsens found out the next week.

"Sorry to take so long," Crystal gushed apologetically, "but you'll *never* guess who I just bumped into in the . . ."

"Cary Grant?" Lauren teased just as Walter beckoned them in.

A moment later they were plunked down unceremoniously in a cluster of small tables. It was a far cry from a banquette. But at least they hadn't been hidden behind any of the massive green-and-white trellised columns, or obscured behind the plastic flora.

Lifting up her briefcase, Lauren produced a handful of manila files. "Just give me a second and I'll be ready," she stated crisply.

Without looking at the menu Crystal addressed the waiter. "I'll have my regular: eggs Benedict. With Perrier . . . now: *What* were you saying?"

"Seafood salad with Perrier," she requested, sharply annoyed by Crystal's ability to devour anything and everything, without jogging an inch or gaining an ounce. That was one more point chalked up for Shirley Temple. "Other than that, I was discussing tonight's stories."

"Okay. No problem." Crystal scanned the dimly lit room and immediately winked over at Ed McMahon. "Just take your time."

From her vantage point, she could see the best and

the biggest reflected in three different mirrors, from a hundred different angles. Johnny was paging Valerie Perrine, and now she was having a phone brought to her table. Lucille Ball was deftly stabbing what looked like sole amandine, and now she was being plugged in as well.

A moment later, Lauren gratefully accepted a light from Walter and thumbed through her files. "First of all, stories from the Futures file. *You* might as well cover the Atlanta bussing story. Contract ratification is set for midnight. The Davis lawsuit file is being updated from New York, together with the States bank bombing. That reminds me: I'll have five minutes with the Villanova tape—scooped *all* the networks on that one. He split for Argentina five minutes later, with two suitcases crammed full of bills. Jewel Beale is going on live tonight with the San Bernardino fire. Are you handling the IRA bombing? In addition to the background, I think London is sending over thirty seconds of eyewitness."

"Right." Crystal rifled through her own executive case. "Now where the Hell did I put that, anyway? Some guy called in from a phone booth. Something about new evidence in the Hoffa case. His name was Randall something. Farnsworth? Farmingdale? One of those WASPy names. Anyway, I'll track that down later. I'm also doing the update on the Soviet maneuvers on the Polish border. That one's going to be beamed in by two o'clock."

"I guess that leaves me with the Harris Initiative. If I have to interview one more damn government clone on the phone, I'll scream bloody murder."

"What are you *complaining* about," Crystal shot back. "After all, you did a good enough job of acing me out of the Begin interview two weeks ago. *Then*

there was that gorgeous hunk on last week's Profile
. . . Speaking of which, whatever *did* happen on that
date with him?"

Lauren stifled a sardonic laugh. How two hundred
and thirty pounds of muscular Los Angeles Ram had
managed to fill a moonlit, smogless evening discussing
his diet, houseplants and troubled knees she would
never know. But somehow he had managed. Capping
off the evening with an off-the-record scorecard on
the latest locker room schoolboy pranks.

For one of the most desirable women in the industry, his performance ranked nothing short of
humiliating. And just in case she needed more
degradation, there was another unannounced
Steinholtz midnight visit. The sort of memorable performance she would give anything to forget.

A dozen phrases drifted across the room, breaking
into her thoughts. "Tatum's a natural," a producer's
deep booming voice proclaimed. At the next table, a
soap opera queen was delicately nursing a glass of
champagne. Between sips, the words, "Signing with
RCA tomorrow . . . Six figures," dropped like pearls
from her heavily glossed lips. From a far corner, the
words, ". . . and they're even throwing in a guest appearance by Streisand," turned at least a dozen heads.

Yes, Lauren concluded, turning to the sumptuous
salad which had just arrived, *this is the Polo Lounge,
alright*. There were other, far more elegant watering
places. But nowhere else did the legendary glamor of
Hollywood refuse to yield an inch to stark reality.

No one talked about debts or arthritis. No one was
growing old, or unhappy. No one else seemed to be in
over her neck in quicksand. Blackmailed by a network
executive whose demands were dragging her under.

Once again, Lauren felt the walls closing in around

her. She felt panic rising to her throat. "Oh damn," she whispered, her fingers desperately ransacking her purse for a half-empty vial of Valium, "I forgot to call in to the office this morning. I'll just be gone for a minute."

Crystal looked over at her wrist and frowned. "Where in hell's Dale, anyway? And *Rob?*"

For one split second, their eyes locked. And the imperious Lauren Conrad of Now News looked suddenly like a desperately frightened young girl.

Wrapping her hands around the stem of her glass, Crystal watched Lauren disappear through the narrow door. She noted the embroidered Blass bolero top and sleek trousers. The aura of confidence and cool once again radiating from every inch of her body.

Then Lauren vanished into the corridor, and Crystal was left sipping her Perrier, painfully aware of the emptiness on the other side of the table. The emptiness seemed to surround her wherever she went. And even the security blanket of stardom was unable to assuage her loneliness.

Twenty

Lauren raced down Santa Monica Boulevard, checking her watch at every stop light. It was already three thirty, and that left her exactly fifteen minutes to snake the Mercedes through a mile of stiff traffic, do a Crystal Cooper-style three point landing at the door, weave her way through the newsroom labyrinth, and slide into The Box.

She cursed herself for offering to do the pre-broadcast news highlight spot this afternoon. Or rather, being pushed into the goodwill gesture. It was either that, or sitting and listening to Crystal go on and on about the latest hassles with Joel, the rift developing between her and her teenage daughter, and God only knew what else. Did she think that she was the only woman in the world with problems?

And Rob and Dale had simply never shown up. In an emergency cancellation, Dale always had her paged at the Polo Lounge, and it was hardly like Rob Steinholtz to miss the opportunity to "press the flesh." Only for him, it wasn't a question of campaign stumping. He was a master of the cheap grab, particularly when he could pull it off in the midst of a roomful of entertainment nobility.

Something was definitely up. Given her precarious

situation, Lauren knew she had to find out in a hurry.

In the meantime, there was fifteen seconds of crucial airtime to get out of the way. The convertible roared into Sunset Blvd, heading toward the RedRock hq.

By the time the valet had approached the car, she was already running toward the entry. No doubt CJ Redfield's hawk-eyed assistant would be peering down at her with the usual disapproving glare. Using the valets violated Redfield's "Maximum Visibility, Minimum Star Profile" philosophy. Which translated into begrudging Down East thrift: if you had to hire the valets in concession to Hollywood lifestyle, you could at least make it a Pyrrhic victory by refusing to use them.

"Barbara and the rest of his brown-nosing retinue can park their own cars and score points as *much as they* like," Lauren fumed, racing through the great sweeping archway. "As for me, I'll leave the parking to the valets, and concentrate on the Nielsens."

She slowed to a brisk trot past the central reception desk. If she touched up her make up in the Box, she could just make it. The producer would be gnashing her teeth. Half a dozen "gophers" would be checking the Now News offices, the dressing rooms, the women's room, the conference rooms—even the men's room. Dale Stevens' office would be going crazy with the calls.

But at least Lauren would show up in the nick of time.

Cutting across the newsroom bullpen, she wove through the sea of desks. Up on the monitor wall, mounted screens kept 'round-the-clock tabs on the three commercial networks, PBS, and two local independents. At a quick glance, the most pressing item there was Mister Rogers.

Stretching back-to-back clear across the room, stationary desks with video display screens bathed the staff writers in a green cathode glow. Twenty-four hours a day they were there, hunched over their computer terminals as they digested and regurgitated information, which was then coded and pigeon-holed in the appropriate story file or date bank. En route, it was retrieved by an editor, scrolled out and corrected line by line, approved, then automatically filed.

A few dozen stories would be filed in reports during tonight's broadcast. But thousands were being written for tomorrow, or next week, or even twenty months from now, when they would automatically be retrieved from the Futures File. In addition, every celebrity or political leader of import already had a place in the obituary file. The moment he or she first burst into the limelight, a new file was created. The material was kept "live"—revised daily, and always printed out in perfect broadcast order. In an emergency news bulletin, all the anchor had to insert was the time, place and circumstances of death into the first paragraph.

Lauren strode briskly through the sea of desks, nodding hellos and avoiding interruptions. Once or twice she paused to chase back up material for her stories. As a rule she kept her distance, and was viewed with a mixture of awe and resentment. Not one soul among them would hesitate to kill just for a shot at her position. For the prestige, the clout, and the quarter of a million dollar salary that went hand-in-hand with them. But beyond that, Lauren insisted upon reworking every story that crossed her desk to conform to her own personal style.

With each stroke of her pen, she transformed the

211

newsroom staff from news makers to mere drones and drudges, a cadré of hundreds of delivery boys. Throughout the newsroom, it had established Lauren Conrad as a gutsy and admired newswoman. And a stunning, gold-plated bitch.

Inside the news editors' office, the usual assemblage of reporters crowded around the desks. But instead of the usual frenzy of activity, the friendly and not-so-friendly competition that kept the energy level explosive, there was a dead silence.

In fact, now that Lauren stopped in her tracks to survey the cavernous newsroom, she realized that something was wrong. Dozens of techies crawling overhead on the catwalks, sixty people pounding the silent keyboards—but every one of them enveloped in tight-lipped silence. No jokes, not even one giggle or whisper.

Milling around in a corner of the news office. Jewel Beale and a half dozen other reporters were looking positively stricken.

Meteorologist Uncle Steve Jaeger's voice came through the doorway loud and clear, like a foghorn. "Calm down, Jewel," he sighed wearily. "What in hell are you and Dave worried about?"

"That's easy for *you* to say," the Lifestyle reporter shot back, her normal syrupy Southern tone evaporating into belligerence. "After all, *you* don't have to consider . . ."

That was all Lauren needed to hear. Now she knew: About Rob and Dale's no-show at the Polo Lounge, the rumors which had been floating past her in recent weeks, the pall which had settled upon the bullpen like a death shroud. After a decade in newsrooms, her sharpened instincts could smell it a mile away.

They cried when it was an assassination, huddled

when it was a declaration of war, and panicked when it was an earthquake.

Now it was a purge. And throughout the miles of corridors, the offices and cubicles, the same eerie stillness would take root. Waiting for the axe to fall, and knowing that *no one* was immune.

Suddenly, Lauren was glad for the annoying promo broadcast. For the next five minutes of isolation and calm awaiting her in the tiny booth.

She waved in the direction of the newsroom, then flew past the row of video-editing cubicles. Pausing one second to smooth her already smooth hair, she checked out her immaculate make-up job, patted away the beads which had formed on her brow, then beamed her electronic smile and entered the booth.

"Had the boys a bit worried darlin'." The voice of Roy Lynn, one of the executive news producers, popped out of the control board as soon as the door hissed shut. "I just got off the phone with Walter. He swore that you just left the place ten minutes ago. Using Uncle Steve's weather chopper again?"

"It's on the roof waiting, Roy. So let's get this the hell over with, as soon as possible."

"My pleasure," he smiled, attempting to cover the edge in his voice. "Now let's hear that voice, good and strong."

"Hello. This is Lauren Conrad, and the stories we'll be . . ."

"*Cut.* That's real fine, Lauren. Okay Mannie, switching central. Live feed on three. *Ten, nine, eight* . . ."

As his upraised hands raced through the count-down, Lauren took a deep breath and glanced at her notes once more, then back up for the "T" signal which meant . . . RED LIGHT.

"Hello, this is Lauren Conrad of Now News. The stories we'll be covering tonight include live footage of the latest bombing to rock Iran, new allegations in the growing NASA scandal. A conversation with the 'Wall Street Embezzler,' Nasen Villanova. A special segment on the Harris Initiative, plus the fire which is still raging out of control in the San Bernardino Forest. Uncle Steve looks at the national weather picture, plus all of the latest stories breaking throughout America and around the world. That's up-to-the-minute global news coverage on this Satellite Broadcasting Network Station. Join us for Now News at five. That's six Mountain, seven Central and eight Eastern Standard Time . . ."

Abruptly, the spotlights blinked off in the broiling booth. Lauren ran a hand down her neck. Now it was just a matter of rapping out a full evening's reportage in the next slim half hour, while the hounds bayed at her door.

"That was very *interesting*, Lauren," called a disembodied voice, in a perfect imitation of another well-known news anchor.

"Winston, get off the airwaves," she barked playfully back into the microphone. She gazed up into the production booth, but found no sign of him up there. Baffled, she grabbed her attaché case and turned toward the door, where the lanky Now News gopher was already waiting.

She observed his loose boned 6 foot body as Winston slid into the box beside her. Beneath his painstakingly coiffed black ringlets, his eyes darted anxiously toward the control panel, waiting for the last lights to blink off.

"Where in hell have you been?" he sighed, on the verge of hysteria. "While you two have been yakking it

214

up at the Polo Lounge with Dale all hell has been breaking loose."

"He never made it there."

"Oh *God*," he moaned, collapsing into the chair. "Lauren, it's bad. Really bad. Up in publicity, Sheila and Brad—that latest assistant of hers—just got canned. Out of *nowhere*. And that's just the beginning. Pink slips and confidential memos have been flying, and all of the brass are 'In Conference.' No one has seen Rob Steinholtz either; and the rumors are . . ."

"Listen," she broke in, struggling to keep his last remark from sinking in, "we have a broadcast to put together. And if you've raced in here to tell me about the rumors, I really can't take the time right now to . . ."

"No wait: there's more. There's a message actually *tacked* to your office door, saying that CJ Redfield is waiting for you. Can you imagine that? *'Waiting!'* I doubt he even does that for the Almighty."

As the message sank in, Winston watched in alarm as the shock waves registered across Lauren's face. She stared at him blankly, her eyes wavering.

"Listen," he whispered, clutching her hand and waiting for the signs of comprehension to return. "There isn't anything to worry about. I mean: how *could* there be? The latest Nielsens are just circulating. Lauren, they're *beautiful!*"

For an instant, a tremor ran through her face, as the control panel loomed up at her and the walls started to press in on all sides. Her hand slipped from his grasp and fell onto the desk lifelessly.

She reached up again and squeezed his hand tightly, then slowly gathered her case and made for the door, her amber eyes once more blazing.

"You'd better look over the Iranian copy for me tonight," she said matter-of-factly, leaping into the cool fluorescent light of the aluminum-tiled corridor. Then with fiercely determined steps, she set off for the familiar bank of elevators, feeling as if she were viewing it all in a dream.

The twenty-one traffic was murderous. And together with the thickening smog, it transformed the broiling street into a disaster area. *Four o'clock.* Crystal stifled a curse under her breath, then thought better of it and cursed out loud.

She was now an hour overdue at the studio. Hadn't even *begun* to hammer out her copy for the evening broadcast. As much as she hated to, she would have to relegate all of the non-essential stories to the newswriting staff.

With the air conditioner on the blink in the BMW, she was forced to choke on the brown-edged air pouring in from the sun roof. At least she was almost there. In the meantime, there was nothing to do but kick off the new gold sandals that were killing her feet, and stare out over the baby blue hood as she inched along.

Rolling toward the intersection of Sunset & Dohney, a black Bentley convertible pulled up perilously close. Crystal glanced over and discovered a frantically honking and gesturing driver, pointing toward the shoulder.

Crystal hesitated for a second, wondering if it was about an ambulance or fire truck mired in the traffic, or an engine ready to explode. She gazed at his old-fashioned horn-rimmed glasses, and the tousled brown hair, the conservatively cut jacket and button-down shirt. If looks were any indication, he was not a rapist or a thug. And his attempts to pull her over were

216

becoming frantic.

As drivers for a block behind her began to lean on their horns, she took a chance and pulled off the road. A moment later the Bentley driver jumped out of his car and dashed toward her.

Instinctively, Crystal leapt onto the tarmac, then headed over to meet him, the gravel on the shoulder tearing through her stockings and biting into her feet. As he came to a halt, she ducked down to check her tires, and make sure that the BMW wasn't leaking a trail of water or gas.

Apparently, all of her gaskets were in place.

The stranger evidently thought so too. As the pavement burned the soles of her feet and the traffic went slipping by, he stared at her approvingly, and flashed a mischievous smile. "This better be a good one," she murmured under her breath.

"Sorry if I alarmed you," he yelled, stepping closer. "I had to get your attention . . . *somehow.*" Crystal felt her annoyance momentarily dissipating as it gave way to curiosity.

Pouncing on her hesitation, he immediately launched into a carefully-rehearsed sales *spiel*. "I recognized you at once. Been watching you and Lauren every night on Now News. And I thought that maybe if I explained who I am, you'd give me a chance to discuss my findings about Laetrile on your Bookends section."

He paused, staring at her in earnest with his long-lashed brown eyes, while his lips slid into an embarrassed, apologetic grin. *Great,* Crystal thought, *another Beverly Hills hustler.* But at least he hadn't called her Lauren, or wasted any more of her time with introductory bullshit. Just how much moxie could a man muster in rush hour traffic. She raised one slender eyebrow inquisitively, amused at the absurdity of the situation. "And?" she demanded, as sternly as possible.

"My name's Doctor Rothmore. Ted. *The Laetrile Alternative* has just been published, but because of A.M.A. pressure the major networks won't touch it. I think that it might change a lot of minds about the therapy. Possibly result in the savings of thousands of lives. But I figured that after you ran that exclusive about the San Fernando radiation leak, *no one* could stop you from exploring a good story. I'm *not* asking for an endorsement. Just a fair chance to bring my message to cancer victims. What do you say?"

Crystal was at a loss for words. First of all because the surrounding traffic was deafening, and she had heard about a third of the sales pitch to begin with. Beyond that, she had been so mesmerized by his soft brown eyes and intense sincerity that she found herself reacting very unprofessionally to the content of his argument.

"I know how busy you must be, Ms. Cooper," he concluded, producing his business card and tipping it into her hands. "But perhaps we could get together over dinner and discuss it . . . At your convenience."

Crystal stared at the engraved lettering, and the Beverly Hills address. One thing was for sure: if Dr. Ted Rothmore was what he appeared to be, then he merited further investigation.

Beneath his blue Oxford shirt and tight French jeans, he also appeared to possess a very nice physique. Slim and muscular, almost boyish. She felt the sort of magnetic attraction to him that lately only Joel had sparked.

"Listen, I admire your nerve," she answered evenly. "But for all I know, you're another Hollywood strangler. If you're serious, you may give my secretary a call tomorrow afternoon."

His eyes lit up behind the horn rims. "I'd be delighted to provide a list of references."

"Not necessary. Our research department is *extremely* competent." She turned, threw him a flirtatious smile in profile, then hopped back into the BMW. Revving the engine, she shot back into the traffic.

At the next traffic light, she caught one final glimpse of him in the rearview mirror. She tossed her blond curls selfconsciously. Maybe Come-Hither Conrad *wasn't* the only anchorwoman in town with irresistible charms.

Dr. Ted Rothmore was a charmer alright. Not many men could turn her on like that—certainly not in the middle of Sunset Boulevard. Maybe their dinner date could even lead to something.

The way Joel had been running hot-and-cold lately, Crystal had alternated between feeling like two Cleopatras—the ones before and after the asp bite.

In her mind, she could hear him pouring out the same old rhetoric about growing and freedom: "I don't own you, and I never want either of us to feel tied down." It was like a mantra that he chanted over and over again.

But half a year down the road, they were still a long way from Nirvana together. Maybe his liberated rap was just a string of words, a subtle rejection that was slowly gnawing away at her. Maybe it was time to start expressing *her* needs. Perhaps the arrival of Dr. Ted Rothmore would shake Joel up, *just enough.*

Maybe it was just time to relax and have some fun, for a change.

That led her to Problem Number Two: *Guilt.* Even

219

if it didn't bother Joel, there was good chance that bedding down with another man would bother the hell out of *her*. Beneath the provocatively flirtatious lilt of her Southern accent, Crystal had remained a born and bred one-man woman. And bed-hopping was one concession to Hollywood lifestyle she was *not* prepared to make.

The very thought of it sent panic alarms running through her mind. What would Marcie think when her mother started introducing her to a string of decidedly laid back beaux? What's good for the goose is orgasmic for the gosling?

And even if Crystal's precocious daughter was safely sequestered for the time being in a New Hampshire prep school . . . what about Crystal's mother? She could just imagine the ubiquitous Rachael Cooper-Smith's voice on the phone, as she followed up the latest reports from her Hollywood spies. "So, what's new? How's Joel . . . Oh . . . that's *nice!* What's this I hear about . . . Oh, a *Doctor! Mazel tov.*"

If it wasn't that, then Crystal's mother would un-doubtedly call up and catch her *in flagrante delicto.* That was also an old habit of Rachael's—even back in the days when the flames of passion were ignited only on bank holidays in Stephen's arms.

One way or another, Rachael Cooper-Smith never missed a trick.

And if her mother could find out, so could Dale or Rob or CJ. That brought up Problem Number Three: The Morals Clause in her contract.

"It's out of the question," she stated flatly, turning into the RedRock drive.

Screeching to a halt before the archway, she yanked up the emergency brake. "Crystal Cooper," she chided, "your pussy is *not* a shrine. Besides, the guy

220

only asked you out on a rotten little date. What in hell are you worrying about?"

The way she was turned on by Rothmore, maybe the answer was . . . plenty. But that wasn't her mother's problem. Or the network's.

The Morals Clause was unenforceable. It *had* to be. If the sinners were ever purged from the studio lots, network hq's and streets of Hollywood, it would turn into a ghost town overnight.

The survivors could probably fit in the back of one Volkswagen. Or maybe there would be enough to run one game show.

Hollywood Squares.

Twenty-two

Lauren sped past the familiar ogling stare of the security guard. She stepped into the glass-enclosed elevator, the door hissed shut and the elevator automatically whisked her up to "Imperial HQ," as the rest of the staff referred to CJ's offices.

Standing alone in the glass booth, Lauren tried to focus on the recent gains Now News had posted in the ratings. Those alone should have been sufficient to make her inviolate.

But in fact, even if Lauren had made it as a broadcaster, Rob Steinholtz may have lost no time in jeopardizing her career. Had those photographs of their first brutal encounter already succeeded in putting her in the most compromising position imaginable?

If CJ had stumbled onto anything between them, she had better come up with a defense—fast. But at least the nightmare would be over. The sheer hell of being an emotional slave to that egotistical son-of-a-bitch. The cheap grabs and the stoned midnight rambles. Having it become past history might almost be worth her job at this point.

Just thinking back on all of those months of degradation, her blood began to boil—with a very unromantic passion. The short hairy fingers which had roamed over every inch of her body. The lips which slobbered over her flesh like—how could she *ever* have imagined that she would be involved in such a nightmare?

Most of the time, the man couldn't even function. In the beginning, when Lauren was still fighting the inevitable, his ineffectual thrashings had kindled vicious abusive fights. At the peak of his fury, in the midst of his curses and occasional blows, Rob would finally achieve erection. For him, it *was* a major achievement. But then Lauren had refused to fight, and his long spindly shaft never made it above half-mast. Instead of giving up, he only grew more bitter—and demanding. To no avail.

For Rob Steinholtz, sex had always been a battle. He did fine with the subservient types—the starry-eyed young actresses and the secretaries desperate for a break. But like a fool, he really lusted only after his betters. His wife Maria, daughter of one of Hollywood's fiercest movie moguls. Then Lauren Conrad. His every attempt to ram through the class and status barrier was doomed to failure.

Would CJ believe Lauren if she came clean and admitted what had been going on? For a man of his rigid puritanical beliefs it could hardly matter. From its tawdry beginnings in Boston a dozen years before, her relationship with Rob was not likely to arouse CJ's sympathies.

But hadn't she already suffered enough for a mistake made years ago? Accepting the RedRock position had catapulted her into a new category of desirability in a town which boasted the most irresistible men in the world. Somehow, all she had collected in fringe benefits amounted to the most miserable half year of her life.

Maybe she would be better off taking the offensive. After all, anchorwomen were human beings, too. They had their needs and their problems—just like anyone else. And whether she was achingly lonely—or just longing for a man's touch—seeking solace in someone's arms was no one's business but her own.

Not everyone could act like Darling Little Crystal, the Den Mother of Network News. Rumor had it that CJ called her every night before she went to sleep— *just to be sure* she was okay. But it wasn't even that Crystal was so discreet with her decidedly low-profile lover. The more Crystal talked about it, the more obvious it was that Joel was the only thing keeping her from playing the sexual field.

From the look of things, the dam was about to break. She was already batting her eyelashes non-stop at anything in jockey shorts. It was only a matter of time before even *she* broke down and joined the human race.

CJ Redfield had asked for the viewers. Conrad and Cooper were delivering. His dramatic little summons was unnecessary—and unreasonable. Particularly when Lauren had a broadcast to pull together. The first time he digressed into one of his famous New England Puritan sermons, she would let him know just where to get off.

She paused to adjust her business smile—warm but clipped—then turned the antique brass knob on the towering zebra-wood doors. Inside, Barbara hung on the phone while sorting through the network chief's piles of afternoon mail and memos. She glimpsed at Lauren, frowned, and decided to postpone noticing her.

"He's *expecting* me, Barbara," the anchorwoman

snapped, after waiting half a minute without an acknowledgment.

Barbara carefully lowered the letter opener she was yielding, ·glared across her desk, then turned and punched the intercom. "Miss Conrad to see you, CJ."

The door to the inner sanctum slid open, and out flew a young ruddy-faced man. Lauren immediately recognized the corporate counsel, and the weary, frustrated and worried look in his eyes. That too was part of every purge. Nodding selfconsciously at her, the lawyer raced out of the office, his shoulders bent forward as if that would help him make headway.

Redfield's voice crackled out of the intercom. "Come right in, Lauren."

CJ stood against the backdrop of the window wall overlooking the Hollywood Hills, his hands tightly clasped behind him. His elegantly tailored button-down shirt outlined his powerful frame well. It was yet another trademark which set Redfield apart from the other network CEO's—who were likely to wear Izod T-shirts at their dressiest.

"How are you, dear?" He turned to stare directly at her, his eyes showing strain and unconcealed concern.

Lauren was immediately thrown off-balance. Instead of the tough and business-minded image she meant to project, her features slid into frank bewilderment. *How are you, dear?*

"Fine . . . thank you," she managed to reply. Above her on the wall, Redfield's ancestors stared down at her with undisguised doubt.

"The rumors are wreaking havoc downstairs. But I wanted you to know the simple facts. We have reached a difficult passage. Your Q Ratings are climbing, and the Nielsens are still edging up across the boards—or at least for many of our programs. We projected our audience share conservatively and have surpassed our minimal goals."

He paused and took a seat behind his antique cherrywood desk. "At this point we're still rising on momentum. Either we trim our sails and try another tack, or we stall and stay right where we are. In irons. Despite strong personal reservations, I am now implementing many decisions reached by the board in the past few weeks."

Lauren nodded. Waiting for the bomb blast.

"I just wanted to assure you how extremely pleased the Satellite Network is with your performance."

Lauren let go a sigh of relief. So that was it. All of the anxieties and desperation tactics she had devised were for nothing. PERSONAL MEMO: *Your personal life is a shambles, and it's starting to corrode your professional abilities. You've just had a reprieve and a warning. Get Steinholtz out of the picture. Anyway you can. Next time won't be a false alarm.*

"I appreciate your concern," she answered, feeling the tense mask of her face dissolving into a smile.

"I know that you've got a broadcast to pull together. But I thought you would want to hear it from me first: Tomorrow morning I will officially announce the resignation of Rob Steinholtz, tendered this morning—under pressure from the board. It will be made clear to whoever replaces him that I personally stand behind the Now News concept. And behind Lauren Conrad and Crystal Cooper. I expect you to weather this storm without getting mired down. I don't want either one of you to worry about this morning's firings either. That's all I have to say for now, except that you are radiant as ever. Any questions?"

"Not a one," Lauren stood up and moved towards

the door, then paused. "Thanks, CJ," she said graciously wondering if he knew just how much she had to be grateful for.

"I'll look forward to watching you at five. Thank you for stopping by."

Lauren rode down in the elevator with mixed feelings of elation and bewilderment. Behind his totally unnecessary pep talk, a new side of the CEO had suddenly emerged. Though his personal life was still clearly off-limits to everyone, Lauren felt she'd had a glimpse at the man behind the myth. For reasons which remained unknown, it was almost as if he was asking *her* for something. If it was a test of loyalty, then she had just passed it with flying colors: at the announcement of Rob's resignation, Lauren hadn't even flinched.

But there was more to it than that. If Redfield understood more than he was letting on, if he even suspected she was involved with Rob — willingly or unwillingly — then why the outpouring of sympathy and concern?

Or was it possible that there was something to Rob's late-night coked-out raves, about getting the low down on "the *real* Redfield"? Was it possible that he and Sloan had found a way to leverage their bid to oust him, and that firing Steinholtz was Redfield's desperation move? That Rob and Sloan had succeeded where the IRS and SEC had failed.

Lauren thought back to the expression on CJ's face when he first turned toward her, and the knotted hands behind his back. If it wasn't just from the boardroom struggle, then perhaps Sloan Schwartz still had him by the balls.

Knowing Sloan, it was probable that she would slowly apply the clamp, turn by turn. And whatever she had on him, it might take the Now News team to swing the balance of power.

In the meantime, there was a broadcast to pull out of the reams of paper on her desk in record time. The elevator clock showed T-minus forty minutes and counting.

By the time Lauren's fingers had begun to pound out her broadcast copy, she was already mentally on her sixth story of the evening. On the other side of the wall, she could hear the rapid fire of Crystal's typewriter. Syncopated by stops, mutters and mumbled curses.

As airtime approached, Winston began to fly all over the newsroom. Above all, his job was to shuttle information between the bullpen, Crystal and Lauren, and the show's producers—one representing the union, and the other management.

At the center of the fray was a frantic Dale Stevens. While barking into one telephone and nodding into the other, he simultaneously kept up a running dialogue between management, reporters, news-writers, both producers, and four dozen technicians. Mind racing, he pored through dozens of updates and last minute breaking stories, searching for material to fill up the ten minute hole in the hour-long broadcast.

Second by precious second of airtime, he filled in the gaps. By now his face was beet red and the veins were throbbing visibly at his temples. At five minutes to five, a conference call with the half dozen key people established the final shape of the broadcast. Which stories would make it in, the order in which they'd be aired, and precise synchronization of input from twelve affiliate stations via satellite, together with fifteen cassettes of footage from the camera crews and video files.

Side by side, Crystal and Lauren raced through the bullpen, then along the darkened, soundproof corridor leading to the broadcast studio. As Roy barked orders into his headset and moved his hands frantically in all directions behind the plateglass wall of the control room, a dozen techies crawled all over the set. A wispy woman flew to touch up the makeup on Crystal's nose, boom mikes rolled across the floor, the production team raced to their battle stations.

"Looking good," Roy called into his microphone. "Switching central. Camera two, let me see how . . . Camera one? *Are you on, Camera One?* Much better. Okay, theme on. Announcer . . . Great! Now dissolve. Wonderful Manny. Now zoom in. Camera Three, no sweep. Now kind of a zoom . . . swe-eeep . . ."

"Hello. I'm Lauren Conrad . . ."

". . . And I'm Crystal Cooper, bringing you Now News on the Satellite Broadcasting Network. In Washington, we'll have a report on . . ."

As Conrad and Cooper sat radiating calm and reporting on the day's events, the control room was full of the usual bedlam. Beyond the swarming production staff and technicians, the wings of the tiny studio were jammed to capacity. In addition to meteorologist Uncle Steve Jaeger and a handful of reporters, a crowd of staff members and anonymous observers always managed to fill up the wings every night. News events occurred all over the globe: but this was the place where the news was *made*.

Off-camera for a moment, Crystal turned and watched Winston burst through the black steel door sealing the studio, wind around the perimeter, and race over to her side of the news desk. He just managed to slip her a hastily written sheet as the producer gave her the five-second signal.

"In a late-breaking development in the La Brea Supreme Court case, witnesses today alleged that . . ."

"*Camera three on . . .*" Roy yelled, taking Crystal's cue and adlibbing as reporter Jewel Beale appeared on his test monitor. "Cross position and widen out. Very nice, you've got it. Now prepare for cassette five. Rolling."

At the rear of the booth, Dale Stevens was craning his neck around a telephone. "Whattt? CJ, *Are you certain?* OhmyGod!" He grabbed Winston's arm and raced below. Edging across the set, he pushed through the crowd milling in front of the corridor door.

On the other side of the hall, he raced through the newsroom, dodging desks until he arrived at the futures obit file. As Winston stood wide-eyed, Dale ripped open a manila folder and, grabbing the first empty typewritter, began pounding out the opening paragraph.

As fingers flew across the keyboard, the Now News broadcast neared its conclusion. Ripping the opening paragraph out of the typewriter, Dale handed the story to Winston, then turned to find a crowd gathered in front of monitor four.

"Ten seconds," Roy announced in the studio. "Five, four . . . music."

Crystal smiled over at Lauren. The red light flashed off, and they pushed away from the desk and calmly stood up, heading for the newsroom.

They entered just in time to see Rob Steinholtz appear on a local station's broadcast.

"*Twelve goddamn years,*" Dale screamed up at him, "You dumb *bastard.*" As the crowd stood there dully staring, he burst into tears.

Lauren slowly saw the face forming on the monitor

screen. Grabbing the bulletin out of Winston's hands, her eyes frantically scanned the words. Abruptly, she spun and took a step toward the studio.

"That's okay, honey," Crystal put an arm around her, tried to lead Lauren into a chair. "Just sit down and relax. I'll take care of it."

Disbelief, shock and then overwhelming relief flooded through Lauren's body. Her voice took on a hard edge. "I'm going to do this bulletin."

"Just take it easy," Crystal purred. "I know how hard this is. What it must mean to . . ."

"You know nothing!" Lauren's hand flew up at Crystal, whipping across her face.

As the astonished anchorwoman recoiled from the slap, Lauren snatched up the script and walked with measured steps back into the studio, oblivious to the hundred pairs of eyes riveted on her.

Later on, there would be time for Lauren to stop, to react, to try to make sense out of the events rocking her meticulously constructed world. But now every ounce of her strength was absorbed in making it through the next minute or two, and keeping her numb legs from buckling underneath her. For years she had been perfecting the ability to store away her emotions and her reactions, filing them out of sight while her calm, even voice reported on cataclysms and tragedies.

"If I can just hold it together 'til I reach the lights," she soothed herself. "Just a dozen more steps . . ."

All eyes focused on the studio monitor as the newsflash broke into the tail end of a commercial.

"This just in from our newsroom . . ." Lauren's voice was serene, her eyes unblinking as she spoke into the cameras. ". . . Robert M. Steinholtz, President of

231

the Satellite Broadcasting Network, was pronounced dead at Santa Monica Hospital, here in Los Angeles, at 5:15 p.m. this afternoon. LAPD spokesperson Gardener Rivlin confirmed earlier reports that Steinholtz had been discovered dead in his Encino home following reports of . . ."

Throughout the red glass monolith, thousands of eyes stared spellbound at monitors in offices or corridors, watching the mask-like features of the newswoman as she pushed through the synopsis of his death. At the conclusion of the bulletin, a freshly developed cassette began to roll.

Lauren gazed stonily into Camera Two. "Three." Roy yelled. "Switching. *One.*"

Before Dale's eyes on the monitor screen, a very dead Rob Steinholtz was being wheeled away on an ambulance stretcher. He leaned against Crystal, every muscle in his body trembling.

Thank God his body was covered with a sheet. Half of his face had been blown away by the shotgun blast. The gun was still clenched in his fingers when the police arrived.

What was it that Rob had started to tell him this morning? Something about CJ—and *Sloan.* Why in hell had he hung up? Now perhaps Dale would never know what had happened in Redfield's office that morning.

But whatever it was, it had cost Rob his life. And for Dale it meant the chance of a lifetime. Filling in his best friend's shoes, as President of the Satellite Broadcasting Network. For Dale Stevens, it was the answer to all his problems.

In the process, Rob Steinholtz had solved his own

difficulties as well.

It was a real photo finish.

Twenty-three

CJ Redfield sat alone in his office at midnight, momentarily letting his thoughts drift away as he surveyed the teeming Sunset strip. Vacantly his eyes wandered over the endless parade of low-riding cars and easy riding women of the night. On the other side of Sunset, he could see the soft shimmer of a thousand lights winding up the Hollywood Hills, and the silhouette of as many palm trees.

Just a few miles to the northwest, cradled against the Santa Monica Mountains, lay Encino. And there, on the other end of the telephone line, Maria Alexander Steinholtz was slowly going to pieces.

"Maria," he urged, as she momentarily lapsed into silence. The next second, she was once again weeping disconsolately. Redfield lowered the volume on the desk speaker, and waited for another pause.

As the only child of Moe Alexander, Maria had grown up in the sort of paradise which only a doting Hollywood mogul could have created. Her world had been filled with movie stars who paid homage to her, servants and studio executives who waited on her hand and foot. She was showered with endless affection. Whenever the motherless girl began to cry, a hundred adults had scrambled to dry her tears.

When they didn't succeed, there was hell to pay.

The result was a fragile woman, one who broke down whenever a cheery show tune or a stunning evening gown wasn't enough to stem the tide of unhappiness in her life. Despite Rob's flagrant and cruel flaws, Maria had always willingly let the wool be pulled over her eyes. Now that her husband was dead, Marie was once again reduced to a child, terrified and alone.

Redfield shifted uneasily in his black leather Eames chair, caught somewhere between guilt and relief at the apparent suicide of the network president. It was only made harder by the torrents of tears cascading over the phone lines.

Rob had always been a high roller, a begrudging and overambitious kid from the un-glamorous Valley. He had struck it rich with the movie heiress. But by then his bruised ego kept pushing him farther. Into the status and power struggles which he *had* to know he could never win.

Yes, perhaps it had been inevitable. But the axe had fallen on his head in CJ Redfield's office, with the network chief as the sole executioner. Nonetheless, he had had little choice. Redfield thought back to the angry meeting with Moe Alexander, just prior to the senior board member's flight to Acapulco.

"*Lissen, CJ,*" the old man had bellowed with rage. "Robbie is *finito*. Kaput. Do you hear me? *Out!* That putzer has just diddled around with me for the last time. This time, I'm gonna fix that ingrate's wagon. I know you don't like it . . . But you ain't gotta choice. So he's out by Monday. Or *we* are."

"*We*" was the Alexander Corporation, a billion dollar holding company which had placed its chairman of the board, chief operating officer *and* president—Moe Alexander—on the Satellite Broadcasting Network board. *"We"* was several hundred million dollars of investor capital, plus invaluable leverage on hundreds of agents, producers and big name talents.

"We" was one of the few forces in the industry who could order CJ to act, then disappear into his awaiting Lear jet to bask in the Mexican sunshine, acompanied by his two young mistresses.

That was exactly what Moe Alexander had done. Leaving Redfield to pick up the pieces.

As Redfield pictured Maria's father—the white leather pumps, red checked sport jacket and riding jodhpurs—revulsion slid down into his gut. Moe Alexander had always been a ruthless bastard. As he entered his eightieth decade, old age brought no dotage. Instead, it had released an even bitterer stream of venom from his fangs.

For the aging mogul, senility was a selective matter: he neglected faithful old friends and employees who had devoted their lives to build his success, when they needed him most. When convenient, he forgot the gentleman's agreements others counted on to survive. Long ago, he had forgotten common decency.

Moe Alexander was no longer making pictures. But he was still making life miserable for everyone around him. Only his ability to forgive and forget was declining. Singlehandedly, he had removed more names from the industry "white list" than the grim reaper, natural disasters, and war all combined.

Now, after pushing Rob Steinholtz into the RedRock presidency, Alexander had removed him—but good. Unfortunately, the ultimate victim was his own daughter, the girl now whimpering plaintively into Redfield's ear.

Moe had always come running when Maria cried. This time when he left Acapulco, his guilt would undoubtedly turn to fury—directed against the nearest scapegoat. If Redfield wasn't forearmed, the victim might turn into the broadcasting network he had spent years and billions of dollars creating.

The only answer was to ward off the attack by showering Maria with kindness. She was Moe's only Achilles heel. For the time being, it was obvious that she was incapable of functioning, let alone up to the massive job of organizing a fitting funeral for her late husband.

Clearly, it was up to Redfield now. To bury Rob in the Hollywood ceremony of a lifetime. *Not* as the uneven president of the budding Satellite Broadcasting Network. But as a tribute to the late, devoted husband of Maria Steinholtz nee Alexander.

"Maria," he whispered more fimly into the phone, his mind finally clear of the day's confusion. "I think I know just how difficult this must be for you. It's not that long ago that Margaret and I . . . lost Kikki. But there are decisions to be made. They can't wait for your father to be located and fly back from Acapulco. If you'd like, I'll personally take care of all the arrangements. I think we owe that, and far far more to Rob."

"Oh CJ," she gushed, "I can't thank you enough. I . . . I . . . It's just so *hard.*"

"That's okay. Listen, I want you to call Dr. Anthony right away."

"He's in Cannes right now. I suppose I could call Ted Rothmore. But it's so late. And I'm sure that he . . ."

"*I'm* sure that he would never forgive himself for failing you at a time like this. I know just how *close* he's been to your *family*. So call him. But I don't want you to be alone. Would you like Margaret to stay with you?"

"No. I'm fine now. Really. I'll just call Ted, then wait for the prescription. But don't disturb your wife. I know how weak she's been lately. I'll be okay . . . Promise. In fact, I'd better go wash off the mascara before it runs down onto the carpet. If you could manage to have breakfast with me tomorrow . . ."

With the president of the network dead and half of his staff fired? Redfield shuddered. "Of course I can manage it," he sighed.

"Thank you so much, CJ. You're a saint. Ciao."

"Goodnight, sweetheart," he murmured soothingly.

Redfield switched off the phone and poured himself a glass of Armagnac. He savored the bouquet, then tilted back the snifter and let the amber liquid roll over his tongue. The day had been full of brutal surprises.

During the years he had known Rob, first as an independent producer and then setting up RedRock, they had learned a great deal about one another. It was no secret that his protegé had harbored a festering grudge. As a surrogate son, and as an outsider who was openly ridiculed by the A Group. He watched the comings and goings from the sidelines, knowing that there were some things even being an Alexander in-law could never bring. Constantly overshadowed by the people jerking on his strings, and knowing that they could be slashed at any second.

CJ was not enough of an egomaniac to be blind to Steinholtz's sporadic hatred. Nonetheless, he had always given Rob the benefit of the doubt. This morning, he had finally discovered just how unwarranted that kindness was. Ultimately, Rob had had a gutter rat's nose for filth, and the evidence was now neatly piled on the antique writing table.

Redfield opened the steel strongbox and thumbed through its contents. He sifted the phone transcripts and bank statements, the numbered cassettes and microfilm cartridges and photographs. In his own way, Rob had been a brilliant detective. Tracing and monitoring Redfield's calls, bribing his way into the data banks, tracking down millions of dollars of carefully laundered and dispersed money, documenting kickbacks.

Over the course of a year, he had done his vicious homework all too well. Enough evidence to earn Redfield a public beheading. And public humiliation for Lauren Conrad.

Redfield gazed at the aging snapshots, and a wave of nausea overtook him. Poor Lauren. He had known about the existence of the photos all along, but rather than risk a confrontation with Rob he had calculatingly allowed him to play his little game with her.

If only that had been the extent of Rob's viciousness. But what amount of hatred had led him to the Redfield family seat in New Hampshire? CJ stared at the telephoto shots of his deranged daughter, then held the movie footage up to the light. There was Kikki, crawling on her hands and knees like an animal. Snarling and drooling and rolling in her own filth.

He struggled to maintain control as his shoulders began shuddering, and his fingers pressed white against the desktop. For seven years, it was a sight that had haunted Redfield, a secret shared only by his best friend in the sleepy New England village.

Every morning he awoke and gazed out at the

phony shrine, wanting to scream. *Yes,* his mind shouted, *you did that to her.*

Hands trembling, he raised the cognac up to his lips and took a long gulp. The liquid burned in his throat and made his eyes water. But his thoughts were still racing, back to the mansion in Pacific Palisades, to the dimly lit den with the fire blazing, casting flickering shadows over the countless horse ribbons and trophies. And over the perfect features of his stunning fifteen-year-old daughter.

How long had her mother been in the hospital this time? Five months? Six? Each time she returned home, it was a little bit worse. Her once beautiful face and healthy, vibrant body a little more frail and shrunken, the life ever so slowly draining from her now almost useless limbs.

In the past few months, Redfield had thrown himself entirely into his investments, and into the agony of his failing wife. He was drinking hard now, too.

He turned to the budding fifteen-year-old girl—a perfect image of the quiet, sensuous beauty her mother had once been. Draining another glass of Chivas Regal, he wearily swirled the ice in his glass, running his hands softly through his daughter's hair, and hugging her tightly against his side.

"Is she dying?" Constance Kidder Redfield's voice stabbed at him in the darkness.

"I don't think so, Kikki," he replied neutrally. *But she'll come back home faded a little more. You have no idea what it means, to watch your lifelong love slowly dying. The spark disappears, but the ashes continue to glow. Maybe for years.*

He got up to pour himself another drink. "We have

to be at the hospital early tomorrow morning. And I'm certain that it's way past your bedtime."

"Daddy, I'm not a little girl anymore. You've got to stop treating me like a child."

He nodded. Staring at her and momentarily forgetting that she was not Margaret. That they were not newlyweds sitting before the roaring fire of Edgemont, the Redfield family estate in New Hampshire. He looked at her slim, full-breasted woman's body, and remembered the incredible passion he and Margaret had kindled, and miraculously sustained through twenty years of marriage. Until the multiple sclerosis.

"Go to bed, darling."

She hesitated, then quietly came and sat on his lap. She suddenly dissolved into tears, burying her face in his chest and clutching him with all of her might.

Redfield tried to ignore the heat kindling in his groin. He kissed the top of her sweet-smelling mane of light brown hair, and threw his arms protectively around her.

A minute later, his left hand drunkenly sought the button on the side table. The butler whisked in, led Kikki up to her room, and CJ was once more painfully alone. He shook his head at the half empty fifth of scotch, then poured himself another.

Settling back into the sofa, he took down a dog-eared volume of Robert Frost. But tonight, he just couldn't focus. Half an hour later, he unsteadily made his way upstairs, into the comforting opulence of his bedroom. Clumsily he laid all of his clothes onto the back of the wing chair, and fell onto the massive bed, head spinning.

In the middle of the night, he awoke to his wife beside him.

"Daddy, I'm scared," she whispered.

He looked at her in the blackness, confused. Margaret? No: it was only Kikki. She reached out and held his hand, kneeling beside him. Forcing his eyes to focus, he glanced at the shadowy features in the starlight. The long, aristocratic nose and the high curved forehead. She shifted before the window, and he could make out the outline of her flat, girlish stomach. The fully rounded breasts and hips so like those he had caressed a thousand times in this bed.

He hugged her to him tightly, and she nestled there beside him in the darkness. He kissed her sweetly on the tip of her nose, then lay back, grateful not to be alone as he had been for so many months now.

He caressed her gently, absent-mindedly, and she returned his caresses with the same soft fervor. His hands roved gently over her shoulders, soothed by the soft warmth beneath his touch. Absent-mindedly they crossed over her breasts, the nipples stiffening at his touch. Then he reached down and lay his hand lingeringly on her thigh.

She froze. "Daddy?"

But his mind was gone now, hearing her lilting voice on another plane.

His fingers probed further, oblivious to her frightened moans and the struggle of her lithe young body. His blood was rushing now, and he ignored the terrified screams as his powerful arms pinned her and his wildly throbbing penis began the assault.

Many minutes later the groans and cries and furious beating hands on his chest subsided. There was a peaceful silence blanketing the mansion, the formal garden, and the Pacific Ocean beyond. Redfield fell back onto the pillows and was immediately enveloped in sleep.

In the morning, he awoke, alone and refreshed. He

thought about the horrible nightmare momentarily, and then resolved to go to confession at once. *Thank God it was only a dream,* he sighed, then immediately slid into his trunks for the ritual hundred laps around the pool.

Over a leisurely three minute egg with protein toast, he scanned a half dozen papers, and left a meticulously detailed memo with instructions for Barbara.

He selected a white St. Laurent three piece suit for Margaret, then went out to the awaiting Rolls. Beside him sat a crisply attired fifteen-year-old daughter, her eyes distant and red-rimmed.

"You look just like your mother—*beautiful.*" He smiled warmly. But she merely turned her head, her fingers desperately clutching the small black leather bag in her lap.

The early morning haze sank back into the hills, and the alcoholic numbness slowly drained out of his blood. Redfield stared at her shattered eyes and realized in horror that it wasn't just a dream.

As dawn broke onto the Hollywood Hills, CJ Redfield turned his haggard features back to the pile of evidence on his desk. He started to view the footage of Kikki once more, then abruptly stopped. Would Rob Steinholtz really have stooped that low? Would he have gone ahead and aired the films? More than that, had he stumbled onto the history of events which had culminated in the girl smothering her illegitimate child, then lowly transforming herself into a mindless, raving animal?

What possible prize could ever have been worth that sort of brutality?

At that point, the questions ended.

Rob Steinholtz was erratic and self-destructive, but

in the end he was nobody's fool. He knew that it would have proven fatal to the declining wife Redfield had been forced to lie to for seven bitter years. Rob Steinholtz knew that he was silently declaring war.

And he *should* have known that Redfield would have blasted his head off before allowing it to be revealed. Luckily, Rob—or someone else along his endless trail of discarded pawns—had beat him to it. The coroner had discreetly ruled it a suicide. But the line-up list of suspects with a motive stretched unbroken throughout the basin, and into the farthest reaches of the Valley.

David had tried to topple Goliath, Redfield mused, carefully tipping the cognac onto the pile of costly surveillance. Thank God he had never had time to get off the last shot.

He lit a match and stared into the glowing head, then watched silently as the reams of paper and cassettes burst into flames and began to consume themselves. With the blackmail material, his own bitterness was being burnt away. Ashes to ashes, and dust to dust.

With the arrival of police officers at the Steinholtz mansion, all of the materials in the SBN sealed case had been discovered. In due course, they had been turned over without question to their legal owner, represented by the RedRock chief counsel.

Furthermore, while Rob was being fired in Redfield's office, the Satellite Broadcasting Network security force had simultaneously taken possession of the files and tapes and shredder in his office below. Of course, that was also standard operating procedure throughout the industry.

The odds were quite good that Rob had not had time to release any of his carefully sequestered information. In fact, since Redfield had had the good sense to have his office, car, home and body monitored, and his every movement under constant surveillance the past few weeks, there were no odds at all beyond a few quixotic and insubstantial outbursts.

Ultimately, it would be a clean sweep all around. Rob's unhappiness was over, and the network would probably move more smoothly ahead with him gone. Maria, not suited to unhappiness, would soon find another protector to worship. Moe would have to be thankful for the tribute paid indirectly to him, and Maria, and for being spared the agonizing details of making the arrangements.

As the last glowing embers faded in the wreckage within the aluminum case, Redfield carefully gathered up the photographs of Lauren from beside it. Together with the negatives, he tipped them back into their yellowed envelope. Then he walked over to Rob's confiscated typewriter and began typing on the outside of the envelope. *Lauren Conrad*, Century Towers . . . and buzzed for the RedRock messenger.

Redfield returned to his desk and lifted up the aluminum case. Foot on the shredder pedal, he slowly sifted its remaining contents into oblivion. Then he removed his antelope gloves, stretched, and sat down once again before the priceless desk.

"Memo," he sighed into the dictaphone microphone, gazing at the amber liquid swirling in his glass. "Barbara, I've decided on Forest Lawn, the Glenwood Memorial Park. Findlay for flowers, and no stinting. Tell him I want it to look like a botanical garden. Tell the funeral directors we want a serene spot in the Court of Freedom. I want to personally go over our official press release. Together with bio and obit, on my desk by 9:30 . . . Milton Williams for

catering. Tell him it's an emergency. My kitchen will be at his disposal. He knows what I like. For family friends and close business associates only. Say two hundred . . . No. Better make it two-fifty. And give him my personal regards. Find out the name of the airplane we hired two months ago, for the Stewart party, and get them on the line for me first thing. That's it for now. I'll call up Fred Hayman at Giorgio's personally, to send over suitable dress for the widow."

Redfield, smiling with satisfaction now, drained the bottom of his snifter. With the arrival of Rob's envelope, Lauren could breathe easier. Then the only bitter taste would be in his own mouth.

That, too would soon fade away, once he had managed to defuse Sloan. Afterwards would come the time when he could concentrate on collecting the debt that Moe Alexander owed him. It would take years, but sooner or later Redfield would seize control of the Alexander Corporation, and boot the aging mogul out once and for all. It was simply a matter of patience.

As for Rob Steinholtz, his vicious blackmailing scheme was over. In time, perhaps the RedRock head would be able to look back on him fondly as the hard-working and brilliant employee he had occasionally been.

In the meantime, CJ's revenge was the ultimate one. Burying him.

In style.

Twenty-four

On the day of the funeral, it was Standing Room Only all along Cathedral Drive. The crowd stretched from the world's largest wrought iron gates at the memorial park entrance, to the Tudor administration building, then past the massive terraced Great Mausoleum, winding on either side of the motorcade route back to the Court of Freedom.

Scattered all over the sloping lawns and terraces ringing the Wee Kirk o' the Heather, stargazers lounged on lawn chairs or blankets, enjoying the perfect weather and a picnic lunch or beer as they waited.

By now, Lauren fully realized what CJ Redfield had been anticipating all along: to the Alexanders and the RedRock staff, this was a private funeral. But to the rest of Hollywood, it was quickly becoming the event of the season.

From RedRock, a motorcade of a hundred cars had solemnly made its way eastward, led by fifteen black Rolls. Just beyond the Universal City studios, they were joined on the Hollywood Freeway by a mile-long motorcade led by Moe and Maria, in a Cordovan Packard Touring car.

By the time they had rolled past NBC, the Burbank

studios and Disney, traffic was backed up for three miles. Slowly the line snaked along the perimeter of D.W. Griffith Park, heading south. As the first RedRock limo appeared at the massive gates, a brief volley of applause burst from the audience. In the front seat, Redfield silently nodded. Behind the glass partition, Lauren, reduced to silent amazement, sat beside Crystal.

Forest Lawn was larger than many small towns, and its current population was pushing a quarter million. For over a mile, the chapels, mausoleums, museum and courts beckoned above the most meticulously landscaped lawns and gardens in Southern California. In every conceivable form, architects, sculptors and painters had erected testaments to the power of the Almighty. And the Great.

Under heavy security they were ushered into the chapel, where Keith Tempkin, the jazz organist who had just released his seventh gold album, improvised on Bach two-part inventions. Between pressing forward and stopping to return greetings, it took the Now News team twenty minutes to arrive in the front pew.

While Bob Hartman—the talk show host who had co-produced Rob's first soap opera—presided as Master of Ceremonies, a number of celebrities mounted to the dais. Finally, after the routine of Borscht-belt comedian Frank Barney—the stand-up comic Rob had showcased in Hollywood half a decade earlier—soloist Joyce Sumner transformed their tearful laughter with her wailing gospel voice.

At last the audience was warmed up and Reverend Stanley Gearhardt ascended to the dais. Lauren gazed at the sought-after A Group religious leader intently. Television cameras had never done him justice. In person, he stood a barrel-chested six-and-a-half feet. His shock of brilliant white hair rose and fell like a symphony director's as he carefully worked the audience.

In the front row, Dale Stevens buried his face in his hands, his whole broad back shuddering as he fought to maintain self-control. On the other side of the pew, Maria Steinholtz abruptly shrieked and then crumpled onto her knees as the Reverend eloquently described the lone royal palm which would tower above Rob's ashes.

"*Maria*," her father hissed, "for God's sake. The entire industry's watching."

A second later, she was sitting upright once again, once more the reigning princess of the ceremony.

The eulogy by CJ Redfield was simple, fervently pronounced, and effective. "Rob was a rarity in this industry. Forthright, compassionate, fair. You could count on him, always. He was a loving and devoted husband; a humble giant who never forgot to be thankful for his success. His passing leaves us all with a great sense of loss, and a challenge . . . Rob, few men will ever be as decent and caring as you. You accomplished many feats in your lifetime. But most of all, you were a real . . . human being. And that is something which each of us must go forward with, and try to emulate in our own lives.

"As Maria remarked, 'Ever since Robbie was a young boy growing up in the Valley, he always treasured the view from the Hollywood Hills . . .' Now he will look across to them . . . for eternity."

Lauren shifted uneasily in the chapel pew, wondering how many people could read through the lines. Rob's lechery and backstabbing had been legendary. Already, she had glimpsed a half dozen faces belonging to people who would have been only too glad to see Rob dead.

But as she scanned the audience out of the corner of her eye, she was amazed to read the beatific smiles on all of their faces. Caught up once again in an intricately woven Hollywood web, bitterness was transformed into quiet appreciation. Whoever Rob Steinholtz might have been, today they were burying a *star*. With a supporting cast of thousands.

"My dear, dear friends," Gearhardt's voice boomed, with the phrase which was his trademark, "in closing, I would like to fulfill Maria's request, by reading a brief passage from Gibran's *The Prophet:*

> *For what is it to die but to stand naked in the*
> *wind and melt into the sun?*
> *And what is it to cease breathing, but . . .*

As the last words of The Prophet fell from the dais, the lights went down on stage. Then the air was filled with the swelling strains of Beethoven known to millions as the Now News theme.

The back rows began to file out the Wee Kirk. Then pandemonium erupted. Outside, the crowd was storming a police barricade as stargazers raced down from the surrounding slopes. *"Please return to your cars,"* a recorded voice bleated over the loudspeakers. *"The funeral service has concluded. Please return to your cars, the . . ."*

While autograph seekers hurled themselvs against the wall of police, press photographers rushed forward. The bright afternoon sunlight was suddenly eclipsed by a thousand flashbulbs as the cameras struggled to capture the hundreds of emerging celebrities fleeing to their awaiting limousines.

Buzzing above the Hollywood Hills, a skywriter

scrawled one final tribute:

So Long, Rob. We loved ya.

By the time Lauren's limo had crawled in the procession along the Ventura Freeway, then dipped South toward Redfield's Pacific Palisades manse, the mood of the funeral party had almost reverted to gaiety.

Except for the predominantly black designer dresses, and the notable absence of jeans and T-shirts, the entire scene was once again straight out of the Polo Lounge. With guests wandering over the expansive lawn with hors d'oeuvres and wine glasses, the hype and glitter had never been more formidable.

"Ah, Lauren Conrad," beamed a portly man, throwing out an arm and linking it into hers with astonishing speed. *"Just* the lady I was looking for." As he playfully swung her toward him, the anchorwoman found herself once more eye-to-sunglasses with Sid Gold.

"Bette, meet the Rock of RedRock, Lauren Conrad. Lauren, of course you recognize Bette Liddleton."

"How do you do," Lauren smiled affably, offering a hand to the New York comedienne. After a minute, she excused herself and headed toward the line of people paying their respects to Moe and Maria, acutely aware of a man's gaze burning into her back. Instinctively, she frowned. Rob's funeral reception *hardly* seemed like the place to encourage a come-on.

Then again, this affair seemed more like a party than a funeral. In every direction, people were talking shop and striking poses. Flirting or scoring points. Even Moe Alexander was breaking into laughter at the moment.

Under the circumstances, her sense of decorum

251

seemed misplaced. Besides, as she turned to face the stranger who had been intently watching her he looked entirely non-threatening. He also possessed smoky grey eyes that were mesmerizing.

"Excuse me," he pronounced in a clear baritone voice. "Lauren Conrad?" A warm smile trickled onto his lips. "I've been wanting to meet you for some time now . . . I'm Bob Radin."

Bob Radin. It was a name which had often appeared in the trade papers. But perhaps . . . yes, it was *definitely* familiar from the society columns. "Bob Radin was spotted last night at Jimmy's, engaged in a *tête à tête* with none other than Jackie Walsh . . ." "In TinselTown last night, the scene was decidedly *de rigeur* at Evie Sandusky's gala reception for Russian novelist Sergiev Kroffsky. Guests included Misty Sanders and her escort, perennial batch Bob Radin. According to your local colorist, the sparks were absolutely *flying.* Insiders predict January nuptials . . ."

Come to think of it, a week never went by without some reference to the latest society figure or starlet he was squiring. And it didn't take much to figure out why. She shook his hand warmly, and found her eyes lingering on the powerful muscles beneath his somber French-cut suit. If the bulges were any indication, then he was built like Michaelangelo's David—all six-feet and four inches of him.

"It's been really exciting to watch Now News take off," he smiled, holding her hand a second longer than necessary. "Even though Redfield wasn't the first to come up with an all-woman anchoring team. Years ago, when I was still working for Fred Friendly, I clearly remember the idea being raised at a network conference. We laughed ourselves sick over that one. Everyone knew it could never work. I want to go on record as apologizing."

"I guess you could say CJ is a prophet whose time has finally come," she replied teasingly.

"Let's put it this way: CJ is *nobody's* fool. Whatever he may have been after in the beginning, at this point you two are becoming an institution. In fact, I actually overheard a news director lately who was complaining. 'Why can't *my* anchors start writing their own stuff for a change?' Not only that, but you've scooped KJJX so many times, Adam Ward has started calling you 'The Golden Retrievers!'"

Lauren laughed. "Well I don't care *what* they call us—as long as they're still glued to the set. At any rate, I *am* delighted to meet you." She stared down coolly at his hand, lingering over her own.

As his fingers drew hesitantly away, she was struck by their surprising softness. She thought of the gossip columns and smiled. Could this be one of those species which appeared to be extinct in Hollywood? A successful, desirable *and* eligible man in his early forties? One who was neither gay nor halfway down the Road of No Return with est, chanting or bioerotics?

Abruptly, the two of them arrived at Moe and Maria, and their conversation broke off. Maria accepted Lauren's condolences and turned to the next well-wisher, while Moe whisked Radin aside for a few moments. Lauren hesitated, but a stunning redhead she recognized from an evening series did not. Within half a minute, she had her arm neatly snuggled into his, leaving Lauren stranded on the sidelines.

"Well, it was wonderful while it lasted," she mumbled under her breath, drifting across the patio.

"Oh darling, *there* you are," chimed in a voice at her side.

Lauren turned to find herself being pecked on the

cheek by Violet Duval. She accepted the older woman's hand gladly, relieved to at least be on warm and friendly turf.

"Isn't it just too sad?" Violet continued in her disarming little girl voice, her fingers tugging nervously at the wide black velvet ribbon caught with a spray of violets which encircled her slender neck. As she spoke, she unconsciously leaned back to accentuate her showgirl figure.

Even at a distance of five feet, Violet Duval looked every inch of the stunning model she had been thirty years before. But on closer inspection, even the former Miss Alabaster Skin's flawless makeup job could not entirely camouflage the fine crow's feet around her eyes. Nor could she entirely pose her way out of gravity's inevitable pull on her still-full breasts and derrière.

Lauren knew from her own experience—even at age thirty-two—just how cruel aging could be in Hollywood. She and Crystal had beaten the odds. Kept their youthful looks and landed anchoring jobs that were usually given to girls in their twenties. But if this Hollywood youth craze continued it would only be a matter of years before they too would be covering their necks, their wrinkles and sags.

It was obvious that Violet had at least one ulterior motive in posing beside Lauren Conrad at that particular moment. She had purposely framed herself right in Sid Gold's line of vision, hoping to catch his attention as he stared at the anchorwoman.

At age sixty, Violet was still waiting for the next big break. The one that would make up for all the years of sliding into anonymity, pursuing one disappointment after another. Perhaps she thought that Sid Gold could somehow carry her back through time, and get her in front of the cameras for a sit com or a movie. Or even a national commercial.

"Lauren, I'm *so* glad I met you at Francesca's soiree last month. Wasn't it simply fabulous? You know, ever since you went on the air, I'd been asking all of my girlfriends to introduce us."

Lauren nodded, for once delighted at the approach of Crystal and Winston. The fact that she had become aware of Violet's desperate posing for the agent made the situation even more embarrassing.

"Violet," Crystal purred, "I'd like you to meet Winston Jerome. Winston, I'm certain you recognize Violet Duval."

"*Enchanté*," he smiled, sweeping into a formal bow and elegantly kissing her hand.

"*Moi aussi*," she glowed, breaking away to hug Crystal. "I was just telling Lauren how lucky I was to finally meet you two. Maybe we'll have another get together soon. I think that I may be throwing a huge celebration party—for something *incredible*. It's still in the negotiation stage, but . . . more about that *later*. I'd better rush off to greet Moe before he gets offended. Particularly since I snubbed his latest invitation to . . . well, maybe I've said too much already. Let's keep in touch. Okay? . . Ciao."

Lauren and Crystal nodded. It was an exit line she had been using for twenty-five years now. "Can she really be sixty," Crystal wondered aloud. "She has such a lost little girl aura."

"She certainly knows how to preserve it."

"I'll say," Winston chimed in. "You know that gorgeous young guy who was falling all over her at the bar? That's her lover! The one with a *Mr. America* body."

"You *would* notice," Lauren teased.

"It's hard enough to ignore. He can't be more than twenty-five."

"You sound jealous." Lauren's voice was tinged with sarcasm.

"Come off it." Crystal sounded exasperated. "So what if he's not even half her age. That's the new trend anyway, and don't tell me he wasn't coming on to you, back at Sloan's little studfest."

Lauren turned back to Crystal with unconcealed distaste. "Well at least *he* isn't letting her come to Rob's funeral without an escort." She saw Crystal wince and instantly regretted the remark. For weeks, Crystal had been complaining about the way Joel refused to get involved in any of her problems, even down to a show of support at Rob's funeral. "I . . . I'm sorry Crystal I didn't mean . . ."

"Forget it. Let's just call a truce for once, okay? We've both got bigger worries right now." Her glance levelled significantly at Dale, who was rapidly downing yet another glass of chablis.

"I'm worried about him too," Lauren offered apologetically. "He's been in his own world for the past three days."

"It's getting worse. And the drinking doesn't help."

Lauren nodded and waved anxiously at Dale to join them. But he stared right past her, seemingly oblivious. Shrugging, she started over toward his table on the edge of the patio.

"I hope," announced Bob Radin, intercepting her, "that we can continue where we left off."

"I'd love to," she smiled. "But Crystal and I have to get back to RedRock. Have you met my illustrious partner? Crystal, this is . . ."

"We've met," he laughed. Lauren's stare darkened perceptibly. ". . . But only for about ten seconds at

256

Genya Ray's party in Malibu last month. Listen: why don't we all get together for lunch at the Polo Lounge next week? It's every man's dream to make an entrance with the likes of Conrad and Cooper in tow. Or vice versa. Definitely front page material for *The Hollywood Reporter,* or *Variety.* And quite frankly, that never hurts in my line of business."

Crystal closed the distance between them and warmed considerably. "Are you a writer?"

He shook his head.

"Director?"

"Nope."

"In this town everyone seems to be one or another, unless they're 'consultants'."

"My dear," he answered with mock solemnity, "every consultant I've ever known in the industry has been perennially unemployed. All the directors have ulcers, and the writers are broke. I hate to confess to being so boring, but I am merely a producer."

"Well," Lauren broke in brusquely, "Crystal and I may be *merely* newscasters. But we'd better tear ourselves away and head down to the studio, pronto. It's getting close to air time. Things are guaranteed to be a mess as is . . ."

"No apologies necessary. It's been wonderful chatting with you. I'll call you soon. À bientôt."

"Ciao," Lauren smiled, locking eyes with him until he abruptly turned away.

"What a hunk!" Crystal murmured once he was out of earshot. "Oh come on, Lauren. Why don't you stop giving me the evil eye? I'm not about to leap into the breach and snag your next *conquest.* Or do you deny that he was already lined up in your sights?"

"Let's just say that Bob Radin sort of just fell into my lap."

"Not yet. But he will," giggled Sloan who had just materialized with Moe Alexander in tow. "Take it from one who knows: Bob Radin just *adores* eating pussy."

No one laughed. Shrugging to hide her disgust, Lauren turned back toward Dale, who was now carefully scrutinizing the group. Crystal came up beside her. "Don't let them get to you," she whispered earnestly. "Things are rough enough as is. First the purge. Then Rob's death. Then this ghastly funeral. Did you notice that no one even mentioned God?"

"They don't speak of Him and Moe in the same room," Winston hissed.

Lauren brushed off the snide remark. Crystal's words had hit home, alright. Most of all the ones about the network. Since the day of Rob's death, it had been plunged into chaos. Dale was doing his best to keep Now News rolling. But for all of his years of experience, nothing could have prepared him for his best friend's death. He was so devastated that he could barely get out a string of coherent sentences—even when he was sober.

While he got his act together, it fell to Conrad and Cooper to cover for him. She stared into Crystal's emerald eyes and considered it. A truce? Why not? She glanced down at her watch, then across to the awaiting chauffeur. "Why don't you and Winston hop into the Rolls?" she replied warmly. "I'll gather up our faithful news director."

As Lauren marched over to retrieve him, Dale's watery eyes remained locked on the group assembled in the far corner of the patio. Moe and Maria stood facing Redfield, who had just thrown his arms around Sloan Schwartz and Jewel Beale.

No sooner were Rob's remains cremated than Sloan Schwartz began sucking up to Redfield, launching her campaign for the RedRock presidency. Lauren shook her head with genuine pity.

Not for the death of Rob, but for the survivors. Crystal was right. The next few days at the network would be pure hell. But especially for Dale, who was in *no* condition to battle Sloan for the Number Two spot.

"You ready?" she murmured placatingly.

Dale was lost in another world. Ignoring her presence, he clenched his fist and stared at the fivesome.

"They're all in on it," he slurred drunkenly.

Then, as Lauren looked on in astonishment, his eyes narrowed. Slowly his lips formed the words which had been burning in his throat for three days.

"*They* murdered Rob."

Twenty-five

Crystal groped blindly for the contact lens case, cursing herself for placing the clock radio on the far side of the bedroom. Lately, just gettting up in the morning was such a struggle that it took all of her efforts to keep from pressing on the snooze alarm and going back to sleep. *"Are jammed . . . a smog alert is in effect for the next 18 hours, when . . ."*

Eyes in place, she immediately snapped off the radio and called in to the service for the morning's messages.

"Oh, good morning Miss Cooper," said the aggressively cheerful operator. "Yes, there are four calls here. One was an obscene caller. He said he was calling long distance—from Atlanta—and didn't leave a number where he could be reached. Number two: Dr. Ted Rothmore. Confirming this evening's dinner date. He'll call back at the office. There was a message from Dale Stevens, 736-2978. Says it's urgent. And I just took a message from Joel Hanson . . ."

"That's Hanlin, I think."

"Oh, no, I'm quite certain he said *Hanson*. Something about inviting you to a screening—I'm afraid that the rest of the message is smudged. I can't quite make it out. And that's it for now."

Crystal hesitated. "Are you sure there's nothing from my daughter, Marcie?"

"What's the last name?"

"It was Benjamin, last time I checked."

"Well no one by that name called. I'm sure we got all the messages. Maybe she'll call later. Have a good day."

"You too," Crystal groaned, wondering if it was in the realm of possibility. So far, she had awakened to a splitting headache from last night's fight with Joel, a smog alert and the news that her daughter had failed to return her third call. If that wasn't enough, in the days since Rob's funeral, she and Lauren had been putting in twelve hours a day, just to keep the broadcasts going.

But at least it was Friday, which meant that the end was in sight. For once, Crystal would be only too glad to turn Now News over to the weekend scrub team. Now that Dale had named Jewel Beale as one of the weekend anchorwomen, it wouldn't be long before her syrupy sweet Virginian rival began to make a play for more airtime on the weekday broadcasts.

In the meantime, it was a question of making it through the day ahead. Based on his behavior last night, postponing a call to Joel was a good step. She listened to the eight-note Now News theme as she pushed the buttons of her phone, then waited to be connected by Dale's secretary.

"Stevens here," he answered too loudly.

"Dale, it's Crystal."

Immediately his voice dropped to a whisper. "Thank God. Crystal, something big is up. Can't talk about it here. I've already arranged for Lauren to meet me at the Century Towers pool at eleven."

"Can you tell me a little bit more? *I've* already scheduled an 11:30 meeting with Winston to . . ."

"Well, change it to the pool. I can't talk here. I've already said too much. The ears have walls. Do you understand?"

"Don't you mean that the *walls* have *ears?*" she laughed nervously.

"*Gottago,*" Dale hissed in a panic, and clicking off.

She stared at the receiver dumbfounded, then placed it back on the cradle. At once it rang again.

With a sigh of relief, she recognized Ted Rothmore's voice, sounding absolutely charged with energy.

"Good morning, Doctor," she replied, giving him the full treatment of her own devastingly sexy Southern lilt. "Yes, I *did* get your message. I was just about to hop into the shower and then . . ."

"You mean we're still on for tonight?" He sounded equally delighted, maybe more so. "I was thinking . . . how about Ma Maison around nine-thirty? Would you like drinks first at the Beverly Wilshire? Or how about . . ."

"Nine-thirty's fine." She paused for a second, then added for effect, "Why don't you pick me up? The Century Towers . . ." On the other end of the line, she could just about hear him bursting, preparing his opening lines to be used over cocktails, while maneuvering her toward the bedroom.

As the conversation trailed off, she felt almost sorry for him. Of course he would arrive to find her for once punctual, dressed to kill and waiting down in the lobby. In the meantime, maybe a bit of fantasy would do them both some good.

She drifted into the shower and thought back to Dale. His voice was clear for a change, but something told her that his thoughts were not. For the past four nights, he had obviously been getting crocked. And when he arrived at the office, he seemed more than a little hung over.

Both she and Lauren had done everything short of making the broadcast calls for Dale since Rob's death. But the way he was slipping, it was bound to be noted up in Imperial HQ. Maybe it was Rob's death—or the pressure of waiting for CJ to choose between Sloan and himself for the network presidency.

Or maybe it was the pressure of the news director's job, finally taking its toll after half a year of frenzied air time. Whatever it was, he was showing signs of disintegration.

Even his personality was beginning to change. Instead of the old, family-minded image, a new Dale Stevens was beginning to emerge. Occasionally, Crystal had had to write off *too* friendly hugs, but suddenly his hands were roving a little loosely. And when it came to ass-grabbing, whether Dale was under the influence of alcohol or overactive glands, it hardly seemed to matter.

Yes, she nodded as the warm shower massage sprayed out from a dozen nozzles in the Delft-tiled bath, *it's time to tell Dale to get his act together. Pronto.* Letting him get away with it—and covering for him—was doing no one any good.

At the sound of the intercom, she dashed out of the shower and threw a bath sheet over her still dripping body.

"It's Federico," announced the doorman. "I jus'

wan'ed to let you know, Senora Cooper. Eet looks like roses, wheech I sent right up."

"Oh *great!*" she replied sarcastically into the intercom.

"My pleasure for the bee-utiful lady," he chimed back, oblivious to her annoyance.

As the doorbell rang, Crystal just had time to throw a green silk kimono around her, the featherlight fabric clinging at once to her still-moist neck and shoulders.

Opening the door, she raced to her wallet for a tip. When she turned around, the delivery boy was rolling on his heels, unabashedly ogling the kimono which was clinging like a second skin. Ignoring the leer set firmly on his unshaven face, she proffered a dollar bill. He stood firm, his eyes locked on the emerald silk draping her body.

What's the matter with this guy, Crystal frowned. Hasn't he ever seen an embroidered dragon before? But then his eyes drifted to the unadorned side of the kimono, then slowly down below her waist.

With a start, Crystal jerked her eyes down. Moistened by her flesh, the pale silk was now about as transparent as saran wrap.

"Here lady," he took a step forward and thrust the flowers into her extended hand. "You can *keep* the change."

She cursed under her breath, then bolted the door on his heels. The card read: "Joel Hanlin apologizes profusely for his uncalled for and childish behavior last night. He will make it up—with interest—at tonight's exclusive screening. Hugh Hefner's mansion, Holmby Hills. RSVP."

"*Shit,*" she screamed at the unheeding roses. "Of all the nights!"

Twenty-six

CJ Redfield vaulted out of his white Jaguar angrily clutching a crumpled newspaper. Instead of a greeting, he tossed the awaiting valet a set of keys and stormed into the arched doorway.

By the time he reached the fifteenth floor, he was no longer on the verge of exploding. But his bronzed skin now shone red with fury, and the veins were pounding in his temples.

"Good morning, CJ," Barbara called to the flurry bursting in the carved doors. "*CJ?*"

He whisked straight past her, sealing the door to the inner office behind him. A moment later, his voice rang out on the intercom. "Hold all calls this morning."

He sank into the burnished leather of his desk chair and spread out the feature article on his desk. Seething, he read it over once more, pausing once or twice to underline sections.

Thre was no doubt about it. The *Tribune* had cashed in on the RedRock media blitz surrounding Rob's funeral. Which network had egged them on remained to be learned. But this much was clear: despite his vociferous legal threats—and many worse scarcely veiled ones—the paper had just published the first in a series of articles entitled, "The Man Behind RedRock."

If the first installment was any indication, it was a carefully pinpointed character assassination. Glossing over his magnificent contributions to the City of Hope and a dozen other charities, openly sneering at his strong public stands against abortion and sex education. Instead of reading about his "A" Group connections, he began pouring over the text outlining upcoming revelations about his "supposed Mafia connections."

"Barbara," he called into the microphone, a bit more calmly. "Get Phil Haas and the rest of the legal staff together for an eleven o'clock meeting. In the meantime, *no one* gets through."

"Trouble?" she probed, already knowing the answer.

"I'll tell you later. In the meantime, take a look at this morning's *Tribune.*"

Clicking off the intercom, Redfield picked up the cradle of his private line and dialled a number he had long ago committed to memory. With a series of clicks, his call was diverted from the New York switchboard to a ranch just out of Reno.

"La Lunette," a thickly accented voice answered.

"Clay Redfield calling for Dom. Tell him it's urgent."

"I'm sorry sir. But he is unavailable for the present moment. I'm afraid that I'll have to . . ."

"Is he with Georgina? Or is it the other redhead?"

"I beg your pardon?"

"Let me try it this way: you tell that wop he has fifteen seconds to call me back. My name is Clayton Jennings Redfield. Got that? What's your name?"

"Julio, sir."

"Well listen carefully, Julio. I don't know how long you've been working for his organization. But I do not enjoy being kept waiting. In future you will not subject me to unnecessary delays. Go ahead and clear it with him. And I *mean* fifteen seconds. Next time I may have to make my point in a more unpleasant fashion."

"*CJ? Wait!*" pleaded a voice cutting in on another extension. "A thousand apologies. We've had some trouble around here in the past few days and . . ."

"Don't bother telling me about it, Dom. I just got a fresh whiff from the pages of the *Tribune*. And it stinks to high hell."

"Oh *Jesus!* I knew that some reporters were sniffing around, but . . ."

"*But nothing*. I detest sloppy organizations. As a matter of fact, I'm cutting off Luna Productions, effective immediately. The papers will be in Sal's hands tomorrow morning, with a courier waiting to fly them back."

"Now wait one fucking minute. You can't just close down the operation like that. It ain't no snap of the fingers thing. We already have our accountants busy with the . . ."

"That's not my concern," Redfield shot back. His words were pronounced meticulously, with a razor edge. Half a minute was always too much of the slimy head of Reno operations, his whiny wheedling voice and his blatant stupidity. "There's a lot more at stake here than your lousy thousand K."

"Please CJ. I need a little time. Just a few weeks. The least you owe me is . . ."

"Forget it. The least I owe you is an order. You just received it. Any further questions will be dealt with by Salvatore. *Capishe?* Or would you like me to go over it with *him*—including ways to improve his staff?"

"I got it," the voice responded through gritted teeth. "I didn't mean no disrespect. *Honest*, CJ. It's just that . . ."

"No explanations. And no harm has been done . . . yet. You'll get in touch with Sal if you need additional instructions."

"Okay CJ. I'll get it done, somehow. I don't know . . ."

Redfield dropped the phone into the cradle and cursed his bad luck. A year ago Sal had approached him, wanting to buy into the Satellite Network. Luna Productions had been a good investor. And one hundred per cent legitimate.

Unfortunately, their money wasn't. Like a thousand other production companies, it was used to launder money skinned off the books. In this case from Mammon Casinos, plus a few dozen less savory organizations. Luna Productions was two thousand carefully monitored miles from Las Vegas. Suddenly, it was far too close.

So far, the *Tribune* had only been able to connect one of RedRock's independent producers to the operation. But the second they got a whiff of the dirty money being laundered, an FCC revocation would be within the realm of possibility.

It was time to launch a counterattack, and fast.

"Barbara," he barked into the intercom, "get Dale Stevens in here on the double . . . and send him right in when he arrives."

His mind was racing now, going over the ramifications. If the story finally broke, the RedRock books would be gone over with a fine tooth comb. With any luck, he could fight fire with fire, and get the *Tribune* to back out *before* the stakes got too high—for the entire industry.

In the meantime, it was time to cover his own tracks. The call to Luna would be a help. But there were a dozen other money faucets which were bound to spring a leak. Shutting them off would have to be a dangerously slow process, or the operating capital of RedRock would dry up overnight.

Above all, he had his network and his family to defend, no matter what it was going to take. Running his hands anxiously through his thinning sandy hair, Redfield stared at the gilt-edged mirror above his Duncan Phyfe harvest table.

The first step was to relax. Regain the confident, crisp look which had brought him through a dozen investigations in the past. If it came to personally going on-camera, playing the part of the stern and abused network executive would outweigh even the most damaging numbers that could be gathered from fine-combing the books.

It was a media lesson that had been learned in the very first days of televised politics and crime reporting. Crooked game show contestants, presidents and endless lesser politicians had used their images in that way for years, with varying degrees of success.

After all, what was a sheet filled with mere statistics against a long-suffering, but still hopeful and handsome face?

As he stared into the mirror, his eyes slowly took on an explosive anger. It was the face which only a select handful of men had ever seen. Two-bit real estate agents who tried to stick him with worthless swamps, underpaid SEC investigators trying to pull together shreds of evidence concerning the manipulation of stocks in a few of his high tech holdings. One and all, he had dominated them by sheer will power, leaving them feeling lucky to be alive.

All without one direct threat. This time, he might have to do a little heavy leaning. But by the time he was done, the *Tribune*, its parent communications company—and even the three major networks—would yield. Either privately to him, or else to public scrutiny. And if every dollar of every television show had to be traced, not even reruns from the fifties would come out clean.

Hastily, he returned to his desk and called Edgemont.

After one ring, Mel Breeden answered with his soft, soothing voice.

"Redfield," CJ announced, although after a lifetime of friendship, it was hardly necessary.

"I hardly expected you to be calling midday on a Friday? Trouble?"

"I'm not sure, Mel. But until I know, I won't be calling Tuesday mornings. Have you noticed anything unusual around the cottage? Wandering hunters or a conspicuous influx of 'tourists?' "

"Not a soul for miles, as far as I know, just your sister . . . and Kikki, of course."

"Any problems?"

"A few things to go over about the main house. But nothing that can't wait."

"I'll be flying in sometime soon. In the meantime, make certain that you get whatever you need wired to you by Barbara."

"If you could just get away for a weekend now, foliage has never been better. But it's not the first time you've missed that. Maybe we can take a day and snowshoe up Elisabeth. With the new trail, it's only a few hours to the first peak."

"I'd love that. Lord, it must be years . . ."

"Eight of them, CJ."

He struggled to keep his mind focused. Mount Elisabeth and Edgemont and the stark beauty of a New Hampshire winter flickered in a smile across his lips, then vanished. "Anything new with Kikki?"

"Afraid not."

"Well, let me try her." His features sank as he heard

the familiar guttural moans and senseless mouthings. He could almost see Mel's broad arms carefully restraining her as she struggled to break free.

"Hello, baby," Redfield cooed, steeling himself. "How's my princess? . . . I love you. Do you understand? *I love you*. I'll be coming home soon now. Promise. Is there anything I can bring back for you?" He waited silently for a minute. "Mel? You there?"

"Yes."

"She didn't? . . ."

"Respond? I'm afraid not. Not this time?"

Or the time before that or the time before that. Not for seven sad years. Redfield nodded silently, fighting back the guilty fury. He thought of the granite shrine they had erected to her memory, following the closed casket funeral. No longer able to bear the sight of it as he plunged into the pool for a hundred laps each morning, he had finally brought in the Japanese gardener to shroud it in a grove of yew trees. But somehow he could see it just as clearly now, burned indelibly into his memory.

Perhaps it would have been better if she had died. Unconsciously, Redfield crossed himself at the thought. "I'll be in touch, indirectly, when I can. Goodbye," he murmured sadly. "Thanks, Mel."

When he looked up from the desk, Dale Stevens was hovering at the door. Looking like he had just seen the ghost of Lazarus.

Twenty-seven

"Just picture it: *Corruption in the Media*. We do it as a full-blown three-part special investigation. *Prime time*, of course." Dale stared down into his half-empty vodka gimlet, and his features grew more animated. "This time, we're pulling out all the stops. You get full use of the research staff, unlimited data base search and computer privileges, the works. A good old-fashioned, open-budget media blitz."

Lauren eyed him warily, taking in the crumpled tie and the odd way his gaze kept shifting around as he spoke. The hype and bullshit were well-delivered, but she was listening to CJ's words—not Dale's. Underneath the mask of his features, something very different was going on in his thoughts.

"Exactly where does the Satellite Network fit in this investigation? We can hardly skip over our own restricted access files, can we? If CJ thinks that he can just maul the other networks and avoid going in to SBN financing, then he's in for a surprise. We're newswomen, not a RedRock SWAT team."

Crystal nodded thoughtfully.

"We said *'total'* " agreed Dale—"and that's what we mean. Anything and everything. CJ swears that the operation is run like an open book. The Good Book, at that. Well, put him to the test!

Lauren's eyes widened. *You'd love to catch him red-handed, wouldn't you?* She glanced over at Crystal and saw two emerald eyes overflowing with visions of news awards and superstardom. So much the better.

The tension and excitement were infectious, Lauren had to fight to keep her thoughts from just dissolving into high voltage bliss. The special segments would be hyped in a media campaign, promos and headlines everywhere from the *New York Times* to the *Enquirer*. It was one prime time series that no one—in the media or out—would dare to miss.

With the right angle, it would provide the kind of thrill and the satisfaction of tackling the power structure which only a handful of events in the history of television had ever captured. But why *both* of them? Why not have Lauren Conrad come out on top? Given Crystal's predilection for refusing to back down from the riskiest stories, CJ might well have to call her off before the Golden Retriever *sicced* the wrong bone. The odds were promising.

If not, then careful study of the data banks was bound to provide Lauren with a dozen other useful bits of information. Particularly if she used them to gain access to Crystal's own personal data; given enough figures, there might even be a discrepancy in the Immaculate Cooper's file.

Dale swirled the ice in his glass and nervously stared up at the towering Century Towers. His eyes quickly darted all around the poolside, then swept over the glass table top. What in hell was he worried about? The investigation hadn't even *begun* yet!

He turned back to the news team, and his lips once again stretched into a grin. "By the time you get back to RedRock, research will be going full thrust. Soon every stringer we can trust will be getting his—or her—little finger into the pie. And with a few judicious probes, we're sure that the birds will begin to sing. They'll be running down a list that reads like *Who's Who* in Hollywood, Washington, Network Row *and* organized crime. Your Nielsens were going through the roof this morning. You've done a fabulous job. So we figured it was time to give you some real *prime time* exposure. It was either that or a raise. Any complaints?"

He threw his arms around them in an expansive gesture. As the women returned his hug, Dale accepted their thanks with a bit *too* much relish. Like a kid out of control in a candy store, he stole one meaty hand downward toward Lauren's derriere. In the meantime, she watched the other paw slide fully around Crystal's slim ribcage, stopping perilously within cupping distance of her left breast.

"To victory!" he said pointedly, pouring out another round of drinks. Lauren traded an unamused shrug with Crystal, then politely clinked his glass. She watched in dismay as he proceeded to down half of the gimlet in a single swig.

"I've really got to get ready for my meeting with Winston," she murmured, setting down her glass and reaching under the table for her attaché case. Dale's hand suddenly reached over, pinning her to the chair with alarming force.

"That's not why we called you here this morning. There's more to it. *A lot more.* This is just the tip of the iceberg . . . I mean, the media investigation. There's something else. I thought that . . . you should know. . . ." His voice trailed off, and he stared intently at the confused gazes of the two women. There was an undercurrent of fury in his eyes.

Or was it terror?

Lauren thought back to his silent pronouncement following Rob's funeral. The past few days, both she and Crystal had arrived at the unspoken conclusion that he was slowly losing control.

She looked into his exhausted, bleary eyes. "*Listen* Dale," Lauren tried to sound harsh, but sympathy was written all over her, "you really should cut down on the drinking."

"I know." His voice sounded pathetically fragile.

"I don't know what's bothering you," Crystal added, "but if it's *your* neck you're worried about, forget it. Not with Now News and your track record. When it comes down to the wire, Lauren and I will personally stand behind you."

Lauren nodded in agreement, knowing that it was only half-true. If Dale kept going at his current rate, then siding with him against Sloan Schwartz would be tantamount to professional suicide.

"Thank you—both of you," Dale mumbled, unconvincingly flashing a smile. He stood up, hesitated, then made for the parking garage, his eyes missing nothing that was going around the pool. His fragmented thoughts sifted down through his alcohol-fogged mind, broken by the gestures of a crowd of women awaiting the valet. One in particular kept looking anxiously toward the garage door, then over toward him. She lifted her hand, as if to signal him.

But a moment later she pointed out something to one of her companions. Did it mean anything? Dale couldn't tell. In the past few days, he had been picking up more and more signals. From news office secretaries right down to the red-jacketed valets. It was impossible to tell how much any of them really knew. But one and all, he noticed their eyes, focusing on him.

At first his secret investigation into Rob's death had been sporadic and inconclusive. Studying the coroner's report and CJ's internal memos, first one phrase and then another had slowly begun to leap off the page. "Shot entered through the right anterior . . ." "According to testimony by the RedRock chief executive, Steinholtz had previously come into his office in an agitated state . . ." ". . . found in his possession at the time of death were a set of keys, billfold, and vials of aureomycin and Valium, traces of which were also present in the corpse as determined by . . ."

Wearily, he sank into the driver's seat of the Brougham. For five sleepless nights now, he had pored over the assembled documents, trying to break the hermeneutic code. Studying the words endlessly, then the careful omissions. He knew just how much had been skirted, left unsaid or hinted at.

He was sure that there was a conspiracy afoot at RedRock, one which had already spread like a cancer throughout the LAPD, the Justice Department. Were Lauren and Crystal already in on it? Hard to tell.

During their meeting, he had listened intently to Lauren's fingernails, and the rhythm they had inter-mittently tapped out on the glass table surface. It wasn't Morse code—but perhaps some other pre-arranged signal between the two.

He couldn't take any chances. Around them, or anyone else. Not even Betty, the housekeeper, could be trusted. Ditto for his fat-assed wife.

It was a waiting game—until the rest of the pieces began to slide together. He had to keep them from finding out how much he suspected. As long as he continued to play the normal unsuspecting fool, he was safe. Day in and day out he would have to stick to the role of CJ Redfield's latest hatchet man. Laughing, stealing quick feels, acting boisterous as he made his way to the top.

It was already hard, and each day's revelations only

made it harder.

He pulled off Wilshire Boulevard and swung into the parking lot of Ship's, anxiously observing a man in a blue pin-stripe suit who arrived right behind him. The man hesitated, and reached for something out of sight beneath the window, then stepped quickly out of his car.

Dale's muscles tensed, and his temples pounded. With relief, he watched the salesman disappear into the diner. He surveyed the empty parking lot, then removed the silver monogrammed hip flask from underneath his seat. He lifted the cold metal to his lips, taking first one hard tug, then another.

The liquor deadened his raw nerves, but the voices ringing in his ears continued. They built up to a crescendo of gibberish, until he thought his head would split apart. Then it was just one voice: Rob Steinholtz, wheezing bitterly through pierced vocal cords. "How could you let me down like this? After all these years?"

"I haven't Rob. Honest. I wouldn't *do* that to you," he mumbled, feeling the words burn on his cracking lips. Dale *had* played along with Redfield, acting the part of the perfect yes-man, and keeping his thoughts to himself. Covering them with a carefully constructed network of hype and glitter. "It was only to keep them off the track," he sobbed. "Of course I wanted the presidency. But not like this. *Not like this.*"

Abruptly, the chorus of voices vanished. Dale looked up over the dashboard, and found the noon sun beating down unmercifully. A concerned-looking girl in her late teens was approaching, wearing a red uniform with a matching cap.

As her hand reached out to tap on the glass, he floored the gas pedal and screeched away into the eastbound lanes.

Twenty-eight

"My *God*," Winston yelped as soon as he was in ear-shot. "You two look like the French troops after Waterloo."

"Thanks," Lauren retorted.

"Better than that, we just finished an exhausting session with Dale."

"Then you know about the special!" Winston's black curls were bouncing excitedly, and he immediately dropped into Dale's chair. "I know that you're supposed to react with cool professional enthusiasm, but how about at least a little smile?"

"Of course we're delighted," Lauren replied. "Who in hell wouldn't be—with a three-part *prime time* report! But we were just talking about a few rotten things back in Denmark. Like a crumbling News Director."

"Was it that bad?"

Crystal shifted uneasily in her chair. "Not that bad. *Worse*. He's playing right into Sloan's hands. He was so blitzed he could barely focus."

"The way he was staring into his glass, you'd think there was a bug in his olive. Not a medfly . . . I'm talking about the electronic variety."

"Do you really think that's so weird?" Winston replied. "I mean, once this investigation really gets underway, a lot of very heavy gentlemen will be more than a bit perturbed. I wouldn't put that past them—or anything else. As a matter of fact, if I were *you* two, I would be awfully careful about . . ."

"Get the stars out of your eyes, junior," Lauren advised impatiently. "The investigation hasn't even gotten off the ground yet. I'm talking about right now. Dale's never been a management flunky. Then all of a sudden, he's talking about 'we' this and 'we' that. You can't just ignore what's happening."

"She's right," Crystal added. "Dale was really flying. And that's early in the *morning*. I walked into his office after last night's broadcast and found him talking to the wall."

Winston shoved aside the comments. "Listen, Dale Stevens has been in this business as long as the two of you put together. He's got credits halfway up his arm. And compared to the shit he weathered back at CBS, Rob's death is like a picnic. Just give him a few more days. He'll snap out of it."

The two women nodded doubtfully.

"I guess there's no need for our meeting now," Crystal shrugged. "Seems like all of the other in-depth reports have been swept clear off the slate. What's RedRock look like?"

"A *zoo!* You wouldn't believe the way CJ has the research team digging. You'd think he was looking for a goldmine. And rumor has it that he's also hired on new staff. I'll tell you this much: I just bumped into his new chauffeur in the john. All two-hundred and fifty pounds of him. If that's any indication, then I would expect some rough going ahead. *Really.* You two had better be a little careful when you're poking around . . ."

"*Conrad and Cooper,*" came a yell over his shoulder. All three turned as the oncomer approached. He was about six feet tall and boyishly slim, wearing a gold embroidered cowboy suit, a fire-red silk scarf and matching Tony Lama lizard boots.

"Excuse me. I certainly *hope* I'm not disturbing you. But I've been watching Now News on the air for months now, and just waiting for the chance to meet you all. I live in the Century Towers, too. I'm Elliot Hirsch."

Pleased to meet you," smiled Crystal, noticing the fact that the young man's gaze had quickly settled on Winston.

The slight figure dropped into a nearby seat. Sighing, she extracted a Sobranie from her case and slipped on her tinted sunglasses.

Hearing Elliot's yell, a half dozen pairs of eyes quickly focused on the gathering. Crystal watched somewhere between amusement and annoyance as others slowly straggled over and joined their table.

"Ah, Jo*Anne,*" beamed Elliot, clearly in his element, "allow me to introduce Crystal Cooper and Lauren Conrad. And this handsome dude is Winston—sorry, I didn't catch your last name?"

"Jerome. Pleased to meet you Joanne." Elliot winked at him, then shrugged apologetically at the newswomen as the ritual handshakes continued around the table. "Joanne is a senior vp with BB & D. But where's the better half?"

The woman's handsome features grew taut, and her full, sensuous lips quivered. "If you mean Andre, I can assure you that he's *not* working at Sassoon. When I left the apartment, he was busy polishing that ghastly coat-of-arms over the credenza."

"Darling," Elliot replied, "I don't know why you put up with the poor, impoverished *artiste.*"

"I'll tell you why," exclaimed a fortyish woman clad in designer jeans. "One: because he's got style, even *if* his claim to be a Prussian count is grating at times. *Two:* Because he's steady, if sluggish. And *Three:* When in hell is the last time you tried to find a straight middle-aged man in this town? They're all a bunch of neurotic freaks, or beach boys who never grew up."

"Bitter, bitter, bitter," chided Elliot.

"Yeah? Well when's the last time *you* tried hunting for a man? A *straight* one, that is."

Elliot ignored her barb, and turned to face Winston, eyes glowing.

"They're plenty of us still around," Winston glowered. Crystal heard the tension in his voice, and saw Elliot lean closer toward him. In the six months that they had been working together, she had at first assumed that he was gay. But when months of observation yielded no confirmation, she had begun to wonder about that. Seeing his skinny frame alternately shy away then lean toward Elliot, she suddenly realized that he was equally perplexed about his sexual orientation.

"Besides, there's always Sam." Elliot pointed toward a slightly paunchy man in his mid-fifties, soaking in the sunshine in a black swimsuit.

Crystal frowned. She had met Sam Hemming at one of Francesca van Rensalaer's soirees a few months back. He had done everything short of rape in his attempts to get her on her back. Given the opportunity, he would undoubtedly have tried that ploy, too.

"If you call that *normal,*" Joanne groaned, "I'd rather stick with Andre. At last report, Sam had clocked in his seven hundredth 'meaningful relationship'. All of them with women half his age."

"The man is sick," announced Fran, a recording studio executive in a pink bikini. "He needs help. They *all* do, around here. I'm about to the point

281

where I'm considering moving to the Valley. Maybe that's the only way to let my sons grow up healthy in this town."

"I used to feel that way too," chimed in a saccharine voice in the periphery. "But that was before I discovered Werner. Let me tell you . . ."

"*Please*. Whatever you do, don't get started on that *est* shtick again. I've heard it all before. How they cram you into a packed auditorium on uncomfortable chairs. You have to sit there for hours. Sweating, bladder bursting, aching for a cigarette. Sounds terrific, huh?"

"That's not the point. You just haven't gotten *it*."

". . . And I don't want to *'get it'*. I've already *had* it—up to *here*! So far, the fabulous Werner has cost me my best friend, my masseur, and . . ."

"What a *freak* show," Lauren whispered in Crystal's ear. In the other ear, a voice was saying, "Personally, I've tried it. And I can do without it. Now Reichian therapy, that's another matter . . ."

Alerted by the familiar click of an attache case clasp, Crystal turned around to find Lauren about to silently exit. "Wait a sec," she whispered. "Can I ask you a favor? I made a date tonight with an author who wants to appear on our Bookends section. In the meantime, Joel has just invited me to Hugh Hefner's weekly screening. I just *can't* turn it down. Is there any chance that you could cover for me?"

Lauren hesitated and continued to make her getaway. "Let me see. I've got to . . . no, that's tomorrow evening. Sure Crys, *why not?*"

Crystal felt a sinking feeling.

"On a scale from one to ten, just how boring *is* this . . . what ever *is* his name, anyway?" Lauren inquired archly.

"Ted. That is, Dr. Rothmore." Crystal thought

back to their meeting two weeks earlier, and the way she had thrilled at the thought of tonight's dinner. "About a four," she lied. "Listen, if it's the *least* inconvenience, I can always call him back and reschedule. Maybe I should do that anyway. I mean, it really isn't fair to . . ."

"Don't worry, darling," Lauren smiled sweetly. "No problems at all. I'd *love* to take care of him for you."

That's precisely what I was afraid of, Crystal thought to herself as her partner headed back into the shelter of her tower. *Just my luck that we've established a truce.*

Since that time, Lauren had been the ideal co-anchor. Friendly, cooperative. Almost responsive. Somehow, Crystal had felt less threatened while they were still enemies.

In the meantime, it was high time to pull out of the coffee klatch.

"I've just heard about a new therapist in town. Dr. Levis. Judith has seen him twice now, and you should hear her rave about it. Personally, it *does* sound marvelous. Instead of a couch, you lie in a warm scented bath throughout the entire session. No lights either. It's just you and the warmth—and him, of course. He claims that he's a neo-Freudian, but . . ."

As Crystal thanked them hastily and prepared to leave, Winston was still firmly rooted in place beside Elliot. Abruptly the conversation turned from therapy to industry gossip.

Crystal glanced from one knowing face to the next, trying to fight back the urge to scream.

Maybe it was the smog, or the Golden Southern California sunshine. Or perhaps it came from the endless barrage of soap operas and sitcoms. The radiation from the picture tube, or just the star-consciousness endlessly ionizing the whole region.

Whatever the cause, there was something which separated Hollywood conversations from the rest of the world. She looked around the table once more feeling totally disoriented.

Sooner or later, she realized, every cliche about L.A. came true.

Twenty-nine

"So how's the most charming publisher in the biz?" Joel Hanlin beamed, strolling into Martina Ferry's office.

As he waited for her to glance up from the manuscript, he struggled to hide his growing anger. He had sat in the *Westwood* magazine waiting room for forty-five minutes, staring at the framed covers, the ASME and Society of Publication Designers awards until he was desperate for a bit of plain white wall.

Five different times, he had been tempted to leave. But each time, one thing kept him pinned to the uncomfortable bentwood chair: *the check*. His account had been coasting on near empty for almost two weeks.

"Can't complain," responded the severely tailored, middle-aged woman looking across the desk. "Our advertising has reached the fifty thousand dollar mark, and we'll be expanding to two-hundred-and-thirty-two pages. Eight four-color signatures. Not bad for the *other* magazine, huh?"

"That's *great*," he smiled, hating the preliminaries. While she was sitting and shooting the shit, the traffic was slowly backing up on the Freeways. Why in hell did editors always have to wax philosophical on Friday afternoons? And particularly when all he wanted to do was take the money and run?

"Keeping busy?"

"You better believe it. I've got two soaps to deliver by Monday, a feature article for next Sunday's *L.A. Times*, plus a backlog booking me solid for the next three months. In the meantime, my agent has given me the go-ahead on the novel?"

"How's the move script going?"

"Slowly," he conceded. Actually, after stringing him along with lousy option fees for over a year, United Artists had just axed his screen treatment entirely, and more than hinted that his latest off-Broadway show might never make it into film, after all. In which case, they could tie it up for six more months.

Damn her and her memory. Why couldn't she have just forked over the check and let *him* decide when to break bad news. After twenty years in the L.A. publishing scene, she must have realized that a writer was not about to hide the existence of a twenty million dollar movie.

"Well listen," Martina continued, "I'm sure that we've both got better things to do than ogle one another in this office. Let's get down to business."

Joel looked at her with bedroom eyes, feigning disappointment.

"I've looked over the article, and so has the managing editor. The content is perfect. But the tone's still not right."

"If you want a few words changed, that's no sweat. I'm sure I can run it through the typewriter over the weekend and . . ."

"No. That's not what I want. We need a rewrite."

"Oh come *on,*" he pleaded, "I already rewrote it for you once." He shot her his most seductive smile, then

286

watched as it hit a brick wall. "I could understand it if you wanted me to change the historical section, but . . ."

"The whole thing. Listen Joel: everyone in this town knows how talented you are. You're a great writer. And to tell you the truth, the style is *wonderful*. But it's not appropriate for a lifestyle magazine."

"What are you talking about? I made every change you suggested."

"No you didn't. I told you that it had to be slanted for our women readers. They want to know about the *glamour* of hang gliding. Not about how much balls it takes. In case you've forgotten, women don't *have* balls."

"Come on, Martina. Be reasonable."

"I *am* being reasonable. You're still in my office, aren't you?"

"What's *that* supposed to mean?"

"I'll tell you: since the day you first walked in my door, you've refused to listen to me. About *our* style, not yours. It goes in one ear and out the other. And two weeks later the manuscript crosses my desk, and it is invariably elegant—and *self-indulgent*. Each time, it takes up more of my copy editor's time, my managing editor's time, and *my* time. Every change I suggest is negotiated or overridden. We both know how charming you can be, but it's beginning to wear a little thin. I'm tired of the way you keep trying to charm the pants off of me, when all I want is the right piece—for the *magazine*. I would hate to give up a writer like you."

"Martina, let's try to keep our heads about this. Tell me *exactly* what you want. And then do you want it delivered?"

"That depends."

"On what?"

"I've already pulled it from next month's issue. How soon do you want the check?"

"Now."

"No way! We agreed that this article would be done on spec. And until it's delivered to my satisfaction, that's the way it stands. So let's get down to the manuscript. I've got to leave in exactly ten minutes. In the first paragraph, you talk about the cliffs and the air currents. That's fine. But then, you suddenly switch to . . ."

Without a word of warning, Joel bolted out of his seat and headed out the door, fists balled in fury. He headed down the hall and burst through the office doors, leaping down the stairs two at a time. "No one treats Joel Hanlin like that," he fumed. " 'Women don't have balls'? Martina sure as hell does. And a big fat carrot up her ass to boot!"

He fumbled with his keys, then jumped into the awaiting MG convertible. Even though no one had ever dared to insult him like Martina, an awful lot of female editors had been pushing him too far lately. Dissecting his manuscripts like they were just slabs of rare roast beef.

One and all, they were short on ovaries. Heavy on manipulation, and light on charms. It was all just one cat-and-mouse control game, based on penis envy.

But they didn't want just his cock. Back East, women knew what they wanted. And it was just what Joel delivered. But in this scene, it was a matter of control.

Even Crystal, with all of her voluptuous sweetness, was into the same control trip. Fidelity and commitment. Acting as if the fact that she shared his bed meant that she owned it.

"Yes," he muttered, crawling onto the packed Freeway headed north, "it's time that Mr. Eight-and-a-Half takes a stand. But starting tonight, it's going to be a whole different ballgame. No more jumping through the hoop at every command."

And Hef's would be the perfect place to make his declaration of independence.

Thirty

". . . So until Monday, this is Crystal Cooper . . ."

". . . and Lauren Conrad for Now News. Have a nice weekend."

The Now News logo flashed on the monitor board. The red light came on, and the studio lights faded.

Lauren carefully blotted the perspiration dotted her forehead, then turned toward the black steel door, moving quickly through the gathered spectators. Just as she reached the corridor, a man wearing tortoise shell glasses broke through to her.

"Hi Lauren," he declared cheerfully, "I'm Dr. Ted Rothmore."

She smiled and stuck out a hand. "Be with you in a few minutes. . . . But why don't you wait in my office? Follow me."

She glanced up at Crystal, who was still sitting at the desk, staring bleakly at them. Lauren blew her a kiss and laughed. Crystal's description had been right on the money, as far as it went. Ted Rothmore was *not* Hollywood handsome by any stretch of the imagination. His glasses were too old-fashioned, his clothing Brooks Brothers conservative. His nose was too big.

But beyond that, his smile would have unlocked any door in the world. And any chastity belt, to boot.

Serves her right, Lauren thought, eyes glowing. She

noted with glee that Ted waved his hand once toward the studio desk, then immediately switched his attention to the woman at hand. On Monday, Crystal could thank Lauren for saving her from succumbing to Rothmore's charms and blemishing her high fidelity record.

Until then, the truce was still in effect.

"I got your flowers just before we went on," Lauren smiled, savoring the thrill of a new seduction slowly coursing through her veins. "That was awfully kind of you." Then she turned and sauntered through the tunnel, letting him fall in two steps behind her; feeling his eyes as they nibbled away at the clinging silk sheathing her legs and derriere.

The ride to the Beverly only heightened her excitement. As Rothmore talked about his Bedford Drive home and his "A" Group clientele—Lauren basked in the opulence of his carefully restored Bentley. The glove leather seats were painstakingly rubbed, and the brass and hardwood trim were equally flawless. The Bentley rolled silently down Sunset Blvd., as if it were a vintage yacht, effortlessly knifing through the water.

Beneath the hotel's port cochere, Smitty greeted them both with a friendly smile. Then they made their way to the entrance and on to the Polo Lounge.

"*Lauren,*" called a husky voice from one of the front tables—Francesca van Rensalaer, sitting alone. With Rothmore in tow she reluctantly walked over to say hello, already sorry that she had insisted on the Polo Lounge instead of the El Padrino Room.

"Oh, darling," Francesca said breathlessly, "I'm *so* glad that you finally met Dr. T. He's been my physician for years, and a hell of a tennis partner to boot. We used to play at the Beverly Hills Tennis Club every week. But lately he's been so hard to get a *hold* of. Haven't you, Ted?"

"Between the expanded practice and the book," he said apologetically, "it's all I can do to fit in the three mile jog every morning."

He grabbed Lauren's arm, and tried to steer her toward their awaiting table, waving goodbye to a forlorn Francesca.

"Not so fast." Francesca made an attempt to flutter her false lashes. "I called you over here to tell you about my *party*. I tell you it's going to be absolutely sen*sa*tional. It's going to be at the Bistro—of course. Casper always treats me so well there. I *do* think that the Bistro is still the chic-est place in town. Don't *you?*"

Lauren nodded, and let Ted take the lead in disengaging them from Francesca, before she could snare them for a round of drinks.

To say that Francesca's soirees were typically Beverly Hills was an understatement. Of course they were catered by Milton Williams, the flowers done by Harry Findlay. In every profession, you could make a check list of the top names, circle the most expensive, and that was whom Francesca simply *had* to hire.

It was more than just a penchant with her, or a natural tendency toward quality. It was a *compulsion*. Her crystal *had* to be Waterford; her sheets Porthault; her china Spode.

From the frilly black lace underwear forcing her overblown figure into a more acceptable shape, to the hand-painted silk scarves which veiled her crepey neck, every inch of Francesca's body simply *had* to be decked in designer fashions. From the right salons.

One day it was St. Laurent, Missoni and Hermes. The next it was Givenchy and Armeni, Balenciaga or Galanos. At the same time, who but the wife of Igor van Rensalaer could manage to strut around with the hem of a six thousand dollar evening dress falling down? Or a split seam in the armpit of her Mary Fadden ensemble—even though it had left the showroom only hours before?

Poor Francesca. Her parties were no different. They had *just* the right components of good food, good music, and ambience. But somehow they just didn't click, and the "A" Group turned her down time and again.

Lauren sat down at their table and glanced across the room at Francesca, still facing an empty chair. Twenty-five years ago, she had been a promising clothes designer, on her way up from working class Italian Brooklyn. Then she had met Igor, a Swiss financier with nothing going for him but unlimited wealth.

Giving up her career to devote all of her time to him might have sounded like a good idea at first. But as the years passed, her creative juices had no outlet. Her acquisition of possessions and need for status turned into a disease.

The right clothing, the right party, the right house. Everything in her life had to be *just so*. At age fifty, she was still holding try-outs for all of the top styles and stylists—looking for a label which would finally mask her entirely.

Whoever the real Francesca was, she had clearly been smothered years ago.

The thought sent a chill running down Lauren's spine. She lifted the champagne glass offered by Walter and tried to focus on Ted Rothmore's toast.

"Anything wrong?" he asked, noting the melancholy look in her eyes.

"Not a thing in the world," she laughed.

"Well then, here's to success." Ted clinked her glass and she lifted it slowly to her lips.

Glancing over toward Francesca again, she saw she

had finally been joined by a familiar-looking black-haired man.

"Just my luck to arrive five minutes too soon," Lauren sighed, watching Francesca lean over and begin whispering in Bob Radin's ear.

"*There* you are," Francesca groaned. "For a while I thought I was being stood up."

"I wouldn't miss this for the world," Radin answered. "I got held up at Steve's office at MGM. Forgive me?"

"Not quite yet. But we'll see. What's doing with MGM?"

Radin chose his words carefully. For months now, Francesca had been hinting that she was interested in backing a mini-series proposal. And for all of the feline purring she put on, he never forgot that she had learned her investment policies from Igor. She never backed a loser or a long shot. Or anyone who showed signs of being snubbed by the "right people." A single wrong word might queer the deal she had obviously brought him here to seal.

"It was just a routine story conference. Nothing that significant. Just brainstorming about a pilot series. Looking for a title, and a leading lady. An older woman. Like Bette Davis. The same kind of directness. But a bit taller. A sad-eyed, strong lead."

"I hear that Violet Duval's been looking into television again."

"Too much of an *ingenue*," he laughed. Sad-eyed, alright. And still stunning. But in addition to the fragility which the camera would expose in a second, Francesca's best friend had one more serious flaw: She couldn't act.

"Bob, darling," Francesca sighed, "why don't you join me on this side of the table? I've come to a decision, and I *hardly* think it should be broadcast all over the Polo Lounge."

Radin slid closer, ignoring the friendly hand which brushed his thigh.

"I finally made the decision last night. I haven't told a soul until today. The only person who knows besides you is Violet . . . Bob, I'm going to open a *boutique!*"

Caught by surprise, he fought back an urge to groan. Is *that* why she had called him to this urgent rendezvous? A *boutique?*

"Surprised?"

He nodded, dumbfounded.

"I'm just *so* excited I can't wait. Igor has already bought the spot on Rodeo. It's going to be sen*sa*tional. Next week I head for Paris and Rome. It's nothing but the *top* names. Then there'll be a gala opening, with my fashions for the winter season. I've been thinking that it really *should* be a boutique for members only. Don't you think that's wise?"

He nodded, holding back a yawn. As her voice droned on about designers and boutiques, his eyes wandered over the crowd. He nodded once at a director staring back at his reflection, then continued scanning the tables until his eyes lit on Sloan Schwartz.

As usual, she was dressed all in black. Her hands were clawing through the air as she gesticulated in the direction of Jewel Beale. He paused for a moment, puzzled. What was the RedRock vice president doing with the young Now News lifestyle reporter? Between Jewel's sicky-sweet, paper-thin charm, and Sloan's aggressive, forceful style, they seemed like an odd couple to be simply out toasting the end of another network week.

Business or pleasure? As he followed Sloan's dramatic gestures, an amused smile formed on his lips. He knew the Hollywood heiress too well to wonder for long.

The answer had to be both.

"Would ya get a load of that bitch?" Sloan sneered, "What in hell is she doing with Ted Rothmore at the Polo Lounge? Just answer me *that.*"

"As far as *I* know, it's business. He's pushing to get *The Laetrile Alternative* on Bookends."

"Business, my ass! She looks like she's about to have an orgasm right here."

"Do I detect just the tiniest note of jealousy, Sugar?"

Sloan glared at the petite reporter. Her long nails seemed about to shoot across the table straight into Jewel's glistening baby blue eyes. "What's eating you tonight, baby? It's sure as hell not me. You haven't let me get within a foot of you."

"I'm sorry, Sloan. I *know* it's not your fault. But you *promised* to land me a prime time special. And now when the big break comes, it gets snatched up by the golden retrievers. It's the same story all over again. I'm just not getting *anywhere.*"

"I got you onto the weekend edition of Now News, didn't I?"

"It's *hardly* the same thing. No one watches the weekend news. I think I was better off as a lifestyle reporter." She shrugged off Sloan's comforting hand, pouting into her Perrier.

"I tried darling. *Really* put myself on the line for you. CJ just had his mind made up. What else could I do?"

"You always manage, when it really matters to you. *Don't* you?"

Sloan shrugged angrily. Because Jewel was an ingrate, and because Sloan always managed to fall for the ice-coated bitches. The impenetrable women who acted like the world belonged to them, owed them a living.

Jewel Beale was a prime example. A perfect body, with firm creamy thighs, and a thin, wispy mound of Venus that was just begging to be loved. Even as she sat there hating Jewel for being such an icy thorn in her side, Sloan's lips were aching for a taste of her.

Jewel knew just how much Sloan needed her. And she knew just how to keep upping the ante, until she finally got what she had wanted.

Sure, Sloan admitted to herself, *I'll give her whatever it takes—unless I get sick of her coyness first.* She downed the rest of her Bloody Mary, and signalled for the waiter. "I need another drink. You could use one too, darling."

Jewel shook her head. "I'd love to join you. But I really *can't.*" She patted her flat stomach and frowned. "Already up to 102. I can *barely* squeeze into my jeans anymore."

"Well, let's get going then." Sloan's eyes were still locked on Jewel's belly when the waiter arrived. "Check, please," she requested curtly.

A moment later they were walking past Walter's station. Jewel sauntering like Miss Universe, just waiting to be crowned, Sloan a few feet behind her, growing more lustful with every voluptuous strut—and suddenly tired of waiting.

Bob Radin smiled appreciatively as Lauren momentarily locked eyes with him, flashed a smile, then disappeared through the doorway on Ted Rothmore's arm.

The gin-and-tonics he had downed in rapid succession had done nothing to dull the irritation he felt toward Francesca for wasting his time with her clumsy ploy.

If nothing else, they had deadened him to the fawning fingers of his aging companion, which kept slipping under the table and roaming over his muscular thigh.

"The house is really too big for us," Francesca mumbled, intoxicated. "Not that I would give up our address for anywhere else in the world. But Igor has been gone *so* much lately. Darling, you can't *imagine* how lonely it gets there. And it's so sad. It's such a *romantic* place. Deep reds with a touch of turquoise. There's a bearskin rug in front of the fireplace—and the most a*maz*ing sad-eyed Modigliani staring down from the mantel. You really should come see it."

Radin nodded distractedly. "Shall we go?" Francesca nodded enthusiastically, and he waved the waiter to the table.

As he reached for his billfold, she grabbed his hand and held it firmly. Then she ran her fingers lightly up his back and over his shoulder. "This one's on me," she whispered, gently caressing his neck. "After all, this *was* a business meeting."

As they stood underneath the port cochere, Radin spotted Sloan's familiar two-tone Rolls. "Excuse me, I want to say hello to Sloan," he said, pecking Francesca's cheek. "Thanks for the drink. And the invitation. I'm looking forward to taking you up on it," Radin lied gracefully.

Francesca's full lips spread into a triumphant, conspiratorial grin as she watched him cross the driveway and head down toward the beige-and-burgundy town car.

The tinted, reflective glass shielded the rear seat from view. But twenty feet from the limousine, he paused. "Puh-*lease*," Jewel's voice rang out, scarcely muffled by the glass. "Not *here*, Sloan . . . My God. Not in front of the Beverly Hills. Mercy sakes! What *has* come *over* you? Sugar, don't. *Please* don't. . . ."

He turned on his heels and headed back to the valet. Handing him a tip, Bob Radin gunned the Mercedes and sailed down the road. For once, he was only too glad to be leaving the whole scene behind.

Francesca crawled impatiently along Sunset, drumming her fingers anxiously as Pavarotti filled the pink interior of her car with a haunting aria. Every other second, she glanced into the rearview mirror, wondering how she had failed.

No, she reassured herself, everything had gone exactly as planned. She recalled the expression of amazement on Bob Radin's face when she announced the creation of her boutique. Obviously, he had been impressed. And rightly so. After all, it *was* quite a *coup*.

She had worked all of her seductive wiles on him. And, when she finally made the proposition, she was startled by the speed and ease with which he had accepted. *"Shall we go?"* Just three words, and that was that. She had always admired men who knew their own minds.

All in all, it was probably wise of him to insist upon leaving in separate cars, even though the anticipation would probably kill her. He undoubtedly knew just how jealous Igor was—and how suspicious. Every conversation with the gardener resulted in an inquisition. She could just imagine what he'd make out of her walking out of the Polo Lounge arm-in-arm with a Greek God like Bob.

"Poor Igor," she sighed. "He's loving, alright. No man half his age can outlast him or match him in bed. But he's just so *boring*. Between his bank and his stocks, his investments and his stamp collection, the man no longer appreciates the finer things in life."

At Beverly Glen Canyon, Radin's silver Mercedes pulled up alongside her. Francesca flashed her most seductive smile, feeling positively giddy. She ran her hand between her legs and the warmth spread out to the tips of her fingers. Giddily, she curled her toes and pressed her knees tight together, the hot moisture seeping onto the crotch of her pantyhose.

There were younger and more beautiful women in Beverly Hills, she admitted. But from the first time she had laid eyes on Bob Radin, Francesca had recognized him as a connoisseur. A kindred spirit who understood true elegance. From his expertly tailored French suits, to his love of fine wines and classical music, he exuded class and distinction. Even the most commercial mini-series he produced had that special touch of class.

And this evening she would possess all of him. It would be just perfect, and she would be the best he ever had. All of her years of experience in the arts of love would be his for the taking.

As the light turned red, she thought of his strong sculpted body rocking gently with her, and glowed with a warmth she hadn't felt in years. Heart pounding, she turned to blow him a kiss.

So she was dumbfounded as he waved goodbye, roaring off into the night and leaving only Pavarotti sadly crooning in the speaker.

Thirty-one

As Joel's MG convertible was buzzed through the electronic security gate of the walled estate, Crystal was struck by the grounds surrounding Hugh Hefner's mansion. Beyond the stone gate and massive hedge, yew trees and cypress cast deep shadows under the full moon. The air was balmy and miraculously clear for early autumn Los Angeles.

Most of all, Joel was at his best this evening. He had shed his habitual jeans and antelope jacket in favor of a tuxedo, complete with grey silk cummerbund. His shaggy hair was just the right combination of groomed and touseled.

Watching him, Crystal was suddenly reminded of the first night they made love, and his gracious—almost formal—manner as he whisked her away from the anonymous world of the LA airport to paradise in Malibu.

Tonight, he was a changed man once again. All of the irritability and restless selfishness had given way to a slow, caring thoughtfulness. It was like being immersed in a hot tub of loving. Slowly, every inch of Crystal's body was warming to its sensuous caress.

In front of the massive tudor house a liveried attendant appeared out of nowhere to help her from the convertible. Before she had taken two steps, Joel was beside her once again, his fingers wrapped gently around her arm, ready to sweep her lightly up the front steps and into the foyer.

His smile was easy and light this evening, not the forced mocking and razor-sharp grin which had flashed so tensely on and off his face during the past few months.

There was no sign of the bitterness that usually hovered just out of sight. The blinding rate which he unbuttoned late at night, venting his wrath in tirades against phoniness, and an entire world which he dismissed as "Hollywood lifestyle." As far as he was concerned, there was nothing to the entertainment world but a sham facade, a painted set with nothing behind it.

Tonight a different Joel emerged. Heading toward one of the ultimate "scenes"—and dressed in a tux—he had never seemed more *relaxed*. Comfortable and in his own element. Without a doubt, Joel secretly thrived on glamourous surroundings. At the core, he was as hooked on Hollywood as anyone she had ever met.

Inside the foyer, several dozen guests were milling about exchanging pleasantries. At the foot of the winding staircase leading to his private quarters, Hef stood alone. Formally attired, holding the omnipresent glass of Pepsi in his hand.

"I'd like you to meet Crystal Cooper," Joel said immediately, sweeping her forward with an expansive gesture. They chatted for a moment, a line of well-wishers forming behind them.

Then they stepped back toward the inner crowd. Crystal glanced once more toward the reclusive Playboy magnate. His eyes were sparkling vaguely as he distantly surveyed the group. Hefner made no effort to join in. He talked warmly with whomever approached, but seemed most comfortable when he was left alone on the periphery, standing outside the crowd and looking in.

"See the fellow over against the balustrade?" Joel whispered. "He's been a guest here for about four months. A mystery writer. And the jetsetter next to him has been here even longer. I recognize about half a dozen other regulars. That's not counting the crowd who use the facilities every weekend. Tennis courts, masseuses, the *works*. I'll give you a tour later."

As hugs and kisses on both cheeks proceeded down the line, Crystal suddenly found herself face-to-face with Cher Allman. One look at her dress and Crystal could hardly keep from giggling.

Joel also paused to ogle her serpentine evening costume; it was hard *not* to. Just before the broadcast, Crystal had rushed into the Right Bank Clothing Company to find a slinky something which would do justice to her in the midst of Bunny Haven. The saleswoman laughed at her selection. "That's the exact one I sold to *Cher* last week," she swore. "But to tell you the truth, it looks a thousand times better on you. It's meant to *cling*—not *drape*."

At the last moment, Joel had vetoed the slinky ensemble in favor of something equally seductive, but more subtle. "Save that one for Betsy Bloomingdale's next week," he sighed. "Or for me. But the Hefner screening won't be what you think. So why don't you wear that formal Blass number? The black one with the chiffon sleeves."

Staring at the performer dressed in *her* outfit, Crystal realized that Joel had been right. So had the Right Bank saleswoman. On all three counts.

As they passed into the adjoining salon, Joel's lips brushed lightly over her forehead, his eyes laughing triumphantly.

Crystal glanced at herself in the gilt-edged mirror

flanking the marble fireplace and smiled. The dress was a killer, alright, but in a subtle way. As she stared at Joel's handsome reflection beside her, she thrilled at the image of the two of them, against the backdrop of elegance.

"The perfect *media child*, aren't you?" Joel laughed, his eyes locking with hers in the mirror. "You seem just as content to watch everything in reflection, when you could turn around and watch it live. You'd *never* make a writer," he teased as he moved toward a silver tray filled with fluted champagne glasses.

Crystal watched in the mirror as he disappeared, then turned her gaze to the rest of the crowd. Slowly but surely, a portly figure in sunglasses was pushing his way over to her, a glass of cognac in one hand and a cigar in the other.

By the time she turned around, Sid Gold's thickset chest was almost nipple to nipple with her own. He threw a hand holding a stubby cigar casually up on the five foot mantel—effectively blocking her retreat. He looked at her with a voracious smile, then stared bluntly at her centerfold bosom.

In reply, Crystal looked stormily at the cigar, whose stench was now flowing directly into her nostrils. "You're polluting my air, Sid," she laughed, "I don't smoke."

"Pity." He removed the cigar from the mantel, but didn't back off an inch. "If you'd prefer coke, I'm sure I could manage it . . . *as your agent.*"

"No thanks," she shrugged, already getting nauseous from the strong whiff of his cologne wafting on the air currents.

"*Look.* You still with Deena Willis? She's no kind of agent for talent like you. Give me the word honey, and I'll renegotiate with CJ on your behalf tomorrow. This evening, if you insist."

"I do appreciate your continued interest. Honestly. But Deena's done a lot for me. She flew out to Atlanta and arranged for the RedRock interviews in the first place."

"Yeah," Sid muttered, swigging his cognac. "I *know*. Be*lieve* me I know. But that was a year ago. I'm talkin' about tomorrow. Crystal, I'd really like to go all out for you. So let's see if we can't close the gap between us." He leaned forward, halving the centimeter between them. "Baby, I already know the facts—and the figures. You got family to look after. And in this town, a lousy two hundred and fifty G will barely *rent* the right place for you."

Joel suddenly reappeared. He hastily planted a glass in Crystal's hands and focused his high voltage charm on the agent. "I'm Joel Hanlin."

Gold nodded noncommitally, reluctantly turning his gaze from Crystal to her escort. "Sid Gold," he responded coolly.

"I know. I've been trying to get through your goddamn defense line at the agency for weeks. Forgive me for being so rude, but if you've got a minute . . ."

"Is it about a script?"

Joel nodded enthusiastically. "It's a screen treatment for my Broadway show. UA is sitting on the option right now, but I'm getting awfully tired of waiting. I thought that if you were interested, then . . ."

"Of *course*, I'm interested. But if you don't mind, tonight is *strictly* pleasure. So why don't you give me a call next Thursday? In the meantime, it's been a real pleasure meetin' you, Joe. And Crystal . . . think about it."

As the agent swept away, Crystal could see the fury building up once more in Joel's eyes. His neck was slowly turning crimson, and his fingers clutched the base of his fragile champagne glass with ferocity. She flinched, waiting for the tirade to begin.

"That was downright rude of him," Crystal said apologetically. "Of all the gall . . ."

"Forget it. Sid Gold is just a mote in God's eye — or less poetically, a pimple on the asshole of city filled with them." He puffed out his chest and stomach, slouching *á la Gold* as he rubbed against her belly. " 'A lousy two tousand G's can hardly get youse a Malibu shack,' " he mimicked with pinpoint accuracy. She snuggled against him laughing.

"Ã toi" cherie" he toasted, letting the tension evaporate with a slow sip of Remy Martin.

"Let's not waste our time talking about an old fart like Gold — or my bruised feelings," Joel said smoothly.

"What I really want to talk about is you. After six months, I *still* can't figure you out. You've got brains, outrageously good looks, and the hottest news show on the air. Five nights a week you come on to millions of viewers like it's nothing. But I leave you for five minutes, and you're so shy that you cling to the fireplace like a vine."

Crystal nodded thoughtfully. For all of her blanket of stardom, she was still uncomfortable being alone in public. When she was stranded in the middle of the Polo Lounge or a party like this one, it was *still* all she could do to stand her ground.

"I'll tell you all about it," she whispered, smoothing out the ruffles on his broad chest. A servant approached with an overflowing tray. "Later, when we're alone."

"The movie is about to begin," called Hefner over the din.

As the lights dimmed, they accepted their silver bowl of popcorn — complete with crystal salt shaker and linen napkins — and seated themselves in the back row of the screening room while Hef and his inner circle lounged conspicuously on special sofas lined up in the front row. Tonight he was previewing a work by a young American named Parnell, a sophisticated modern life comedy.

Pressed against Joel in the darkness, Crystal struggled to focus on the move until the first intermission. Then, gently motioning Joel to join her, she stepped out purposefully past the crowd at the bar, and ducked into the hallway, out the door, and onto the crisply manicured lawn.

Stealing through the darkness, they arrived at the Grotto, the massive cut stone swimming complex in back of the mansion. Stopping once or twice to admire the unconcerned flamingoes, they inspected the jacuzzis.

"Rumor has it," Joel laughed, "that one of these has a nozzle at *just* the right height."

"Oh *really*," Crystal replied with girlish wonder. "Tell me: does it suck or blow?"

"Touchè." Arm around her waist, Joel escorted Crystal into one of the changing rooms. She stared at the array of bathing suits, hair dryers, cosmetics. Even *toothbrushes* were provided for the comfort of Hefner's guests.

"You ain't seen nothing yet," Joel howled. "I think that Hef even has his own zoo, somewhere on the back forty."

"Do you mean a bunny farm, by any chance?"

"Nope. Just a petting zoo, my dear. But I've got a better idea. Why don't we head over to the playhouse?"

Arm-in-arm, they strolled across the lawn, heading for the smaller replica of the great mansion. Peering through the leaded glass panes, Crystal saw a crowd of people, busily shooting bumper pool and playing Pac-Man.

"I see what you mean by 'play house'," Crystal laughed. "Hef really *is* the *perfect* host."

"Almost," he replied, as she approached the first vacant machine and pressed the reset button, then the controls. Nothing happened.

"Don't tell me you have to use real money," she groaned.

"I'm sure the money goes to charity," Joel sighed. "But in the meantime, I'm Hollywood rich." He turned out his empty pockets to emphasize the point. "So unless you feel like pawning your diamond earrings, I suggest we stick to the exploring."

In back of the playroom, a corridor led to a series of doors. The first opened onto a bedroom, once again equipped with every convenience imaginable. The second door revealed an even grander suite. In addition to the rows of toilet items, it featured a massive circular bed, and a fully mirrored ceiling.

"Is that *all?*" Crystal laughed, wide-eyed.

"Well, I'm not sure. I imagine that there are some rather arcance pleasuring devices stashed somewhere in the vicinity. Other than that, I've heard some quiet rumors about hidden cameras which are automatically triggered by heavy motion—or was it heavy breathing? Just rumors, at any rate."

Shutting the door behind them, Joel switched on the lights and threw himself down on the circular bed, then pulled Crystal playfully on top of him. She could feel his massive cock straining upward, and her own body melting into his arms. "Joel," she whispered, acutely aware of how much her own body was ignoring her better judgment, "I really don't think that we should . . . I mean, I never *did* want to be a movie star. At least, not like *that*." She eyed the ceiling and walls uneasily.

"*Of course not*," he chuckled, rolling them over effortlessly and nuzzling against her breast. Annoyed with her lack of will power, she felt herself giving in.

Then abruptly, Joel tore himself away and rolled onto the far side of the bed, no longer laughing.

"I've been thinking about us all afternoon," he said, folding his hands under his head and gazing at the tableau in the overhead veined mirror.

"So have I." Crystal curled against him and put her head on his chest. "I just don't understand *you* at all. One day you're a million miles away. It's all I can do to get you on the phone. And when I *do* see you, you treat it like a business lunch. The week after, we have a night like tonight." She ran her fingers softly over the tanned contours of his face, pulling it to her. She wished that he had ignored her protests, and was already naked and pressed to her.

Languorously, she brought his hand over her breasts, then insistently urged it downward, showering his neck with hot, wet kisses.

As his hand slid over the flat of her stomach, he broke away from her and looked into her half-shut eyes. "Sometimes you're so easy to please," he murmured.

"And the rest?" In a panic, Crystal felt the bubble bursting. The calculated solicitous charm and tenderness he had showered her with was vanishing once again. It was a game she had played for too many years with her husband. He had always peeled off the layers of charm and civility along with his custom-tailored clothes, allowing her to beg for love and be rejected, month after month.

"Crystal," Joel breathed, pulling her back into the confines of the huge bed, "you want too much."

"*Why?*" she shot back, "because I want to know when I'm going to see you again? Because I like to plan five days ahead of time? Because I want to be your *lover*—instead of the stacked blond you carouse with when the mood strikes you? Is that *really* all you want from me? Don't you understand that a human being needs to *share* with someone . . . And to have emotional security. Even Stephen Benjamin understood that much!"

"I am *not* your goddamn ex-husband. In case you forgot."

"I . . . I'm sorry," she pleaded. Knowing that it was too late to stop the downhill slide from turning into an avalanche. Or the familiar tapes from playing into their lives one more time.

"What makes you think it would be any better the second time around?" he spat. "You haven't even dealt with Marcie yet. Let alone another spouse. That *is* floating around in the back of your mind—*isn't it?*

His attack hit right on target. "I'm a different person now. I've had my whirl on the celebrity circuit, and my high society fling. It's *lonely* out there. When the lights go out and the cameras stop rolling, it's sometimes miserable. I'm not ashamed of wanting stability."

"Personally, I think that what you really want is slavery."

"That's simply not true." Crystal felt the anger and sadness filling her eyes. But she refused to back down or give in. "Joel, I *do* want a solid marriage. And I want to bring Marcie back and give her a real home life before it's too late. I've been tasting your brand of freedom on and off for months now. Quite frankly, it's exhausting. Instead of being committed to my lover, I feel chained to half a man—the half that occasionally responds to my needs, showers me with love, and really helps me to focus on the other important things. Like family and work and myself."

"Well what about *my* career?" he lashed out. "In case you've forgotten, I'm a long way from making a casual quarter-of-a-million-a-year. I'm not like a t.v. star. I have to have room to move and explore. Personal space. Do you really think it's that easy to make it as a writer in this town? Do you think I enjoy the sneers when my rusty MG rolls up to elegant restaurants? Sometimes I feel like a zoo specimen. You know: *Step right up. Feed the starving writer some peanuts. Only five cents* . . . The cage bars are tight enough . . . without having the gorgeous lion tamer in the teddy back me into a corner, make me leap through her honey hoop, then doff her tophat, show a bit of tit and ass, and bow to the audience . . ."

His voice took on a softer tone. "Crystal, I do love you. You know that. But this year has been a professional and emotional disaster for me — except for you. At this point, my career has to come first."

Before her eyes, Crystal suddenly saw the rift widening. She knew now that sooner or later she would lose him. She thought back to the loneliness of her last season in Atlanta, to the sterile confines of the studio, and the years of emptiness which she had hoped meeting Joel would finally end. *Not yet*, she thought, *please, not tonight*.

"Of course your career is more important." She hated herself for giving in. But right now, having Joel was more important than anything.

Pulling him tight against her once more, she moved her lips hungrily over his face, then knelt down and began unbuttoning his shirt. As she buried her mouth in the cleft of his chest, her hand slid feverishly down to his already straining cock. "Please Joel," she moaned, "I need you so much."

"Let's-just-lie-here-for-awhile," he replied without emotion, this time making no move to remove her caressing fingers.

Long minutes passed. He began to respond—grudgingly at first, then with increasing passion. As his own hands began to explore her, they exploded into an animal frenzy.

There was no tenderness in Joel's touch, just desperation. Wildly he began to tear at her clothes, and Crystal knew now that there was no holding back. As she held his head in her hands, he greedily began nibble her flesh. His probing mouth was by turns gentle and brutal, and she felt no joy; only a bittersweet ache she had never before experienced.

Now there was only his burning lips and fingers. His shoulders and back and buttocks, straining underneath her clawing fingers. As his head slipped down between her thighs, Crystal stared once at the mirrors and then surrendered. She knew that their passion tonight was only half-love.

And half hate.

Winston stumbled blindly out of the club on Sunset, his muscles floating in a sea of Quaaludes. He tripped on the curb and almost fell into the path of a stream of cut-down low-riding Chevys, roaring past in a fierce procession.

At 2 a.m., Sunset was a battleground. Clusters of men in tight-fitting leather jackets, hookers staking out their corners, bikers and low-riders and gangs of teenagers all maneuvering on their turf.

He tried to focus his vacant eyes on the distant towers of RedRock, but they were lost in the haze. Somewhere in the back of his mind, he registered a note of alarm. Was it the street toughs, or the beers with which he had chased down the muscle relaxers?

Or maybe the thought of Elliot, dressed in a sequined midnight cowboy outfit, clutching onto his arm.

"I'm parked over here," Elliot called, half-dragging him around the corner.

"Wait a minute," Winston mumbled. "Where in hell did I leave my car?"

"Oh come on. You couldn't even see the steering wheel. I'm taking you home. So let's get going."

Winston struggled with the seat belt as the car headed west on Hollywood. Instead of turning south on Crescent Heights, the Jaguar zoomed north into the hills. The wrong direction, he wryly observed.

Ten minutes later, he was sprawled on a massive waterbed in the seedy, but magnificently appointed carriage house of a 1920's Tudor mansion in the heart of the canyon. As Elliot lay down beside him, he felt a wave of revulsion sweep through him. He tried to struggle, but every muscle in his anesthetized body remained still, refusing to obey.

"You made the right decision, baby," Elliot leered, turning off the lights and gently kissing him on the lips, while his hands frantically reached for the flesh beneath his jeans.

Thirty-two

At precisely 7:59 a.m., Lauren woke up and slammed off the alarm clock with the first click, hitting it before the arrival of the piercing wake up tone.

She curled into the peach satin sheets, pulled back her tousled mane of hair, then bolted into an upright position. Filtering in through the creamy silk brocade curtains, the sunlight diffused the room with a cool, even glow which was murder on her throbbing eyes.

"Oh God," she moaned, shaking the sleep from her head and smoothing out the silk surface of her lavender Dior nightshirt. "When will I ever learn how many martinis are enough!"

Pulling aside the pleated drapes, she stared at the tiny store fronts and cityscapes of the Twentieth Century studio lots. Far off in the distance, the Pacific loomed like a massive, landlocked grey cloud. "Still there," she muttered ironically.

But in fact, on mornings like this one, it still came as a shock that she was no longer in Eugene or New York or Boston. She was now *the* Lauren Conrad of Now News.

"She paused for a moment to let it sink in, then padded off to the dressing room, throwing off her night shirt en route. Rolling out the exercise mat, she chose a medium weight warm-up suit and slipped the pullover on, all the while carefully examining her profile in the floor-to-ceiling mirrors.

Much as she hated her latest exercise regimen, it was definitely working. Her hips were a fraction slimmer, her buttocks high and firm. Flat stomach, small high breasts. They all looked exquisite—and not one ounce of cellulite anywhere on her body.

Gathering her hair into a ponytail, a smile of self-satisfaction crossed her lips. The early morning aerobics made her ache in all the wrong places. And half of the time, the daily three mile jog was a crashing bore, a real pain in the ass.

But the day she signed with RedRock, the pace on the success treadmill had begun to accelerate. At thirty-three, Lauren knew that she was still devastatingly beautiful. But she also knew that as the situation at the network intensified, it would become a matter of running faster and faster just to stay in the same place, and by the time middleage set in, she like more of the lesser newswomen, would begin to drift out of the klieg lights.

Lauren was determined to beat the odds, and knew she was just about to reach the ultimate heights. That knowledge thrilled her, and goaded her to push harder with the body-beautiful regime day after day. In the industry, looking great was more than the best revenge against middleage.

"In terms of survival, it was the only one.

Her workout concluded, she stepped into the Florentine shower and shot piping hot jets of water to pummel her shoulders and back. Even more than the exercise regime, she ached from the tension which had been building up on her date with Ted Rothmore.

She edged the shower control a fraction hotter, and thought about last night's battle of wills.

Midway through the evening, things had begun to get out of hand. Instead of just baiting the trap and waiting for Ted to succumb, she had somehow found herself responding to his overpowering magnetism, drawing herself closer to him as he drew farther and farther out on a limb.

Not that he was indifferent. Far from it. But Ted Rothmore handled her with a calm reassurance which was disturbing. Not to mention vaguely infuriating. Punctuaring her overtures with a devastating smile, or a light brush of his fingers which left her begging for more.

Even when she announced her intention to call it a night, Ted was hardly nonplussed. Far from being crushed, he barely even batted an eye. At the same time, his good night kiss had incredible voltage in it. And by the time Lauren had reluctantly climbed out of the Bentley, they both knew that it was only the beginning.

A surgeon's gentle hands and a Zen mastery of mind over body—her body. It was a dangerous combination. Particularly since it came in such a controlled, unassuming, package. "After all," she thought, "he's just a Beverly Hills doctor. Soft-spoken, conservatively dressed, affluent. Like a hundred other guys scattered throughout Los Angeles."

But she immediately reassessed her words and shook her head emphatically. There was something dazzling about his smile, and more than a little hypnotizing in his eyes. The way he seemed to be staring right into her core, brushing aside all of the preliminaries. Stroking and egging her on. All of the while suffusing her in raw unspoken sexuality, while his eyes looked vulnerable, yet unyielding.

If that was how he talked and acted, she could just *imagine* what his lovemaking would be like. There was no doubt in her mind now that she would find out— soon enough.

Lauren stood under the paralyzing intensity of the icy cold water for a few seconds, then gasping, groped for the shower control. As she patted her skin dry and slipped back into the dressing room, a wry smile crossed her lips.

Was it just the tv appearance that he was after? If so, Ted had gotten what he wanted, without her even putting up a fight. By the time she invited him for a Monday morning taping session, it was already a *faît accompli*. Come to think of it, they hadn't even discussed *The Laetrile Alternative*. How he had done his research, who he was treating, not even how the book was selling.

In fact, all night, he had sat there with his soothing, bedside manner, and said not one thing about himself. Where in hell had her mind been? Not on the business at hand, that was for sure.

Behind his bedroom eyes and warm, slightly lop-sided grin, Dr. Ted Rothmore might well be the greatest con man she had ever met. She knew that he lived in Beverly Hills and seemed to know everyone she had ever met in Hollywood, from Moe Alexander down. Surely that was *some* sort of recommendation.

Lauren pulled on her running suit and began to stretch her back and legs in front of the mirrors. One thing was certain: Where Ted was concerned, Lauren Conrad was thoroughly taken.

Whether it was with him or by him remained to be seen.

Thirty-three

CJ Redfield walked briskly through the French doors connecting his dressing room with the upper level patio. With measured steps, he descended the wrought iron stairs and headed for the pool.

His dive was clean and effortless, as were the hundred laps which followed. Just as he did every morning, he swam across to the ladder, and accepted the awaiting towel from his houseboy.

"Up early today, sir."

"Breakfast meeting," he grunted. "And a full schedule afterwards. Tell Thomas that we'll be leaving for RedRock at 10 a.m. in the Maserati. In the meantime, breakfast for myself and Sloan Schwartz on the east terrace at 8:30."

He ran the thick velour quickly over his arms and shoulders, then tossed it aside as he was helped into his robe. "Is Mrs. Redfield awake yet?"

The other man nodded. "Lillian wheeled her into the front room a few minutes ago."

"Fine, fine," he replied distractedly, as his eyes lit upon the grove of yews on the far side of the pool. "I think I'll just pop in and say good morning."

Ten minutes later, immaculately groomed in a steel-grey pinstripe suit and burgandy silk tie, he emerged into the marble-tiled corridor, stopping across from his wife's sitting room to double check his appearance. In profile, the sandy hair was clearly receding back on his forehead, and his sideburns were almost entirely grey now. The telltale lines on his brow were deepening, and his tanned skin had an uneven, wide-pored complexion.

"Weathered," he noted. He had never gone in for the facials and eye tucks which kept most of his contemporaries looking twenty years younger than they had a right to.

But at the same time, without going to extremes, he had always carefully maintained his physique and muscle tone. With pleasure, he noted that there was not a spare pound of flesh anywhere on his broad figure. All in all, he was in better shape than most men half of his age.

A healthy mind in a healthy body. It was an aphorism which had been drilled into him from childhood on, and had stood him in good stead. At age fifty-eight, he was even sharper and more single-minded than he had been two decades earlier. And without the broken family life or personal excesses which drained so much out of other media figures, he was able to devote a hundred per cent to the network.

It was a fact that was occasionally overlooked by the board. And certainly by Sloan Schwartz, immersed as she was in her own visions of grandeur. He knew why she had suggested this Sunday morning meeting. It was a bold step, and one that he had to admire, despite the revulsion he felt at the thought of having her invade his private world.

At the same time, it was the perfect opportunity. By giving her more than she had set out demanding. Letting her think that he was weakening, while he bought time and tried to strengthen his position, arming for the battle they both knew was coming.

With any luck, Sloan could quite easily dig her own

grave, given enough time, and her penchant for gathering up dirt.

Glancing down at his wafer-thin Piaget watch, Redfield lightly rapped on the door of the room adjoining his own.

"Is that you, darling," a shaky girlish voice called out. "Come right in."

Surrounded by the white velvet shawl, propped up against an eyelet and lace pillow, Margaret Peabody Redfield was almost lost in the background. Her skin was a translucent milk-glass color, and her white gold hair hung limply around her painfully thin face.

Despite the great pains she took with grooming before her husband's appearance every morning, the aura of illness was ominously present. Even the well-intentioned touches of lip gloss and rouge did nothing but highlight the pallor of the rest of her features.

"Feeling better?" he asked, coming over to embrace her.

"Much. I think I may even venture out to the pool today. How about that?"

"Fantastic," He noted the icy temperature of her long delicate fingers with alarm, and wrapped her shoulders in another layer. He brought the hand up to his lips, glancing at the massive emerald-cut diamond which had marked their latest anniversary.

"It is Sunday, isn't it, CJ? I really must get out to the shrine. To see Kikki."

"Of course," he agreed soothingly. "I'll have Arthur cut some roses." Redfield hugged her gently, and prayed for the intercom which would cut into the silence, and send him hurtling back into the world of RedRock, to the upcoming showdown with Sloan.

Death could always sit and wait, laying siege to him as it had for a decade now.

* * *

"Damn it Sloan," Redfield roared in the isolated den he had chosen for their meeting, when breakfast was finished. "I refuse to let this conversation stoop to the level of hearsay and character assassination. We are talking about the Satellite Broadcasting Network. Not about the personal life of its news director."

". . . and that's exactly what I mean," she shot back. "It's not just our image he's tarnishing. *I'm* talking about morale. Have you ventured down into the newsroom lately? It's like a morgue."

"I'm well aware of what's been going on down there. But Rob's death was only a few weeks ago. Of course the news team's upset. They're human beings, not machines. What else would you expect?"

"I'll tell you what I'd expect. No, what I'd demand. Some leadership down there. We've got our ratings riding on Now News, and we can't just let them slip down and out of sight because of Rob. Listen, I was as close to him as anyone. But it's time for some positive action, if you don't want to see the whole thing crumble."

"And just what do you suggest," he snapped back, reddening.

"I'll be honest with you, CJ. I think that you have to fill Rob's vacancy—and now."

"Needless to say you're volunteering for the position."

"No one was more on top of what Rob was doing than me." She paused, letting the remark sink in. "And I also know that without strong guidance, Dale isn't worth shit. We both know that."

"I can't afford to lose Dale," Redfield retreated. "Not now."

"Personally, I think that we can't afford to keep the pervert on board much longer."

"I refuse to listen to . . ."

"To *what?* Come off it, CJ. You said that this was going to be an off-the-record chat, so we could talk honestly. I'm telling you that the man is crumbling. Drinking on the job, scrambling at the last minutes just to pull off the daily news broadcast. Let alone the specials segments, and setting up the futures editor with a coherent program. How much longer do you think Lauren and Crystal are going to put up with that?"

"As far as I'm concerned, their loyalty remains unquestioned."

"Yeah? Well their brains are unquestioned as well. You may not care that the News Director is getting done at a bondage house when he should be putting in office time, but they're bearing the brunt. In return for which, they're now totally forsaking the image guidelines we spent months working out. With the way they've been delivering their stories, it's a wonder we haven't lost our audience share by now."

"So far, it seems to be working just fine," he replied obstinately. Sloan's eyes bore down on him and he intentionally let his eyes wander onto the photographs and awards plastered on the wall behind her. Exeter rowing, Class of '46. Harvard Hasty Pudding. Kikki's dressage ribbons, gathered in a corner. With Sloan's eyes following, he stared at the newspaper photograph of the RedRock groundbreaking ceremonies.

"Sloan," he said pleadingly. "I just can't let Dale go."

"Then have it your way. I suppose that he's got no more to hide than half of the board anyway, huh? But for God's sakes, get him where he can't do any more harm, will you? You want to give him time to come around? Fine. While you're shopping around for a replacement, why not let me oversee the rest of the News Department. Tighten up the images of our reporters."

"You're an ambitious woman," Redfield smiled bleakly. "We may have had our personal differences in the past—and I'm sure we will in the future. But I appreciate your frankness. And what you say makes a lot of sense . . . I'll speak to the board tomorrow morning."

He stood up, hands clasped behind his back, and turned to stare at the distant shrine, feeling Sloan's triumphant glare cutting into him.

"Thank you CJ. You won't regret it."

"I'm sure I won't," he replied evenly, while the butler appeared silently and escorted her out to the awaiting beige-and-burgundy Rolls.

Thirty-four

"*Alright already!*" Crystal snapped at the tenth ring. "I'm coming." She pressed her lensless eyes to the alarm clock and read the time: 8:15. "What in hell is the telephone service doing, letting calls go through at this hour? . . . *Hello.*"

"Good morning Crystal," bubbled the voice on the other end, gratingly cheerful. It answered her question: It *was* the telephone service.

"Good morning, Sylvia," Crystal sighed. "How are you doing?"

"Can't complain. I went to the most fabulous screening last weekend. Goldie Hawn was there, sitting two seats away. Can you *believe* it? And I went up to her and chatted afterwards. She was so friendly— not at all stuck up. Really a terrific person and—"

"That's great," Crystal groaned. *So much for the rhetorical how are you.* She wondered how wise it was to have gone with this latest answering service. Personal Service was everything it threatened to be, and more. But at least the operators weren't botching calls yet, like the previous two.

". . . I've just got to tell you how *wonderful* you were on Friday's broadcast. Absolutely sensational. And that story about the welfare children—it just blew me right away."

"Thanks, Sylvia. I appreciate it."

"Anytime, Crystal."

"Now, uh . . . about the messages."

"Oh yeah. I almost forgot. Now, let's see. Where did I put those . . . Oh. Here we go. *Wow*. Three obscene phone calls. I think that's a new record. Dale Stevens will see you at the office. Joel Hanlin will call you, ditto. Lauren said she'll be in at eleven this morning. Wait a minute. There must be a mistake. Today's *Sunday*. Maybe she meant . . ."

"No mistake. We've got an in-depth report to . . ."

"Well, I think you ought to talk to the union. A woman in our position must have a thousand better things to do than . . ."

"I'll think about it. Any call from Marcie?"

"Not that I see. But you know how teenagers are . . ."

Barely, Crystal stormily mumbled. *These days I don't even know how adults are. Including myself.* "Uh, huh. Well, thanks for the wake up call and messages. I'll call in around nine this evening."

"Okay, we'll be waiting. Have a nice day."

Crystal hung up the phone and slide back between the soft eyelit trimmed sheets, tired of waking up alone in the morning. Especially when it was a grey and dismal Sunday. For once, the electrifying tension awaiting her in the newsroom held no joy. Particularly with Dale on a binge.

Undoubtedly Lauren had been up for two hours. Stretching, running, grooming. Stalking her next conquest, now that she had landed Dr. Rothmore. At the thought of the two of them at Chasen's, she felt her face flush with jealousy. And whatever had happened on their date, she knew it was a subject Lauren was not about to confide in her. All the same, she had no doubt that it would be written all over her partner's face the moment she stepped through the door.

Heading into the shower, she tried to content herself with the fantastic lovemaking at Hef's two nights before. But there was no joy in her body, just an aching emptiness. Happiness was something which wasn't provided for, in her quarter-of-a-million-dollar contract, or her network schedule.

All she had to show for it was bags under her eyes in the morning, a beautiful penthouse apartment she saw only at night. An exorbitant wardrobe she had little time to appreciate, a baby blue BMW, and a home life which consisted of bi-weekly telephone calls to her distant mother and alienated daughter.

For a life with all of the fringe benefits, it seemed to have very few of the basic satisfactions. She thought about the hundreds of other celebrities scattered throughout town. All of the gossip about their wild revels, tempestuous affairs, sightings at the right places, with the right people. Then again, if you could believe the Hollywood reporters, the same was true of her.

She could just imagine Hank Grant's report of Hefner's screening. "A gala formal affair in Holmby Hills . . . Making the scene were Cher Allman, and RedRock's blockbuster Crystal Cooper, spotted in a quiet *tête à tête* with none other than the ubiquitous Sid Gold. Insiders predict that the wedding announcement is only a week away . . ."

If only there were someone to even talk to. She started to dial her mother in St. Petersburg, then thought better of it. Hearing about Mrs. Rosenberg's gall bladder operation was not the sort of communication she needed.

Then she thought of Violet Duval. If ever there were a lady who understood loneliness, it was Violet. For weeks the two had been swearing they would get together. Maybe a nice quiet dinner. Somewhere inconspicuous like the Westside Cafe or at Marty's. Just to get off the roller coaster for an hour or two.

Lauren rounded the corner and headed back along Wilshire, eyeing the conspicuously magnificent Los Angeles Country Club. Enclosed by Beverly Hills, Century City and Westwood, it was worlds away from the exclusive industry watering holes. These days the top rung of Hollywood figures eventually found their way in, but the scene there was still dominated by names like Cartwright. Settling families who had moved out to Pasadena mansions and beyond, at the time when antics like creating parade riots for the benefit of Keystone Cops footage had given film-makers a decidedly dirty name.

As the Avenue of the Stars came into sight, she stepped up the pace, lifting her aching legs higher and smiling triumphantly as her body finally came into its stride. She was suddenly breathing more easily, her heart and arms pumping in perfect rhythm as her feet flew across the pavement.

It was the moment she waited for every morning. When groaning muscles and burning lungs suddenly gave way to perfect control, a feeling of totality. No network pressures and phony smiles. As her breasts heaved and her slightly open lips sucked in air, her features broke into an expression of sheer exhilration.

As the Century Towers loomed up before her, Lauren entered the home stretch. Coming to a flying halt, she jogged in place, for once oblivious to the admiring stares and honking horns as she waited for a break in the traffic.

She was just about to cross the boulevard when a familiar Bentley pulled up alongside, blocking her progress. Brushing aside her annoyance, she flashed her best smile, suddenly acutely aware of the sweat drenching her back, and the suit clinging to her soaked stomach.

"Looks like I'm just in time," Ted beamed. "Listen, hop in and let me give you the grand tour. I was just on my way to the sauna. But what the hell, I'm sure Ginna can wait a few minutes."

"Ginna?"

"The *masseuse*, Lauren. Actually, she's better known as Golden Fingers. And the way she charges, that's no understatement. Listen, you look like you're ready for a hot oil treatment as well. Why not make it a doubles set. My treat."

"I'd love to. Honestly. But I really have to get down to RedRock. Like I told you last night . . ."

"I know. I know. The investigation which has the whole network hopping. At least let me give you a sneak preview of the Club. That's a proposition you don't get everyday."

Lauren hesitated. "I'd really love to. But maybe you can give me a rain . . ."

"*What?* At least do me the courtesy of stepping inside the car. I can barely hear you through the traffic."

A minute later, they were zipping through the security gate. Lauren's eyes scanning the golfers strolling across the rolling fairways, as Ted began a perfectly timed tour guide spiel.

"On the left is Mrs. Astor. I can't quite make out her escort. But based on the pork pie he's wearing, I'd bet anything that it's Fred Vogal. Did you see the portrait of the Royal Wedding he did? *Sensational*. But his best works are all sitting in the atelier of his place in Truesdale. Paints them in front of a tiny Franklin stove. Even in the middle of the summer, while the air conditioners are blasting everywhere else in town. Arthritis. That little guy in the golf cart is Calvin Jones, the plumbing magnate. Partial colostemy . . ."

"Okay. Who's that stunning redhead who just sailed past us doing fifty miles per hour?"

"I clocked her at forty-two. That's Cindy Leighton. But I don't see anything stunning about her at all. First of all, she's anorectic. Positively anemic. And talk about drug abuse. Her intestines are halfway rotted."

"Oh? I thought that the nostrils were the first to go in this town."

"That all depends. You're talking about cocaine. But very few people understand the dangers of patent drugs. No, if I had my way, the first drugs I'd remove from the market are laxatives."

"And then what? Vitamins? How about aspirin?"

He turned to her with eyes suddenly very earnest. "Maybe valium."

Lauren started. "Oh come on, Ted. Half of this country lives on that drug. You don't mean to say that . . ."

"Of course there's no harm in it. When it's carefully prescribed by a competent physician. But like any other drug, its use has to be carefully monitored, not just refilled at a patient's whim. Anxiety is a national problem. And it should be dealt with, not merely masked."

"That's quite a crusade for a Sunday morning, don't you think."

Rothmore slowly turned the Bentley off onto the shoulder. "Let's be honest, Lauren. I could tell from the moment I met you that you were popping tranquilizers. It's just no good."

Lauren stared out at the club house colonnade, feeling his eyes pinning her to the seat. "If you don't mind, Ted, I'd rather not discuss . . ."

"Please, Lauren." His eyes were pleading now.

"This is my professional responsibility. I also care about you. I'll bet that you're wearing yourself down. Admit it: *You haven't even had breakfast yet.*" He exploded into laughter, defusing the tension building up.

"*Mea culpa*," Lauren roared.

"Then it's settled. Breakfast it is." He grinned mischievously as the Bentley headed for the parking lot.

"I can't go in there looking like this!"

"Like what. You are absolutely stunning. And that's my professional opinion."

"That's very nice Ted. But in case you've forgotten, I happen to be Lauren Conrad of Now News. Not just another jogger."

"Alright, if you insist. But we are having breakfast—and now. Doctor's orders."

Once again Lauren was floored by the man's arrogance, and the way she seemed to buckle in to his charm, his manipulations. At the same time that he was bending over backwards to impress the hell out of her—with no small degree of success. He was constantly on the offensive. Pressing her ever so slightly, then immediately backing off. There was also something disturbingly similar to Skip Collins in Dr. Ted Rothmore. Nothing she could put a finger on—but a vague feeling that she had been down this road before.

She looked up just in time to see him pointing at an imposing Tudor bungalow. "Marlena Dietrich's old place," he smiled, pulling into a circular driveway several houses down. "And this is the Rothmore diner."

She gazed at the elegant old Spanish mansion in admiration. Like most of the houses in the heart of Beverly Hills, the surrounding properties seemed a little too close for true elegance. But then again, it was just a few blocks from the Club, and an equal distance from the Rodeo Drive shopping district.

"It doesn't look like much," Ted shrugged, "but the food's great."

As he opened the massive iron-bound door, Lauren let out a gasp. Inside, the cathedral ceiling towered thirty feet above her. The front third of the mansion was an entirely open space, broken only by an ascending series of wood parquet platforms. Priceless medieval tapestries hung from the center of the room, bathed in clerestory light from a series of concealed skylights.

"Hanna, I'm sure Miss Conrad would appreciate a shower," Ted announced to the stoop-shouldered maid who silently appeared. "In the meantime, I'll see how breakfast is cooking."

Lauren glanced once in the direction of the dining area, taking in the simple tubular steel Breuer chairs, then smiling quizzically as she noticed the single spray of lilies-of-the-valley—her favorite wildflower—placed in front of two already laid table settings. Was it just a coincidence, like Ted Rothmore's appearance at precisely the moment she rounded the corner at the club? Or did he know a lot more about her than he was letting on?

Like everything else about him, it left a bittersweet taste in her mouth as she followed the maid upstairs and into the master bath, marvelling at the sparkling, almost antiseptic cleanliness of every inch of wood trim, carpet and tile.

"Oh . . . Ted," Lauren murmured two hours later. His knowing fingertips and lips were playing her pliant body like some soft and acquiescent instrument until every inch of her was moaning with desire.

"Mmmmmm," she moaned, as he finally thrust between her achingly ready thighs, rocking in an easy
counter-rhythm to her own mounting desire. He was
slow and controlled, moving first hard and then
gently, full thrusts and then gently rocking hips. She
drew him urgently deeper and deeper, running her
fingernails up and down his back, clenching his rock
hard buttocks and pulling them to her, faster and
faster.

My God, she groaned inwardly, an hour later. *Isn't
this guy ever going to come?*

She had long ago succumbed to a shattering
orgasm. But the moment her body relaxed into fluid
bliss, Ted slowly began to make love to her once more.
With no sign of slackening. There was just the cloying
sweetness of lilies-of-the-valley mixed with cologne in
her nostrils, and the insistent rocking rhythm of the
unhurried stallion pleasuring her flesh as the minutes
flew by.

"*Damn it*," he roared, missing a beat, as the bedside phone erupted into a piercingly shrill ring.

"There'll be other marathons, you know," Lauren
laughed fondly, more than a bit relieved.

Ted Rothmore had no desire for coitus interruptus.
Thrusting harder once more, he reached over and
grabbed the receiver. "Hul-lo," he barked in rhythm
to his thrusts. "Ted Roth . . . more."

As the other voice responded, he cradled the phone
to his neck, then quickly rolled over with Lauren, until she was straddling him. "MMmmhmmm," he
mumbled with increasing excitement. His palms softly
cupped Lauren's breasts, easing her up and then
down as her tousled mane trailed languorously over
his chest.

"I'm so happy for you . . . Mom."

Lauren burst into hysterical laughter and flopped

down onto his chest. But now Ted's hands were insistent as they clamped around her slim hips and pressed them up and down.

"And how about Mrs. Stewart?" he whispered hoarsely. "Is she coming too? That's just terrific."

Lauren shook her head firmly, but Ted held his grasp, thrusting harder into her. As he mumbled into the phone, his eyes took on a sheen of desperation. With the phone still resting on his shoulder, Ted pulled her down onto him and groaning, began covering her neck with kisses.

'N-no," he stammered, as his breathing grew louder. "It's just the asthma . . . yes . . . I will . . . oh yes . . . mmm. I promise . . . sure . . . okay . . . Mom . . . I love you, too . . ."

As Lauren heard the other side of the line click off, she felt Ted tremble uncontrollably deep inside her, then grow still.

"That was downright nasty," she chided.

"What could I do?" he shrugged, the familiar boyish grin creeping onto his slightly downturned lips. "I couldn't hang up on my mother."

At a loss for words, Lauren flopped over onto the other side of the bed and began searching for her hastily discarded champagne glass. Refilling it from the chilling stand which had been magically transported upstairs, she debated the wisdom of asking the doctor for a cigarette.

"Ted," she crooned, as sweetly as possible." I'm just dying for a cigarette. Don't you think that I've . . . Ted?"

For a moment there was dead silence, as she surveyed the empty place beside her in the tangle of satin sheets.

Then from out of the master bath, she heard a torrential blast of water, and a soft bass voice singing obliviously in the shower.

Thirty-five

Crystal thumbed through the burgeoning folder in front of her one last time, pausing once or twice to doublecheck the information.

Just a few days into the probe, and already there was a growing mountain of information on her desk. Countless columns of data from the computer bank, plus ream after ream of telephone transcript, and—

"Excuse me, Ms. Cooper," grinned a slightly star-struck newsroom gopher as he swayed uncertainly at the half-open cubicle door, yet another pile of papers in his hand.

"Never mind. Let's just have it," Crystal shot back, then returned to the computer print-out beneath her aching eyes. She nodded absentmindedly as the newest folder was plopped onto her desk, then consulted her watch.

It was already half-past one. Time for the meeting she had scheduled with Redfield. As she picked up the inter-office phone and dialled Imperial HQ, she was once again acutely aware of the silence on the other side of the wall. "Eleven o'clock my ass," she breathed angrily into the phone. "Where in hell *is* Killer Conrad, anyway?"

"CJ Redfield's office," came the crisp greeting on the other end of the line.

"Oh, Barbara. Don't tell me he's got *you* in here on

a Sunday, too."

"I'm *always* here Sunday afternoons," the assistant replied huffily.

"No offense intended, Barbara. It's just that I thought . . ."

"I understand, *Miz* Cooper. In the meantime, CJ is expecting you to . . ."

"I'm on my way up," Crystal answered, once again giving up on breaking through the wall of ice surrounding Redfield's woman Friday. It was going to take a sledge hammer, at the least. And about ten times as much effort as anyone on the news team was going to have in reserve for weeks to come.

"Fine. I'll let him know," Barbara said mechanically, and clicked off the line.

Hurriedly, Crystal threw her presentation into her Gucci case and sped through the newsroom, almost colliding midway through the sea of desks with the oncoming blur of Lauren Conrad.

"So nice of you to show up," she glowered, while a dozen faces momentarily left their terminal screens.

"Sorry I'm late, darling," Lauren smiled noncommittally, maneuvering around her. "I was going to call and let you know. But I figured that you'd probably just be arriving yourself."

"With a meeting for Redfield scheduled for 2:45?"

"It wouldn't be the first time."

Wordlessly, Crystal spun on her heels and continued marching toward Redfield's private elevator in the hallway beyond the door. *That settled it.* "Someday," she fumed, conscious of the crimson fury slowly rising in her temples, and feeling rather than seeing the other newswoman saunter easily back toward her office. "What a gold-plated bitch. After I set her up with Rothmore, the least she owes me is an apology. And maybe a gold plaque—with the word SUCKER written all over it. I really blew my chance with that one. But good. And then she has the nerve to waltz in here like . . ."

"*Pay up*," hissed a voice somewhere in the cavernous room, cutting into her thoughts. "That's ten smackers, right now."

"Wait one minute, there, buddy. You said ten to-one-odds that the truce wouldn't last 'til the end of the month. That was just a little lover's spat. Nothing serious. As far as I'm concerned, there have been no declared hostilities and I'm not about to fork over until . . ."

"Until *what*? The blood starts flowing. Sally's the referee, right."

"Right," came a laughing woman's voice from across the aisle. "Sorry Bill. But they've just ruled that round one is over. Hand it over."

Gloatingly, the researcher pocketed the bill, then hunched once more over the green cathode lights. "Anyone else interested in a little wager? Fifty bucks says that by Wednesday Dale's gonna be fielding complaints from their agents. Any takers . . . No? I'm surrounded by cowards."

With a disgusted shrug he began punching access codes into the computer, then impulsively grabbed the phone. At least there was always Jonathan Reed over at KJJX.

And Adam Ward's personal assistant was such a betting fool, he had already dropped two hundred bucks on Cooper-and-Conrad wagers.

"Come into my parlor, said the spider to the fly," Dale Stevens whispered to Crystal the moment she appeared at the doorway of Redfield's inner sanctum.

As surprised as she was by his presence in the private meeting with the RedRock head, she was more startled by his appearance. The beefy features which had taken on an increasingly flushed and drink-saturated hue were now ashen. Above the nervously grinning and drawn lips, his eyes were sunken.

"Don't just stand there Crystal," he said louder, shrugging off her concerned stare.

She gazed over at Redfield, standing like a pilot at the helm of his ship, both arms grasping the top of an eighteenth century cabinet as he surveyed the teeming vista beyond the curved glass wall.

"If this is a summit meeting, then maybe we'd better call in the other half of the anchoring team as well. I didn't really realize that . . ."

"Don't worry about it," Dale laughed hollowly. "I just thought that I might sit in on your meeting with CJ—if you don't mind. I just thought that it might be good for me to know what's happening as News Director. They haven't stripped me of that title . . . yet."

Her face dropped and she searched his blank features for confirmation of what she already knew. He stared right through her, refusing to meet her eyes. "Do you mean that Sloan just weaseled her way into . . .?"

"Ah, Crystal. Good," CJ called across the room, rushing over to kiss her lightly on the cheek. "I've been waiting to see this for days now."

He pulled up a ladder back chair for her, wasting no time in dropping down on the other side of the broad desk, thumbing through the report and then reading the series of figures supporting it. As anxious minutes passed, she found herself staring at Dale's wildly fidgeting fingers. His knee bobbed uncontrollably up and down, and the rest of his taut frame seemed about to break into a frenzied St. Vitus dance. The blasé demeanor he had spent so many years keeping up at any cost was shattered.

She bit her lip and turned to stare at the wall, sadly realizing that she was looking at a man who was clearly walking the tightrope of sanity. And showing every sign of losing his balance any second.

"No," Redfield concluded with soft determination, tossing the stack of papers lightly across the desk.

"Forgive me," Crystal agreed. "I knew I should have postponed the meeting until I got more solid backup. But I'm pretty sure of these facts, and I knew just how anxious you were to have a look, so I decided to go ahead with it and . . ."

"Quite the contrary. You were right to show it to me today. The problem isn't the fact that the charges are unsubstantiated. I'm sure that everything you say can be easily documented with another few days of research. But if that was the extent of what I was looking for, I would never have asked Conrad & Cooper to direct the investigation. This falls far, far short of what we need to really make an effective report."

Crystal shook her head and stared down at the carefully prepared summary. "As it is, I think that half of the initial findings are going to bring lawsuits raining down on us, no matter *how* true they are. Dale told us to go all out, but . . ."

"But what? Do you really think that a few more legal battles are of any concern to us? I sent you out there to look into the payoffs and kickbacks. What you brought back is the most sugar-coated kid glove treatment I've ever seen. What we are talking about is an invasion of the media by organized crime. You and I both know that, don't we?"

"But it's all hearsay. And the first rule of journalism is . . ."

"Forget the rules. The figures we're talking about are not members of the boy scouts. Take Kornreich. The head of a network. What does he do? Sign a series of expenditures checks and charge it to a sit-com—with the *star's* signature. You did an excellent follow-up on that—as far as it went. But *everyone* knows about that one by now. A man worth twenty million dollars stealing out of the cookie jar. When the other networks took over the story, they had a field day with the court proceedings. The net result: his wizened old psychoanalyst makes an impassioned plea to the jury, explaining the underlying childhood causes. Kornreich agrees to continue his therapy. Angry victims are paid off or fired, and the story dies. But didn't you wonder about the real motivations? . . . Mental illness, my ass. Try getting in touch with the Sands Casino, for starters. Then try and figure out what the FCC would say about him writing personal checks to the mob. That's where the story is."

"Well what about the data on the Cruise of Fools sit-com? That's something which no one has come up with yet. And I think that I might lead to . . ."

"It's small-time, Crystal. Everyone already knows that there are two producers who have this town sewn up. The question is not how they pull it off. The question is: who's behind them? We're talking about billions, not a million dollars here and there. The fingers that dial the numbers that turn on the strikes, not the figureheads and puppets. Fred Stanwith is dead—and the entire nation dismisses it as an over-dose. Susan Drabble is strangled in the Hollywood Hills . . ."

"*Rob Steinholtz is murdered,*" Dale hissed quietly between his teeth.

As the words fell on Crystal's ears, her mouth momentarily dropped. Her eyes raced from Dale, once again obliviously drumming his fingers on his knee, to Redfield.

He paused for a moment, staring across the room at

the family portraits on the wall behind her, then shifted in his burnished leather chair. ". . . Furthermore," he continued, his face growing darker, "I find the private sexual references to other network heads both cheap and offensive . . ."

"I figured that in the case of Stalfort, it might shed some light on a few of the questionable pay-offs. But I never intended to use those as the basis of investigation."

"Fine. I intend to hit below the belt. But this is not going to be a character assassination. We are looking for an industry-wide indictment. And individual personalities are irrelevant. We'll save those for the *Enquirer*."

"Now wait one moment," Crystal shot back, her emerald eyes glowing with fury. "If you think that I'm going to sit here and listen to . . ."

"I'm sorry, Crystal. That was not meant as an insult. But I hired you in part because of your tremendous mass appeal, and in part because you were the kind of woman who had the guts to take on the entire city of Atlanta when you had to. This time, you have our full support. And my personal guarantee that putting *whatever* you find on the air—wherever you find it—will be equally supported. You can have it in writing, if you would prefer."

"Your word is good enough for me," she backed down, struggling to bury the anger still boiling inside her.

"Have you got anything to add, Dale?"

"Not a word, CJ. I agree with you all the way down the line. So I guess it's time to head back to the drawing board. Right Crys?"

"Sure." The simpering yes-man tone in his voice haunted her as she rode down the elevator. In the movies, it was enough for the hero to turn to a guy like

340

Dale, slap him hard across the face and snarl, "*Snap out of it.*"

But this time, it was going to take a harder jolt of reality than that. Maybe a few days with Sloan as the RedRock President would be enough to bring him back. If not, the going would be that much harder. For all of them.

Passing by Lauren's office door, she paused to catch her up on the latest developments, then thought better of it. For once, Lauren Conrad could come to her.

Back in her own office, she tossed the attache case on top of the latest pile of data to appear, decided to let it wait. Gazing at the photographs clustered around her typewriter, she grabbed the phone and determined to get through to the Wyndale School, and the daughter who had been dodging her attempts at communication for the better part of a month.

"Third floor," came a sullen reply, echoing faintly.

"Marcie," she announced triumphantly.

"Uh, hi mom."

"Didn't you get my messages? Sweetheart, I've been trying to reach you for *weeks*."

"Sorry. People around here are really sloppy about pinning messages on the dorm board."

"Never mind." She heard her daughter slipping away into defensiveness and tried another tack. "I tell you, two months up North, and you practically sound like a Yankee. I haven't spoken to you in so long I barely recognized your voice."

"Uh . . . Mom. Listen. Someone else is standing here. Waiting for the phone. And I have a shitload of homework to do. So . . ."

"Well they can *both* wait a second. Darling, I miss you. And I want to know how you are . . ."

"Fine."

"Well, good. I'm really glad to hear that. It may be

341

old hat to you in New Hampshire. But as far as I'm concerned, I have just sent my baby off to prep school and I've been worried sick. Do you need anything? Should I send you a check? *Besides* the birthday check, I mean."

"Not really. Daddy already sent me one."

"Well that was very nice of your father. I guess that about takes care of things, doesn't it? Well listen, Thanksgiving is just a month away. The headmaster told me that you can take off the entire week. So I thought that maybe you and I would spend a few days here and then maybe we could go up to San Francisco and visit . . ."

"I really can't, Mom. I already promised that I'd go down to Atlanta."

It was a possibility that Crystal had prepared for. But as the words reached her ears, she felt the tears welling up in her eyes, and her fists clenching with frustration. According to the divorce agreement, Marcie was to spend Thanksgiving with her. Whether they lived in Georgia, California, or Outer Mongolia. No court in the world would dare to deny a mother's right to see her daughter. Not even the ones that Stephen Benjamin could buy for *anything* else.

If it came down to that, then the ultimate decision would belong to Marcie. It was a vicious thing to submit any child to. And the way things had been going between them, Crystal herself might end up being the one brutalized, when Marcie did make the decision.

"Of course," she stammered, wondering if Marcie heard the cracking in her voice. "That was silly of me. I'm sure you miss all of your friends back home. I know *I* do. Besides, Daddy must be dying to see you. And I'm sure Jeffers and Mary just can't wait, either."

"I really 've got to get off the phone now, Mom."

"I'll call you again mid-week. Try to write me if you

get a moment. And don't forget that I love you."

"I-love-you-too," the girl responded automatically as the phone clicked off.

Crystal stared at the neutral beige walls surrounding her and carefully got up and locked the door. For once, she decided, the thing she needed most was someone to talk to. Anyone.

In the absence of that, maybe giving in to a good old fashioned cry would have to substitute.

The phone rang and she watched it through teary lenses. If it wasn't Joel, then it was sure to be her mother. And as far as she was concerned, at that moment they were the last problems in the world she needed. Maybe the best thing was just not answering for once.

Then she heard Lauren Conrad curse on the other side of the wall and grabbed the receiver. Letting the phone ring off the hook was the sort of lapse which Miss Cool, Calm and Collected next door was sure to observe. And capitalize on.

"Crystal Cooper," she stated defiantly.

"Finally," came the burst of laughter on the other end of the line. "Lady, you are harder to get a hold of than Dr. J. on the court. How you doin', Crystal."

"Just fine, Mitch. It's nice to hear from you."

"So far, so good. Now if I can just dribble past your defenses and make the pitch . . . How about it, Crystal? I've been asking you out ever since we met at Sloan's. I've got two tickets for the symphony on Wednesday night, and . . ."

"I'd love to . . ."

"Thank goodness. I was beginning to wonder if you would ever come around."

"But right now things are too busy around here I can't even find a minute to . . ."

"No need to go any further. One week you're busy,

the next week you're tied up. Then you can't find the time to . . ."

"I'm not brushing you off."

"I'll believe it when I hear you finally say yes."

How about a drink right now, she thought. *My God, I could use some conversation. And some tenderness.* But with the bruises of her recent passion with Joel still dotting her body and her mind, she knew that it would be a mistake.

"I'll give you a call when I can get free," she offered.

"I'll be here," he answered neutrally. "Nice talking with you, Crystal."

"Thanks for calling me."

"Anytime."

She hung up the phone and suddenly felt drained. Grabbing her attache case and clutch, Crystal slid silently out of her office, taking the rear entrance to avoid the chance of any collision with Lauren or the newsroom staff.

Beyond RedRock, there were hundreds of miles of LA Freeway. And at the moment, nothing seemed better than humming along doing fifty-five, heading nowhere. Ignoring the honks and the waves, and letting the empty afternoon pavement envelop her in nothingness.

Thirty-six

"Good evening. This is Lauren Conrad. And tonight on Now News Bookends, we'll be discussing a controversial . . ."

"Cut," Roy's voice barked through the speakers. "Manny, we've got an audio problem registering on B. See if you can't . . ."

Lauren straightened out the waist of her unusually decollete dress. Aware of the eyes silently lapping up her svelte form from the tubular steel armchair across the glass coffee table set up in the studio.

She felt at home now. And behind the cameras, the facade of supreme confidence which she struggled to project in her private life was transformed into an ease and gracefulness which anyone would have admired.

Even so, she knew that she was in especially top form. This morning, she had jogged her three mile course easily—and with no interruptions. She had chosen the clinging blue Missoni knit dress carefully, for effect.

The reflection of Ted Rothmore's eyes on the table top confirmed what she already knew: this morning, Lauren Conrad of Now News was absolutely irresistible.

Now the seduction could continue on her terms. The ball was in her court, and she knew just how to slice it. Soaring and unapproachable, she wanted him to be blinded as he stood there observing, and realize just whom he was dealing with.

Yes, Lauren smiled, as his eyes continued to survey her shapely legs primly crossed just below the knee, she wanted him to be starstruck, and more as the lights bore down on the two of them. *Without a doubt, she wanted him to positively drool at the sight of her.*

Coyly, she kicked off one shoe, and shifted, allowing the insides of her thighs to press against one another. His eyes shifted uneasily beneath the tortoise-shell glasses, following the almost imperceptible motion of her legs. Unaccustomed to the blazing lights, the make-up and the inevitable stage fright which even the most accomplished non-professionals suffered, Ted looked beside himself. Like he was ready to bolt at the next delay.

"Feeling better?" she grinned. He had presented her with a newly filled prescription for Valium—in her name, the moment he arrived. Wordlessly, she had slipped the vial into her handbag—but not before the good doctor had casually downed two of them.

"I've never been in a studio like this before."

"Oh?"

"I mean . . . well, it must be two hundred degrees in here. When in hell are the cameramen going to stop crawling all over the ceiling and . . ."

"Those aren't cameramen in the flyloft. Those are technicians. The cameramen—and women—are out there. In front of the cameras. Don't worry. They'll be rolling soon enough. In the meantime, I can have a drink brought for you, if you'd like."

"It's a little bit early in the morning, but . . ."

"Coffee? Or water? Anything else looks livid against the tangerine backdrop."

"Water," he shrugged doubtfully.

Lauren relayed the request and leafed through the pages of *The Laetrile Alternative*. She carefully noted the important dates, places and statistics, then turned to examine the serene and hypnotic expression in the author's photograph.

"It may seem like dry stuff at first," he began defensively.

"Not at all. Just remember what happened to a little biological study called *Human Sexual Response*. But what I was really admiring was the shot on the back. It's absolutely stunning."

"You really think so?"

"Positively," she nodded, turning to stare at him with the full intensity of her violet-edged amber eyes. "A mixture of passion, but control. It looks like you could hold that position — or any other — for *hours*."

For the first time since his arrival at RedRock, Ted burst into a full smile.

"That's better," Lauren laughed, winking at him as the cameras began to warm up once again.

She had done a lot of thinking about Dr. Ted Rothmore in the hours since yesterday's afternoon delight. He was an odd combination of charmer and snake in the same basket. Alternately supremely confident and desperate for approval. One moment disarmingly straightforward, and the next about as sincere as a bad check.

He was a far cry from marriage material. But just the same a superb lover. A man who knew how to have fun. How to keep his hips moving indefinitely. And more importantly, he obviously knew how to keep his mouth shut about it. Even when his nerves were frazzled by the pre-taping agony, Ted had never even come close to an indiscretion, or even a knowing glance.

"*All right. Countdown,*" announced the production booth. She turned and shot a reassuring wink in his direction.

"Our guest on tonight's Bookends section is Beverly Hills doctor Ted Rothmore, author of the controversial new book, *The Laetrile Alternative*. Dr. Rothmore, what exactly is laetrile, and why is this a cancer treatment which has been generally dismissed in this country?"

As the camera zoomed in on him, Ted Rothmore once more reverted to his easy, self-assured bedside manner. He shifted back in his chair and smiled broadly. The moment for bringing his message to bookbuyers across the nation had finally arrived, after so many months of planning. Where his efforts to reach Johnny Carson and Phil Donahue had failed, Lauren Conrad had finally come through.

Launching into his meticulously crafted sales pitch slowly, a warm smile eased itself onto his features. "Well, Lauren, let me begin by saying that the medical basis for laetrile treatment goes all the way back to a Greek surgeon, two thousand years ago. He discovered that for some serious ailments, giving a patient the smallest dose of a toxin—in this case from apricot pits—would simultaneously trigger the body's own immune system, while killing off the . . ."

Crystal wound slowly around the gallery of the taping studio, followed by Sloan, Dale, Jewel Beale, and an entourage of men and women in sober business suits.

They stopped at the center aisle. The strangers quietly traded observations and nodded with self-assurance after each remark. "Obviously the *ingenue*," a slim man in his early forties noted, eyeing her as if she were a mannequin or a still photo. "Good expression in the eyes, and that pulled back hairdo is just the perfect quality for her . . . Crystal, do you mind turning around for a moment?"

His eyes trailed slowly over her body, starting at the neck and winding their way down. They showed a mixture of personal excitement and professional appraisal. Oblivious to everything else, including the broadcast tape being concluded with Dr. Rothmore. And the increasing irritation lighting up Crystal's features.

"Okay, fine," he said with a dismissing shrug. Crystal continued to face the group of news imagists, amazed at the way the men and women alike were content to treat her not only as an object, but as one in definite need of modernization.

"I agree with you, Bill," offered a thirtyish, heavy-set woman, "from the neck down, she's a disaster."

"Now hold on one minute, lady," Dale bristled, stepping toward the group.

"Back off, Dale," admonished Sloan. "Let Sarah say her piece. For what we're paying them in consulting fees, we can't afford any scenes. We'll discuss it with the news team later."

"No insult intended," the woman continued, "but there's no sense in beating around the bush. These women are professionals, and I'm sure that they understand that our observations are objective. They deal with image and role modelling—not personal critiques. In addition to the standard voice training, we try to establish comfortable roles for the news team, to enhance the clarity of the product. As it stands now, there are simply too many inconsistencies. Give us a few minutes and I'm sure you'll see what we mean."

Upon the stage, the lights dimmed out. A weary Dr. Ted Rothmore fell back in his chair, then turned to

Lauren. "I feel like I've just been put through the Boards all over again."

"Never mind," she laughed, "you did just fine. Listen, about ten percent of our guests get so tense that they have to rush off to the wings halfway through. Some of them get sick backstage, some of them collapse. Believe it or not, you breezed through."

His lips broke into a crooked smile. "Well, how about a celebratory drink? . . . Is that Crystal standing over there in the shadows? Maybe she would . . ."

"That's Crystal alright," Lauren pronounced flatly, as her eyes adjusted to the dark and took in the new hairdo and body molding Calvin Klein slacks.

Crystal felt Ted Rothmore turning on the charm with every step he took toward her. Two paces behind him, Lauren was already at a slow boil.

"Ms. Cooper," he announced, loudly enough for everyone to overhear, "you look absolutely stunning. And that hairdo. I mean it. I've never seen you look better—and I've been watching Now News every night. I was just about to head out for a drink with Lauren. And I thought that maybe you could join us. How about it?"

"Lauren, darling," Sloan called out in the background, "why don't you c'mon over. I'd like to introduce you to Bill Myers—and his staff. Imagus International. I'm sure you've heard of them . . ."

"Afraid not," Crystal answered Rothmore, turning to him as Lauren brushed by her with ill-concealed annoyance. "It's already too close to broadcast time. Besides, I think that we're going to be working in the studio for a few minutes."

"Maybe a raincheck, then?"

"Well," Lauren interjected, "so much for our drink,

350

Ted. Looks like we have a family portrait to attend to."

"How about dinner? We could . . ."

"Better give me a call later on," Lauren shrugged, quietly ushering him off to the side.

"Going to a costume party?" Lauren sneered, pasting on her best smile as she sat across from Crystal. Around the studio, still photographers were busily snapping their shutters. "I mean, between the hair and the nails, you look positively *theatrical* . . . Or is that a sample of the Imagus image?"

Crystal ignored the barb, quietly pleased at the jealous undertone. When Lauren began to lose control, she always *knew* that she was looking good. "How long are these jokers going to be around?" she sighed.

"Who knows?"

"Come off it, Lauren. I can't believe that you like it any more than I do."

"Quite frankly, Crys, I don't give a damn. They can play their little games for as long as CJ cares to pay them. I for one have not spent years perfecting my broadcast style just to throw it away the first time a panel of 'experts' decides a change is in order."

"*Alright. Profiles,*" called a voice over the speaker. "*Face one another. A little more, Lauren. Perfect.*"

"That's 'Ms. Conrad' to you, Jackson," she whispered through clenched lips.

"I don't know about you," Crystal confided, "but my smiling muscles are killing me."

A moment later, Dale led the crowd up on the stage.

"Well, we've certainly got our work cut out for us," sighed the group leader. "Please forgive me, Crystal . . . Lauren. But I've got to be honest with you: It just doesn't work."

"Just exactly what are you referring to?" Crystal answered as sweetly as possible.

"The *geist* of the thing. You know, the point of departure. The news content is fine, of course. But on the tapes I've seen, the rest of it just isn't quite right, I mean, there just isn't a uniform image. A clear statement."

"How about the ratings, then?"

"Crystal, *all* of the news anchors feel that way. At the beginning. But once we've had time to clarify your image, you'll see results. It's the little things we're talking about. Like that silk blouse. It may look fine on you off camera but it doesn't go with the sort of warmth we're looking for from you. A sort of ingenue, melding a big sister image with Hugh Hefner's girl next door. If you want to keep the Southern inflection, fine. But we see it as more subtle. With a little bit of coaching . . ."

Crystal glowered silently.

"Fine, fine. Lauren, we'll see if we can't brighten up your delivery. You know: A bit more splash. And a touch of wry humor. At the same time, we want Uncle Steve to tone things down a little. A bit more of a father image . . . Remember: the key is *identification*. We want every member of the audience to identify with the characters you portray on the news. As a wife, or a sister, maybe just a friendly secretary in the office."

"Oh, *I* get it," Crystal broke in sarcastically, "sort of like a smorgasbord. With a little bit of everything thrown in."

"Precisely. Let's just say that the em*pha*sis has been on the wrong syl*la*ble. Now why don't we all head back to Sloan's office. We've got a little presentation on the Imagus International philosophy."

"Sounds too good to be true," Crystal groaned,

wondering if all sarcasm was lost on children and hypesters.

"Well, here comes baby sister," Lauren hissed at the evening broadcast's conclusion as Jewel Beale came on with a dubbed-over lifestyle report. "It *was* raining in *Los* Angeles this evening," she beamed over the monitor. "And that made for *some* rough going for Trick-or-Treaters as they sludged through ankle deep puddles en *route* to the door . . ."

Lauren stared at the made-over reporter and prayed that a lemon chiffon or banana cream pie could somehow fly across the airwaves, and *right* into her *clearly* revolting new image. The old one had been hard enough to tolerate. But between the broadcasterese accent and the familiar sickly sweet drawl, every moment of the broadcast was nauseating.

At last the red light flashed on, and Crystal took up the cue. "Until tomorrow evening, this is Crystal Cooper . . ."

". . . and Lauren Conrad. Wishing Jewel Beale and the rest of our trick-or-treaters a Happy Halloween. Have a good night. And a pleasant tomorrow."

Thirty-seven

"Francesca, would you please shut off the tube, and put away those stupid lists?" Igor roared across the king-sized bed.

"The broadcast's almost over," she sighed wearily.

"What do you mean? I have to lie here with my aching shoulders and wait for the end of the credits for a goddamn massage? Don't I work hard enough to have you do something for me, without having to beg?"

"Darling, please don't be petulant. I just can't take it right now. My nerves are shot. Why don't you get me a drink?"

"Get it yourself."

"What has gotten into you tonight? Just because I want to sit and watch my friends for half an hour a day, that's no cause for a tantrum."

"I-am-not-throwing-a-tempers-tantrum—or whatever you may call it. But I am sick and tired of it. Conrad & Cooper *this*, Conrad & Cooper that. You act like those two dames are God. Glued to the set every evening."

"Please darling. Don't get your blood pressure up over nothing. In this town, *everyone* is watching Now News. Besides, Lauren and Crystal just happen to be my *friends*. I care about them—and what happens on their broadcast. It's also the best national news show around. You *used* to watch CBS every right, anyway."

"I'm sick of the whole scene. If it's not them, then it's the party. I thought that buying the Rodeo property would help things. But ever since I started the negotiations, I get no peace at home. To tell you the truth, Francesca, I'm thinking of calling off the deal."

"You wouldn't."

"Oh no?" He seized the remote control and snapped it off, then tossed it onto the loveseat in the corner of the bedroom. "Don't bet on it."

Wearily, Francesca tossed aside the invitation list headed *Chez Francesca: Opening.* Soothingly, she leaned over and began kneading the taut muscles bulging from his thick neck.

"A little lower," he moaned. "And right . . . *there.* Yes. The right shoulder is killing me. I work too damn hard. And tomorrow I may have to fly to Zurich again."

"The factory?" she asked gently.

"And the bank. I tell you I am surrounded by fools and incompetents. And by an ungrateful wife who just doesn't appreciate how much I do for her."

"Of course I do," she sighed, kissing the broad red bald head, and wishing he was already back in Switzerland. Just for a week or two, so she could finish the preliminary plans for the boutique opening before flying to Paris. "Igor, you wouldn't really call off the deal now, would you?"

"For the factory in Taiwan? Of *course* not."

She roamed her fingers gently over his back. "I meant for the boutique."

"Why shouldn't I?" Beneath the ripples of fat, she felt a new line of tension stretching taut across his broad sea of back.

"Darling, don't tease me. Not about that."

"Who's kidding," he spat, rolling over to expose a

thickly forested chest of long grey hairs. He gazed at her lavisciously, while his broad palm sought out the fullness of her massive breasts beneath the thin Dior peignoir. "You're too clothes crazy already. In case you forgot, Sweetie, I did not pay two hundred dollars for you to hide your magnificent breasts from me." His stubby fingers grasped the thin silk and began to tug at it.

"Stop it," she begged, "you're going to *rip* this."

"I'll buy you another."

"That's not the point," she protested, struggling to free the peignoir from his grasp. "This garment is a work of art, and it demands respect. Honestly, sometimes you are positively vulgar. There is more to appreciating art than merely possessing it."

"Nonsense. I bought it, and I'll do what I like with it." With a satisfied groan, he tore the flimsy aquamarine neckline down to her navel and lunged onto her pink Rubenesque belly. "You're so beautiful," he sighed, groping for the lush delta of black hair outlined in silk.

"I will not be treated like a part of your collections. In case you forgot, I am not a rare coin, or a stamp or a butterfly. I am a human being."

"No. You are more than that: you are my woman. And I want you. *Now*."

His fingers thrust greedily downward, piercing into her. She struggled to free herself from his grasp, tears running down her cheeks as the fabric gave out in a final heart-rending rip. "*It's ruined*," she shrieked. "You just destroyed it."

"I said I'll buy you another," he replied calmly, cupping hands around the twin globes of her ass and drawing her toward him.

"Well, you cannot buy my love," she snapped bitterly.

"Oh no? My pet," he leered, punctuating his words with fierce licks and nips on her breasts, "I already *own* you. And your boutique. And I am suddenly tired of your silly little girl games. Now either you do what a good wife is supposed to do, or we forget about Chez Francesca. Understand?"

She stared at him in a state of shock, her once beautiful features looking old and miserable. Nodding blankly, as the tears streamed mascara over her puffy cheeks, down to the corners of her mouth.

"Good." Abruptly Igor pushed down the lavender Porthault sheet, to reveal a short thick penis, its head already strainingly red. "Now suck my cock. I'm horny." He grabbed her neck beneath the long curly black hair and brought it forcefully down to his lap.

"Igor . . . *please*," she pleaded as he bobbed her head up and down.

"Later, my pet," he softly replied. "I detest people who talk with their mouths full."

The massive red knob pushed through her thick lips and began thrusting deeper and deeper. *He does love me*, she thought, as he rammed against the back of her throat. *I know he does. He'll apologize—just like always*.

In the meantime, there was the boutique to think about. And all of the arrangements. The Bistro, upstairs was already booked. And by the end of the week, she would have to decide on the announcements.

She felt herself gagging as he clamped her head down and began speeding up the assault. *Violet will be there, of course. And Lauren . . . And Crystal. This time, the entire "A" group will show. Even Jody Jacobs. Maybe even the Fred Astaires. The crème . . .*

Igor came in a vicious torrent, his massive body rippling, then growing still.

Slowly he came back to life, his fingers now caressing her softly. "Francesca?" he whispered hoarsely. "*Francesca?* Are you okay? I—I'm sorry. I feel . . . so ashamed. Please. I didn't mean to . . . I just lose my head."

Trembling, he raised himself up and curled around to face her. "Tell me . . . you forgive me. I'll never do that again." Frantically, he pressed his mouth to hers. "Oh baby, I didn't . . ."

"It's okay, darling," she sighed, lifting up a pendulous breast to his lips, and feeling desire seep through her tired limbs as he began to suck feverishly. "It's alright . . ."

Thirty-eight

"Ah, *there* you are," Bob Radin's voice boomed as he
finally spotted Lauren entering the newsroom.

"What's left of me," she smiled wanly, allowing him
to take her arm and escort her back toward her office.

"Rough broadcast?"

"No. The news show was fine. Like clockwork. It's
what went on before and after that was sheer hell.
You ever hear of the Imagus School?"

"You mean the one which turns out news clones?
Like the wind-up doll news family at KJJX?"

"The very one. Weird, unnatural speech and type-
casting straight out of 'Leave it to Beaver.' Well, one of
their branches—Imagus International—was just called
in by Dale—at the insistence of our new president."

"Good old Sloan," he laughed. "She never did waste
any time. How many cub reporters has she snagged
for the course in advanced clonography?"

"None. The list begins with Conrad and Cooper.
Uncle Steve. Jewel Beale . . . and it's downhill from
there."

"You've got to be kidding. With your ratings, she'd
be crazy to touch Now News. Furthermore, I don't
believe that your viewers would stand for that kind of
sit-com news crap."

"With any luck, they'll never have a chance to."

"Do I hear a mutiny brewing in the background?"

Lauren shrugged. "God, do I ever need a . . ." She froze in front of her office door, as the word *Valium* gushed up to her lips. *I really do need one*, she grimaced. *It's getting to be every four hours, like clockwork. That's the last thing in the world I want to tell Bob Radin.*

She shrugged off the sentence and gathered up the awaiting stack of messages in silence. What was it about Bob Radin that did that to her? At Rob's funeral, when she spotted him at the Polo Lounge, now, when she bumped into him after a broadcast. She always felt so comfortable in his presence that it was positively unnerving. *Remember where you are*, she chided herself. *One wrong word, and it'll end up on the front page of Variety. In Hollywood, the only safe secrets are the Sins of Omission.*

Her eyes pored over the slips of paper as she slid open the door. A call from Geneva, refusing to supply information on a series of deposits the media investigation had turned up. Maybe that banker husband of Francesca's could unlock a key or two. An obscene call. An anonymous tipster: Will recall. Two messages from Dr. Ted Rothmore within the last fifteen minutes.

"Now what was I saying?" she smiled, staring up into his serious grey eyes.

"I think it was along the lines of 'I need a drink.' I'll tell you something else: I could use one too. It's been a vicious day. I haven't had so many deals fall through in years. Or maybe decades. I stopped by on the rare chance you might be free to join me."

"Well as a matter of fact, I . . ."

As the telephone rang, he stared down at her expectantly. In reply, Lauren grabbed her coat and attache case.

"Well, that's what I call a woman of action," he

beamed down delighted. "But what about the telephone?"

"Persistent. Isn't he?"

"He?"

"I mean the telephone." She stared up at his imposing presence, then down at the phone ringing off the receiver, never doubting for a moment that it was Ted Rothmore. But he would have to wait. From the moment she had laid eyes on Bob Radin, Lauren had been waiting for the opportunity to get to know him better. And more than little piqued at the fact that he seemed to pick up her vibes, but had never ventured to give her a call to follow up. Clearly, this drink was one opportunity she couldn't refuse.

She slammed the door shut and locked her arm in his, shaking her head at the outraged ringing echoing within. "Such endurance," she marvelled.

And staying power like you wouldn't believe.

Ted Rothmore slammed down the phone and vaulted out of his office chair.

"That *bitch*," he fumed, throwing on his jacket and heading out the door. "I *told* her I would call after the broadcast. Now where in hell is *she?*"

He gunned the Bentley and screeched onto Bedford, heading for Number One Sunset Boulevard. Pulling up to a stoplight, he angrily noted the ache in his left testicle. Gonorrhea? A sea of bacteria and fungi danced in his head. If she had given him the clap, then . . .

But hadn't he showered thoroughly immediately after making love? Of course—with surgical precision. Besides, it was only yesterday, remember. That's right. Symptoms wouldn't show up for seven days to two weeks. Maybe that redheaded babe he had tailed in Malibu?

No. He had suspected her from the first, and wisely used a rubber.

There were certain occupational hazards to being a doctor. Especially for a hypochondriac. A lot of knowledge could be a very dangerous thing.

"Relax, Buddy," he sighed, snapping a cassette into the Dolby. "It's probably just the prostatitis kicking up." He pulled off onto the side of the road and fumbled frantically in the glove compartment. In the midst of a jumble of vials he located a label identifying one as Gantricin. Popping one, he slipped the cannister into his pocket, making a mental note to continue the dosage for two weeks.

Breathing a little more easily, he cruised past Sunset Strip, in a cloud of symphonic sound. Slowly, he came to the realization that Lauren would probably be long gone. In the future, he would have to keep closer tabs on her.

In the meantime, he still had a dull ache in his groin to contend with—together with the dangerous build-up of bodily fluids which it represented. Foul humours. He knew all too well—from a clinical standpoint—the dangers of failing to release them. Particularly given his condition. *An orgasm a day keeps the humours at bay.*

"I should never have prolonged orgasm like that," he said firmly. As if he had a choice in the matter. Someday, they would find the miracle drug to cure situational impotence. In the meantime, he would have to remain the hottest stud in town—and halfway down the road to priapism, unless he acted fast.

As the Bentley glided past Mann's Chinese Theatre on Hollywood, the street action began to pick up. He gazed at the decidedly punk streetwalkers and ejected the Guillini tape, in favor of a new wave recording.

At once the interior was flooded with a chorus of "*I*

362

want to be Jackie Onassis/I want to wear Big Sun-glasses/Oh yeah." He mussed his hair a bit, tossed the jacket into the back seat, and cruised to a halt at the corner of Yucca and Vine. Beneath a colossal Zig Zag Moderne facade stood a long-legged girl of about fifteen. Maybe thirteen, if the barely budded breasts were any indication: no zigs and no zags. He loosed a grateful sigh and stared at the skin tight black tee shirt, with the word "Expensive" emblazoned across the chest in rhinestones. Given a choice, he never went in for mushy boobs.

He rolled down the window and stared at her tufted silky blond hair, with a tiny orange ducktail pointing down from the peak of her forehead. Once again, he could feel the pressure building up in his groin.

"Hey. Human Sexual Response," she yelled.

"In the flesh," he snorted.

"No. I meant the tape you're blasting. That's the name of the band."

He felt his cock prodding the waistband of his jockey shorts and nodded. "So tell me," he grinned, pulling out a wad of bills, "the sign says *expensive*. How much?"

"That depends." She sidled up to the car and smiled provocatively.

"On what?"

"What you're interested in buying."

He laughed and put the money down at his side. "What're you selling?"

"Speed. Quaaludes. Got some STP-base mescaline, but it's a little raw to be honest."

"Not what I had in mind. My first name happens to be 'Doctor.' "

"Fantastic. In that case, I got a better proposition. Pussy for pills. We make an even exchange."

"Hop in, and let's get this deal under way." As she

bounded around the Bentley, he carefully locked the glove compartment. A moment later, she was all over him. One hand running over the nape of his neck as she stuck her tongue into his ear. The other losing no time in stroking his balls. "Listen," she whispered, breathing heavily into his ear, "can I score some reds from you? It's been so long, and I'd do *anything* for a good old-fashioned round of downers. What about it, handsome?"

"What's your name, honey?" He drew away and stared at her lips in the shimmering high intensity crime light. No obvious lesions on her lips, and the color of her eyes showed no signs of hepatitis.

"Jeannie."

"My name's Ted. And I'm a magician—but not in public. So just sit back and let your fingers do the talking—discreetly—until we get back to my place."

"Anything you say, Doc. But listen: Nothing too kinky. I'm only seventeen."

"And a liar," he laughed, flooring the accelerator.

"This machine really moves," she cooed, increasing the pressure and pace of ten tiny fingers curled around his cock. "Is it really yours."

"All twenty-three feet of it. Honey what you're doing is fine, for now. But I want to pleasure you as well, so just hold tight and relax. We're almost there."

As the car stopped at his Beverly Hills mansion, he could feel her excitement growing. "It's . . . enormous," she groaned. "I thought you'd bring me to some dump in West Hollywood."

"Not Dr. T., baby. Tonight we do you in style." He led her silently through the cavernous living room, and up the spiral staircase. As soon as the bed loomed into sight, she did a fleeting strip tease and tossed a carefully preserved pack of prophylactics onto the pillow.

She nodded lasciviously, then arched her back until her tiny swollen nipples pointed tantalizingly at the ceiling. He gazed hungrily at the skinny buttocks, then at the scanty wisps of hair dotting her mound. "How about a massage shower?"

He scrubbed her thoroughly with the antiseptic soap, delighted to see that she was already virtually spotless. Then he quietly uncapped a small bottle and poured a handful of pale yellow fluid into his cupped hand, allowing her to squirm playfully as he inserted it into her tiny vagina.

"Oooh, that tickles," she giggled, moving in slow circles against the bone of his palm. "What is it?"

"Lemon scent," he gleamed with his devastating smile. Actually it was lemon juice, and she had just passed the Sailor's test. The slightest lesion would have produced a bloodcurdling howl from the acid burn.

Shutting off the water, he gently patted her dry, wondering about the anal absorption of vitamin C. In all probability, that was how they discovered the cure for scurvy on those long, lonely voyages to Africa. Devilishly clever, those British.

Soon they were locked together, Ted, as usual, expertly pumping away. Despite the friction which excited him, he was no closer to orgasm than an hour ago. Tonight none of the fantasies seemed to do it for him.

Pulling out, he propped himself up against the pillows, then directed her disappointed lips onto his cock. With a shrug, she began her ministrations while he casually reached for the telephone and dialed.

"Hello," came his mother's cheerful voice on the other end of the line. "Hello. *Hello*. Who is this? *Harold*. Ohmigod. *Harold*. We've got a *breather* on the line. What do I do?"

At last, he sighed, letting the phone drop onto the

bed as his balls reared up and then finally let go.

"Can I have the pills now?" Jeannie wearily gurgled. "I mean, you don't want to fuck anymore, I suppose."

Wordlessly he reached for his prescription pad. "Take this to Rowland Pharmacy downtown. I'll give you ten. That should last 'til the end of the week. Give me a call then. And keep this quiet—or it's the end of a beautiful relationship."

Thirty-nine

Crystal cruised down the San Diego Freeway, basking in the relatively smog-free sunlight pouring in through the windshield.

It was barely 10:30 in the morning. Yet miraculously, there was not a trace of dream-laden sluggishness in her blood. She felt awake and vital, driving effortlessly, listening to a talk show rambling on in the back speakers of the BMW. Things had gotten off to a great start, for a change.

"Maybe I should cut down to three hours of sleep every night," she mused, zipping around the cloverleaf and heading west on the Santa Monica Freeway. Whatever had possessed Joel to break down and spend the *entire* night for a change, she had no idea. Hopefully it wasn't just guilt.

Whatever the cause, there were concrete results to show for it. Like the contented smile she had awakened with after last night's second round of fireworks, and the afterburner still quietly warming her insides with an effusive glow. The second stage had been spectacular, alright—and easily worth a week's sleep deprivation.

The question remained: was it worth the rest of the bullshit she had been contending with? Joel's sporadic bursts of selfishness, his on-and-off passion?

Luckily, it was a question that could be filed away—for now. At least when he was on, Joel was *really* on, and on a night like last night, he was indescribable, insatiable, indefatigable. And *in-* more ways than she could ever have imagined.

Waking up with him on a morning like this, it was impossible to be anything less than charged by his infectious energy.

After breakfast, she had amazed herself even more by strutting past the graveyard shift in the newsroom without a trace of the normal I-need-another-cup-of-coffee-before-the-blood-starts-circulating look. And that at 7:30 in the morning! It would sure as hell give the newsroom gossips something to chew on—and undoubtedly to bet on as well. "Wonder if I could get in on one of the sidebets?" she laughed to herself.

To top it all off, the media investigation was finally getting into the swing of things. Whatever else she had to say about the RedRock accounting staff's whiz kids, they were like bloodhounds when it came to sniffing out laundered money. Next time she met with CJ, she would have some concrete facts and figures to show . . .

Come to think of it, they seemed to know a bit too much about the whole laundering business. Well, there were ways of finding out about RedRock as well. It would be easy enough for Winston to have one of his little friends in the programming department disguise the ID readout on the computer tabulations for the Satellite Broadcasting Network. To submit it as a run from CBS' own limited access files, after adding six decimal places. Not a bad idea at that.

If not for Sloan and her little Imagus power play, things would be going great across the boards. If the training sessions could be cut down to a bare minimum, she was confident that Redfield would be brought around to realize that the school for reporters was a waste of time and money, as far as RedRock was concerned. As long as the network continued to flaunt the trend by having two women as co-anchors, the rest of the "news family" modelling was bound to fail, anyway.

If and when the Now News formula was altered, the shit that hit the fan would make the Imagus school the least of their problems. Either way, it made the nuisance of voice, image and grooming suggestions seem like a pretty insignificant problem. But a grating one.

She pulled into the parking lot of the Women's Institute and gathered her attache case. Just in case, she dropped the miniature tape recorder into the breast pocket of her blazer.

"*Nice groceries*," yelled a man in a hard hat, leering down. "Whoooeeeeee."

"Hey, that ain't just some broad, Charlie. That's *Crystal Cooper*."

"You mean that broad on *KPTL Cincinati?*"

"What are you? Some kind of clown. She's a reporter. Now News. Brenda watches it every night. And to tell you the truth, she's a hell of a lot more interesting than Dan Rather—from my point of view."

"Well, from here, she's a dead ringer for Dolly Parton . . ." He cupped his hands to his mouth. "*Good morning, Ms. Cooper . . .*"

Pulling her jacket a bit more closed, Crystal waved up at them and smiled easily, ignoring the whistles and the words ". . . watcha doin' after the broadcast? . . ." as she slid through the sliding glass doors.

Inside, the scene was no different. The building reeked of fresh plaster and paint. Hordes of workers mixed with the harried staff dressed in pale green scrub uniforms, all preparing for the approaching opening of the center. Stopping constantly for greeters and stargazers and autograph-seekers, she eventually wound her way down to the office of the director.

"So pleased to meet you," exclaimed the doctor, extending a gentle hand as she swept Crystal into the still unpainted office. "I'm Dr. Hussein . . . Sandra. And this rather unimpressive set up is going to be my office. I just called in to RedRock, to request that we shoot the story tomorrow . . . if possible. I'm afraid that there isn't a square foot of quiet space in the building today. In addition, there's an emergency meeting of the board of directors. Two operations at the old facility scheduled for . . ."

"No need to explain," Crystal interrupted. "I always like to set up the shooting on a story like this before the camera crew arrives anyway. Sometimes they get so hung up on the original story that they miss something equally important right under their noses. So, quite frankly, a day of lead time is good for me as well."

"You are very gracious," the other woman replied. "Also for agreeing to do the story in the first place. I realize that this is a small health facility, and—"

"And also the first of its kind in the nation. It's the sort of story which deserves national coverage. I understand what the federal cutbacks have done to your program, and what this center would do if you had the funds to complete the other wing. So look at it as a public service announcement. Maybe it will even open a few pockets in the private sector."

"I certainly hope so," Dr. Hussein shrugged. "Otherwise, the construction comes to a halt next week. Our staff has already been cut in half. As a result, our appointment list has grown to the point where some women are waiting months to see a doctor."

"Are you talking about women who call up because they're ill?"

"It hasn't come to *that* yet. It may soon. But even for women who want to schedule a routine pelvic exam and pap smear, it is going to result some very disastrous personal consequences."

Crystal nodded, beginning to jot down notes furiously. "How much difference can a month or two make?"

"Forgive me," Dr. Hussein smiled gravely, "but that simply isn't the issue. For most of these women, the examination is months *overdue*. Often *years*. Either they haven't got the money—and haven't heard of us—or else they think it doesn't matter. It's remarkable how even intelligent, highly educated women ignore the routine exam. When we say once a year—and twice a year for the women who are DES babies—it is for a very good reason. But so many ignore it. Among your colleagues, do you think it is any different?"

"I really couldn't say," Crystal shrugged.

"And yourself?"

"I . . . mmmmm. Let me think: If Marcie is twelve-and-a-half, then . . . I really . . ."

"Can't remember?" Dr. Hussein shrugged, then turned back to Crystal, this time with the softness in her almond-shaped eyes gone. "This is what the story might also be about, Crystal. Perhaps you should consider having the examination yourself, to explain what it is like."

"I'll think about it," Crystal smiled.

"The examination takes no more than twenty-five minutes—including waiting for the test results. Under the circumstances, I would be pleased to conduct the interview in an examination room—after you have had a routine . . ."

Crystal thought about it. It was the sort of story which would probably bore the male half of her audience, and possibly threaten a good deal of the women as well. Definitely out of character for the chaste-yet-sensuous image the experts were cooking up.

And if it managed to challenge them, and save a few lives as well, it would be worth every bit of the flak.

"You're on," Crystal smiled. "Tomorrow morning?"

"Ten o'clock. The camera crew may want to wait half an hour. I just hope that there won't be any delay in the waiting room."

"Without a wait I would hardly feel like I was going to the doctor," Crystal laughed, standing up and following her out into the unfinished corridor. "See you at ten."

"I'll be he's really dynamite," Crystal brooded out loud, as Lauren's gull-wing Mercedes roared into third gear and screeched around Mulholland's torturous curves.

Lauren gripped the steering wheel a bit tighter, but her face remained calm, impassive. Maybe even the slightest bit friendly.

She glanced over at Crystal, studying her in the twilight for the thousandth time out of the corner of her eye. Tonight, the Rainbow Kid had pulled out all the stops. From the lip gloss and deep eye shadow and upstaging new coif, to the piercing turquoise contact lenses. To the purple silk blouse which—she couldn't help noticing—had set a new low in her phenomenally plunging record of necklines.

She thought back to Crystal's grand entry yesterday, at the tail end of the Rothmore taping. The way she had immediately made a spectacle of herself for his benefit, smiling and posing and sweet-talking, playing the Southern belle for all it was worth.

All right, darlin', she remembered thinking, *if thayat's the way you wan' it: Why Sugarplum, that means WAR!"*

Somehow, sitting beside her as they sped toward the awaiting studio bash, Lauren found herself in the unthinkable position of almost liking her nemesis. Definitely a first.

Come to think of it, in light of the Imagus invasion and the need for daily cooperation on the media probe, it made sense. And while there had been nothing spectacularly pleasant in the truce after Rob's death, it had proved pretty useful.

". . . To tell you the truth," Crystal rambled on in the dark, "I knew it was a mistake the moment I introduced the two of you. I should've known that he'd take one look at you and . . ."

"Ted?"

"Just who did you think I was talking about?"

Lauren shrugged, smiling as she recalled once again the morning jog which had dissolved into a champagne breakfast. Then done a languorous fade upstairs in his bedroom. If he never made the *Guinness Book of Records*, he had already warmed a niche for himself in the Conrad Hall of Fame. "Guess I owe you one," she said, not unpleasantly.

"At least."

But in fact, at the moment, Dr. Ted Rothmore was a million miles from her mind. He had been ever since the appearance of Bob Radin. For the twenty-four-hours, she had been virtually drifting on automatic pilot. Feeling like the world and the newsroom could be someone else's burden for a change. For all she cared at the moment, Crystal Cooper could do a striptease on Now News.

Given the chance, she probably wasn't above it, either.

The worst part of it was, Lauren hadn't even rolled between the sheets with Bob. Not that she didn't want to. And he was certainly just as eager. But there was something so damned unhurried about the man. Like waiting all of that time just to get in touch with her, and follow up their introduction. Then being content to just sit and chat the night away in a quiet jazz club. A few tender squeezes, one prolonged kiss goodnight. And that was that.

He may have been an older man—but he wasn't *that* old. There was just something about him that exuded calm. And sufficiency. Whatever made him tick, he was like no one she had ever met. Certainly not like the stereotype of the Hollywood producer.

For starters, there was clear admiration glowing in his eyes. But not hunger. He didn't seem desperate to ravage her. Or even the industry. At forty-nine, he had a list of credits a mile long. four or five big box office movies, including two supersellers. Yet even more than success, he exuded an aura of contentment.

Apparently it was infectious. For the first time in months, Lauren's constant companion—the little Valium vial she kept at her side, remained undisturbed. *If only he could find a way to bottle it,* she grinned, pulling into the driveway and catching her first glimpse of the plate glass living room wall, and several dozen figures writhing in ecstasy, silhouetted in soft neon light.

"Feast or famine," she sighed as the gull-wing door hissed up toward the sky. She remembered hearing of a French disease referred to dubiously as *crise de foie*, caused by too much of the good life. She thought of a steady diet of Rothmore and Radin, and felt a shudder of delight run down her spine.

Eyeing her strangely, Crystal remained sitting in the passenger seat.

"Well, what are we waiting for?" Lauren shrugged, turning toward the pathway leading to the front step.

"For the answer to my question: How in hell do I open this thing?"

"Snap off the release, push up the lock button, then pull back on the handle."

"Oh, is that all?" Crystal performed the sequence indicated and watched with amusement as the gull-wing door actually did spring open.

"Sorry I didn't hear you," Lauren offered, as the two wound their way up a spiralling flagstone walkway.

"Do you mean when I said 'How in hell do I get out?' for the second time or the third? Or about a dozen other things I mentioned on the ride over? Now don't get angry at me: But Lauren, you are downright spacy these days."

Ignoring her now with malice of forethought, Lauren sped up the remaining tier of steps and through the bulbous art deco door. "It must be more serious than I thought with me," she frowned. "I never thought I'd see the day when Crystal Cooper could call *anyone* spacy."

Crystal paused at the door to smoothe out the gathered waist of her ruffled silk St. Tropez dress—and also to give Lauren enough time to make her entrance. Things were going well between them, for a change. And she was *not* about to fuel the fires which had taken so many months to lower to a slow burn.

Glancing at the mushrooming stained glass framing the squat arched doorway, she grasped the handle and pushed through, wondering just how high-powered this party's greeting line would be. If it was like half of the other industry soirees the RedRock publicist wangled them invitations to, the sky was the limit. The last one had featured a guest list that read like the credits trailing at the end of half a dozen current movies. Between spending half of the evening *saying how-do-you do's,* and the other half saying farewells, she had never even made it to the buffet.

Once again, Joel had cancelled at the last minute. In spite of the fact that he knew how much *she* disliked going to these things unescorted. And although she understood how much *he* hated these things, it did little to make her feel better as she burst into yet another Hollywood scene alone. "Maybe it'll be different, once he finally scores the big one," she sighed. Knowing that at the rate his novel and screenplays were going, it might be one hell of a wait.

On the other side of the foyer door, the sculpted art deco hall was virtually deserted. The rock music was at once ear-shattering. Hovering at nose level was a cloud of marijuana smoke which *had* to be sufficient to set off any smoke detector designed.

And spread a giggly contact high throughout the block.

"Whatever their latest box office blockbuster may be," she groaned, "it *isn't* the Sound of Music." Vaguely searching for Lauren—or any other familiar face in the crowd—she wound her way through the immense library, along the ringing gallery of the solar greenhouse, and into the cavernous living room.

For once, she was in no danger of being cornered by a hungry agent, a horny plumbing fixtures magnate, or anyone else. In fact, the house was decked wall-to-wall with zombies so stoned that they could only writhe to the jackhammer beat, or nod out silently in cushions scattered along the glass wall.

She gazed at the tableau with wonder. It was pure Hollywood alright. Gauging from the dozens of faces she recognized from the Polo Lounge, *The Hollywood Reporter*, and the tube, it was decidedly upper crust. Tonight the theme was definitely Cooler-than-Thou, and they were playing it to the hilt.

Normally sedate Sassoon groomed hair was frizzled and teased into careless manes, and Galanos and Beene hadn't made it past the door. It was rhinestone jump suits and feather boas. Peek-a-boo blouses and leopard-skin belts. And the ever-present red glow of joints and pipes, lighting up the faces which tossed her a knowing nod, then focused on the matter at hand: getting blown away.

"I'm Steve Welborn," yelled a voice in her left ear. Crystal turned to find herself staring at a thirtyish man in full punk regalia. "Glad you *could make it.*"

"*Quite a scene,*" she replied *dubiously*, staring at the host. Suddenly, it all added up. This was a party to celebrate the conclusion of shooting for *A Nymphet Vampire in Rome*. A film which had the *dubious* distinction of being the first combination kid porn/horror flick to achieve major studio backing. And an ad and promo budget guaranteed to make it the most vaunted film of the year.

"*The Klone Tones are fucking incredible,*" he snorted. "*New wave band from the big apple.*"

"They're *too much,*" she nodded, while her eyes sought an escape route. Next thing she knew, this undernourished exploitation artist would ask her to dance the robot with him, or else . . .

"Care for some toot?" he nudged her.

"Some what?"

"You know. *Toot*" He mimed a line of powder sailing into his flaring nostrils, punctuating the demonstration by squashing one side of his nose with his finger, while the other nostril made a weird sucking sound.

So that was how you did it. How glamorous. "Not just yet," she said smiling graciously.

"Whenever you're ready, Crystal," he shrugged, turning to intercept a more promising guest. "Lemme know when you're ready. In the meantime, the bar is set up in the game room. And remember: *Mi casa es su casa.*"

Not in your life, she laughed, nodding as he bade her *ciao* and sank back into the crowd.

Fending off the sporadic invitations to dance that were screamed in her ears, Crystal headed upstairs and burst through the bathroom door, determined to find a moment of peace and quiet. But the noise blasted in through the air ducts, while a rumbling bass riff plowed through the walls and the muffled groans of the crowd echoed in the tiled room.

In the muted golden light splashing down from silvered bulbs concealed behind a carved mahogany valance she spied a row of apothecary jars lining a shelf in the corners. "Sopors," "white crosses," "reds" and "poppers." If the first three were anything like amyl nitrate, then it more than accounted for the gonzo look in the guests' eyes. "I think I'll check into the rest of these tomorrow," she said, putting a few of each in her purse. "They don't look like aspirin to me. Maybe Ted Rothmore knows more about them. It might be a good excuse to . . ."

"Mmmmm, Mick," cried a voice in the shower stall. Startled, Crystal turned to find a couple casually exploding into a pretzel-shaped love act.

"Heyyy," he cried, "aren't you Crystal Cooper? Listen luv, there's plenty of room in here. Why don't you join us?"

She stared for a moment at the rock star's shattered pupils, then at the dull leer of his companion—through the doorway. As she ran out, she heard his drugged out, sing-song voice mumbling, "Those American news bitches are so damned tight-assed. Back in England . . ."

Pausing to accept champagne from a passing servant in jeans, Crystal headed onto the balcony, gratefully breathing in the sultry and sullied night air, and what would have to pass for silence.

"Crystal, *there* you are," an attractive, slim woman called out from the other end. Nearing the petite figure leaning dramatically against the grillwork railing, the flickering tiki torch cast shadows on a familiar face.

"Violet," she gushed with relief, "what's a nice woman like you doing in a place like this?"

"Simply reeling," she laughed. "From the decibels, darling. And trying uselessly to keep my eye on Rick. Anyway, allow me to introduce a very *sympatique* rival of yours. Adam Ward, *je voudrais te presenter ma chère amie*, Crystal Cooper."

"I'm *delighted*," he grinned, sweeping into a formal bow and brushing her hand lightly with his lips. "Welcome to the Hollywood Old-timers Club. Our motto is: Over thirty, and *Thank God*." He slid over next to Violet, and made room for Crystal on his other side, appraising her every curve as she settled onto the lounge chair.

"I don't care if he *is* from KJJX," Violet beamed, "I still say that it's high time you two met."

"No politics tonight," he laughed with a dismissing wave of his hand. "I've waited too damn long for the introduction to let it stoop to shop talk . . . Though the keys to our network are yours, my dear, the moment you give me the word."

Crystal stared at his profile, taking in the satin eyepatch she had spotted several times at the Polo Lounge. He was conservatively dressed—almost formally—in a serge French-cut suit which made him stand out from the rest of the revellers like a diamond ring in a gumball machine.

"I think I'll case the joint for my randy Greek God," Violet said bravely. "In case I don't make it back, Crystal, let's get together soon. If you could just free up a lunch or . . ."

"I'd love to. As a matter of fact, I tried you on Sunday, but . . ."

"I know. You hit the machine. Did you like it? I mean, Lady Macbeth."

"Of course," Crystal hedged.

"No. I mean *really* like it? I put it on expressly for David Zanuck. In case he needed to get in touch with me about . . . Well, I'll fill you in on that one later. In the meantime, I'll leave you to this perfect gentleman, while I track down my own knight in tarnished armor. Some day . . . *À bientôt.*"

"*Ciao,*" Adam whispered, immediately rivetting his attention on Crystal. "I hardly would have expected you to turn up at a soirée like Wellborn's. Or myself, for that matter. To think that a third of those folks have *kids* waiting at home—and appearances to make tomorrow—dressed to the nines. Sometimes I think we're all a bunch of chameleons in this town. I'll bet half of those bumping and grinding corpses are closet conservatives."

Crystal nodded, wondering just how many shades Adam Ward could turn when he wasn't putting on the charm. The way he was pouring it on tonight, she might never know.

One thing was for certain: in Hollywood, nobody made it to the top just by hard work and Dale

Carnegie magic. Sitting at the head of his rival station, Adam undoubtedly had his own share of hatchets to bury.

You're getting cynical, she chided silently, his honeyed words trying to make inroads on her senses. She gazed intently into his strong, handsome features made more exotic by the eyepatch, remembering Maxine Hong Kingston's remark about Americans and how their piercing gazes always seemed to search for lies.

Her ears perked up as she heard the faint echo of a familiar laugh, issuing from the parked cars below.

"You *weren't* kidding," Lauren laughed, staring at the silver gull wing Mercedes parked directly behind her own.

"Of course not," the tall dark haired man agreed in a rich bass voice. "Not about our similarities in cars—or music. As a matter of fact, I had an ulterior motive in luring you out here. Just two minutes from here is the most spectacular collection of classical records and tapes you've ever seen. It'll put your old radio studio to shame."

"I know when I'm being challenged," she bantered back. "I'm right behind you."

Crystal watched the twin Mercedes roar down the driveway with envy. Then she made a determined effort to turn her attentions to Adam Ward. Maybe she could salvage the evening with a dinner invitation. Why should *she* spend the night alone?

"Quite a view, isn't it" Bob Radin smiled proudly, as Lauren, sliding into the magnificent marble tub beside him, let the steaming water slowly creep up her body onto her breasts.

Her flawless skin glinted golden in the light of the tapered candles. His eyes lingered longingly over her, with an intensity which startled her. Everywhere else there was only calm now. A pile of birch logs momentarily flared in the fireplace, then returned to a quiet glowing red. Beyond the open curtains, West Hollywood and Beverly Hills winked lazily on and off in the hazy evening air.

The Bach recorder sonatas faded out, only to be followed by the languorous strains of Pachelbel's canon. Lauren wondered if Bob was always surrounded by sumptuous music, like the aura of peacefulness he never seemed to surrender. Somehow, it hardly seemed her speed. And yet . . .

"I was hoping you might show up at Wellborn's crazy as that seems." Bob punctuated his words with gentle sponge strokes, caressing her neck and back with unconcealed tenderness.

"Mmmmmm," Lauren replied, shifting into his hands and closing her eyes as the heat slowly engulfed her in hypnotic bliss. Through her half-opened lashes, she could just make out the massive redwood beams supporting the coffered ceiling, the antique lacquered chests scattered about on Chinese rugs, and the elegant oak four-poster dominating the room.

Sliding down a fraction more, she turned toward him, allowing the silky soft sponge to lick the inside of her arm, urging it to stray onto her breasts. Her thoughts wandered back to Ted Rothmore's Beverly Hills mansion, and the medieval tapestries ostentatiously hung overhead. The two men could not be more dissimilar in taste.

Opening her eyes, she found them locked in a gaze with Radin's—gray, open, loving. Physically, there was no comparison between the two men. Bob stood almost a head taller than Ted. His proportions were sinewy, not stocky. Between the fine aquiline nose and the shock of silver tinged-black hair curling at the back of his neck, Bob Radin was second in pure physical presence only to Michelangelo's David.

"Your turn," she laughed, playfully snatching away the sponge and eagerly applying it to his muscular back. On the far side of the tub, she could just make out the tips of his toes, startlingly distant from the rest of his body.

She traced the outlines of his powerful biceps with her fingertips, allowing the sponge to plunge noiselessly onto the marble ledge. *If only he had the Rothmore spark.*

But there was no driving competition as he turned toward her and gently raised his tender hands up to her face. No challenge as she brought her lips forcefully to his own, probing his mouth hungrily with her tongue.

Lauren slid his hand down onto her breast, pressing it hard between them. Arching her back, she pulled him onto her, feeling his massive cock rigid against her navel.

Sliding back onto the heated marble slab floor, she thrust her pelvis toward him, wrapping her agile legs around his hips. The quiet, controlled motion of his lips and hands was maddening. Lauren sank her fingernails into the small of his back, wanting to ravage and be ravaged. To flail against his massive sculpted form, have it thrust into her with crushing force, bearing down as she heaved tirelessly upward, sending them both into orbit. *What in hell would it take to speed up Radin's fuse?*

As if in answer he lifted her in his arms, and gently laid her on an oversized, suede chaise longue. "I promised you tonight wouldn't end in a wrestling match," he said softly in his matchless baritone. "And I intend to keep that promise."

He brought a slender taper up to her face, then

purposefully trailed it over her shoulders and neck. He stared long at the flickering shadows toying with her breasts, then continued the downward sweep of the candle. "You're even more beautiful than I dreamed," he marveled, placing the dim light off to the side, nuzzling his cheek gently over her abdomen.

She clutched his head between her hands and pressed him to her, then pulled him up to her lips. His tongue danced on the soft folds of her neck, then hungrily sought out her own.

"*At last,*" Lauren groaned with relief, when his fingers began to lightly trace circles over her moist labia, increasing their pressure as they parted her willing lips and lingered on her clitoris. Spreading her legs with a guttural moan, Lauren reached out with both hands, wrapping them around his straining cock and leading him in.

Instead, Bob pulled away. He gently moved his mouth down her neck and slowly caressed her hard nipples, following the candle-lit path. With stubborn insistence he shrugged off her frenzy, kissing every inch of her body until his tongue reached its destination. Only then did he respond, moving his head faster and faster in counterpoint to the arching of her spine.

A few seconds later, Lauren's madly gyrating hips crashed down into a spasm of relief. *He barely even got started,* she realized in astonishment, surrendering to the scattered sensations battering her body and drawing up her knees with a cry.

For a moment there was only the dancing strings of a Mendelssohn concerto. Lauren felt her legs slowly being lowered. She spread her thighs once more to receive him.

Then he was surrounding her, his massive chest blanketing her as his lips paid homage to her. He thrust fully into her, exploding with a fury she would never have believed, kindling an even more blinding response inside her.

He made love to her until dawn.

"Thank you for giving an 'un-hip' man a terrific evening," Adam laughed. He kissed her "Hollywood style"—a quick peck on each cheek, then shut the door and escorted her to the tower.

"Well, he certainly lived up to his reputation as the most honorable bachelor in town," Crystal observed with a shrug, watching the Lincoln Continental with the KJJX license plate recede into the traffic on Avenue of the Stars. "Three hours of pure charm, a ride home, and not a single paw print. Even opened the door for me. What a perfect gentleman . . . maybe he could tutor Joel. At least about being a gracious escort."

On the other side of the entryway sat Juan, busy leafing through a racy paperback. Stealing peeps over the pages as she struggled with the massive glass door.

"The senora ees so *bee-u-tiful,*" he exclaimed when she pushed through, tossing aside the book to ogle her cleavage more fully. "And on such a night . . . *Estas magnifico, guapa.* May I help you upstairs with your things?"

"You mean my handbag? Or my silk jacket?"

"Anything the senora wants."

"I think I'll manage. But maybe you can manage the door next time?"

Quien sabe?" he pouted, leaving her to push through the second door and into the lobbyway.

Talk about laid back men she fumed. *Maybe Adam Ward can do seminars.*

* * *

"That fucking bitch," Dale screamed at the steering wheel, "de*mand*ing that I ask CJ for a raise—or better yet, Sloan. That's a laugh—ISN'T IT?"

The car lurched to a stop, narrowly avoiding a culvert.

"Just who the hell does she think she is anyway?" he slurred drunkenly. "Trying to pussywhip me like that. *Sheesh.*"

"She's your *wife* Dale," admonished a voice.

"*Your wife, Dale,*" echoed the chorus. "Your wife. Yourwifeyourwifeyour . . ."

"*Shaddup,*" he bellowed, slamming his fist against the steering wheel and recoiling in pain. "Shut up . . . Please . . . please don't start again. I beg of you . . . I'll do anything you say."

Whimpering, he took a last slug from the pint flask in his pocket and tossed it away into the bushes, the tears rolling uncontrollably down his cheeks.

"You're all crazy," he hissed at the voices in the shadows. "You're crazy. But *I'll show you!*"

Lunging across the gravel parking area leading to the West Hollywood bungalow, he slammed against the front door and began pounding on it. "Open up," he pleaded, kicking it. "Open up, it's Dale."

"There's no one home," called a voice in his brain. "No one at all."

"Please . . . Penny I know you're . . . in there. Let me . . . in."

He crumpled on the stoop and shuddered, oblivious to the creaking of the rusty hinges. "Look at you," Penny cried, "you're a fucking mess. Stevens, you're a worm. You disgust me."

Cringing, he stared up at the woman dressed in black leather, shivering at the sight of the bullwhip clenched in her dragon-nailed hand. "P-Penny," he whispered in astonishment.

"It ain't the cops. Though you're gonna wish it was by the time I'm through with you tonight. Dale, I'm going to whip you black and blue." She threw back her long, dyed hair and laughed.

"You *are?*" His foggy eyes glimmered with excitement.

"You've been very naughty, haven't you?"

He nodded enthusiastically.

"Then you need to be punished. But first you have to lick my boots. Now get your ass in here. *Quick.*"

Trembling, he stumbled back onto his feet and plunged through the doorway. A second later, he doubled up in pain as her razor-sharp heel dug into his belly.

"You're a worm," she sneered, slamming the door behind him. "So crawl like one . . ."

Forty

"Crystal? Is it really you?"

"Who in hell is this?" she demanded, staring into the receiver. At 3 p.m., sitting in her office, who else would be trying to prepare a broadcast?

"Are you wearing that slinky golden silk shirt again, the one that wraps around your boobs like . . ."

"You-lousy-stinking-pervert," she spat, slamming down the phone. She clutched her hands to her breasts and felt her heart pounding furiously. Then her left hand slid down to the pea-sized lump Dr. Hussein had discovered.

Fourteen hours. She shuddered. In fourteen hours, she would be back at the Women's Institute, lying on the operating table, in the O.R. she had visited with the camera crew this morning. Knocked out, with an IV tube plunged into her arm, while the scalpel penetrated her and isolated the tiny tumor. Next would come the decision about whether they would remove her breast—or how much could be saved.

Since this morning's "routine" exam, she had been walking through a living nightmare. Waiting powerlessly for the broadcast to be completed, so she could grab the suitcase sitting in the corner and drive to the hospital. Gazing down at her shaking hands, she could just imagine the green-gloved fingers as they . . .

"*Snap out of it,*" she screamed to the wall, "you're

only making it worse. Come on, *Que sera, sera*—and all the rest of that bullshit." She wondered if the coiner of that timeless phrase had ever faced a mastectomy in the morning.

All the frightening questions she had ever heard and read raced through her mind. What if it is cancer? Could I accept a mastectomy? How would I look with only one breast? My breasts have always been such an important part of me; would men be repulsed? What about Joel—he's always talking about my breasts or my ass—how would he feel? *Would I ever be the same?*

Trying to still the voice inside of her, Crystal finally told herself, "It's only a biopsy. Get ahold of yourself!"

Once again, she turned to the piles of news stories scattered across her desk. How much could the stock market's dropping two points really matter at a time like . . .

"I got your message," Dale pronounced flatly, barging in through the unlocked cubicle door. "Just now. But before we go into whatever you have to say . . . We had a meeting today about the initial Imagus report. It was hardly encouraging—where you and Lauren are concerned. Sloan is furious, and I don't blame her one bit."

Crystal was dumbfounded. By the News Director whose voice she barely even recognized. And by one of the clumsiest examples of bad timing she had ever seen. All day long, she had been debating whether or not to tell him what was up. But looking into his distant eyes, framed behind the square glasses, she suddenly realized that she could no longer trust him.

"We want you to ease up. RedRock is paying a staff of two hundred to dig up the news and write it. Look at you: two hours to broadcast, and you're swimming in unwritten news copy. Crystal, all your contract calls for is promotional appearances, sitting and reading one hour a day and a few special features. That's all we're expecting from you. If you would only stop trying to perfect the broadcast, and leave that to me, you would have some time to work a bit more on your image. Including cleaning up the accent a bit."

"I'll take it under advisement, Dale. In the meantime, I have to take off the rest of the week. Personal reasons. I left a message for CJ and . . ."

"Does Sloan know about this?"

"I didn't really see any need to inform her personally."

"Oh you *didn't?* And just what — if I may ask, is so pressing that you have to disappear with five hours notice? I'm sure that if it's that urgent, you can divulge the problem to your News Director."

"I said it's personal. Family emergency."

"That is hardly sufficient," he growled, reddening. "Now tell me: what the hell is going on?"

"I don't want to discuss it. It's a personal emergency. And that's in my contract, too. Section 43A."

"I'm sure CJ will understand," he said sarcastically, backing toward the door. "But the rest of what we said stands. Whenever you return from your little secret crisis. It's time for you to stop banging your head against the wall. And making enemies in the newsroom. Keep your nose clean and leave the dirty work to the rest of the staff. Got it?"

"*Get out,*" she snapped, watching in distress as he immediately turned and bolted from the office.

For a minute, Crystal looked at the second indicator sweeping around her digital clock in silence. Then she finally resolved to place the call to the Wyndale School.

"Marcie Benjamin, please," she ordered the voice on the other end of the line.

"One moment. Who may I say is call . . ."

"Just put her on the phone."

Her fingers drummed mindlessly on her typewriter, as the girl breathed a series of expletives under her breath, then dropped the phone with a loud crash.

"Hullo," came the lifeless greeting from her daughter. "This is Marcie Benjamin."

"It's Mom."

"Oh. Listen, I'm in the middle of studying for my midterms with a whole group of kids. Can I? . . ."

"No. You can't call me back. I . . . I won't be at home. I'm going to be checking into the hospital for a few days."

"Is something wrong?"

"I don't really know, darling. But the doctor found a lump in my breast and said it really couldn't wait. I'll find out tomorrow morning."

On the other end of the line, Marcie started to say something, then hesitated. "Uh, let me know how it turns out. Okay?"

"Of *course* I will." Didn't she even understand?

"Hey, Mom. Good luck, huh? Break a leg." Before she could reply, the phone clicked off.

"Crys?" a voice called at the door. "An hour 'til broadcast. Can I come in?"

"Sure, Lauren." She watched her enter, staring with envy at the superbly healthy body sweeping toward her. Was there just a hint of gloating in the amber eyes? "What's up?"

"I brought you a present," Lauren replied matter-of-factly, with a sheepish grin.

"I'm *not* sick yet."

Shrugging, Lauren brought her hands out from around her back, then deposited their contents on Crystal's desk. A glass of orange juice, and a small capsule. "It's fresh squeezed," she noted. "Now bottoms up."

"Thanks But I'm not interested in taking any of your . . ."

"Well, I'm not interested in hearing any of your bullshit. You have exactly two seconds to down that Valium, before I *shove* it down your throat. I heard your little exchange with our illustrious News Director. And I've also been watching the way you've been wandering around the bullpen this afternoon. You're not functioning. And if you can't be persuaded to take it out of self-preservation, then let me try another tack: *no one* is going to fuck up tonight's broadcast. Now *get going*." She planted her heels defiantly in place, crossing her hands on her chest.

Crystal stared tentatively at the capsule, then surrendered.

"Thank you," Lauren said, turning and heading back into her own office.

A second later, her typewriter was clicking furiously on the other side of the wall. Sputtering on and off, and occasionally interrupted by stifled curses.

"What in hell has *her* so shaken?" Crystal glared. Yet somehow it comforted her to think she might be the cause. Settling in to her typewriter, she began once more to plod through tonight's stories, the tranquilizer slowly weaving its way through her system.

Ease off? She rifled through the growing pile of news stories, grateful that she was once more into the frenzy. *The hell I will.*

There was more to anchoring a news show than reading idiot cards and monitors. It was all well and fine to leave it to the pros. But was it really that long ago that President Carter's aborted attempt to rescue the hostages resulted in disaster? Leaving it to the pros, an LA anchor had insisted on telling one-and-a-half million viewers that only three men had died—while the rest of the world was already mourning the rest. So much for the pros.

If not for crawling in behind the scenes, she never would have visited the Women's Health Center in the first place. At this point she almost wished she hadn't.

". . . Now here is the first in a three-segment report on health care in an era of shrinking government funding."

Crystal felt her mouth miraculously tightening into a smile. And holding it as the cassette began to roll . . . .

"I'm standing in the heart of the unfinished Women's Health Institute of Greater L.A., with Dr. Sandra Hussein, the program chairwoman. Next week, the workers will disappear, and construction in the main wing will grind to a halt. As in so many other facilities around the nation, the dollars have stopped trickling in . . ."

Crystal stared blankly into the dots of light in the studio monitor, the smile pasted firmly on her lips. This was where Dr. Hussein explained that only two per cent of women examined actually turned up symptoms of possible cancer. "Welcome to the top of the class," she could hear herself thinking while the camera swept across the exposed girders and half-mounted electrical lights.

Across the news desk, she could feel Lauren's eyes, burning into her with high intensity *sympathy*. It was easy enough to feel now? Wasn't it? Especially when as of tomorrow, Lauren might be Now News—in its *entirety*.

Crystal ripped through the final minutes in a fog. The second the lights went out, she leapt from her seat and made a beeline for the steel door, brushing hurriedly through the crowd of puzzled spectators.

"Crystal," Dale called out, grabbing her shoulder as

393

he raced to keep up with her ferocious stride, "I wanted to apologize for . . ."

"Don't bother," she shot back, turning to look at his bloodshot eyes, and catching a whiff of the tell-tale aroma of breath freshener. "I mean, no apologies are necessary," she softened, relieved to see him accept the remark, and give up the idea of another cross-examination.

He nodded knowingly, and dropped away, wandering over toward the wall monitors.

Throwing open her office door, Crystal bent down to grab her overnight bag and was immediately caught in a bear-hug embrace.

"I came the moment I got your message. I just don't know what to say. You don't think they'll . . . " Joel blurted out.

She shrugged and buried her face in his chest, pulling him tighter to her. "Let's get going," she sighed.

"I thought that we could have a little candlelight supper first. Then I'll . . ."

"No food. Doesn't mix with the anesthetic."

"It all seems so rushed. Don't you think that you should get a second opinion. If it were my body, I'd sure as hell . . ."

"Honey, don't treat me like a dumb blond. Investigative journalism happens to be my profession. I already spoke to a second doctor. And a third and a fourth and a fifth. There's no choice but a biopsy. It's already *way* overdue." She kissed him lightly on the lips and shook off the next round of questions. "You drive."

"Where're we going?"

"The Century Towers."

"And then?"

"You are going to make the most breath-taking love to me imaginable. You are going to tell me how much you love me—whether you really do or not."

"Of course I love you. You know that."

"Then it should be very easy for you. Afterwards, we will drop me off at the hospital. Now no more questions: I want to get the hell out of this place."

On tip toes, she kissed the tears from his eyes, then pressed her lips tenderly onto his as he held her gently in his arms.

In silence she handed him the suitcase, locked the door, and strolled down the corridor. Defiantly she wrapped her arm tightly around his waist as they cut through the newsroom. Nodding affirmingly to the gaping gnomes peering out from over their terminals.

Forty-one

Lauren paced wearily back and forth in the waiting room, like a caged animal.

She focused on the smugly blank face of the ward nurse, wanting to wring some information out of her flabby neck.

Six stinking hours. So far, all she knew was that the operation was over. How in hell did they ever get the goods on Reagan's gunshot wounds so fast? Recovery room security here was tighter than a nuclear plant. Not a hint of anything beneath the mechanical half-smiles and unseeing stares of the clones in surgical green and white.

"Maybe if I called Ted?" She raced to the phone booth and stepped inside. Fishing for change, she hesitated. After discussing Crystal, she might have to do some explaining—mainly about the way she had simply vanished for two nights, ducking his phone calls left and right. Besides, Dr. Ted Rothmore had no relationship to the patient, as far as she knew.

Then again, what relationship did Lauren have to Crystal? Half a year of antagonism. And despite a bit of occasional camaraderie, forced upon them by round-the-clock proximity, they had remained adversaries.

Perhaps Crystal had helped fan the fires. But Lauren had to admit that hers was the motivating force. Because from the very beginning she had been terrified of Crystal. Instead of waiting for the slow siege which never did materialize, she had rushed in like a crusading knight, capturing the first prize and then immediately launching her next attack.

Each clash led to the next. Automatically. From make-up skirmishes to air-time battles, or arguments over lead stories. And then came Ted Rothmore. Taking him by storm—right out from under Crystal. That had been a *real* victory. And a blow below the belt.

The way they bickered off-camera, it was as though Crystal's neckline mattered more than Sadat's funeral. "Did she ever suspect," Lauren wondered to the randomly selected page of the phone directory, "that I might be every bit as sick of it as she? Of the war of attrition wearing us both down?" Of spearing the brass rings as the carousel spun faster and faster around. Each time she had to lean farther and farther out, until her balance began to slip.

Crystal, Bob, Ted. RedRock and the Imagus School. The media investigation which kept pulling her deeper and deeper into shark-infested waters. They were all swirling through her mind now, racing and racing until the faces blurred and became indistinguishable.

Each big break and each sexual conquest just led her to another. Unless she found a way to break the cycle, once more her ladder to the stars would leave a series of enemies on each rung. *Casual* casualties, just like Crystal. In the end, that's what they had become, and that was the end of it.

Why had she come? Just to bury Crystal's career, to certify that she would be mained—*finished?* Wasn't it just the tension of not knowing for sure that had driven her here, when she should have been back at Number One Sunset, working with Jewel Beale on the first post-Crystal broadcast?

What other possible explanation could there be? She stared out at the rows of plastic chairs and grim faces. Still no sign of Joel. Maybe that was why she had come: *Because she knew no one else would.* Because beneath the professional bonds which tied them to one another like bitter Siamese twins was an even stronger link: loneliness. She thought of confessing this to Crystal and burst into laughter. It was all too absurd. *Hysterical.*

Loneliness. Crystal would never believe that one. And yet, it was true. They were each alone in a fight for identity and survival in the cruelest jungle of all: Hollywood.

Somehow, Lauren knew that if the situation was reversed, Crystal would drop anything to be there with her. "Well, I'm glad I did it," Lauren thought proudly. "Someone has to be with her when she wakes up. Where is that bastard Joel anyway? I bet he won't come. She'll be heartbroken."

Lauren walked to the florist shop off the lobby and purchased a dozen long-stemmed roses. On the card, she printed "Get out of that hospital bed and into mine as soon as possible. Love, Joel." That sounds like him, she thought wryly. She instructed the clerk to have the flowers delivered to room 601 immediately. Mission accomplished, she crossed the waiting room, hands trembling as she paused to light a cigarette.

"Any news yet?" she snapped at the ward nurse. But the nurse shrugged her off once again.

Lauren rushed to the drinking fountain and downed another Valium. She glanced at her watch and hesitated before picking up the receiver on the pay phone by the fountain. "Well, here goes," she thought. "I never thought I'd miss a broadcast for *anything.* Live and learn." The thought made Lauren grin as she heard the ringing over the line.

"Hello. SBN," came the operator's sparkling voice.

Probably a new one, Lauren snidely observed. "This is Lauren Conrad. Please put me through to Dale Stevens—no, Sloan Schwartz, at once."

"Yes, Ms. Conrad," the voice bubbled. "Right away."

As the muzak bleated over the line, Lauren anticipated Sloan's high-pitched drone and a screaming battle about her own "urgent personal emergency," and the fact that poor Jewel Beale would have to go it alone.

A promising fight if ever there was one. And Lauren intended to enjoy every second of it.

Crystal cowered in the back row of bleachers. The auditorium lights blazed down on her, and she felt the oppressive heat causing rivulets of sweat to pour down beneath her borrowed graduation dress. She could picture the crescents of moisture forming under her arms. And just how her junior high classmates would have a field day with that one.

She gazed down at the oversized dress hanging limply on her skinny frame, and wanted to die. If only she had known, she could have saved up the money for a new dress in her bank account.

But neither she nor Rachael had ever dreamed that Sam Coopersmith would walk out on them—until it happened. One night he drove to a "poker game" and never returned. Taking his *schiksa* and all of the money in the joint account. Leaving them with a bankrupt, antiquated paper box company, and a collection of debts they could never repay.

She watched as people greeted her mother, revelling in sympathy in the front row. Milking it for all it was worth. Adolescent rage and guilt boiled up inside

Crystal, who fought to control the tears already beginning to fog up her tortoise-rimmed glasses.

She had been Sam's favorite all of her life. Now she could no longer defend him against the torrent of her mother's vilifications. Instead, when the screams became too vicious, she had to run out of the house clamping her hands over her ears.

At home, the remaining furniture was already covered. This afternoon, the moving van would arrive to cart it all away to the dreary row house in downtown Baltimore. The servants and the boat were already gone.

On Monday, Rachael would start her new job as a dry goods clerk. "Maybe then she won't make me call up Uncle Sollie any more," Crystal sighed. Perhaps the worst part of it all was being schlepped to the phone when the bills piled up, to call Daddy's brother and beg for help.

She stared at the row of boys flanking her and the tears renewed. She was skinny and gawky, and the butt of every whisper and wisecrack hissed across the tiny stage.

"At least I'm leaving here," she bitterly acknowledged. Moving downtown to a new school. There she would be anonymous. "And someday," she wearily told herself, "I'll be rich again. Glamorous. Not stodgy like Mama—but *chic*. I'll stand in front of crowds and there'll *never* be snickers. Or *pity*."

"*Crystal,*" boomed the loudspeaker, shaking her out of her reverie. Her hands dropped limply to her side as the girls in front of her whisked aside their satin and organdy gowns, content to let her wiggle down between them.

Seeing their condescending eyes, a shudder ran through the girl. She hesitated, eyeing the long, lonely distance to the podium, wondering if her legs would hold out.

"C'mon *Bean,*" sneered the gangly boy beside her, giving her a nudge with his elbow and waiting for her to dry out.

Tense seconds passed as she stood frozen, framed by her well-dressed classmates, the entire room staring at her.

Pulling her head even higher above the crowd, she straightened out her spine and forced her hands to unclench. "It's almost over," she coaxed herself, launching her slim legs slowly down the risers. Raising her budding breasts up defiantly, she walked with slow graceful strides toward the awaiting principal.

"Yes, I'm going to be beautiful," she declared, peering out of the thick lenses and searching for an affirming glance. She found it at the rear of the auditorium.

Looking small and vulnerable, his robust olive complexion pale and sickly, Sam was swaying nervously back and forth. Their eyes locked for an instant and she glowed. Sam had come to see her graduate. He loved her. She radiated the broad, effortless smile which her father recognized so well.

She reached out her arms to him, but he remained pinned in place. She struggled to break free as she stood still. Heads began to turn to the rear of the auditorium. Embarrassed, Sam bolted to the door.

No, she screamed, *don't leave me. I know I'll never see you again. Daddy . . .*

"*Crystal,*" boomed the principal's voice. "*Crystal?*"

Arms pinned, she struggled to break free. Her eyes opened hazily to a jumble of tubes and wires.

She sucked in air and felt the dull numbness in her chest. The faces were looming down at her. Lauren. "No," she moaned dully, feeling the empty ache growing sharper. "Nooo. Oh God, they . . ."

"It was benign!" Lauren shouted at her. "We just got the lab report. You're okay. Do you understand? They didn't have to operate."

She looked up at the animated features and exaggerated smile, trying to piece together their meaning. "Did they operate yet?" she moaned. "Tell them to hurry up and get it over with. The pain . . ."

When she drifted back into consciousness, her left hand was gently cradled over her breast. Beneath the bandages and the sheets, she felt it throbbing. Living, rising and falling gently with each breath.

"It's all there," Lauren assured her.

"Thank God. I was so afraid," Crystal whispered weakly. "I'm glad you're here, Lauren. Where's Joel?"

"He was here all afternoon," Lauren said soothingly, wondering if Crystal would detect the lie. "He just left. But he brought you the most beautiful long-stemmed roses. Look . . ." she pointed emphatically at the bouquet. "Here's the card."

Lauren was glad to see Crystal's smile while she read it. But she was furious with Joel for forcing her into this charade. Didn't that man have any compassion? Even she, who was hardly known as *Miss Caring Person of the Year,* had enough feeling to know that Crystal needed love and support now. How could a man who claimed to love a woman be so oblivious to her needs? Lauren shook her head. "We both need an infusion of new men in our lives," she thought.

Lauren idly flicked on the television news. It was about time for their daily broadcast. On the screen, a doll-sized Jewel Beale was delivering the Now News broadcast with an oddly-inflected sugary drawl. Crystal stared at the girl's toothy smile, then over at Lauren, trying to place what was wrong.

"Why is she doing our broadcast Lauren? Why aren't you up there telling Americans how they should think today?"

"Because I chose to be with you, curly top. That's why." Lauren felt slightly embarrassed. Kindness was a new experience for her.

Crystal immediately understood the sacrifice Lauren had made to be at her side. She had given up a chance to shine on the nightly news alone, sharing the spotlight with no one. Moreover, she had turned over the spot to Jewel Beale, who would be only too happy to have it permanently.

They watched in silence as Jewel delivered the newscast almost letter perfect.

"Boy, she's pulling out all the stops tonight," muttered Lauren. "She's probably sent mailgrams to all three networks, *Variety,* and the *Hollywood Reporter.*"

"Don't worry Lauren. She can't touch either of us now. She's no threat," Crystal reassured, squeezing Lauren's hand. "I won't ever forget your being here with me tonight. I didn't expect it, but I sure am grateful. Maybe now we can be friends, as well as partners." Crystal sank back into the blissful unawareness of sleep, still holding Lauren's hand.

Lauren sat there until dawn, trying to sort out her conflicting emotions. Slowly, a strange new feeling came over her—a feeling of peace.

Forty-Two

Crystal tied the sash of her Lucie-Ann maribou trimmed peignoir, then slowly made her way around the apartment, straightening as she went.

"A few days has done wonders," she observed glowingly. "For the apartment, for my head—even for my figure." She stood in profile before the full-length mirror, still giddy at the sight of the healthy, shapely contours of her body. Dr. Hussein's exercises had hurt like hell. But if they made her feel this good, she might even keep up with them. At least for a while.

For the first time in ages, there was real food in the fridge—not just yogurt, bread and coffee fixings. With all of the bouquets which kept arriving, it was starting to look like a botanical garden. Or something out of *Architectural Digest.*

She gazed at the spotless tile kitchen counters, the humming oven timer, and burst out laughing. Souffle in the oven, champagne in the freezer, and a waxed dining room table elegantly set for two. "How very *un*liberated," she nodded, loving every minute of this little domestic charade. "Maybe I should rush down to *Aprons Only* and pick up a frilly cover-up while I'm at it. That would give Joel something to think about."

And herself as well.

When the doorbell rang, she was ready for once. Perfectly curled wisps of golden hair framing her delicate face, and an irresistibly sexy negligee. Just in case he was thinking of her delicate condition—and planning on escaping untouched.

She leaned seductively against the doorframe, took a deep breath, then pulled it open and leapt into his arms.

"Well, *hello* there," Winston shrieked, a bit taken aback. "I knew you missed me, but . . . wow."

Caught up somewhere between amusement and disappointment, Crystal led him into the living room, wondering if it would be possible to clear him out in five seconds. But it *was* great to see him. Besides, he had already dropped melodramatically into the velvet chaise.

"Did you get my flowers?"

"You bet, Winston. That was awfully sweet of you. Especially the card. How many shifts did it take you to collect all of those signatures?"

"Actually I had to forge the last few, but it's the thought that counts."

"Don't keep me in suspense. How are things at RedRock?"

"Wild. Crazy. Throat-slitting. All of the usual stuff. Sloan is pushing her weight around a lot. And making quite a little stir with her latest flame."

"Don't tell me it's another one of the fair-haired adolescents from Sid's Agency."

"Wrong on both counts . . . it's Jewel Beale. And if you ask me, they could both do better."

"I *didn't* ask you. As far as I'm concerned, they *deserve* each other. But tell me about Dale. He called once and seemed pretty together, but it was early in the morning, and . . ."

"Well, he's wised up. A little."

"Thank God. His drinking was beginning to . . ."

"What I mean is: I *think* he's switched to vodka instead of scotch. Smelling like a rose. But polluted as ever."

"Oh."

"What're you frowning about. He'll pull through the crisis. Just like the rest of us . . . But tell me about you: you look good as new. Even better. Come to think of it, if the delicious aroma of food is any indication, I'd say that good old Winston just popped in at the wrong time."

"Not really. I'm *delighted*. Really."

"You sure? I simply *had* to see you, and I figured that since I was passing by on my way home . . ."

"From Sunset to West Hollywood via Century Towers? Now that's what I call creative driving."

"I've moved."

"Apparently. But I thought you loved your apartment. You certainly *spent* long enough locating it. And a fortune having it redone."

"Yeah, but the new place is . . . well it's really different. A little bit funky. Actually *very* funky. But the view is incredible. It's a carriage house on the old Valentino estate. And the main house is not to be believed. Faded elegance just bursting out all over."

She watched the tension spreading through his boyish features, and the misery settling in on his brow. "Considering the fact that it's so magnificent, you don't look particularly elated."

"It's Elliot's place. It was *his* idea."

"So?"

"So I'm a *queer*."

"What do you want me to say? That I'm *overjoyed?* I'm not. But I'm not shocked or disgusted, if that's what you're afraid of. As long as you're happy with it . . ."

"I'm *miserable*," he shouted. "I'm a lousy stinking faggot. Mrs. Jerome's nice sweet Yiddische boychick is a *feigalah*. I've got the guilties so bad I'm waking up in tears every lousy morning. What's worse, he's just *using* me to break into tv, the P.R. side of it. I *know* it. But I just don't have the guts to break loose. Every day I decide I'm moving out. Then I get home, take a few snorts, Big Daddy shows up, we start popping pills, and the next thing I know, we're back down on the Strip, cruising the bars."

"No wonder you can't make the decision. Sounds like you're tripping every second he's around. Just what on earth are you shoving into your bloodstream?"

"You name it. Speed, downers, coke, mescaline . . . Crystal, I'm *scared.*"

She threw an arm comfortingly around his shoulder, and felt his entire spine tighten.

"I'm sorry," he sobbed, making a beeline for the door, "I really didn't mean to lay my problems on you. But I can't really call you from home. And I needed to . . ."

"I'm *so* glad you did stop by," she soothed, genuinely concerned. "I just wish that it wasn't so bad with you."

"Well at least one of us is doing *great.* I really miss you around the newsroom. Things just aren't the same without the golden curls whipping around the corner like a speeding bullet . . . Well, hiyo Silver. See you Monday?"

"Right," she smiled, hugging him. "We'll talk some more."

"Woman-to-woman," he shrugged archly, ambling off to the elevator bank.

You'll never guess who I just bumped into," Joel chuckled, locking his forearms around Crystal's waist and bear-hugging her into the apartment. "Going about ninety miles an hour."

"He just left here."

"What? Made a cuckold by Winston? Who'd a thunk it?"

"Hardly. He just stopped by to chat. Got a real problem to work out."

"I'll say. The way he was mincing like a New York Doll, I'd diagnose it as lack of balls."

"That's not funny. And you don't have to go on the attack, feeling threatened by every man who fails to come on like King Kong. Speaking of which, why don't you loosen your hairy arms long enough for me to get the souffle out of the oven? You're late, and you must be starving . . . *I* am. You'll have plenty of chance to prove your masculinity—and my femininity. Later."

"So I'm a coward," he shrugged. "I freely confess. I can't stand the challenge of a man coming on to me . . . Or the sight of blood. Every time I drive past a hospital, I break into a cold sweat. It's a lousy excuse for not coming to see you. I'm a shit and a heel, and I feel awful about it. I haven't been able to sleep a wink since I drove you to the hospital. That's the honest truth. I've been miserable. But I know it's no kind of excuse."

"You could've called," she said wistfully.

"Have you forgiven me yet?"

"I'm working on it."

"I'm sorry as hell. You *know* how much I've wanted to be with you. In the meantime, I've been keeping busy." Fishing in his briefcase, he produced four clumsily wrapped packages. "Eh, *voilà*. Two vintages, red and white. This . . ."

Crystal carefully removed the ribbon, then tore off the wrapping on the record.

"Nothing like Ravi Shankar," Joel mused. "After

408

the way you made love last time we listened to the sitar, I decided that it deserved a command performance. You command—and I'll perform. We're going to have a lot of catching up to do."

With an automatic response, Crystal's insides began to flush with warmth as she recalled the sensuous strains of Indian music, and how Joel had rocked her gently to the rhythm. Fluidly and gently. For what seemed an eternity.

"And finally," he grinned, unwrapping the third present behind her back, then pressing close and draping the enameled choker around her neck, "a snaky something to decorate your beloved breast. Can I make it up to you, Crys?"

"The wounds are healing," she nodded, feeling his arms encircling her and thrilling to his scent closing in on her senses. She let the negligee fall open, and brought his palms up to her breasts, allowing his fingertips to roam over them, lightly brushing the bandage. "It's still a bit tender," she whispered, "but not *too* tender."

"Are you certain? What did the doctor say about . . . ?"

"She said not to let you stroke it too passionately. Just enough."

"That's all?"

"Well, if you really must know, she gave me one other warning: Never stick anything in your vagina that you wouldn't stick in your mouth."

"You're giving me ideas," he beamed, falling to his knees and cupping her wounded breast tenderly. He kissed it gently. Pulling her down to him on the thick white carpet, he trailed his tongue over her body hungrily.

"You're forgetting one thing: dinner."

"Let's take the good doctor's advice: *Fuck it.*"

"That's not what she meant."

"In that case, let's have it for dessert. Crystal, I want you so much—every inch of you. Let's put on the Shankar album and turn down the lights."

"Wait a minute, Joel," Crystal whispered, disentangling herself. She jumped up and found a parchment scroll she had placed on the cocktail table. "This is *my* present to *you*, darling." As she handed the scroll to Joel, an excitement sparkled in her wide, green eyes.

"You look about twelve years old right now," he marveled. "Like a little kid who has a naughty secret."

"Open it," she commanded shyly. "I had a lot of time in the hospital so I indulged my secret wish to write poetry."

Joel unrolled the parchment and read aloud, *"Ode to Joel's Cock."*

> *I get a high from your prick*
> *Its phallic mushroom head.*
> *Its shaft so long and thick.*
> *Your velvet-covered, steel-hard pleasure stick*
> *Turns me on*
> *I need it like a fix.*

"Crystal, that's fantastic, wonderful. I want to use it in my book."

They both collapsed on the floor like two children, laughing and hugging. "I had better infuse you with a double dose of cock, so you'll stay hooked," teased Joel. Suddenly he turned serious. "I love you so Crystal." He showered her with kisses as he swept her up into his arms and walked towards the bedroom. "Do you want me to carry you over the threshold?"

"I do," she exclaimed. "I do, I do, I do."

With a wave which revealed nothing, Lauren

gunned her Mercedes and disappeared around the bend of the winding driveway.

Ted jammed his hands down into his pants pockets, then turned to Smitty with a satisfied smile. He stood jauntily, rolling back and forth on the balls of his crepe soles.

Drinks with Lauren had gone even better than expected at the Polo Lounge. No wait. And a table on the right side, to boot. They had acknowledged—then pointedly turned away from—the winks and waves from a dozen other tables. Just an intimate *tête-à-tête*, holding court for the biggest and the brightest.

"Good for business," he reflected. In Hollywood, even doctors were subject to a certain prevailing fad mentality. Boredom and caprice were heavy factors in the choice. And once the star patients switched, the news slowly filtered down. As momentum grew, a physician could easily be toppled from the select ranks of the "right" doctors.

Pointedly ignoring the outstretched palm of the valet holding open the Bentley door, Ted made a quick inventory of the spotless interior, then discovered a wad of spent chewing gum in the ashtray. With a shudder, he sealed the compartment, making a mental note to have it washed out. Of all of the body's orifices, none was more filthy than the human mouth. Especially when it was the vastly over-exposed yap of a grime-covered car attendant.

Once again, his thoughts turned to Lauren. Her personal hygiene seemed adequate, in terms of the garden variety airborne microbe strains. Her skin was close-pored and unbroken, carefully scrubbed to maintain uniform skin cell growth. And a glowing, attractive complexion.

Good skin always turned him on. Particularly when it comes with a package like Lauren Conrad. In the week since their first Polo Lounge date, things had been going great. The reliability of his laetrile clinic and book had shaken up a few of his patients. The SBN broadcast and coverage in national papers, however, set business booming. Overnight, the clinic had a waiting list. Book sales were up in the thousands—and a mass market paperback deal was almost a certainty. Prodigal clients were returning to the fold—and not just for prescription refills.

"Still," he mused, feeling the pressure building beneath his skin-tight jeans, "she's a dangerous proposition. With the stir created by the Presley trials, it's hard enough to get Vals refilled. And that prick at Rowland—actually questioning me on the Demerol and Dexedrine orders. Better move them to a different pharmacy for a while."

As if the media saturation wasn't enough of a problem, Lauren had to go and ruin things by spending the night at Bob Radin's. Didn't she realize the dangers? If his hot tub temperature dipped five degrees, the microbes would start to bloom. Moreover, the guy wasn't even Jewish.

If he wasn't circumcised, then God only knew *what* he might be storing in his prepuce. A cold sweat broke onto his forehead as the word hovered at the antipodes of his mind: *smegma.*

Maybe the risks were too high. The prudent thing to do would be to cut off the relationship right now. From here on in, Lauren Conrad could only mean anxiety. There were thousands of nymphets—flat as a board and tight as a glove—just waiting. Like that chick he had picked up yesterday at the Store 24. Now *that* was a superb fit. Wouldn't even accept the money he stuffed into her training bra.

More his style. Grateful and obedient. Sparing him the necessity for prolonged foreplay, a further strain on his already weary prostate.

With it all, his thoughts and fantasies just kept running back to Lauren. It was illogical. She wasn't even his type: over twenty. The mere thought of her, straddling him and bucking like a bronco, her long mane of tawny gold hair, flowing over the flat of his stomach was enough to drive him wild. Enough to make him willingly cater to her expensive tastes. "She's living testimony to the fact that you don't have to be Jewish to be a Jap," he mused wryly.

"So what, I can afford her," he admitted to himself. "The dividends just better be worth the investment." The profits so far seemed promising. There was nothing like the thought of Lauren moving her lips teasingly up and down his cock, while he deliberately dialed his mother and . . .

"Speaking of which," he mumbled, "better call in to the office." Snatching up the microphone, he switched on the CB and broke in to the static on his wavelength. There was a faint buzz, then his secretary's voice broke through. "Dr. Rothmore?"

"Yes. I'm just finishing up the Beverly Hills house call. Nothing serious. Any important messages?"

"Irv Flax says his pancreas is kicking up again. Francesca Van Rensalaer called, needing a refill. You had it tagged for a hold, so I scheduled her for an appointment next week. Some bad news from Dr. Gutierrez. He says you're urgently needed at the clinic. About that actress who showed up last week. He says she's too advanced. And in view of the publicity, maybe she should be released."

He nodded grimly. "I'll take care of it. Anything else."

"Just a kid who says her name is Jeannie. No last name, I've got her hanging on the other line. She says that . . ."

"I'll fill you in later. A very . . . delicate case. Put her through."

A series of buzzes and clicks. "Ted?" came the distant voice.

"I'm calling from the Bentley. On *open* airwaves. You understand."

"I copy."

Smart cookie, he nodded. "You understand just how serious this complaint of yours might turn out to be?"

"What? I, uh didn't."

"Maybe I should rush over right away. Exactly where are you?"

"Downtown in Hollywood."

"Excellent. I'll pick you up in fifteen minutes. Where I did last time. Be there."

"Breaker, breaker," came the fuzzy voice. "This is Sourdough Jack on the Pacific Coast Highway. I heard your little distress call, good buddy. Need a little hand? I'm just south of . . ."

"Dr. Feelbetter signing off," he shouted back, snapping off the set.

Fishing out a new wave tape, he yanked off his tie and shook loose his hair. "Thank heaven for little girls," he crooned to the rhythm of his pulsing groin. The pressure was mounting dangerously. No time to lose. He gazed through the tinted windows frenetically, mapping out the most discreet route for their hour of hands-on medical training.

"Didn't Lauren look luscious tonight?" Violet asked pointedly as she swept out of the cotton-candy interior of her vintage Cadillac.

"I didn't notice," Rick shrugged.

"Then *why* were you staring at her like that? It was downright embarrassing. I hate to think of what Ted

Rothmore was thinking. Let alone the rest of the Polo Lounge."

"Why bother?" he countered angrily. "Who cares what they think? *Any* of them."

"*I* care," she retorted, following him into the light-drenched kitchen, unconsciously rearranging the silk violets around her neck. "Especially after you made such a big deal about taking me there. I don't even know why you *brought* me, if all you wanted to do was ogle other women."

"I wanted to celebrate, that's all."

As he brought her a glass brimming with champagne, her anger subsided. "I didn't think you'd remember," she exclaimed. "Is it really our year and a half 'anniversary'?"

"Nope," he clinked her glass, then downed the wine, giving her backside a goodnatured slap. "I got a call today . . . from Sid Gold."

"Oh Rick. That's wonderful." She threw her arms around him and sighed. "My star pupil," she beamed. "Well, what are you waiting for? Let me have it."

"Over hors d'oeuvres," he stalled, producing a dip platter and turning his attention to the cutting board. "Fresh cut vegetables, hollandaise sauce, and just a wee bit of beluga and cream cheese. Then we'll have . . ."

"Stop torturing me darling. I can't stand the suspense. What did Sid say?"

"Well, since you insist. He's taking me on as a client. Already got the contract drawn up. Plus, from now on he's going to have Sampson Associates in New York handle the Coast gigs.

"*Sampson?* You've got to be kidding. They turn *down* a hundred bookings a week. Not to mention thousands of clients." Her features grew momentarily cloudy, as she remembered the stack of rejection letters they had sent her over the years. "I'm so happy for you."

"There's more. Sid took me on because he landed me the spot as spokesman for 'Man Handler' cigarettes. I'll be doing all their commercials and making personal appearances everywhere. He's even got me doing the national print ads. That's why we're having this celebration. Because I owe it all to you."

"How *sweet*," she gushed, wrapping her arms around him and clinging to his young sleek body. Relieved, she remembered how she'd always feared this moment—never doubting that it would come. How she'd been terrified by the thought he'd someday forget her, once he finally got a major break.

Contritely, she realized just how wrong she'd been. How she'd let her insecurities and fear of rejection run away with her. Maybe now that he'd taken the first step, Rick would be less restless. There'd be a bit more money to spread around as well. Rick needed that too.

"Violet," he sighed, staring down into her eyes with the look that had never ceased to thrill her, "I'll never forget what you've done for me. I'm going to be running my ass off for a while. I'm sure that it'll be really hectic, but . . ."

"What does that matter, darling," she whispered, hugging him tighter. "I'm sure we'll make time."

"Speaking of making time," he laughed.

"Exactly what was on my mind," she giggled, running her fingers over his almost hairless chest.

"Not now," he smiled apologetically. "We'd better hurry up with dinner. I've got to catch an eleven p.m. plane. Got a big conference scheduled for eleven in the morning, New York time."

Her mood sank, and she felt his shoulders stiffen. "Well, I suppose if you must . . . How long will you be gone? I hope not for too long. We've got the Davis party coming up next weekend."

In silence, she watched his fingers deftly slicing the carrots and celery into neat slivers. Just as he had learned back on Ventura, at his father's souvlaki stand. *Snap, snap* . . .

"Man Handler's agency is in New York," he called over his shoulder in rhythm to the knife strokes.

"But that's *crazy*," she protested. "If you're working there four or five days a week, then how do you expect to . . ."

"I'm *moving* there." *Snap snap.*

"Moving there?" She arched one eyebrow questioningly, as the words began to sink in. "You . . . you're leaving me?"

"Don't think of it that way, darling. But it's the break of my lifetime. I just *know* it. My career has to come first. We both know that."

"You . . . can't . . ."

"*Lighten up*," he snapped. "I'm sorry. But don't make it any harder than it is. We both agreed that . . ."

"You can't leave me," she cried, digging her nails into his steel-like biceps. "Do you *hear* me? I won't let you. Not now. Not when I need you to . . ."

"To *what?*" He shook off her clutching hands and waved the knife menacingly. "To be your house pet? To haul your ashes because you can't find any other pretty boys to do it for you? Or to carry you like a dead weight on my back? To keep the invitations rolling in so you won't notice that you're a wrinkling hasbeen?"

"NO. Shut the hell up. You're lying. You vicious, UNGRATEFUL . . ."

"You disgust me," he intoned fiercely.

Violet dropped her champagne glass, blankly staring at the shattered slivers of crystal. Slowly she levelled her eyes back at him, red-rimmed and murderous. "You stinking son-of-a-bitch," she screamed shrilly.

With a shrug, he dropped the paring knife and began to slip off his cook's apron.

Springing to the counter, Violet seized the knife and lunged at him.

"Cut the dramatics," he shouted, clamping down on her swinging wrist and forcing the knife back onto the counter. "You never could act worth shit."

Violet slammed her knee into his groin, then attacked him with her fingernails as he slumped forward. She wrestled him to the ground and began striking out with her fists.

In a rage, Rick grabbed her wildly flaying right arm and twisted it around her back. "*You crazy bitch,*" he roared, sending her flying across the floor. "*You useless hag, I ought to . . .*"

With a sickening crunch, he heard her head thump against the broken glass, then raced out of the kitchen and vaulted up the stairs two at a time. Grabbing his already packed suitcase, he sped toward the front door. "I'm sorry it had to end like this," he called into the kitchen. A fitting farewell—a bit overused: Just like Violet.

Glancing into the room, he saw her lying motionless in a pool of blood. "Violet?" he called, but there was no answer. He saw the labored motion of her ribs and realized she was hurt. "Shit, she's not going to stop me now," he vowed. Then he called the para-medics and headed for the airport.

The distant whine of an ambulance siren raced up Benedict Canyon. Violet slowly stirred. Sitting up, she ran her hands over her aching forehead and cheek.

They fell back into her lap. Moist and crimson.

She stared at the fluid pool beside her, then back at her hands.

Below her on the tiled floor was the reflection of a woman covered with blood. Running down the side of her face was a five inch gash, the sliver of Baccarat still embedded in it.

"My . . . face," she wailed, crumbling onto the ground. "My *face. Oh my God, my face.*"

Forty-three

"Thanks for coming here on such short notice, Bob," Lauren smiled tensely. *God, he looked magnificent. Every inch of him.*

"Are you *kidding?*" He replied tersely, with a sharp cutting edge just below the surface. "This is the closest I've gotten to you in a week-and-a-half. What gives?"

"Just like I said on the phone. We're almost ready to begin taping segments on the media probe. I just wanted to ask your opinion on a few pretty hairy situations which have turned up. Under the circumstances, it seemed better not to talk on the phone. And if possible, I'd like to get some of the conversation down on tape, as possible back-up, in case . . ."

"That's *not* the answer I was looking for. I meant: why in hell haven't I seen you in the past few weeks. I just don't understand. Lauren, we've been together for three months now. Sporadically, I admit. And maybe I don't really have a right to probe into the rest of your life . . ."

"I'm sorry Bob," she said flatly, directing her eyes into the list of questions on her lap. "Things have been crazy around here lately. I barely even have time to . . ."

"No need to explain," he answered earnestly. "If that's the reason, then I'm sorry I acted like such an ass just now. I thought that maybe you were breaking things off. Just sort of letting them slide into oblivion. You know how I feel about you."

"And as soon as they let me out of the cage for an evening, I'll let you know just how I feel about *you*. After all, I am *not* about to let Hollywood's most desirable bachelor slip through my hands." Tiptoeing to the door and locking it, Lauren hopped into his lap and began planting tiny nipping kisses all over his lips. "See what I mean?"

"I'm beginning to get the message," he responded, hugging her as his exploring hand ran gently over the contours of her bottom. "Now if only we could cut out all of the interference."

"You do know, don't you, you smug producer?"

"What's that?"

"You are truly the most remarkable man I have ever met. That's all. And the most incredible lover. As a matter of fact, now that we're alone, I've a good mind to cancel the taping altogether, and head back to that marble hot tub for a few hours of R & R: Romance and Restitution."

"All of that in a few hours? I figure that I must have a month of back pay coming to me. Besides, you know that when a man gets to be my age, it takes that long just to get past foreplay."

"Amen," she laughed, sliding her hand down his thigh and softly stroking his willing cock into an erection. After three months, she never ceased to be startled by the intensity of his lovemaking—or his love. It was so strong, it was sometimes almost smothering.

Maybe *that* was the answer. Something had to be. Week after week, she returned to Ted. Balling the night or afternoon away. He was technically superb as well. Actually indefatigable. Deep down inside, though, she knew that there was something strange going on there. Ted's cleanliness fetish, the weird habit he had of calling his mother, then letting Lauren listen in as they pumped away in silence: it was downright kinky.

But exciting. Everything Ted did was exciting. And so easy. He never drained her the way Bob seemed to. She never had trouble meeting him for brunch-in-bed, then rushing back to the office to prepare the evening broadcast.

It was deliciously illicit—something that Bob could never understand. And much as she hated to admit it, there was a challenge in laying out her schedule with the precision of a master engineer. Both tracks running continually, criss-crossing and overlapping, passing within a hair's breadth of one another, but never colliding.

Sooner or later, she sighed, I'm going to have to jettison . . . the buzz of the telephone jarred her back to reality. "*Damn.*"

"It's just as well," Bob laughed, lifting her onto her feet. "In addition to being an outstanding reporter, you are one of the most insidious cockteases I have ever known. Another five seconds, and it would have required half an hour in an icy shower."

"I see what you mean." Angrily, she snatched up the phone. "Gloria? What in hell is this about? I distinctly *told* you to hold all calls, and . . ."

"Do I sound like Gloria?" Ted laughed on the other side of the line.

"No . . . not exactly. But how in hell did you get through the switchboard?"

"The powers of gentle persuasion."

"I can imagine." She glanced over at Bob, relieved to find him examining the Heiman Award she and Crystal had just received. Somehow or another, Ted *never* missed a chance to run interference with Bob around. Or else to hound her with a telephone call the

422

second she returned home from one of their all-night trysts. The most extraordinary case of ESP she had ever witnessed.

And at times the most annoying. Particularly when he used his hypnotic charm to slip past the defenses of the switchboard. "I just have to see you."

"I'm afraid that's impossible."

"For you? Nothing is impossible. Tell me what it'll take. Anything."

Bob shot her an inquiring glance. Lauren felt her heart skip a beat. In her mind's eye the trains were speeding downhill, heading for a collision. Only this time, it wasn't just a game. There were two relationships, and three very bruisable human beings involved. She had to pull a switch, and fast. "Maybe if you call back later, we can discuss this at greater length."

"What's to discuss? I'll pick you up at twelve-thirty." She glanced down at her Rolex as the phone clicked off. So much for lunch with Bob. Now she was going to have to come up with one hell of a whopper. Meeting with Sloan? Hardly convincing. Maybe a . . .

"Trouble?" Bob inquired, his face registering a bit too much concern.

"Just my broker," Lauren blurted out. "Guess those guys really know how to push when it comes to shove."

"Are you buying? Or selling?"

"I'm not really sure," she shrugged, running interference with her smile.

"Miz Conrad?" came a muffled voice as a series of sharp raps invaded the office.

Venting her anxiety in rage, Lauren threw open the lock and pounced at the doorway.

"Beverly Florist, Ma'am," the boy mumbled, taking a step back as she glared down at him.

Lauren closed her eyes and screamed inwardly, as the trains headed into the tunnel—this time from both sides. She was riding each of them as they hit the darkness, watching herself watch herself as the two worlds collided. *You snake,* she screamed at Ted, leering at her with his hypnotic eyes as they barreled on to certain disaster.

With a start, she turned back to the bewildered boy, who was anxiously pocketing the five-dollar bill Bob had quickly produced. "If you don't mind, Miz Conrad," he stammered as her eyes stopped glaring, "my boss was wondering if you could possibly . . . I mean, I know how busy you are, but he told me not to come back without a . . ."

"Autograph? Why of course, step right in." Lauren removed an eight-by-ten glossy from a stack on her desk and hastily scrawled a line. "Thank you for the flowers," she smiled.

"Oh, they weren't from me, Miss. They were from a Mister, uh Doc . . ."

"How-about-an-autograph-for-you-as-well?" she interjected, the warmth of her smile dropping below the freezing point. "And one for your mother?"

"Really?"

"Of course. Now why don't you run along . . ." *And play in traffic. Before you do something we'll both regret.*

"Now, shall we?" she laughed in Bob's direction, gathering up her notes for the taping session.

"I just don't know how you do it," he shrugged.

"Do *what?*"

"I'm not quite sure." His eyes scanned her features closely, then burst into a broad grin. "But the most *I* ever get from my broker is coupons."

"Isn't it just too marvelous for words," Jewel cooed,

dropping the latest Imagus report back onto Sloan's clutter of messages and folders.

"I'm so glad for you, darling," the petite woman responded, hugging her and slowly insinuating her knee between Jewel's legs. With a throaty groan of pleasure, she began to bump and grind, almost toppling them back onto the desk. "So . . . delighted."

"The way Lauren and Crystal keep getting panned, CJ is going to have to sit up and take notice. Don't you think?"

"Of course, darling." Sloan slipped her hand down onto Jewel's crotch, groping through the thin layers of silk.

"Not now, Sugar," Jewel resisted. "I just had my hair done by Fleming."

"So I won't go near your face. Okay?"

"Please Sloan. You know what it does to me, when we . . ."

"*Sloan?*" Dale Stevens barked, "*You in there? I have to . . .*" As he knocked harder against the door, it flew open. The two women jumped.

"Just what in hell are you doing? Bursting in here like that. Stevens, I have a good mind to . . ."

"*I gotto speak to you.*" He glared over at Jewel, hastily rearranging her skirt. "Alone."

"Oh you do, do you? Well, speak to my secretary. I'm sure he can . . ."

"I don't think it can wait. Jewel, you'd better excuse youself for a few minutes."

"In case you've forgotten, Mr. Stevens, let me refresh your alcohol-ridden memory. This is *my* office."

Leering as he waved a dog-eared manila folder in her face, he inspected Sloan's new furniture and frowned. "At least Rob had taste," he hissed.

"When it came to teeny-boppers. Well, since you insist on speaking to me, why don't you at least compose yourself. Jewel, that'll be all for now. I guess I'll just have to humor our distinguished News Director. Shut the door behind you, okay? . . . Now Dale, what the hell is the meaning of this?"

"Thought you had us fooled, huh?"

"I haven't the slightest idea what you're talking about."

"Thought you had it all sewn up, didn't you. The perfect crime. A perfect, closed circle. No witnesses, and no clues. Well I caught up with you."

"That's very nice, Dale. Now if you don't mind, I have a lot of work to catch up on. Why don't you just write it up in a memorandum, and . . ."

"You don't understand," he laughed. "I finally did it. It's taken months, but I've caught you. The blood is all over your hands."

She felt her face go white, and swivelled around to the wall. *It wasn't possible. Was it?* Out of the corner of her eye, she glanced at the computer sheets he was fanning before her pointy nose. The thought hit her like a mortar shell, ripping through her gut: Cooper and Conrad. Somehow they had stumbled onto the link. Once they found the dummy checks, it was possible that . . .

"Is it Lauren and Crystal?" she probed. "Because if *they* came up with anything, I'd give it a very careful scrutiny before I started making unsupportable accusations. Particularly to my boss."

"You kidding? Trust them? You've got to be kidding. No way, Sloan. I know they're in it with you. Just like CJ. Baby, it's just you and me now. I *own* you, Sloan. And you will live to regret . . . what you did. For starters, I am giving you exactly five days to clear out of here. You'd better resign by Friday afternoon. Or else."

"You're *crazy,*" she shrieked. "Certifiably gonzo.

426

Now either you drop this insanity this instant and get a grip on yourself—or I call an emergency meeting of the board, and . . ."

"It won't work this time," Dale chuckled. "You're too late. Just remember, Sloan: *five days.*"

Mumbling to himself, Dale marched out of the room with an odd, rolling gait.

Sloan watched the broad shoulders bounce out of sight with bitter irony. Dale was cracking, alright. Just this morning, CJ had finally faced up to the inevitable, and authorized the search committee to find a replacement. Dale's termination was already zipping through the cogs of the legal department.

The problem was that it was a little bit late.

And maybe—just maybe—Dale was still a little too sane.

"What do you mean, 'They're threatening to go out on strike?'" Redfield bellowed into the intercom. "There's no justification for it whatsoever . . . *I* know all about their demands for time-and-a-half. But I also know what the contract calls for. Why in hell did we go through all of those weeks of negotiation? Get them back on the job . . . *Now.*"

"I'm trying, CJ," Sloan's voice whined at the other end. "I even took Ralph aside and pleaded with him. When the strokes to his ego failed, I offered him a little incentive."

"How much?"

"Ten grand."

You stupid fool, he thought. *If only Rob were still in that office. He would've had the man back on the job in two seconds flat . . . then again, and you might even be sitting at my desk . . . as the network's Chairman of the Board! . . . Get a hold of yourself, CJ.*

Loosening the tie which was suddenly choking his

neck, Redfield took a deep breath. "Alright, Sloan. I'll go down there and see what can be done. In the meantime, I want you to have Dale send down Conrad and Cooper. To soften them a bit, and urge on the necessity of working *together* for a change."

"It's awfully close to broadcast," her voice insisted. "I'm sure that the three of them are running around trying to pull it together. Maybe we should send Jewel down instead."

"I said Conrad and Cooper. I meant it. Unless we have technicians to run it, there won't *be* a broadcast. Or did you forget that? I'll meet them in the studio in exactly three minutes. Make sure they're there."

He snapped off the intercom and stared at the ancestral portraits, feeling their eyes bearing down on him, a hint of mockery in their stern Puritan lips. Lately, it all seemed to be flying apart. And each day his world was harder and harder to keep together. RedRock was in perpetual chaos, as if the sins of the father were indeed visited on his children.

"I never should have hired her," he burst out. Pointedly ignoring the fact that he really had no choice in the matter. It was just a matter of buying time. But the price was getting higher every day. Strikes, low morale, resignations and firings. The problems kept reappearing and multiplying. Whatever Sloan's talents as an administrator, she was a miserable bureaucrat and negotiator.

"Just rose too far, too fast," he concluded. It was a plague in every industry. The whiz kids were catapulted into the upper echelons overnight, without enough time to master the basics. They stalled right before reaching the top of the pyramid, and just began to flail out desperately, trying to grab the golden ring anyway they could.

No patience, and no understanding of the need to

get along. Particularly with employees. That summed up Sloan alright, with one added factor: the one thing she had managed to grab a hold of was his balls. And every day, she attempted to squeeze just a bit harder.

He had to get her out of the way—before her destructive fury toppled the whole network. In the hands of a master, Divide and Conquer was an indispensable rule for governing a network. With Sloan, it was just ripping things apart at the seams.

"And slipping off to Edgemont for a few days didn't help. Did it?" he admitted. "Just more self-flagellation. *Mea culpa mea culpa mea culpa.* But it didn't bring Kikki back, did it?"

For four days, he had locked himself into the Edgemont world. Spending hour after hour in Kikki's carriage house. No, make that "cell"—because that's what it really was. And she'll have to do life without parole.

When it grew unbearable, he would join Mel to go snowshoeing, covering mile after mile in the blanketed valley, or making their way to the top of Mount Elisabeth.

Nothing seemed to help. Kikki was with him wherever he went. Her idiotic leer and meaningless grunts and moans always waiting when he returned. "She's gone," he dumbly nodded, wondering how in hell he had ever been left with this animal changeling.

Of course, he knew every step in the path to losing her. Beginning with the footsteps which had brought a fifteen-year-old daughter to his bedroom door.

With his beloved wife slowly fading and beyond the point of return, there was only RedRock left. Listlessly staring out the mullionless glass, Redfield was only faintly aware of the ant-sized figures scurrying up and down Sunset. He turned back once more to level a commiserating glance at Calvin Jennings Redfield.

With the death of Kikki's son, the Redfield generations had come to an end. The fertility problems which had plagued each succeeding generation had finally taken their toll. There was no male heir left to pass on the name—and no female to pass on the genes.

Only RedRock remained. And unless he bounced back, and moved into action, the Satellite Network would fall apart as well.

"Barbara," he pronounced briskly into the intercom, "get Dale Stevens down to Studio C. Pronto. And get Vincent C. on the line."

A moment later, a faintly echoing voice sprang out of the speaker. "CJ?"

"Ah, Vincent." He felt his heart begin to pump faster. "Got a problem, I'm afraid."

"D'you think it could wait 'til tomorrow? I was just packing it in for the night, and . . ."

"Afraid it can't." He listened intently to the silence, trying to gauge the hesitation. If he was losing his power base back East, then it spelled trouble.

"Okay," the distant voice sighed. "Shoot."

"A bit of a labor problem. I want you to place a few calls for me. Nothing heavy. Just a few reminders." He could imagine the obedient nod on the other end of the line, sensing the flow of power across the lines even before Vincent's voice confirmed it. *Thank God.*

"You got it, buddy," the man sighed with good-natured weariness. "How soon do you need results."

"Yesterday," CJ laughed broadly. "But I'll settle for fifteen minutes. Just as long as the technicians and drivers are back on the job before the Now News broadcast."

"As they say out in Hollywood, I'll stroke 'em."

"I owe you, Vincent. I won't forget." *And more than you know.* Snapping off the phone switch, he paced across the room, carefully dotting the perspiration from his brow and straightening out his striped club tie. Once again, he was the captain of his ship. Trim, confident, unyielding.

"I'll be down in Studio C," he waved to Barbara, smiling as the elevator whooshed him once more down into the fray. His blood raced with the thrill of the upcoming battle of wills. And the victory he now knew was certain.

Walking down the streamlined hall, he made a mental note. Tomorrow, St. Paul's would receive another $100,000 check.

Marcie Benjamin curled up on the bed, eyes glued to the miniature color tv. Outside fierce Arctic winds were buffeting a row of gnarled oaks. Sheets of rain slammed fiercely against the sagging leaded windows.

Spellbound, she reached over for her navy school blazer, shivering as fingers of cold air raced up her spine. She took another long tug of apricot brandy.

"In Washington today," Crystal Cooper's smooth voice reported, "another demonstration by the United Labor Front. Following last September's record-breaking crowd, a quarter of a million union members, students, and welfare activists gathered. Protesting the administration's latest social services cuts, angry union leaders vowed to . . ."

Marcie slowly poured the last of the pint down her throat, eyes still riveted on the outlines of her mother's face. "You stinking bitch," she sobbed. "I hate your guts . . . Do you *hear* me? I HATE YOUR GUTS. If you loved me, you never would have left Daddy and me!"

"Lights out," a voice called down the corridor, hours later. Room swaying, Marcie stumbled to the tv, and turned it off, staring drunkenly at the dying glow

431

of the picture tube.

Laughing senselessly, she stumbled back to her bed in the blackness, peeling her clothes onto the cold pine floor. Then she waited, half-conscious, for the familiar footsteps.

She was awakened by the jingle of the nightwatchman's keys. "J-Jack?" she mumbled uncertainly.

"Who else did you expect?" his young voice hissed in the darkness.

"Did you bring it?"

"The bottle? You bet I did. Almost got caught by the Headmaster, too. It's *crème de mênthe*. I ripped it off from his study."

"Give me a sip."

"You got to be kidding. You're already ploughed."

"I don't care," she slurred, lunging for the bottle.

Forty-four

Lauren burst back into her apartment just after dawn. She drew back the brocade drapes and stared out at the endless sprawling suburbs of Los Angeles, waiting for sleepiness to overtake her.

She was at the point where exhaustion had turned into a humming, restless energy. After twenty-one hours on the go, her system had no intention of shutting down. Pouring herself half a snifter of cognac, she rolled it over her tongue, watching red streaks of sunlight slowly spread across the distant mountains.

Midafternoon, the RedRock data had begun flowing out from the line printer, its identity carefully hidden. The analysts would be pouring over the figures for the next few days. But by now, even she was able to sniff out the obvious: someone was dipping their hand into the till. Whoever it was, the transfers were pouring into a numbered account in Zurich, via New York and Bermuda.

It was a neat, steady conduit, diverted through half a dozen troughs. Perhaps so carefully entrenched that it would be impossible to uncover in time for the media probe broadcast, now just weeks away.

Perusing the copied raw data from her attache case, she pondered the question of where to dispose of the priceless information. CJ? Sloan? Moe Alexander? Maybe she would show it to the wrong one. With millions of dollars involved, who *knew* which one to trust.

They all had mansions without mortgages, Rolls Royces and warehouses full of priceless antiques. Paintings by masters worth hundreds of thousands, conservatively. On the surface, they were all fabulously wealthy. At the stage where money, in itself no longer mattered. It was just one more tool, a weapon added to the arsenal. Without a doubt, what each of them sought was just more power. Pure unadulterated clout.

It was a heady thing, being at the top. To them opulence was merely a token. The tip of the iceberg. Underneath it lay the ultimate trip. One and all, they lived to create and dominate. Living like gods, and paying out endlessly for the privilege. Nothing was more expensive than the Hollywood game. Being served like royalty, having the right entourage, the right champagne, the right address.

Maybe it was the challenge of the thing. Skimming off the cream from the top of the profits, thrilling at the thought of being caught. More than one major network head had been caught at that in the past. Forbidden fruits always were the sweetest.

Or maybe the weight of constantly living life to the hilt, and pushing the limits was too much of a strain—for one of them. Maybe there weren't enough liquid assets to pick up the tab. To keep the wheels of the Alexander empire grinding. Or to keep Sloan's nostrils filled with coke, and finance her increasingly opulent entertainments.

She thought of CJ Redfield. Yesterday he had appeared with a show of strength, to quell the union uprising. The familiar ruthless power had never been more apparent in the way he twisted the union rep's arm.

Even as she stood there, she had marvelled at the

perfection of his performance. The cool evenness of his voice, the unshakable resolve with which he had dominated the gathered crowd. A masterful, undiluted outpouring of personal power.

Clearly it was as much for the benefit of the Now News team as for the striking workers. Instead of settling it behind the scenes, he had purposely decided upon a show of force. After his absence, and the way he barricaded himself in Imperial HQ upon his return, it was reassuring.

But the pointed absence of Sloan might be another indicator that things weren't quite as rosy as they seemed. If it wasn't a matter of cash flow, then he might have other reasons for siphoning cash. Reasons why he had to avoid any connection to some massive funding. Maybe even the FCC.

Rolling a sip of cognac over her tongue, Lauren stared out past the meticulously decorated apartment, letting her eyes focus on the distant row of million-dollar Malibu cottages, then on to the shifting black surface of the Pacific. In the pale dawn light, the mansions and the palms seemed to fade into obscurity, as the land contours once more swept to the sea.

"Everything here has built up much too fast," she thought, shifting her gaze to the endless canyons and hills. "Every year, the mudslides bring them crashing down. The overnight stars become has-beens, the movie moguls go bankrupt. The next day, there're two more to take their places, straddling the scene just as precariously. Glorious facades, with not enough support to sustain them."

She nodded self-righteously. Then it struck her that everything she mentioned was true: *About her.* "The Conrad Heiress." The words stung her tongue. No doubt, when the holdings finally did pass to her hands, there would be trusts within trusts, and boards of overseers and advisors. At the moment, her monthly check barely covered the bills on Rodeo Drive.

The story wasn't much different with her RedRock salary. If she didn't allow her accountant to bury it in tax-free investments, then the lion's share would be swooped up by the federal eagle's claws. Either way, nine thousand dollars a month trickled down to her, and the rest was out of reach.

In this town, it was barely enough to pay for the essential grooming, let alone the Mercedes which sucked up money like a vacuum. Even with the expense account, there could never be enough to feed her growing hunger for extravagant living.

It was an Achilles heel that Sid Gold seemed to regularly puncture, drawing her closer and closer to signing on with his agency. And much as she hated to admit it, decadent opulence was a great deal of Ted Rothmore's overwhelming charm. The way he showered her with jewelry, set siege to her lust for the good life, firing it with dinners at Chasen's and L'Hermitage.

"The right addiction in the right town," she grimly observed. How much charm would the guy exude if the millions powering her decadent lover's batteries of opulence ran dry? If the faces in the Polo Lounge no longer acknowledged him? How much would his outrageous little-boyish pleasures count for then? Or even his indefatigable sexual acrobatics.

In the meantime, there was Bob to consider. From the first time they spent the night together, she had felt the warmth coming through from him. And for the first time in her life she felt herself responding on more than a sexual level. Compared to the rest of the Hollywood crowd, his life was as solid as his sturdy redwood and glass Hollywood hills home. It would sure as hell outlast the garish houses scattered over cliffs, or climbing up the quake-prone sheer rock surfaces.

Last night had gotten off to a shaky start. Particularly since the backstage maneuvers to ditch Ted had taken their toll. For once Bob had seemed moody, almost distant. It had taken all of her defenses to deflect his piercing glances, and stop short of laying out the whole situation.

Last night had been like a battle of wills, with Bob withdrawing, and Lauren following in hot pursuit. It had taken half of the night to seduce him. And the rest of it to enjoy the results.

"No sense trying to fall asleep," she shrugged. "Not with my stomach still churning like this." She pressed her hands to her abdomen, recalling the sensation of Bob thrusting deep within her, his luscious aroma filling her senses.

Abruptly, she turned to the closet and rolled out her exercise mat. Throwing on her sweat suit, she began the prolonged ritual of warm-up stretches. Maybe today she would cut short the run, just loop around the Twentieth Century set and unwind.

Lacing up her New Balance shoes, she grabbed her keys and dropped them into the waist pocket of her pink satin shorts. She was just heading out the door when her private phone rang.

"Oh my God—the sapphire earrings," she laughed. It seemed that she always left *some*thing at Bob Radin's bedside. Marking her turf? Maybe. Whatever the deep underlying significance, the effect was sure. Romantic morning-after calls were getting to be a pattern. Propping up the pillows on her untouched bed, Lauren curled up with the phone in her lap and breathed a warm, "Good morning."

"Lauren?" Ted's voice was laced with accusation. "I tried to reach you last night, but then it started getting late. Anyway, you haven't been out for the morning jog yet, have you?"

"Well, actually darling, I was . . . uh, no."

"Great. I was thinking that we could drive out to the Malibu Colony. A friend of mine has a great house there. We could jog on the beach. Afterwards, there's a great brunch place I've been wanting to . . ."

"Actually, I was thinking of sleeping in this morning."

"Are you alright? Not coming down with anything, I hope."

"No, I think I'm fine," she yawned. "Just tired." It was true, her stomach was tied into a hundred knots, but the rest of her body suddenly felt totally drained and lifeless. Numb.

She stumbled apologetically through the rest of the conversation, then cut it off at the first chance. Then she reached for the latest vial of Valium and popped two in succession.

Slipping down between the peach satin sheets, Lauren felt absolutely drained, a good deal less happy than she had moments before. As she stumbled into oblivion, words from an English poem began to spin across her mind. "Of two minds/ Like a man and a woman/ And a blackbird."

She felt the sharp beak jabbing into her gut as the blackness spread over her.

"Orange County," Joel exclaimed over the hum of the MG engine. "Newport Beach, here I come."

"How can you be so enthusiastic at ten in the morning?" Crystal felt the residual puffiness still clinging to her sleepy eyes.

"When I'm leaving L.A.? It's easy. Besides, if you didn't get plenty of sleep last night, don't blame it on me."

"I did just fine, thank you," she yawned. *And what if she hadn't? Would it have mattered anyway?* "Get

438

much done on the book this week?"

"Dribs and drabs. Listen, no business today. Professional, personal, or other. Just you and me. The beach and the sun . . ."

"The shops and the restaurants. You've got a deal." She leaned over and stroked his thigh drowsily, then placed a wet kiss on his cheek. "Wake me up when we get to Newport."

When she reopened her eyes, they were high on a plateau overlooking the ocean. At their feet lay Newport Bay, Balboa and Lido Isle. She gazed around at a scene of boats, docks, houses and condominiums and realized that they had indeed entered a new brand of Southern California.

Although it was just an hour's ride from Beverly Hills, the change was dramatic. The houses were newer, less ostentatious, more open to the eye. Instead of walling in their opulence, they presented simple, almost subdued facades of Spanish colonial or deco style. "Cozy," she nodded, seeing his eyes ablaze with appreciation. Many had magnificent views of the beach and harbor.

"I've been waiting to drag you down here. One of my favorite places. In fact, I was seriously considering buying a house here. Should've, while the getting was good. These days, I couldn't even *touch* the beachfront property."

"Invaded by the Dream Machine? If you wanted to find a reason to resent the industry, at least this would be a good one."

"Not quite. Take a look around you. No Polo Lounge regular would be caught dead here. It's a whole different kind of money. Most of it distinctly top drawer, of the old WASP variety."

Hand-in-hand, they descended the beach walk to a surprisingly narrow band of sand. "People say it used to go out three times as far," he observed, as they watched a line of sailboats, sails billowing, disappear around the island. "But it's still a terrific place to dive in. C'mon." He tugged at her arm impulsively, and she soon found herself being carried into the surf.

The waves broke over and around them. Joel pressed close to her, arms locked around her waist. Crystal felt more alive than she had in months.

"I've never seen you look more beautiful," he sighed, holding her at arm's length. "Or more lovable." He ran his fingers lightly over her finely carved features, staring into her eyes without holding back. "It's days like this that make me think it could go on forever."

His kiss was long and unhurried. Crystal's arms wrapped passionately around him, urging him further. The chill of the autumn ocean subsided. Minutes passed, and the rest of the world seemed to fade into limbo. There was only the lapping of the waves and the warmth of Joel's embrace.

"He's like a changed man," she thought, staring at his muscular chest as he gently wrapped a towel around her, feasting on the curves of her body. "He has been ever since the operation. Maybe it really shook him up."

"Ready for the tour?" he called out, tossing on a French sailor's shirt and some white duck pants. She shook her head, marvelling at the way he could effortlessly fit in to any scene. Get absorbed in it, to the exclusion of anything before and after. "And where do I fit in?" she murmured, sliding into a slightly too-Hollywood cotton print beach dress. "*Nowhere:* Unless I can get this zipper unstuck. *Joel?*"

"Let's see now," he wondered aloud a few hours later, "we've been to the old Ferry boat house, the pier, to the open air fish market, to every boutique on every narrow little street within sight. Promontory Point, the boat channel. I want to show you UC Irvine, but we can swing by on the way home. Have we missed anything?"

"How about lunch. My stomach's growling and my feet are aching."

"Good point." He nodded at an unimposing restaurant on their right, as the MG ground to a halt. "Ring any bells?"

"Only a vague alarm. Look at that line. And if they make the regulars wait, then lord knows how long it'll be before they'll seat . . . ."

"This isn't Beverly Hills," he retorted. "Seating is strictly democratic. As a matter of fact, the Crab Cooker is a sort of local legend that way. Can you imagine Walter letting Richard Nixon wait his turn? Well this joint did—until he walked out in a huff. And the meal he missed. Lobster, gulf shrimp . . ."

"Okay, okay. Just let me slip on my espadrilles. But what about the painting?" Joel had just bought it for her at an art fair near the beach.

"Do you really like it? The woman reminds me of you."

Her eyes drifted dreamily to the inscription Joel had scrawled on the back. *To the most exciting and beautiful woman I have ever known. May our love last as long as this painting.* "It's the nicest painting I've ever owned," she whispered.

"Are you sure? Be honest. I know just how diplomatic you Capricorns are."

"And I know just how much Leos hate rejection. The answer is I adore it. And the man who gave it to me. So let's go do our share for democracy, and get in line before it stretches around the block."

Afterwards, they rode back in easy silence, listening to the low rhythmic throb of the engine, and feeling

441

the sexual energy building up unbearably. Crystal watched the sun grow larger and hazy, finally sinking down into the blue-black slab of ocean.

"Did you really mean what you said on the beach?" she murmured, twirling the hairs on his chest as he threw his arm around her.

"You mean the bit about sailing down to Baja? I've always wanted to."

"I mean about wanting it to go on forever."

" 'Forever and a day,' " he recited. "That's Shakespeare, for you."

"But what I wanted to hear was Joel."

"How about this then: 'Men are April when they woo, December when they wed: maids are May when they are maids, but the sky changes when they are wives.' Not bad, huh?"

"Terrific," she said sarcastically. Up ahead, Los Angeles twinkled in the thick evening air. And in the car, the silence was suddenly dense. A return to status quo.

"Well, here we are," he announced as the car pulled up to the massive tower. "What a perfect day," he said, stretching. "Just what I needed."

"I almost think we should have stayed there," she sighed. "The night air is too smoggy to be perfect. With a little bit of sitar music and wine, however, I'm sure we'll manage."

"Not tonight," he shrugged. "I think I want to be alone. Do some writing. And some thinking. Got a lot of things on my mind."

"So do I, Joel," she whispered in his ear, "and every one of them is X-rated. Be a gentleman . . . Don't make me beg."

"Will you settle for a goodnight kiss and a raincheck?"

"Absolutely not. Please Joel. Make me beg, then. I

need you tonight. Don't you understand that? Don't leave me yet . . . Don't leave me alone—"

"It's been a wonderful day. Don't spoil it," he said icily, opening the passenger door and fishing on the back seat for the painting.

Crystal stormed past the doorman and up to the elevator. The low rumble of the exiting sports car still ringing in her ears. She threw open the apartment door and dropped the canvas limply, feeling the lonely silence slowly pour into her, echoing with Joel's parting shot. "Stop acting like a child. You can do without my services for one night."

"How is it possible?" she wondered. "One minute everything couldn't be finer. And the next . . ."

Shrugging wearily, she threw herself onto the bed and prepared for a good cry. But tonight, the tears refused to come. "Why in hell am I being rejected? For being a woman? And wanting my man?"

Actually, he was withholding sex as a punishment. Joel's cock giveth. And Joel's cock taketh away. Especially the latter, whenever the sacred covenant of his freedom was breached.

"If he wants his freedom that badly, he can take it," she barked at the eyelet pillows piled against the headboard. "But I'm sick and tired of being a slave to his whims. He's got his needs. *And I've got mine.*"

Blood racing, she snatched up her address book and leafed through the pages. The phone rang endlessly.

"Well, maybe it's just as well," she reasoned, feeling her frustration rising to a crescendo. Just as she was lowering the receiver back into the cradle, she heard the deep baritone voice answer.

"Hello?"

"Oh, you're home. Mitch, this is Crystal. I've got a free night, and I was wondering if . . ."

Forty-five

Francesca's private phone rang just as she was undressing to take her bath. "Oh, it's *you*. Violet darling, where in earth have you *been?* I've simply been trying for days."

"Moe's just got the most *splendid* villa in Cannes. And while Rick is out of town, sealing the deal on a *very* big project, I figured . . ."

"Don't be coy with me, Violet. Everyone knows that Moe has been sighted in Acapulco, shacking up with one of those ghastly little tarts. It was in *all* of the columns, darling. And there was also a note in the trades about Rick's becoming the 'Man Handlers' man in New York. Poor thing—you should have confided in me. I'll bet you've just been crying your eyes out at home. And you haven't told anyone else either—*have you?*

"I . . . I just *couldn't,*" Violet sobbed uncontrollably.

"Listen. You just sit right there. Francesca is coming right over. I've got a few little errands to do, but I suppose they can wait."

"Oh, don't bother," Violet got out between her tears. "I'm fine, really."

"*Nonsense.* I'll throw on something right now and rush . . ."

"I'm not at home. I'm at Dr. Sapir's. The *Clinic*."

Francesca started. Unconsciously, she lifted her fingers up to her neck, feeling for the tell-tale scars. *A lot of good it had done.* No wonder the "A" Group had switched to Dr. Burrows. Maybe next spring, she would spend a few months in his Swiss hideaway. It would have to be booked right away—at least six months in advance. But if Violet had resorted to Sapir, it must have been an emergency. "I see. What are you telling people?"

"Nothing . . . yet. I haven't spoken to a soul. Except you . . . ."

What on earth was she doing with that butcher? After what he had done to Francesca? Not to mention half a dozen other women in their group.

"Francesca, I . . . have to ask you a tremendous favor."

"Anything you want darling. *Honestly.* Now what can I do?"

"I know it's asking a lot. But I just don't know what else I can tell everyone. Do you suppose we could say that I was . . . acting as your assistant buyer? On an advance trip to Paris and Rome . . . Maybe Brazil as well. That would give the scars long enough. Maybe I'm asking too much. If it's impossible, just let me know. I'll understand."

Francesca bridled with disgust. *Of all the nerve.* Violet—a buyer? Who in hell did she think she's kidding? She couldn't even *afford* an Andre Laug—let alone select dozens. It was simply out of the question. As a friend, of course she would have been willing to. But as a couturier catering only to the *right* people, Violet simply wouldn't do.

She patted the chiffon sleeves of her peignoir and reflected. She had spent a lifetime building up her image—and it was not one to be trifled with. Every painting, every dress—even every pillow case in her universe was carefully selected for the right effect. It was a world she would only share with her exclusive clients. One which, for all of the friendship between them, Violet was simply not privy to.

"I'm sorry . . ." she blurted out. She thought of Violet's face, aching under the itchy, foul-smelling layers of bandages and gauze. If she was refused now, who else could she turn to? Frieda Salkin? Hardly likely. There was no one else who could possibly do this for her. If she was really that desperate, could Francesca possibly turn her down? "I'm sorry I hesitated. It's going to take a little bit of planning. And coaching—for when you get out. How long from now is it?"

"Eight weeks. Francesca, I don't know how I can repay you."

"You can't. But that's what true friends are for." She felt her teeth clenching, as her tongue tried to wrench out the promise. "I'll be sure to tell *everyone* I see you're in Europe, darling." *If they ask.*

Slipping into the bathroom, Francesca slowly peeled off her peignoir in front of the mirror, then watched the tub filling up with steaming water, a froth of bubbles floating on the surface. "Just right," she nodded to the aging Swedish maid, a stocky wide-eyed woman named Marta.

"I'm glad Madame likes it. Will there be anything else?"

"Yes," she lowered herself into the tub. "Bring me my ebony lap board. I'll need a stack of invitations, and the master list located in the rosewood secretary . . . I'm also expecting a call from a Mr. Robert Radin. I'll take it in here."

"Very good, Madame." Marta bowed stiffly, then set off to locate the invitations. Francesca watched her broad-backed frame recede and nodded with approval. She was just as good as the agency's references promised. Certainly worth all of the expense of having her shipped over. There was a certain graciousness in Old World maids that the California stock couldn't hope to match. Class, and style.

It was the bond which had first drawn Igor and herself together. And kept them intact, throughout all of these difficult years. Even when he had selfishly insisted upon the abortion, and terminating it resulted in her inability to conceive again. He could be cold and hard, but she knew that when she really needed him, Igor generally let the best of himself come out.

The lap desk slid over her foam-covered legs, resting on the bathtub ledge. She watched it glide to a stop an inch short of her pendulous breasts, then nodded with satisfaction as the fountain pen and invitations were set in place.

"Just right," she mumbled to Marta, the perfect combination of helpfulness and homeliness. Igor could be such a bore with the younger au pairs. She reached for the ringing bathside phone, then hesitated, waiting for the maid to formally announce Radin's call. He would appreciate that, knowing that she wouldn't speak to just *anyone*.

"Hello, darling," she breathed huskily. "You just caught me in the bath."

"Sorry, Francesca. Your message said call as soon as possible. If you'd like, I'll call back in a while."

"Not at all, my dear. I can think of nothing more divine than sharing a steamy sensuous bath with you." She felt a rush of excitement trickle down to her toes, waiting for his witty rejoinder. The silence began to annoy her. After letting her down at the Polo Lounge, his growing inattention had begun to worry her.

Luckily, she *did* have the boutique to lure him with. The patina of glamour and elegance which she

447

had carefully impressed upon him. Besides, there was still the pilot he was trying to sell her.

"I've found the most wonderful writer for us," she murmured.

"I thought we had already settled that one. Ray Novell. He's got a solid track record. And I've worked with him before. He was in on the Middle East documentary I shot for CBS last spring."

"I know darling, but the man I'm thinking of is . . . quite exceptional. He wrote a very fine Off-Broadway play. And it's so exciting to discover a new talent. The final decision will be yours. Of course. But I've set up a meeting for the two of your. Nothing formal. Just drinks at the Rangoon Racquet Club. Can you manage Thursday, say, five o'clock?"

"I'll make time," Radin sighed. "What's his name?"

"Joel Hanlin. A *very* dear friend of Crystal Cooper. If you catch my drift. Now let me tell you about Chez Francesca. This very afternoon, I'll be sending out the advance invitations. That's for friends, columnists and magazine editors. Things are just going so fast, my head is spinning . . ."

Forty-six

"You just can't do it," Marge stated with finality, her eyes avoiding Sloan's.

"What do you mean I can't do it? I *am* doing it. You take care of the arrangements. And let *me* take care of the rest."

"No, Sloan, you're being a spoiled brat."

"May I remind you exactly who the fuck you are addressing?"

"I know quite well, thank you. But where in hell are you going to find the dough for this kind of extravaganza? And two hundred people. You're not being realistic. Ever since you were named network president, you've been out of control. Jewelry, formal gowns. Twenty people one night. Fifty people the next."

"I have to do that, darling. You *know* that. We can borrow the money now, and simply repay it in a few months. By then the stock market will be back up anyway. If it's absolutely necessary, I'll dump the rest of my Cinearts holdings. But right now it's essential that I keep up the image. It's an investment."

She watched with growing annoyance as Marge shook her head, folding her arms firmly across her chest. "Why don't you get in touch with reality, honey. The way the stocks have been dropping, you couldn't *give* Cinearts away. You've just *got* to cut back. And that's final."

"I love you when you're so manly," Sloan replied drolly. "Now be a darling and get a pen and note pad. And the snuff box—and I'm dying for a little toot."

"I'm not backing down this time. We've been through it a dozen times before. I'm tired of having you cry on my shoulder about the bills. And sending *me* out to run interference when the collectors come. God knows where you got the money to pay for the last bash. In case you forgot, you had to agree to signing the Faberge egg on as collateral. The way payments are mounting up, I wouldn't be surprised if they slapped a lien on the estate."

"They wouldn't *dare*," Sloan screamed, clutching at Marge's shoulders. "They couldn't really . . . could they? I . . . I couldn't bear it."

Marge gazed down at the trembling head, the waist-length black hair unfurled, draping Sloan's skinny shoulders and back. It was amazing how a woman could be so abrasive on the exterior. Yet so needy and insecure beneath the façade. She cupped her breast to Sloan's mouth, and felt the waves of passion crash down on her as Sloan's pursed lips suckled greedily.

"Darling," Sloan moaned plaintively, "go get the coke. And let's go back to bed. I just can't cope with the rest. Not now."

Sloan took up Adam Ward's card, twirling it absent-mindedly in her hand. Once again, she went over the possibilities in her head. Maybe there was nothing behind Dale's crazed threats. The way his behavior had gone from unstable to bizarre, he would be a raving lunatic before long, if not already.

"You always were a careless fool, Rob," she recalled bitterly. "Between your big mouth and your oversexed cock, you really screwed things up. But good, didn't you?"

She unscrewed the top of the cloisonné snuff box and dipped in the sterling coke spoon. She felt the numbness clamp down on her nose, then drift down onto her lower lip. Impulsively she brought the container closer, and filled her nostrils twice more.

Things could have gone so smoothly. It had been an easy enough matter, between Moe Alexander's support and Rob's own twisted genius, to have Steinholtz appointed as the network's operating president. It had been even easier to play on Rob's insatiable greed, and his Napoleon complex. Even more than he needed to augment his salary, he needed to steal it out from under the ruling powers at Number One Sunset Boulevard. To laugh in their faces as he dipped his hand into the till. Like a kid stealing candy. Just because he was a nothing from the nether world of the Valley. Because everyone knew it; and they would never let him forget it.

Fifty-fifty. That was the arrangement. The money was siphoned off from three dozen different accounts. Maybe twenty-five dollars a day. But it added up, smoothly, electronically. Invisibly. Half of it in routinely issued miscellaneous expenses. The other half was wired directly from the bank to Bermuda, after the computer had checked the report, and found that the balance in general accounts matched the accountant's figure.

A trifling discrepancy in each account. The kind which would only be discovered months later. A small tidy sum, perhaps $45,000 a month. Wired to a numbered Swiss account, through an untouchable intermediary in Bermuda. Just enough to tide us over, until we could oust Redfield and enter the big stakes.

You wanted Lauren Conrad, and I let you have her. But you just didn't know when to stop, did you? First it was taking on CJ, gathering evidence for blackmail.

Understandable enough, perhaps. Then it was upping the ante, and those ridiculous forged checks billed to sit-com accounts. Then came *the most foolhardy move of all.*

You knew I could never afford to let you have seventy-five per cent. Especially since it was only a matter of time before the pattern of our anonymous mutual fund was discovered and the invisible pipeline was shut off. Smart of you to hire a programmer with a "hidden" record. "Once a felon, always a felon," you laughed.

Maybe I was stupid to be the one to sign those checks. And you were always so careful to get my fingerprints on every one. But blackmailing me? Come on, darling. It was a bit much, really.

Just a little bit much.

Sloan shuddered as the cocaine buzz came on. As long as CJ thought she still possessed the blackmail evidence of Rob's little secret scandal—whatever it may have been about—he wouldn't dare touch her.

But Dale Stevens, that was another story entirely. There were no traces of reason left in the man. He was operating on one track: Revenge. No way to make a deal.

The more she went over the situation, the more clear it became. In some perverse way, Rob had wanted to be caught. Perhaps it was via an access code. Or a sloppy trail of recorded memory bank searches. But *how* was immaterial. Somehow, Rob Steinholtz had never learned to just take the bucks and run. He *had* to savor it right then and there, just as he had always *had* to seduce that latest receptionist at Redrock—no matter the cost. The way he *had* to make cheap grabs at Lauren, whenever she was near.

Ever since the start of the media investigation, Sloan had been forced to lie low. Letting the account pile up for month after month, untapped. Muscling her way into CJ's position was going to take money. Lots more money.

As long as Dale stood in the way, it was impossible. She had begged CJ to dump the sot, tried to pressure the board into action.

Now that he was on the way out, it came just a few days too late. Even though he was already well on the road to the funny farm—

Abruptly, she spun through the Rolodex, stopping when she reached his number. Fingers flying, she punched the seven digits. What in hell was that tight-assed social-climbing bitch's name? . . . "Hello. Regina, this is Sloan Schwartz . . . Yes, darling, the very one . . . I hope you don't mind me calling you at home. Is Dale at home? . . . He *is*. I see. That's exactly why I was calling. Quite frankly, he's beginning to worry me. There have been a few *extremely* unpleasant episodes this week. I had the devil of a time keeping them from developing into full-blown scandals. I understand just how horrible that would have been for you. Moreover, I'm convinced that he's showing signs of a nervous breakdown. I know how much you want to protect him, darling. But let me be frank. He's starting to get violent. I don't think a confrontation would be wise. And this couldn't come at a worse time: he's scheduled for a $15,000 merit raise in two weeks . . . That's right, *fifteen* . . . *thousand*. If only there were some way to get him to take the two-week vacation he's got coming, and get him somewhere where he could relax . . ."

She nodded absentmindedly. "Of *course*, it's hard for you to deal with. We're all suffering. And believe me, we love Dale, just like you do. But short-term institutionalization is the obvious thing, as you say. Give Dale two weeks, and he'll spring back—into a higher salary—better than ever. Luckily, I've got a friend who has a *marvelous* private hospital. Totally discreet. But let's not be hasty. Let me call you tomorrow, and see if things are any better . . . No, don't mention it, darling. It's for the best interests of all of us."

Breathing a sigh of relief, she dialled the private number Adam had insisted on scrawling on the back of his card. He snatched up the phone on the second ring. "Ward here," his confident voice proclaimed.

"Ward, this is Sloan. You told me to give you a buzz the second I made my decision about the telethon. Well, I think that it might be possible for you to have Conrad and Cooper for a few hours this Friday—providing that certain conditions are met: First of all, there will be no other news celebrities present. Secondly, they are to be introduced as 'the Satellite Broadcasting Network's star newswomen, Lauren Conrad and Crystal Cooper, who co-anchor SBN's nightly prime time Now News program.' I'll send you a confirming memorandum tomorrow via courier, but I want to be quite clear on the exact wording. *Third:* There is to be no reference to KJJX prime time news while they remain on air. Four: All incidental expenses are to be . . ."

Forty-seven

"There you are!," Joel called out to the imposing man who stood off to one side of the packed bar, surveying the crowd. He waved above the throng, then wove his way through the bodies. "Francesca told me just to look up, and I'd find you . . . Guess she wasn't kidding. I'm Joel Hanlin."

"Bob Radin." He smiled, taking in Joel's shaggy mane of sandy hair, and the cocky, self-assured stance. Antelope sport jacket, Levi's—definitely not Hollywood chic. Above his slightly prominent nose, Joel's ice blue eyes darted nervously back and forth, with the wary, uncontrollable energy which always singled out a born New Yorker.

"Glad to meet you, Bob. Listen, I'm already drinking a Jack Daniels. What can I get you?"

"A martini's fine, no olive." He followed Joel back to the table, wondering if the Rangoon had been his choice. The crowd here was a different slice of the media world. Writers, junior executives, and more stunning young women than a studio cattle call.

Bob dropped down into the leatherette banquette. If nothing else, the place did have atmosphere. And the best scotch eggs in Beverly Hills.

"So what's it like, working with Francesca?"

"I can't really say, Joel. I'll let you know if we ever start working."

Joel laughed. "She's a strange bird. I can tell that much. And that accent. I had it down in a flash. Saturday Night Italians, as they were known back in the *Brawnx*. Does she come onto every guy like that? One more round of drinks, and I think she would've clawed through my jeans. Not to mention the paw prints all over my shoulders. If I had a dollar for every time her jewel-encrusted fingers slipped under the table, I'd probably be living . . ." His voice faded out, and he took another tug of the Jack Daniels.

"Anyway, let me tell you about the script. The treatment is pretty damn impressive. But the way I see Betty Jean, there's more than just desire and lust. Hunger, yes. But a vague notion of revenge against her past. She's not just a sex kitten—she's an angry tiger. Behind the camouflage of purring seduction, she's out for blood. That's where John Randall really fits in. I mean, it's fine to having her clinging to a sympathetic doctor. But if she's out for his balls, it adds a whole 'nother layer. Gives it some depth. Then, when . . ."

Bob twirled his martini pensively, ticking off his impressions. As Joel's voice rattled on, he felt the hackles slowly beginning to rise. It wasn't that the new slant was bad . . . far from it. Interesting. Maybe even a mini-series in it. But the problem was clear: Joel Hanlin wasn't talking about Radin's story line . . . he had immediately tossed it out the window, and substituted his own. A hard kind of writer to work with. Verbose, self-indulgent. Especially now that he was warmed up, and slowly moving the conversation toward his obviously favorite subject: himself.

"Jeez, I'm really waxing philosophical tonight, huh? I guess my feelings about women and relationships come through in my screen treatments."

"Interesting," Bob nodded, feeling a growing dislike

for the writer. Was it just a question of experience, and the fact that Bob was older? Perhaps. More likely, it was the self-righteous way he kept tilting at windmills. And women—using his cock instead of a broadsword. Sex as a weapon. "Since we're sitting here, why don't you tell me a bit more about your novel. Sounds like it might have possibilities."

"In some ways, it addresses the problem I was talking about in the treatment. Feminine romantic bullshit on the one hand, and the real world on the other. I mean, historical romance is fine, when you're living in a castle. But what the woman of the eighties is looking for is realism. Good, tight sex scenes. Action. Not just emotional masturbation and endless foreplay. Who in hell is going to believe that crap—the trembling kisses, the quivering thighs, the pledges of enduring love? It's all passé . . ."

Poor Crystal, Radin thought. *Beneath his smooth veneer, this guy's just one more old-fashioned male chauvinist pig. I'll have to mention that to Lauren.* "How does that fit into the story line? From what you mentioned on the phone, the protagonist was a woman."

"Got to be, in today's market. But a lot of the more *penetrating* moments are from her boyfriend's point of view. Lots of flashbacks—a natural for fade-ins; I've done a good job of setting up the camera work for a movie tie-in. At any rate, it's a sort of Cinderella story, a tryst between a superstar performer and a screenwriter. She's torn between having her cake and eating it. He tries to show her the real meaning of freedom. But she's so caught up in Hollywood, and a dream of family life right out of the Doris Day mold . . ."

"Sounds more like the *'Cinderella Complex'* to me. And maybe just a bit autobiographical."

"I write what I know," Joel shrugged edgily. The

tone in his voice was beginning to rise along with his alcohol intake. "There's a bit of Crystal Cooper in the heroine, I'll grant you . . . But she's hardly the first babe I ever tumbled—or the last. Jessica is a composite, with the real focus on the lives women live in the media. They get unbalanced. It's almost inevitable. Let's not talk about Crystal. But take her partner, Lauren Conrad. Ever meet her?"

"Once or twice," Bob grinned, glad that the conversation would finally get a little more interesting.

"She's got a great body. Maybe a little short on jugs. But that's a matter of personal taste. No dummy either. The way she comes on to every man in the room, you'd think she was living the Great American Dream . . . But no way. Instead, she's popping pills left and right. And rather than balling her ass off and having the time of her life, she gets hooked up with some oddball Beverly Hills doctor."

"Doesn't sound like the Lauren Conrad I know."

"That's just the point. *No one* knows. But it's a fantastic story. Just picture it: some schlemiel of a quack doctor, kinky son-of-a-bitch, at that . . ."

"You're not talking about Ted Rothmore, are you?" He lowered his eyes to the table, where a third martini had mysteriously appeared. Of course, she had mentioned his name a few times in passing. But she had mentioned dozens of men.

"I wasn't gonna go into names," Joel grinned conspiratorially as he downed his fifth Jack Daniels, "nothing I hate worse than TinselTown gossip. But can you picture this guy, pumping away at a broad like that like he owns her? Calling five, six times a day, whisking her off for midday lays whenever he goddamn chooses."

Bob tried to shut out the image. Ted's manicured surgeon's hands slipping down the straps of Lauren's silk evening dress, roaming down her tight, straight spine. His wide, crookedly grinning mouth sliding over the soft mounds of her breasts, teasing her nipples into arousal, then devouring them. He thought of the prolonged absences. "Work," she said. The lockets or diamond earrings that suddenly appeared one night, only to be replaced with new ones the next time they went out. The awkward silences, and the almost apologetic way she . . .

"You get the point," Joel laughed. "*Any* man would. But there's just something in women that shies away from reality. For years I've wanted to see just one realistic novel on the subject make it to the top. I guess I finally decided to write it. You've got to admit it's got possibilities."

"Possibilities." Bob nodded, wanting to beat the cocky asshole into a pulp. Instead, he watched the possibilities slowly congealing into a certainty. For the first time in twenty years, he had fallen for a woman. That was the phrase, "fallen for it." Hook, line and sinker. Opened up to her, shared incredible nights together, thought about marriage.

All that time, she had been leading him on. Perhaps for reasons even she didn't understand. He had known from the first that there was a side to Lauren Conrad that baffled him. A side that might take him years to explore fully.

Apparently, someone had beaten him to it. Even if Joel had exaggerated, the essential situation rang all too true. That brought up another certainty: Bob Radin and Lauren Conrad were just about to go their separate ways.

"Well, you've certainly given me some stuff to think about," he announced, fishing out his card caddy and smacking down a sliver of plastic, as the hovering waitress bent over invitingly, then winked as the tray was whisked to the register. "I think I'd better get going now . . ."

"So soon?" Joel asked, watching the same waitress bouncing delectably back toward him. Ignoring him, she flashed yet another come-on at the producer, her tempting lips turning into a pout as he ignored her. *What was he, a queer?* "Before you go, I just wanted to go over the financing once again. And we still haven't really settled on a figure for the new treatment. I was actually hoping that . . ."

"I'm sorry, Joel. But I just don't see this script in the same light you do. Under the circumstances, I don't want to play games with you. I figured you'd want to hear it up front."

"Uh sure. No problem, Bob." His face fell, then slowly rose again, blazing with fury. *Why in fuck did he invite me here in the first place? Probably had another writer in mind from the start. Is that this tight-assed producer's idea of Victorian professional courtesy? Doesn't he think a writer like me has better things to do with his time than sit around and give him a script analysis—and a dozen ideas he's just lapped up—for gratis? Or was it Francesca's idea? Just to get me between the sheets? Jerking on my chain. The thought of bouncing up and down on those silicone-bloated jugs was enough to make any man seasick.* "I do have a lot of other screenplay ideas on the back burner."

"I'll keep that in mind," Bob shrugged. "Well, nice meeting you. Sorry I couldn't have a different response for you." A barely sufficient goodbye. But under the circumstances, it was all he could muster.

Bob drifted out of the bar to the awaiting parking valet, surrendering his ticket with a five dollar bill. The silver gull wing Mercedes raced up the ramp and screeched to a halt. In the red neon light, he had momentarily mistaken it for Lauren's identical one.

He crumpled into the driver's seat, suddenly feeling a thousand years old. Punching in a tape cassette, he roared up Santa Monica Boulevard, oblivious to the rusty MG in his rearview mirror, or the flushed face of the angry writer driving it.

He turned up the volume, flooding the car's interior with the ordered strains of Bach's second Branden-burg Concerto. At the next stop light, he eased the treble up a notch more, until the flute became a shrill flutter, blocking out the sounds of the street.

But the image of Lauren, lying naked in the candlelight beside the sunken marble tub, persisted. A Mona Lisa smile, with uplifted, beckoning arms. And the silhouette of Dr. Ted Rothmore indelibly engraved in her amber eyes.

Forty-eight

"But I tell you it's real," Crystal insisted. "I think I ought to call the police. And stop telling me to take it easy. This was a threat."

"I know you're upset, Crys. I would be too."

Crystal shook her head doubtfully. "No you wouldn't. You'd keep right on working, wouldn't you?"

"I meant if it was a real threat. But why go to pieces over one crank call? We get dozens of them every day. They can't all be like your Georgian breather. Just stop and think. Two months ago, there was the guy who was going to Tommy-gun my Mercedes—because I reported on a leftist demonstration. The woman who was going to blow us up because Uncle Steve said it was going to rain, and then it didn't. And don't forget the guy who cast a voodoo spell on you last week. That was a real one too."

"He didn't threaten Marcie. That's different."

"Sure it is. But why get upset over nothing? He didn't call her by name, did he?"

"He mentioned New Hampshire."

"All that proves is that he reads the scandal sheets. Probably picked up the info from that item in the *Hollywood Reporter*. Together with the information on the media probe. One nut wants to protect the NRA, the next one wants to protect CBS. You should have kept him on the line long enough to find out what planet he was calling from."

"It's not funny. I am scared for my daughter's sake. The way this investigation's been going, I wouldn't be surprised if the mob started playing rough. Have you forgotten the Bolling case? Or what about the Washington reporter whose investigation led to a vial of acid in his face? Is the Karen Silkwood case really that different? We're talking about millions in payments and kickbacks here. I don't know why you find it so funny when some maniac threatens to abduct my daughter."

"Why don't you just . . ."

"If you tell me to 'Take it Easy' one more time, I'm going to scream."

"I was just going to suggest that you call your daughter and make sure she's okay, before you send out the National Guard." Lauren reached over and put a sympathetic arm around her partner's shoulder. "Make sense?"

For the first time in half an hour, a wary smile crept across Crystal's lips. "I guess you're right. I am making a mountain out of a probable molehill. The way Sloan's been pushing us the past few days, I don't suppose I'd be human if I didn't explode. And springing tomorrow's telethon on us. Where in hell does she think she's getting off?"

"The same place Dale is headed, with any luck."

"Did anyone hand him the pink slip yet?"

"I doubt it. Bad news travels slowly when the victim still has his network issue shredder. Although in Dale's case, the most damaging thing they're likely to find is little green people, living in the walls."

"It's just not right. He did a hell of a lot for me—for both of us. The most decent caring man in the industry. Don't you even feel guilty about it? Every time

I see him in the newsroom I cringe."

"Of course I feel like shit. Don't you think I have feelings, too? . . . I may not wear them on my sleeve in public—"

"*Or* in private, nine-tenths of the time."

"Touché. But do me a favor. Grant me the privilege of belonging to the human race. I've got my share of problems, too. Sit down with me some long weekend and I'll reel them out for you, if that's what you really want. You and I may have more in common than you know."

"I'm sorry, Lauren. I really didn't mean to . . . I mean, things have been going so much better lately. I'd hate to . . ."

Shrugging, Lauren lit another Sobranie. "Apology accepted and really Chrys, I understand how upset you are. Next topic. Any word from Joel?"

"Sure. He's still 'mulling it over.' Whatever that's supposed to mean."

"Then let's get down to the one other matter at hand. What in hell are we supposed to do about the money disappearing from RedRock? Ignore it?"

"CJ said he wanted a thorough investigation across the boards. As far as I'm concerned, we go public."

"Are you crazy? Just because they ask for honest reporting, doesn't meant they'll take it sitting down. This is a commercial network, not Nader's Raiders. And in case you've forgotten, you tried pulling that number once before. Back in Atlanta. It hardly earned you a standing applause, as you'll . . ."

"I-think-I'll-go-call-Marcie," Crystal replied from gritted teeth, slamming the door behind her.

Lauren slumped back down into her arm chair, closing the RedRock folder which had been haunting her for days now. "Really blew it with Crystal . . . again,' she admonished herself. "What the hell is wrong with me. If I gave her half a chance Crystal would probably turn out to be the best friend I ever had—maybe the only one?"

Pausing, she picked up the phone and dialed Bob Radin's number. "Oh damn . . . Hello machine. This is a lonely lady over at RedRock, calling for the second time. I'll be at home. Ciao."

At Wilshire, she noticed the yellow Pinto still hovering in the rearview mirror, half a block back. "Wasn't that the same car I saw this evening at the entrance?" she mused, fishing in her attache case for the silver cigarette case. "On second thought, maybe it's time for another Valium. The tension must be getting to me."

With alarm, she watched in the rearview mirror as the car slowed down, keeping the distance between them. At Avenue of the Stars she turned, with the Pinto nowhere in sight. As her car crept towards the Century Towers driveway, it appeared once more. In a panic, she swung screeching toward the entry, only to watch the Pinto go zooming past.

"Must be watching too many reruns of *The Untouchables*," she laughed, still feeling the chill running down her spine. With exaggerated carefree steps, she strolled into the tower and up to the elevator. By the time she reached her penthouse, she was once again calm and in control.

A half block beyond the driveway, the yellow car ground to a halt. Hidden in the darkness, the driver slowly lifted up his dashboard mike, reporting her return to Century Towers.

Forty-nine

"Well, another day another dollar," Lauren grinned at the broadcast's conclusion.

"Not so fast," Crystal declared. "We've got four gruelling hours in tonight's telethon to look forward to. I don't know about you, but I'm going to be catching a quick nap. I thought that maybe we could have a drink after the broadcast."

"Sorry. Ted's going to take me out afterwards to some party."

"Then maybe you can do us both a favor. When's the last time you had a good talk with Winston?"

"You've got to be kidding. All I ever got from him in the first place was bitchy one-liners. A good talk with Winston? Sounds like a contradiction in terms. As far as I can tell, his switch has one position: *on.*"

"Lauren, I'm serious. I'm *worried* about him."

"It's just the fact that you're a frustrated Jewish mother. I swear, Crystal. Sometimes I think you worry about whether the sun's going to rise or not." Lauren threw on her raincoat and turned toward the exit. "We'll talk about Winston later, if you insist. Right now, there's a devastatingly charming Beverly Hills doctor waiting in my office. With all due respect to our fay news gopher, I think he can wait."

"Just do me one favor," Crystal urged, pressing a dog-eared piece of paper into Lauren's hand, "ask

Ted about these drugs he's been taking. I tried calling the Help Hotline, but all they wanted to do was talk me down from a bad trip. I tried NORML as well. Once they found out I don't smoke pot and don't care one way or the other about decriminalization, they pretty much lost interest."

Lauren glanced down at the scrawled list and nodded patiently. "I'll ask him about it after the telethon," she promised, sauntering toward the door.

Crystal stared at the message on her office door and felt the blood suddenly racing through her exhausted legs. Throwing open the door, she sprang to the phone, already knowing the news awaiting her on the other side of the line.

"Wyndale School," yawned the night switchboard operator.

"This is Crystal Cooper calling for Mr. Hemmenway."

"I'm sorry Ms. Cooper. But office hours are from nine to five. If you'd like to leave a message, or call back tomorrow . . ."

"I need to speak to him now. It's an emergency."

"That simply is not possible. Mr. Hemmenway has just left with the football team. Tomorrow *is* the Windale-Exeter game."

"I'm afraid I don't understand."

"Tomorrow morning, our football team is playing Exeter. It's the biggest game of the season. Of course, there are a lot of important alumni who attend the game. Mr. Hemmenway . . ."

"Well, put me through to *someone*, then."

"Anyone in particular?"

"Someone who knows where the hell my daughter is."

"What house does she live in?"

"I really don't know off-hand. But her name is Marcie Benjamin."

"Marcie Benjamin. Ah yes. It seems that I've heard that name before. In late night calls from the Head Resident. Making quite a reputation for herself—"

"Just put me through to the Head Resident," Crystal snapped, hearing the woman's tongue clucking a *tsk tsk* in the background. Several clicks later, a brisk Bostonian accent announced, "Maudlin Gardner."

"This is Crystal Cooper. Marcie Benjamin's mother."

"Oh. Doubtless calling about Marcie's whereabouts."

"You mean you know something."

"Only that she failed to sign out for dinner. Or show up for evening study hall."

"Don't you have any *idea* where she is?"

"No more than usual. Your daughter, as I'm sure we are both aware, has quite a mind of her own on these matters. As well as showing up for classes, preparing her assignments, and wearing appropriate clothing."

"I've never heard a *word* to indicate that . . ."

"As I understand it, Mr. Hemmenway has felt that to date you were far too busy to trouble with the discipline problem. Personally, I would have preferred to discuss her problems much earlier. I must admit that I'm astounded to hear you so surprised. In two months, your daughter has established quite a solid reputation as . . ."

"Listen, I want you to call the police—immediately."

"Oh, I wouldn't worry so much about it," the woman laughed patronizingly. "I'm sure that your daughter will return, safe and more or less sound, in a

468

few hours. It's not the first time that one of our little angels has gone AWOL. I can assure you that they've always turned up and—"

"I want you to call the police. Do you understand me? I have reason to suspect that—"

"I'm afraid that's not possible. The campus security have already been alerted, and—"

"Then *I'll* call the police. What's the number?"

"You don't understand. The nearest police car is in Sandwich Township. It's a good forty-five minutes from here. At the moment, there is a blizzard going on. Besides, until such time as Mr. Hemmenway decides to alert them, it remains an internal matter for Wyndale. Mr. Hemmenway is—"

Crystal slammed down the phone and flew through the corridor.

"Good evening, Crystal," beamed the night-watchman as she raced into the elevator. "I caught tonight's broadcast, and wanted to tell you that . . ."

"Thanks," she interrupted as the doors hissed shut and the glass elevator whisked her up sixteen stories.

"Gotta speak to CJ," she muttered to Barbara as the massive doors burst open.

"He's in a conference right now. If you'd like to leave a message, or wait in the outer office, I'm sure that . . ."

Crystal raced across the floor, dodging Barbara's attempt to block the path. *"CJ, I'm leaving for the East Coast tonight."*

Startled, he looked up from his desk, looking surprisingly old and tired. "Mel, you there? I'll call you back." He hung up the phone and his features immediately reverted to his familiar vibrant, measured expression. "What seems to be the problem, Crystal? It's okay, Barbara. And please shut the door behind you. Now . . .?"

469

"I've got to fly to Boston tonight."

"Well, I really don't see any trouble. We can easily reschedule our meeting to Monday. The telethon will be over at 11 p.m. After that, wherever you choose to go on the weekend is your own business. Of course, I had hoped that . . ."

"Midnight is too late. The last commercial flight leaves at nine."

"In that case, I'm certain that whatever your personal business is, it can wait until—"

"I'm sorry. It just can't.

"Then perhaps we should discuss the matter with Sloan . . . and Dale. I must admit that I'm a little reluctant to agree to it. After all, we're dealing with a national telethon appearance. Thirty million viewers. I don't think it's in our best interests—or yours—to have Lauren go on alone. You can't disappoint your audience like that and not expect a ratings backlash. And in view of the fact that there was a similar emergency last month, I would urge you to reconsider. Maybe you should call up Deena, and see if your agent doesn't agree. But as far as I'm concerned, unless there is . . ."

"CJ, my daughter has disappeared."

"How long has she been missing?"

"Six hours."

"Well don't you think that's a little premature for pushing the panic button? I mean, Wyndale is a fine school, though Wynnies have always had a reputation for being a little footloose. I just happen to know that this weekend they're playing my alma mater. As a matter of fact, it wasn't *that* long ago that I was playing in those games. We always managed to ship up a carload of Wynnies for the post-game beer blast. As a matter of fact . . ." His voice drifted off and his eyes suddenly sparkled, with the memory of boyhood backseat bliss.

"Terrific," Crystal glared. "Just what I needed to hear. If Marcie isn't being kidnapped, then she's probably getting beers shoved down her throat, while some horny quarterback—"

"Kidnapped? Isn't that being a little dramatic? I mean, even Kikki occasionally took off for—"

"There was a call yesterday morning. Some guy threatened to get her, if we didn't stop the media probe. I was all set to call up the FBI when Lauren stopped into the office. By the time she was done, we were laughing about the whole thing. It just seemed so far-fetched . . . I mean, why should one more raving lunatic turn out to be for real?"

"So you just let it go at that." His voice had a pained, accusing undertone. "You simply laughed the matter off."

"Of course not. We're talking about my *daughter*. I called up immediately, and left a message for her to call me, as soon as possible. It's not unusual for her to wait a day. Or two. I just left the studio to give her another call . . . when I found a message from the headmaster."

"They've now alerted the police?"

"*What* police? From the sound of things, the police there consists of one cruiser. In snow up to the windshield. That's why I've got to—"

"No police?" He stared past her and nodded. "Good."

"What do you mean *good?* My daughter is out there missing somewhere in a blizzard. I mean, if *you* can't arouse any more emotion than a dull nod, then . . ."

"*Stop!*" he bellowed. "Before you go on and say something we're both going to regret." His eyes shone fiercely, cutting through the distance across the broad table. "Don't think for an instant that *I* don't understand what you're going through. In case you've forgotten, *my* only daughter was just fifteen when . . ."

"I'm sorry," she whispered, staggered by the explosion.

"No need." His grey eyes scanned the corner of the room. Unfocused. Searching. "There are times when the authorities get in the way. *Most* times in fact. Once they're involved, resolution of personal differences can become . . . cumbersome."

"You mean . . . you think that the threat was real? Don't mince words, CJ. I'm going to know soon enough."

"I think nothing. But one bereaved parent in perpetual mourning is enough for this network. I just wish you had contacted me sooner. Let me make some calls before you rush up to Wyndale. I'll have my Lear jet standing by, just in case." He reached for the phone and pushed the memory.

"Thank you CJ," Crystal sighed, picking up her Gucci case and moving impatiently as he raised his hand with a stern gesture, commanding her to wait.

"CJ here, Thomas. Tell John I want the Lear jet ready for take-off at eleven-thirty. We'll be flying into New Hampshire. Logan or Hartford, if the snow hasn't lifted. I want you to arrange for a car at either end. Yes. I want you to be prepared for . . . exactly. We'll be travelling with Crystal Cooper. One photographer's photo, and I'll have your shaven head on a platter: you got that? Whattt? Of *course*, Mrs. Redfield will be informed. This is business, man. I'll see you in a few hours."

He stared across at Crystal Cooper's tense form, and suddenly burst into laughter. "A slight misunderstanding," he chuckled. "Apparently, he assumed that you were my . . . uh, mistress."

"I don't care what he thinks. Or the whole god-damn industry . . . as long as we get Marcie back. I just don't know how to thank you enough. Or ever repay you for . . ."

His eyes raced over her sumptuous curves, and the answer flickered briefly across his mind, then vanished. "I expect you to proceed as scheduled with the telethon. Lupus has always been a special crusade to me, and I will count that as a personal favor. In the meantime, I will do what I can through private channels. With any luck, that will be sufficient. Otherwise, Thomas will personally be there at the telethon's conclusion, to drive you to the airstrip."

She thought of the hulking, ape-like chauffeur and shuddered.

"Don't worry," he continued, reading her thoughts. "He's entirely harmless. Until given the command. And one other thing, which you should also communicate to Lauren: effective immediately, I am suspending the media probe, pending resolution of this and several other matters."

He watched the blur of red silk disappear into the outer office and his features broke into a self-satisfied grin. "Beware the fruits of sin," he chided himself, pouring a carefully measured half-inch of cognac. He stared at the golden liquid, and pictured once again the grateful look of the voluptuous newswoman as she paused before the outer door. In that instant, he finally knew that he had her unquestioning loyalty come what may in the future.

His thoughts turned back to the more urgent problems at SBN. From the moment of Rob's death, he had never doubted that Dale would have to go.

A lesser man would have removed him immediately.

Pink slip and a six month's pay guarantee, never looking back on 25 years of dedicated service in the news media. Instead, Redfield had fought to keep him on, knowing the inevitable outcome. Thwarting Sloan's every attempt to oust him, knowing that she would only fight harder in a senseless ego clash. By the time she succeeded, her shrill anger had already made a lasting impression on the board.

"The poisoned pawn," he tersely noted. The opening gambit had been played superbly, and now it was time to push toward the end game. For months now he had been strengthening his defenses, waiting for the moment to attack.

"Barbara," he said softly into the intercom, "get me Tony Firestone." He snapped off the intercom and listened to the stillness surrounding him. Confident in the knowledge that she would be there ready to act on command. Firestone, his long-time rival, would be there, too. Ready to pounce on the opportunity his network needed: an out.

"Hello, CJ," came the puzzled voice.

Redfield slowly exhaled, then breathed in again, silently. Content to let him wait. And knowing that this was one call the multi-millionaire would hang on for indefinitely. ". . . CJ? You there?"

"Yes . . . I'm here." Should he toy with Firestone first? Draw him out and gently probe to find out how much he knew. No. *A stupid, childish display of power. A waste of time.* "I need some information. And I'm willing to *"pay"* for it. Crystal Cooper's daughter has disappeared. I want to know where she is."

"I dunno what in blazes you're talking about. I didn't even know Cooper had a daughter."

"When you've been making job overtures to her for the last two months?" He heard the man's defenses

474

dissolving and smiled. "I haven't got time to bullshit. I want that child returned unharmed."

"This is bizarre. Do you realize what you're . . ."

"Of course I realize what I'm saying. Let me be more explicit. I told you I have no time left for bullshit. Now either you get your seedy friends at Mammon to find her, or else we run the exposé, as scheduled. If you'd like me to be more explicit—*over the phone*—just keep playing dumb. Surveillance is random, and you can always take your chances."

"I'll see what I can do."

"You're a reasonable man. I'll be waiting for your call."

He went over the checklist systematically, rattling the names off to Barbara. One by one, the edgy voices came over the speaker. One by one, the carefully researched scandals fell, setting off an endless domino chain. Two dozen reputations left intact. Each one of them tilting toward New Hampshire.

Tens of thousands of hours of research, perhaps two hundred strategic bribes, all falling by the wayside. An expensive pawn sacrifice.

He sipped the still, dark liquor and thought of temptation. Liquor, women. Years ago they had taken their toll. Still beckoning. But easily swept aside.

And what about Marcie? Would he have made this sacrifice if it weren't for his guilt about Kikki? The media investigation had never been more than a bargaining chip—one which he had intended to save for the moment it would do him the most good. Would he regret calling in his chips now?

A useless question, leading nowhere. No point in engaging in flagellating self doubts, when they were mired in the past. The media scandals had been quietly smothered and pronounced dead. The final rites would come in a matter of weeks.

Whether Marcie was out on a precocious lark, or bundled up in the trunk of someone's car, she would be returned. No names, and no questions asked. *Fact*. With no one the wiser, he had finally maneuvered between the shoals, and out into clear seas.

"A little chancy, Clayton," his father would have admonished. "Cutting it a bit too close to the wind."

Nonetheless he had steered clear, with the patience passed on by eleven New England generations. The moment had passed, but the success would linger. That was another fact.

Fifty

"Sloan? Is this you?"

"Yes. But Regina darling, you'll have to speak up a little. I can barely . . ."

"He's downstairs in his office," she hissed through clenched teeth.

"So soon? I thought for sure that he'd still be en route. Listen, I want you to bundle up the boys and get them out of the house."

"But what can I tell him? Sloan, I'm really *terrified*. The way he's been rattling on to himself, and slamming furniture around. I . . ."

"Tell him you're dropping off the boys at the club for racquetball lessons."

"But Sloan, I . . ."

Stupid of me, she thought. On the money Dale makes, they could *never* afford those lessons. Maybe even any club at all. "Don't tell him *anything*," she ordered. "Just get them the hell out of the house."

Regina Stevens meekly agreed. Almost gratefully, Sloan observed.

"They'll be there any minute, darling. I'm sure it'll be fine. The papers have all been drawn up and signed. I know it's hard, but you've got to be strong. I'll drop by later if possible, just to make certain you're all okay. But the most important thing now is to prevent the boys from seeing it. Later on, when he's a little more stable, I'm sure they'll be able to understand. But it's important for their relationship with Dale—and for his own peace of mind later, to keep them out of the way. A straitjacket may be necessary. And that something a child should never have to witness. Now you'd better get going."

"I'll do it," she whispered, gently clicking off the line.

Dale waited a full half minute, until Sloan hung up and the line went dead.

That traiterous bitch, screamed the voice in his head. *Kill her now.*

He coiled the nylon tight around his fists, thrilling at the way it cut into his meaty palms, streaking them with white, while the surrounding flesh flushed a choked scarlet.

Blood is going to flow, murmured the chorus. *Rivers of blood.*

He crept stealthily up the carpet, egged on by the voices as each foot rose and fell. Higher and higher, to the sacred altar.

Already, he could hear the nylon fibers, singing out for the life of the sacrificial lamb.

She stood in the kitchen, bent over the counter, hastily cramming her wallet and checkbook into her Vuitton bag.

"Too late," he hissed, his voice distant and tinny, as he floated toward her effortlessly. His hands flexed and then loosened the garotte, drifting with a life of their own to the beckoning softness of her throat.

She looked up in terror and he felt his desire blossoming.

Act normal, she intoned, closing the distance between them. The psychiatrist's words became a mantra, flowing around and around her brain, as he approached. *Act normal act normal act normal.*

She saw the knotted cord, and the leering lust in his eyes. *Act normal.*

She clutched the countertop and felt her legs give way. His eyes nailed her to the corner as he swept closer, arms extended. *Act normal. Act normal.*

"Dale," her voice shrieked as she cringed, paralyzed. "What in hell do you think you're doing with my new stockings. Put them down. *This instant!*"

His twisted features froze. He hesitated.

Regina watched in a dream as he dropped the knotted hose, then turned and ran out of the kitchen.

The front door creaked lazily shut as he gunned the engine and screeched down the driveway to freedom.

"Ted, what can you tell me about Quaaludes?"

He stared nervously at the road up ahead, his eyes combing the sidewalks as they raced east on Sunset. "Uh, Quaaludes? They're a muscle relaxer."

"Addictive?"

"Let's just say 'habituative.' "

"How about white crosses? What are those?"

"Speed. Low grade amphetamine."

"Addictive?"

"Habituative. Again, strictly speaking. When you've been doing a lot of them, cutting off the supply leads to some very serious metabolic problems. And an extremely poor sense of humor . . . Jesus, are we ever late."

Lauren checked her watch, then held it up to her ear. "It's just that your clock is fast. It's only six-thirty."

"Stopped at seven fifteen this morning." He shrugged absent-mindedly, once again focusing beyond the windshield.

"Slow down. Listen, it's *my* telethon, and I say we're early. What in hell is this rush about?"

"Sorry." He made no attempt to slow the Bentley. "By the way, I have some business matters to catch up on before I pick you up."

"There's really no need to. I already told you that I wanted to have a drink with Crystal afterwards, anyway. So why don't we just call it a night at the studio?"

And let you escape into Radin's arms? "I'd love to see Crystal. So we can make it a threesome."

She scanned his tensed features and it struck her: lately, his veneer of affectionate and witty charm had begun to grate on her nerves at times, wearing progressively thinner. Tonight it was altogether vanished. She found herself looking at an irritable, self-involved Hollywood doctor. Pompous, moderately attractive, and infinitely resistible.

"Now how about amyl nitrate? Poppers?"

"What in hell is this, the med boards? Who's who in best-abused drugs?". As Lauren stared stonily out the window, a young girl in a rhinestone-studded T-shirt suddenly lunged out at the car, frantically waving. The Bentley swerved quickly across the yellow line and back, accelerating.

"Who was that?"

"Who was what?"

"We just almost ran over some kid, trying to flag us down. Do you mean to tell me you didn't even *see* her? I'm sure that she wanted to . . ."

"Probably some autograph hound."

"At night? When you've got tinted windows?"

"Listen, you're the investigative reporter. *You* figure it out. I've got enough on my mind tonight."

"Like what?"

"Like the fact that we lost a patient at the Clinic today. A four-year-old kid. The leukemia was too far advanced before he arrived. I knew there wasn't really a chance but we gave it our best. No sooner has rigor mortis set in than his socialite mother is slapping a law suit on us. In Mexico and in America. Sometimes I wonder why I bother."

"I'm sorry," she murmured, "You should have given me a warning."

"I suppose you're right. And . . . I apologize for being such an asshole this evening. I'll make it up to you, I promise. Beginning as soon as the telethon is over."

"Maybe it's better if you waited until tomorrow morning. I have a lot of pressing matters as well. Maybe we should make a date for—"

"*Please,* Lauren. I think we really need to talk it out. And the thought of not being with you tonight . . ."

As the parking valet approached, he held her fingers tight. "May I see you, later?"

Once again, he offered the familiar boyish grin. The pleading bedroom eyes anxiously promising her anything and everything, in return for tonight. "Well, I don't know," she sighed, feeling her resistance being sapped away.

"Say yes, then."

As the valet opened the door, he squeezed her hand gently.

"*Yes,*" she sighed, freeing her fingers with a yank, quickly escaping inside the KJJX broadcasting station. Directly ahead was an entourage of staffers, with Crystal holding court at its center.

"Only five minutes remain in this telethon," Crystal smiled, feeling the corners of her mouth about to drop off. "Our telephone volunteers are still waiting for your calls. And so are the thousands of children across this country. Lupus erythematosus isn't a household word. We don't have the time or the money to launch a national campaign. Instead, every cent we receive goes into research and treatment. Won't you help us? Contribute a dollar—or a thousand. But call in your pledge right now, and give us your support . . ."

"In the few minutes which remain," Lauren added, "we'd like to thank all of the generous organizations which have helped to make this crusade against lupus a reality. Our heartfelt thanks to these volunteers, who have given generously of themselves and their time. You've done a fabulous job. Without you, we never could have accomplished so much this evening . . . Please pick up your phone right now, and dial 800—745 . . . . To the Kittridge foundation, special thanks for providing . . ."

As the announcer's voice cut in, Crystal dashed to the wing of the studio, her eyes searching for Redfield's hard-to-miss chauffeur. She picked up her suitcase and headed toward the exit.

"Crystal, this just came for you," Adam Ward yelled, waving a blue-and-white envelope.

She tore it open and scanned over the telegram once, then twice. Then again.

Adam smiled vacantly. "I hope it isn't . . ."

His next words died in his throat as Crystal threw her arms around him and hugged as hard as she could. "I can't believe it," she groaned, planting a kiss on one cheek, then the other. "I just can't believe it." She hugged him once more, then grew limp in his arms.

"Adam, excuse me," she laughed, as the tears slipped down her cheeks. "I . . . it's just. The telegram's about my daughter. I was so afraid that . . ."

"No excuses, please," he laughed, hugging her once

more for good measure. "I don't know about you . . . But it's the best news I've had in months."

"Hope we're not interrupting anything," Ted Rothmore called out as he approached with Lauren. He looked down at the suitcase and grinned wryly. "Not planning on eloping, are you?"

"Or maybe moving to KJJX?"

"I only wish," Ward smiled. "And you can make that official."

Crystal excitedly exclaimed, "She's okay, Lauren. Marcie's safe!"

Lauren stared back blankly. "Well, that's great. But we found *that* out yesterday."

"But this evening, after this broadcast, I got a call from Marcie's School. I spoke to her Head Resident, and found out that . . . God, it's a long story. Much too long. But that's why I had my suitcase here."

"It seems like a happy ending, anyway," Ward grinned. "And since you're obviously in the mood for celebrating, why don't we all head to Scandia? I mean, after a night like tonight, it's well-deserved. Our treat, of course."

"Love to," Ted answered before Lauren could accept. "But Lauren and I were just on our way out the door, heading to a party out in Beverly Hills. It was a great offer, though."

"I'll call you tomorrow," Lauren whispered to Crystal, shooting a look of barely disguised disdain into Ted's back. "And congratulations . . . About Marcie, I mean." She nodded pointedly in the direction of Adam Ward, then sauntered coolly out along with Ted.

"Unless I'm mistaken," Adam whispered to her, "Dr. Ted Rothmore is not one of your favorite people?"

"It's not that I *dis*like him," she shrugged.

"But you just don't like him."

"Let's just call it a chemical dislike. You are very perceptive."

"And you're very beautiful. I've been wanting to get to know you better for months. Supper tonight at Scandia would be a perfect opportunity."

"I'd love to," Crystal accepted.

She knew he had lost the sight in one eye from a permanently detached retina, and wore the silk eyepatch because he detested dark glasses. It gave him a rather romantic air, and there was something very sensitive and vulnerable about his manner.

The rest of him was right out of the media mold: slim, bursting with energy, and positively hypnotic. Crystal was more intrigued by him than by any man she had met since Joel.

"You'll have to tell me all about the *real* Crystal Cooper." He smiled knowingly. "I think there's a lot more to her than meets the eye. There's a haunting quality about you," he added, picking up her suitcase.

Crystal was surprised, yet relieved that Adam Ward had seen through her bubbly facade, to the loneliness which clung to her like a shadow.

As he lifted her suitcase into the back of his Seville, then swung open the front door and waited to help her in, she thought of Joel and frowned. He never opened doors, or carried her bags.

For Joel Hanlin, sharing anyone's load but his own was always too much of a burden. And once again when she needed support, he was conveniently absent in the flesh, whatever his claims about the heart.

"Just who are the Stangs anyway?" Laren probed, as the Bentley headed into Benedict Canyon and slowly began to climb.

"Well he's a cardiac bypass, with ulcers and

degenerative arthritis. She's that greatest wonder of all. A perfectly healthy specimen. But actually it may not be that much of a miracle. She *is* a fraction of his age."

"Another May-September marriage?"

"More like early April-late December."

"Actually, I was inquiring about their occupations. Seems like I've heard the name recently."

"I wouldn't be surprised. He works at Paramount. A vice president and his former secretary. I hear that he's marvelous at dictation. Or was it lactation?"

"Very funny." It was a lousy joke, but at least his mood had picked up. And finally the night was showing some promise. Having Bob fail to return her fourth call was hardly a great beginning.

"Herb Stang," announced the balding, heavyset host. "I'd recognize Lauren Conrad anywhere. This is my wife, Suzanne. Darling, meet Lauren Conrad. I'm sure you recognize Ted Rothmore. Dr. T. is the biggest pill-pusher this side of the Rockies. Aren't you, Teddy? Actually, I'm just kidding. I love this guy. Known him since he was in knickers, dissecting his first alleycat. Or was it playing doctor with Cristina? I noticed that you were scrupulously avoided in that book . . ."

As Lauren was introduced around the room, the extent of her ignorance about the movie world grew more evident. Every other face in the room was vaguely familiar to her. She also recognized the names. This was the crowd who Bob Radin had been sitting in story conferences with for the past three weeks.

She settled warily on the edge of the sofa, eyes scanning the couples drifting in from the patio. As a tall, wavy haired giant broke out of the darkness, her heart skipped a beat.

Then she saw the red servant's jacket, and the tray

resting on his uplifted palm. Suddenly, she wanted to get out of there, away from these people, away from Ted.

"So the judge says to her: 'Lady, let me ask you one thing? Why did you throw your husband out the window?'

"She shrugs and says: 'Vell, I tell ya. I figure *at his age, if he can fuck he can fly.*' " The joke-teller turned to face her and said, "I'll bet that's not the sort of story they tell at RedRock. CJ Redfield would probably have a stroke."

"Probably," she agreed dispiritedly, focusing on a cluster of Beluga which dangled from the corner of his moustache. Ignoring the sudden quiet which settled on the group, she snatched up her handbag and crossed over to Ted. "Take me home," she ordered.

"What's wrong?" he said soothingly, rubbing his free hand over her bare shoulders. "Got a headache?"

"No. I'm nauseous. And if I have to sit and listen to these creeps for one minute more, I'm going to puke."

"Listen, simmer down. We just got here."

"That was your idea, Ted, not mine. I didn't ask you to bring me here. But I'm telling you to take me home, now."

"I promised Francesca Van Rensalaer that we'd meet her here. She's really dying to see you. Besides, we just got here fifteen minutes ago."

"I'm sorry about Francesca. Tell her anything you like. But let me know if you're not going to give me a lift, so I can call a cab."

Pasting an apologetic smile on his face, Ted pushed the horn-rimmed glasses back on his nose and followed her down the driveway. "I just don't understand you," he growled.

"That makes two of us." *Or what in hell I'm doing here with you in the first place, when the only thing I* can think of is Bob. Maybe it was the way Ted always seemed to hypnotize her, sap away her will. Or maybe it was the fact that it was so easy with Ted, just glamour and laughs and acrobatic sex. There was a mystery behind his horn-rimmed glasses, a hint of naughtiness and forbidden fruit for added spice. A vague notion that he was always concealing something, which kept tantalizing her reporter's instinct.

Whatever the thrill of Dr. Ted Rothmore was, it seemed a million miles away as they silently rolled through Beverly Hills. Why in hell wasn't Bob there? Was it merely a coincidence, or had he deliberately avoided her?

"Well, we're here," Ted announced, as the tires crunched on gravel.

Lauren gazed up at the stately mansion and shook her head.

"Please, sweetheart. I'm sure you're just exhausted. C'mon in. I'll fix you a good stiff drink, and have the maid run a bath. After an oil massage, I'm sure you'll feel more like yourself."

"*Home*, Ted. *My* home." She drew away toward the window, brushing off his softly caressing fingertips.

"But you're so seductive when you're like this. I just want to run my lips all over your body, and . . ."

"If you really get off on my fury, you're about to get a lifetime supply, unless you get this machine moving."

"But Lauren," he cried ten minutes later, as they rolled up to the Century Towers. "We haven't made love in a week."

Eight days, she thought, arriving at the penthouse door. Then she corrected herself.

"We've never really made love at all. Have we, Dr. Rothmore?"

Fifty-one

Lauren slammed down the phone and picked up the slim golden key ring.

She started to take another Valium, then reached for a cigarette instead. In the past half hour, she had already taken two tranquilizers. Maybe three. "Anything would be better than waiting here," she thought, grabbing her shoulder bag and racing down to her awaiting Mercedes. "Even if he doesn't show up alone."

The lights were out as she approached the redwood house. She screeched to a stop, and leapt out of the car. His Mercedes was gone from the carport.

Lauren felt her muscles knotting tighter as the doubt began to grow. What if he didn't show up at all? What if it was all one big misunderstanding? Maybe Bob had simply slipped out of town on business for a few days, and she hadn't gotten the message? She could just play it cool, end the affair with Ted — and no one would be the wiser.

She shrugged and turned back to her car, feeling a little hysterical and foolish about the whole thing. Maybe it was just her guilt feelings about hiding the relationship with Ted which had manufactured the entire crisis.

She looked back at the silhouetted peak of the soaring roof. After all, Bob *had* presented her with a key, hadn't he?

She tip-toed across the cold slate floor in silent darkness, heading for the bedroom. Lighting a crystal circle of tapered candles around the black sunken marble tub, she opened the swan-winged golden faucet and tipped a stream of Vitabath from the hand-blown decanter into the steaming water.

She carefully selected a tape of the Goldberg variations—some of Bob's favorite music—and opened up the curtains of the plate glass wall. Gazing out at the winking lights of the city, she slowly stripped off her sheer georgette blouse, then her black silk pants, feeling as though Bob were somehow there in the sunken tub, watching her every movement.

For a moment she stood there, naked and beautiful, and then the fantasy vanished. After touching a match to the pile of logs in the mirror wrapped fireplace. She moved wearily across to the tub and slid into the soothing, lemon-scented heat.

Far in the distance, Hollywood glistened before her. Daring her to tear her eyes away. The Polo Lounge, Rodeo Drive, Chasen's, her penthouse, a hundred places and impressions joined together in her mind. She thought of her childhood words, late at night in the bedroom studio in the Conrad Compound. "It was marvelous. Simply marvelous."

After so many years of stalking success, she was finally on top. The recognition she had so desperately and ruthlessly pursued was finally hers. It seemed that everywhere she now went, there were smiles of recognition, requests for her signature, photographers just waiting for her to do anything. Smile, and she made the pages of the *Enquirer*. Frown, and the trade press began digging for the reason why.

There was no longer a wait at the Polo Lounge, either. Crystal and Lauren were always seated immediately, on the right side of the room. Perhaps a quarter of a million dollars in salary wasn't that much in Hollywood. But sooner or later she would inherit the Conrad furniture fortune. In the meantime, there was always enough to keep her flow of designer clothes from Saks, Giorgio's and upstairs at Gucci. And her bi-weekly beauty treatments at Elizabeth Arden.

The rest she could easily have showered on her by Ted Rothmore or a hundred other men just like him. Charming, loaded and willing to give it all to her, in return for love. Or a fuzzy equivalent.

"You've got everything you've ever dreamed of," she observed, watching the foamy bubbles slowly pop on the water's surface. "So why in hell are you so miserable? You can have anything you want. Any man you set your sights on . . ."

Except, possibly, Robert Radin. She thought once more of Ted, and the compulsion which kept driving her back to him, time and again. The paper-thin charm, the careless opulence. Had that really been worth the threat of losing someone like Bob?

She gazed into the crackling flames as the warmth of the perfumed water enveloped her. Why hadn't she realized sooner that she had always needed someone protective, anxious to shield her from anything unpleasant? Sometimes it had been oppressive, but now that it was no longer there she felt a giant emptiness. When would she ever grow up and stop trying for just one more brass ring? Ted's kind of excitement was short-lived—she realized that—but if she could only figure out the hypnotic hold he seemed to have on her emotions. She knew she could never spend the rest of her life with him. Who would she spend it with—Lauren Conrad wasn't getting any younger. Most women her age already had husbands and families. Would she end up alone?

She gazed out the windows and thought of ten thousand has-beens scattered throughout the Hollywood Hills. Women like Violet Duval, trying to keep up her appearance at any cost, taking on younger and younger lovers as she grew older and more flawed. Waking up in the morning and crying bitterly into the mirror because life was too short, and growing old too debilitating. Staring at your reflection one morning and knowing that unless you hired a plastic surgeon in a hurry, the dream would suddenly shatter.

The world would keep on spinning, either way. Faster and faster.

She remembered the giddy feeling of riding a painted pony on the carousel. Going up and down, up and down, as the calliope cranked out a waltz. Starting slowly and revolving faster and faster, until the faces beyond the wooden gate were just a blur. She leaned over and speared one brass ring, then another. They kept disappearing and the row grew smaller, more distant. But way in the back was the golden ring, just a little bit larger and brighter than the rest. She tried unsuccessfully for the gold ring that day.

The next morning she was back there again, her pudgy baby fingers grasping the iron wand and thrusting time and again. Her bottom was aching and she felt nauseous, but she refused her mother's pleas to come down off the carousel. Finally, she leaned way out and speared the golden ring, scattering half a dozen others into the park grass.

Closing her eyes, she held onto the carousel pole with all of her might, just waiting for the triumphant moment when she would present it to her mother. The calliope music slowed, and she kicked her feet gaily in the stirrups. As the attendant lifted her up out of the saddle, she clenched onto the golden ring with all of her might, refusing to let it go.

"Look lady, you handle this," he hollered, as she

sank her teeth into his prying hand. "I don't know what's wrong with this brat."

"Lauren *darling*," her mother sniffed angrily. "What in heaven do you suppose you're doing?"

"I got the golden ring, Mommy. I got the golden ring."

"There ain't no golden ring, chubs," growled the angry carousel operator. "That one's just a little scratched, that's all . . . see?" He yanked the metal out of her hand and displayed it with an angry smile. "That's what your 'Golden Ring' is. Just a bit of scratched paint."

"Lauren, darling," her mother angrily drawled, "don't be so boring. You know how it upsets me when you act like a little brat. Come along."

The snap of a twig just beyond the patio door broke into her reverie. Lauren listened intently. The footsteps were muffled. Gripping the side of the tub in terror, she watched horrified as a silhouetted figure moved across the darkened glass door.

Was it possible? After all, CJ had just *cancelled* the media probe. Why in the world would anyone be watching her in the shadows? It was ridiculous.

There was a scratching sound on the glass. Her eyes stared wildly into the darkness. The rosebush brushed against the door again, and she saw the tall bulky shadow and laughed.

The Santa Ana winds. Too many negative ions coming down off of the mountains. Maybe that was why she felt so shitty and on edge.

It was only the wind.

"Oh, they're gorgeous," Crystal exclaimed, examining the photograph in the center of the carved oak mantel. "But they look awfully young."

"Seth is six, and Alexander is three-and-a-half. We had the half birthday last week. Anya was only twenty-six when they operated for the first time . . . Would you like to take a look at them?"

"Why not?" Slipping off her heels, Crystal tiptoed on stockinged feet across the thick pile carpet. She peered in beside him in the darkness, allowing a crack of light to shine upon the twin golden heads, lying side-by-side on the king-size bed. "Somehow or other, they always end up in my bed," he laughed. "Lord knows how. The governess swears that they're tucked in in their own rooms every night."

"Looks pretty snuggly to me." Crystal thought of Marcie, and how seldom she was even permitted to kiss her only child. The thought of physical affection between them was inconceivable, right now. But soon she would buy a house somewhere and bring Marcie home. Hopefully, there was still time to break through the wall between them

"Just one problem with the arrangement," Adam chuckled, shutting the door behind them and leading her back to the glowing sunken hearth. "For two kids with barely eighty pounds between them, it's amazing how much they can hog the covers. It was even worse when Anya was still home."

Anya Anya Anya. Didn't the poor guy ever stop thinking of his dead wife? "You must have really loved her," Crystal commented as he brought back two brimming sherry glasses, and joined her on the pillows stretched in front of the fire.

"Of course I did. She was beautiful, loving, supportive. The best wife and mother you've ever seen. I never forgave myself for cheating on her. Still haven't."

Crystal sipped the sherry and gazed into the anguished lines of his face. "You're not the first loving spouse who's done that . . . and regretted it. I've never really told anyone this before, Adam, but I was unfaithful to my husband as well. Once, in the beginning. I was pretty young and our marriage was in trouble from the start. I'll never know what made me do it. It was quick, painless, joyless. He never found out."

"No. It was like a disease with me," Adam said. "Maybe it was the pressure of just starting at KJJX. Maybe it was the last dying throes of bachelorhood. Whatever it was, I think she knew. And that thought used to torment me, when we found out she was dying. Somehow, we never got around to discussing it. I learned a bitter lesson. I won't repeat the pattern the next time. I want real commitment if I re-marry."

They watched the glowing embers fade in silence. Crystal felt his arm drift down around her shoulders, and her head dropping onto his chest. His heart beat drummed softly in her ear. She thought about a hundred thousand couples enacting the same scenario in front of fireplaces or television screens. Rich and poor, young and old. Were any of them truly happy? Was it possible that life was really *that* miserable?

There was something about Adam Ward. She felt so drawn to him, so close. It was almost as if they had known each other in another life. Crystal could hardly believe the "magic" between them. Maybe she had finally found someone to replace Joel in her emotions.

"God, I hope so," she whispered softly. "I think Adam could break Joel's emotional hold on me." Adam had children, a lovely home filled with antiques and paintings, warmth of a family life. He understood love, marriage, commitment.

As if he read her thoughts, he tenderly cupped her chin in his hand and spoke to her earnestly. "You know, Crystal, you're the first woman I've even really

494

looked at since Anya. The first woman that I could even conceive of . . . as a permanent part of my life." He lightly urged the sherry glass away from her lips, replacing it with his soft, yearning mouth. "I know that this is presumptuous of me . . . but is there any chance? Do you think you might spend the night with me? I don't want to let you go. 'Ever.' "

"Oh, yes, Adam . . . yes," she whispered, enfolding him in her arms and feeling their bodies topple back onto the cushions. He pressed into her, filling her senses with his warmth, and driving away her aching loneliness.

"Not here," she breathed into his ear. "The children."

He paused and looked around him, searching. "The governess is barricaded in her room tonight. That leaves two other beds. They're a little bit narrow, I'm afraid. We'd also have to share them with a few stuffed animals . . ."

"Then we'll have to cuddle all night. Could be worse."

"In that case, how do you feel about Mickey Mouse designer sheets?"

"They're lovely—in the dark."

"I'll go and get your bag."

She watched him make his way out the door, then disappear around the corner. The contours of his body were different from Joel's trim, muscular back and buttocks. What *would* Joel be doing ten or fifteen years from now? Still driving around in some rusty sports car? Lashing out at the world with his typewriter and his cock, proving that he was right and Hollywood was wrong? Clinging to the perverse notion of freedom which kept him from forming any permanent relationship?

How different it was to at last find a man like Adam

495

Ward. One who wasn't afraid to speak of marriage, or to show tenderness beyond a virtuoso technical performance in the sack.

Adam Ward needed no encouragement that night. He made long, passionate old-fashioned love to her. It was so intense, they were both shaking with emotion. Crystal was overwhelmed and she fell asleep with his arms wrapped lovingly around her. They made love once again just before dawn, escaping out the front door just as twin sleepy eyed heads emerged from their father's bedroom.

Crystal looked out at the rose-colored mountains in silence, then over at Adam. At the golden, handsome face, the black silk eyepatch, the square shoulders raised confidently as he drove her home through the dawn. "Yes, this might be the one," she nodded dreamily. He smiled at her fleetingly and she smiled back, ignoring the inexplicable sadness suddenly overtaking her.

Dale Stevens stumbled out onto the dirt driveway and crashed to the ground.

"*And stay out*, you lousy excuse for a pervert. I'll tell you something, buster, I met a lot of kinky johns in my day. Never had any complaints from 'em either. But you are really sick. Come around again and I'll call the heat. I swear it."

He gazed up at the lady in black leather and shook his head. Hadn't he just said what The Voice told him to? Why was she so upset?

Pay no attention. Let's go.

Nodding feebly, he fumbled in his mud-caked jacket pocket and fished out the key ring. *Look at that smudge on the passenger seat. A handprint?*

They know where you are, Dale.

He gunned the engine and let the tires spit gravel as

the Brougham swerved onto the deserted street.

"W-Where to?" he mumbled feebly.

In response, The Voice cackled maniacally. The chorus wailed in unison, then began shouting at him in jumbled fragments.

There's no where left to go, Dale. . . . You spineless coward. Just go ahead and ask CJ for a raise, Dale. I mean, if Conrad and Cooper each make a quarter of a million you've got to be worth . . . Believe in the Lord Christ Jesus and remember to pray. BELIEVE IN THE LORD CHRIST JESUSAND REMEMBER-TOPRAY. BE . . .

The sirens pounded in his ears. *You're trapped.*

"NO!" he cried, racing through the hairpin turns of Coldwater Canyon. "They won't get me." He smiled confidently and began to laugh in a croaking throaty chuckle. "They can't get me. They don't dare. Not with what *I* know. How could they? The letters would be too damaging . . ."

He looked up and saw the black Impala bearing down on him, its brights blinding him as it approached.

"Those fools," he laughed confidently, yanking on the steering wheel.

A second later the top of his head burst through the windshield, as the car bucked momentarily against the guard rail, then broke free.

It turned three lazy somersaults then met the earth far below.

"Nice night out, Ms. Schwartz," mumbled the nightwatchman.

"Huh?" She heard him pronounce her name and shuddered faintly. "Oh yeah. Terrific night. Just the kind of night for spending in the office. You know: The network never sleeps." She managed a throaty chuckle.

"Apparently. CJ just left here half an hour ago."

At least he was gone. She held the pen up to the personnel sign-in sheet and faltered. There was no way to avoid it. She scrawled her last name and the time, then headed for the central core.

Inside the computer room, climate control fans hummed wearily. She pulled the black mink jacket tighter around her freezing shoulders and dropped into a chair.

Her fingers punched in an access code and the magnetic drives behind the glass partition blinked on and whirred into life.

DEPARTMENT . . . AUTHORIZATION NUMBER . . . LINE PRINTER Y/N . . . The routine words scrolled across the screen in green letters, and her fingers punched in the appropriate responses. Feverishly she gazed around her at the yawning bank of computers. It was dangerous, doing it this way. Risky. But she needed the money, and fast. By tomorrow, they would all know about Dale's death. As soon as his body was discovered, the call would be placed. The code would be killed. The faucet would dry up.

IDENTIFICATION CODE . . .

D-S-N-E-W-S . . .

OPERATOR ERROR.

D-S-NEWS . . .

OPERATOR ERROR.

Cursing to herself, she automatically began to type in her own code. S-S-I-S-S-I.

LIMITED ACCESS, the terminal shouted. INSUFFICIENT ACCESS CODE. JOB TERMINATED. XN03 OIR. 2:45 AM EXIT.

"I'm the President, you imbecile," she screamed, slamming the desk and breaking off one two-inch long mauve fingernail. *"You goddamn idiot computer."*

NON-FUNCTIONING UNIT, it flashed defiantly.

NON-FUNCTIONING UNIT.

The power unit switched off, leaving $120,000 of desperately needed electronic money locked inside.

On the verge of hysteria, Sloan burst back into the elevator, and pressed the button for the fourteenth floor. Skirting past the executive offices, she thrust her key into the private elevator, then headed back down to the newsroom.

Avoiding the skeleton staff through a series of maze-like back halls, she arrived at Dale's office. The key turned effortlessly in the lock and she slipped inside.

Lowering the levelor blinds, she produced a flashlight and began to search. Five minutes later, she spotted the folder.

She dropped down into Dale's still-warm chair. *Five days Sloan,* she heard him cackle in her weary mind. *You've got five days . . . I own you . . .*

Then her eyes fell upon the contents. There were senseless scratchings all over the page. Circles and arrows describing nothing. Red underlining in random spots. Exclamation marks and questions.

Staring at the crazy coding, she burst into tears. "All for nothing," she sobbed, feeling her body collapse. "One more day and he would have been gone from the network for good."

Her head crumpled onto the stack of neatly-typed letters, addressed to President Reagan, The Supreme Court, The Postmaster General and the Pope.

Fifty-two

Bob Radin stared silently at the mane of red-blond hair, and flickering mounds and shadows as Lauren floated in the candlelight.

He felt the indignation rise up to his throat and die there. She stretched languorously, invitingly unaware of his presence. It would be so easy just to slip off his shoes, strip down and slide in beside her. To make love to her once more on the warm unyielding floor. Pretending that it was one more movie-perfect romance. No lies, no betrayal. Just sensuous perfumed golden flesh.

He took a step toward her and hesitated, seeing the long-lashed eyes slowly flutter and open. Their eyes met and locked in the darkness in silence.

He flipped on the lights and saw her recoil, as if struck by an invisible hand, "Here," he grunted, throwing her an over-sized terrycloth robe and for once averting his eyes as she stepped from the sunken bath, cowering at the cold touch of the air.

"I'm sorry, Bob," she implored nervously. He shrugged and her face fell. "I don't expect you to forgive me. But I came here to tell you something tonight, and that's what I'm going to do. I gather that you found out about Ted. I don't really understand why . . ."

He listened to the wavering voice in silence, weaving

through the facts and feelings. Finally she finished and stood there beside him, waiting.

"I'm sorry," he said evenly, his deep baritone voice moving quietly over the words. "It's not just the infidelity. We all make mistakes. But there's a wise old African proverb that goes, 'He who shits upon the road meets flies on his return.' It stinks—every goddamn moment we've spent together is covered by the stench. Believe it or not, I'm still in love with you. Crazy, isn't it? But there's just no way—"

The phone rang and he stared at it expressionlessly. Then he swooped up the receiver and barked. "Who in hell is this?"

He listened for a moment, then placed the phone back on the table, leaving the cord dangling down, slowly rotating in space.

He gazed at her bewildered stare and an ironic smile crossed his agonized features. "For you, Lauren." He spun around and retreated into his study slamming the door closed as he yelled, "It's *Ted.*"

Lauren awoke to the sound of Ted screaming on the other side of the wall, in his office.

"What do you mean you can't refill the prescription? My client needs those pills. Listen, Lester, I *know* the authorities are cracking down. Okay, okay. I'll cool it on the amphetamine prescriptions. But I'm telling you *as her physician* that this routine refill is okay. *No, I'm not going to give it to you in writing. You think I'm nuts?* If you're smart, you'll shut your mouth and keep it shut. I do thirty thousand dollars a year with you, and there are plenty of other pharmacies in Beverly Hills if you're getting cold feet . . ."

The voice died down to a dull, insistent murmur. She heard his returning footsteps and decided to feign sleep. "I'm heading out a little early this morning," he called in from the door. "Got an emergency with a patient. Lauren? You awake?"

She nodded lazily and rolled over onto her stomach, pulling the covers up over her shoulder.

"I must've been better last night than I thought," he laughed. "Guess you can find your own way home this morning."

As he headed down the stairs she rolled onto her back and stared up at the textured ceiling, waiting.

The ride back down from Radin's had been gruesome, as the Mercedes stumbled along and she tried to see beyond the tears cascading out of her eyes. Ted was waiting in the circular driveway, also in tears.

How in the hell had Ted ever convinced her to give him one more chance? Now she had closed the door forever on any future with Bob. Too late, she realized that Ted meant nothing to her.

Even the flowers, the diamond necklace, the contrite pleas—none of them had cast the spell this time. But somehow she needed to know for sure. She had drunk champagne joylessly, pasting the cool smile in place. She had let his hands roam over the supple curves of her body, following him hesitatingly upstairs.

He had hovered above her expertly, thrusting, withdrawing, dipping, soaring, dipping again. Hour after hour they had thrashed together, until the friction grew unbearable. She had faked an earthshattering orgasm, just to put an end to it.

Ted had smiled down at her with self-satisfaction, then rolled onto the other side of the bed. She was grateful for the distance separating them. As the numbness slowly crept over her, the tears wet her pillow as she thought to herself, "Boy, Lauren you've really fucked up. This time your self destructiveness has done you in."

"What a waste of time," she now reflected, gathering up her carefully folded clothes and slowly slipping into them. She paused for a moment, revolted at the thought of driving home with the feeling of Ted still clinging to her skin. Then, throwing her bag under her arm, she straightened out her clothes, drew her hands once over her freshly brushed hair, and stepped into the hallway.

Lauren paused at the landing, waiting until she heard the Bentley gently hum down the boulevard. Crossing over to his office, she slipped a credit card out of her billfold and pulled it upward against the latch, feeling the lock slowly give in to the plastic wedge.

Unhurriedly, she shifted through the scrawled notes and printed forms lying in neat piles on top of his desk. Knowing that an anal compulsive like Ted kept notes on everything.

ROWLAND APOTHECARY—*good for vals only*
JOHNSONS DRUG—*too much heat; lay off*
WALTON—*suspicious of Quaalude orders*
LECHMERE—*no amphetamine*

She copied down the information, then continued through the stack, pausing momentarily when she reached the invoice headed, *Joseph Black, Private Investigator.*

"Lauren recoiled in horror.

"So I *was* being followed!"

Fifty-three

". . . And then, after Dale's death, it was all I could do to get up in the morning. I guess I felt almost guilty. I mean, I walk into the office with stars in my eyes. Adam calls, tells me how much he cares for me . . . And then the news about Dale . . . It was horrible, Dr. Fielding . . ."

Crystal felt the tears welling in her eyes and tore at the handkerchief in her hand. "I know that he was having personal problems. But I think that if only we had helped him a little more . . . I mean he was just such a decent man. In an industry which is hardly known as a wellspring of human kindness. Dale did a lot for me. He really . . ."

"Tell me about Adam Ward again?"

"There's not really much to tell. The morning after Dale's funeral—he accompanied me, of course . . . I was seeing Joel again sporadically, but he would never have dreamed of supporting me that way . . . Anyway, the next day he calls me up with an offer from his network. He's got it all figured out. I refused of course. *I* couldn't leave RedRock at a time like that."

"Why not?"

"I couldn't even conceive of it. I told him that. I could sense the displeasure on the other side of the phone. I asked Adam if he was annoyed, or resented something I'd said. 'Of course, not, darling,' he replied . . . Just like that . . . Said he was going away on business for the week but he would call me back the second he returned . . .

"I never heard from him again." She stopped to wipe her tears away.

"I left him three or four messages, but he never returned the calls. How could he be such a bastard? I thought he really cared for me. After that night we spent together. Was it all an act just to get me to leave Now News and sign with him? Or is he just one of those men who like the thrill of the chase and then lose interest after the conquest?" Tears of frustration streamed down her face. "Damn him, I really fell for it. God, I feel so cheap. So used!"

"I've heard enough," Fielding interrupted. He slid his hands down into his pockets and his eyes bore into hers. "Crystal, I've sat patiently and listened to you for forty minutes now. And quite frankly, you could go on and on like that for hours. We'd simply never get anywhere. I don't know what you expected from this office visit, but it's obviously not help. I suspect that all you want me to do is nod and look sympathetic while you rattle on about how bad you feel because of the tragedies in your life. Well, I'm not biting. Life isn't fair, and that's all there is to it. Of course I empathize with your feeling of loss at Dale's death. And I'm sorry that RedRock can be so stressful. Honestly. But I'm not about to congratulate you for martyrdom, or for drowning yourself in depression because of things you can't change anyway."

"I'm not being a martyr."

"Of course you are. Just look at the way you got angry when I suggested it. Do you have any idea how furious you look right now?"

"I have a vague notion," she nodded between clenched teeth.

505

"You came to me for help. That's what you're paying me $120 an hour for, and that's what I'm going to give you. And the first thing I'm going to tell you to do is listen to the tapes, start throwing them away and making new ones."

"Precisely what 'tapes' are you referring to?"

"The ones in your head. The early childhood programming that you got from your mother. The message that says things like: Just smile and look pretty. Wear pretty clothing. The world will be wonderful. You'll find a nice boy and settle down and make a happy little nest. Nothing will ever go wrong, and you'll live happily ever after. Don't you hear yourself saying that?"

"Not exactly, I confess."

"You're going to try to, if you want to get better."

"I didn't think I was crazy. At least when I walked in the door."

"I didn't say you were crazy, but it's time to realize that you are looking for the father you never had. You destructively pick men who are destined to desert you, just like he did. Joel told you from the beginning that he was a loose fish, yet you persisted. And Ward's admission of his infidelities should have given you fair warning."

"So what should I do, Doctor?"

"Start processing data from the outside world. Everytime an unsatisfactory message comes in, you get depressed or file it away. Instead of living in the eighties, you're suspended in a little fantasy cocoon."

"I don't think that wanting a regular family life qualifies as an escapist fantasy."

"As a mature and quite perceptive adult, have you ever met one of these idyllic happy families? Have you ever thought about the possibility that they don't exist? They're a hangover from a repressed Victorian

506

mentality. An emotional dinosaur. Remember the old song, *Love and marriage, Love and marriage: They go together like a horse and carriage?* Well, it's what you might call a Freudian irony. And unless you want to be wearing that yoke and bearing crosses for the rest of your life, you'll throw out the tapes. Learn to live for the moment. You enjoyed your moment with Ward, didn't you? What else do you want?"

"You mean you don't believe in marriage?"

"I prefer to put it this way: sexual bonds and chemical attraction are unlikely bases for a stable, rational lifestyle. That means picking an environment for growth and personal development which is not about to fluctuate on the basis of a bad night or two. In order to give myself and my son a positive, nurturing environment, I live in a combined household of four men and three children. Two boys and a girl. With our pooled income, we can all afford the very best care for them, and the personal space we each need. At the moment, I'm also living with a woman. Debbie is a wonderful person, and we enjoy a solid, mutually beneficial arrangement. An open relationship, in which we are both entitled to sexual diversity."

"It sounds more like musical chairs than love to me."

"You're showing hostility again. I sympathize with you. As Fritz Perl taught us, 'To change your life is not an easy thing.' But I can honestly tell you that it was a tremendous growing experience watching Debbie make love to my best friend. No bruised ego, no guilt or possessiveness. I suggest you try developing the same kind of adult relationships."

"Well, *if that's your thing,* as they say, more power to you. But it's simply not what I'm interested in. It's not what I want, although it may work just fine for you. You really have no right to sit there as a therapist and try to push your own ethic onto me."

"I'm-here-to-help-you," he responded emotionlessly. "If you're serious about dealing with the problems that brought you here . . ."

"So it's agreed then?"

"Right," affirmed Lauren. "We turn the evidence over to CJ. Now that I've tied Sloan's name positively to the Swiss account. Igor did it as a personal favor—in return for a minor sexual assault in his office. God, what a pig. The very thought of it makes my skin crawl."

Crystal swerved the car onto Sunset. "If you don't mind, maybe we can cancel the Polo Lounge today. After my bout with Dr. Fielding this morning, I just don't think I can cope with another high intensity dose of California lifestyle. Matter of fact, I would prefer Hamburger Heaven."

"Just so you can lord it over me and drown yourself in a cheeseburger and fries, while I'm counting the calories in my radishes? Actually, after last night with Ted, I feel too nauseous to eat, anyway. And please don't give me the 'I-told-you-so.' I feel shitty enough as is."

"Did I just detect a four letter word escaping from your lips? That's not like the Lauren Conrad we all . . ."

"Knock it off, Crystal. I'm not in the mood." Lauren stared moodily out the tinted windshield. "It's not her fault," she thought. "I haven't even mentioned a word about Bob last night. As long as I keep smiling and looking like I'm on top of the world, why in hell should she suspect what's up?" She stared into her compact mirror, half-comforted and half-tormented by the cool, self-confident features staring back at her.

"Anyway," Lauren continued aloud, snapping the mirror shut, "I want the Rothmore case for myself. Now that I have a few names to go on . . ."

"Wait one minute there. You can't just cut me out of the scoop. Just because you've got a lead on it. Don't forget that I told you a month ago that there was something suspicious about the way he kept handing out the drugs to everyone we've ever met. Besides, it might not look good. Considering the fact that you just broke up with him this morning. I mean, the connection hardly looks great. However discreetly you think you handled it, I'm sure that there are quite a few people around who know what was going on."

"Certainly a few more than I thought," Lauren mumbled, staring bitterly out the window.

"What? I didn't hear what you . . ."

Lauren's eyes shifted onto the passenger rear view mirror. Abruptly she froze. "We're being followed."

"You're going to have to speak up. The way the engine is roaring, I can barely even hear myself . . ."

"*We're being followed.* Don't look back into your rearview mirror yet, but—"

"Too late. But I didn't see anything suspicious."

"Did you notice the yellow Pinto three cars back? No, why should you? That guy's been following me for over a month now. I'm sure of it . . . No. Don't turn off Sunset."

"But I thought we were going to Hamburger Heaven?"

"Forget it."

"That's easy for you to say. But my stomach is already growling, and . . ."

"I'm *serious.* I owe you a lunch at the Bistro Garden."

"Can I get it in writing?"

"*Can't you see that I'm serious?*"

"Just calm down," Crystal answered soothingly. "Take it easy."

"You sound like me," Lauren laughed. "Next thing I know, you'll be offering me a Valium . . . Now listen: he's still behind us. I want you to drive past RedRock, and keep on driving."

Crystal cruised down Sunset slowly, noting the fauna parading its streets and shaking her head occasionally in amusement. She stared at the leering rock posters, the rhinestone tee shirts and punk hairdos. Rolling past Schwab's pharmacy, she glimpsed a girl frantically writing down numbers at the pay telephone. The word "tapes" flashed into her mind.

What was it about Los Angeles that could make a lunatic like Dr. Fielding seem almost sane? That's what it had come down to: either he was crazy, or she was. She stared at Lauren, struggling to maintain control at any cost. Out on the street, there were nothing but easy smiles and confident, laid-back strutting. If life was such a miserable experience, why were these people laughing?

Back in Atlanta, a question like that would never occur. Who thought about facades, or the *right* watch on your wrist, or waiting for a *maitre d'* to recognize you at the Polo Lounge, and devoting a year to accomplishing that achievement.

She glimpsed the hood of the Pinto in her rearview mirror and smiled. Probably just some stargazer down from the Valley. "Maybe I should never have come here." She tried on the thought and threw it angrily away, glancing at the receding towers of Number One Sunset Boulevard.

"Come off it, Crystal," she sighed. "You're as hooked on Hollywood as any woman alive. Maybe there is something a little strange in the air. And more than a little strange in the lifestyle. But you love it. It's just a matter of coping with California — or at least going down fighting."

As they approached the wasteland near the Hollywood Freeway, the Pinto was still fifty yards behind them. "Well, here goes nothing," she laughed, creeping up the ramp and heading north. As the BMW slowed to a crawl, she watched the Pinto come racing up towards them, then immediately slam on the brakes. She sped up and slowed down, watching him maintain an even distance in the rearview mirror.

Crossing over to the left lane, she let the cars pile up and lean on their horns, as the BMW did a cool fifty-five miles per hour. As the Hollywood Bowl exit appeared up ahead, she dropped down to thirty-five, keeping her eye glued to the passenger-side mirror. As they came level with the exit, she floored the accelerator and swerved sideways through four lanes of traffic. The engine revved into a protesting whine as she cut through a row of trucks and bounced over the median strip. As they shot down the off-ramp, she could just make out the Pinto, stopping a quarter of a mile beyond on the freeway.

"Well, we did it," she yelled, slamming on the brakes and skidding toward the stop sign.

Lauren nodded weakly, the color draining from her face. "Ever thought of trying out for the Indianopolis 500," she gasped.

"Nineteenth Precinct," issued the voice between recording bleeps, "Sergeant Nunez speaking."

"Yes, officer, I want to report a crime."

"Exactly what sort of crime?"

"I'm not sure what you call it. See, I was dating this Doctor. And he's been giving me illegal drugs. Lots of them. And he's made me have sex with him, too."

"How old are you, Miss?"

"Fourteen."

"Name?"

"Dr. Ted Rothmore. Bedford Drive in Beverly Hills."

"I meant your name."

"You think I'm crazy or something? I don't want to get a reputation in school. He's made me perform some acts that . . . well, forget about that part. This guy is stockpiling drugs like he's trying to corner the market. Not only that, but he always keeps a few decks of smack under his pillow. He gives those to little girls, too. Listen, I've got to get off the phone before he grabs me and rapes me again. Please help me."

She snapped down the receiver, and fumbled with the string of plastic Mardi Gras beads hanging onto her shallow cleavage.

"Who were you speaking to?" Ted demanded.

"My girl friend Saundra."

"I told you I don't like you using my phone."

"Lissen, can I have those reds now? I'm late for biology. Unless you want to fuck again."

"No. Fine. Here." He tossed the vial onto the bed and headed out into the corridor.

"You think I'm really stupid, don't you?"

"No, Jeannie. I told you before, I think you're a clever girl. That's why this little arrangement has worked out so satisfactorily."

She pointed to the photograph on his dresser and smirked. "Lauren Conrad. She's your girlfriend, isn't she?"

"Listen, I've got some patients waiting for me and . . ."

"She was in the car with you the night you tried to run me over."

"What in hell are you talking about? I told you before . . ."

512

"You told me lots of stuff." She threw on her T-shirt and arched her back brazenly, sensing his eyes once more crawling all over her. "But I'll bet you suck *her* pussy, don't you? I'll bet you just lap it up . . ."

"I've told you. It's nothing personal. But the vagina is one of the filthiest organs in the body. I'm just not into . . ."

"Eating *mine*. I know. But a woman's got her rights. And if you're not going to satisfy my needs, then I'm not going to satisfy yours. You can just find someone else to suck your cock . . . *while you're dialling your mother.*"

"Are you quite finished?"

"No. I think you're *extremely* bizarre. And despicable. A real sick-o, you dig?"

"GET OUT OF HERE!"

She ducked away from his knotted fists, glancing once more at the glassine envelope of heroin peeping out from under the pillows. *A whole week of her allowance down the tubes. And worth every penny of it. Hell hath no fury like a girl scorned. Or however it went.* "Goodbye, Dr. Rothmore."

She undulated down the stairs, throwing him a practiced come-hither look. Then, bouncing toward the front door, she tossed her book bag over her shoulder, and proceeded down the stairs.

Leaving the door wide open, she cupped her hands to her mouth and screamed at the top of her lungs, ". . . *And you're a lousy lay, too!*"

"That lousy pubescent little slut," he glared, watching her stick out her thumb and pick up a ride from a passing Rolls. "That was really a low blow. But the next time, she can come crawling to me if she needs reds. They always *do* come crawling back."

As the telephone rang, he yanked it up and cradled

it in his neck. He removed the sphygmomanometer from his satchel and wrapped the band tight around his forearm, pumping it up as he spoke. "Dr. Rothmore, speaking." *One-forty over eighty-five. That lousy bitch.*

"This is Joey. Joey Black."

"Yeah, what's up?"

"I just lost her."

"You whaaaat?"

"She was driving on the Hollywood Freeway. With that Cooper dame. Talk about lady drivers. Jeez. One minute she's doing thirty-five. The next she swerves across four lanes doing ninety. She almost killed them both. The Pinto just couldn't keep up."

"You were tailing her in a Pinto?"

"You said nothing obvious. I figured . . ."

"You're *fired.*"

He glanced at the pressure indicator, suddenly hovering at one-eighty.

"Lauren," he moaned, "what are you trying to *do* to me? Don't you understand that it's for your own good? Those guys like Radin are going to destroy you. God only knows what they transmit. For all you may know, they're slurping water from public fountains. Sitting indiscriminately on toilet seats. They're walking *carriers.*"

He scrubbed down his hands, then took a pulse reading. *Ninety-five. Five milligrams of Valium. Better make that ten.*

He opened a bottle of mineral water and gulped them down greedily.

Then, grabbing his keys, he bolted down the steps two at a time, praying that she would be waiting, untouched, at Number One Sunset Boulevard.

The police sergeant met him at the second step.

Fifty-four

Lauren collapsed onto her bed and switched on the local news.

She watched the set, the laughing family chatter as the reconstructed anchors at KLJA warmed up for the report and felt her exhaustion flare into anger. Imagus had struck again. The one decent local affiliate had finally caved into the industry pressure. Two more newscasters replaced with changling clones. Strong father type, young eager-to-please woman co-anchoring.

At least when Cronkite was still telling it the way it was, news reporters had a *serious* anchorman to rally around. But lately they were dropping like lead-winged flies. Glittering up the news and going light on the content. There was no news like show news. For the first time, Lauren began to feel like an endangered species. Or a fossil at thirty-three.

As the slight Oriental woman began her second story, Lauren's ear could already detect the queer inflection of Imagus reporterese. "In Los *A*ngeles this afternoon, police ar*res*ted a Beverly Hills doctor described as . . ."

"I don't *know* why they even *bo*ther," Lauren mimicked. She shrugged and turned to the alarm clock. "Eleven fifteen? My watch says eleven ten. Better stop off at the jeweler tomorrow morning."

Suddenly, she caught a glimpse of something on the screen. As the smiling face of the television reporter faded from view, she was shocked to see Ted's haggard face trying to hide from photographers and cameramen.

"Isn't that Dr. T? Igor, are you listening? Ted Rothmore is on the local news."

"That's very nice, Francesca." He studied her features carefully. Her tennis dates with Rothmore had seemed innocent enough. But you could never tell with Francesca. The corners of her mouth wrinkled up into a smile and he grimaced. Thank God he had put an end to their little *rendez-vous*.

"Wait a minute. They're . . . they're arresting him. Can you *imagine?* Arresting Ted Rothmore. It's horrible."

"He must have done something, my pet. I *told* you I didn't like that doctor."

"That's just because you thought that he and I were making love on the sly. You really thought that I would stoop to the level of a common doctor, didn't you?"

"I said no such thing. Never made a single accusation."

"But you thought so."

"Well . . . *were you?*"

"Of *course* not, darling. And thank *God*. Can you imagine what a disaster it would be? My God, *quel scandal!* What with the boutique about to open? I think I'd rather *die*. . . . It's going to be enough of a problem as is. The seating arrangements have already been made. Ted was going to sit between Georjeana Mayer and that marvelous new actress that we met at the Astaire party last month. I guess I'll have to call Georjeana right away. Who in hell can I get for her dinner partner? She despises Robbie Mann. I guess there's always Roger Spears. But his new building is creating such a stir—I'd hate to waste him like that."

Her porcelain fingernails scratched rapidly through the stack of invitations, until they lit upon the one marked *Urgent: Dr. Ted Rothmore*. "One thing is for certain," she mused, dropping it back onto the table and offering the remainder of the pile to Igor. "Until this matter with the police clears up, I can't take any chances. Dr. T. is *out* of the 'A' Group invitation list. If I have to invite him, he goes out with the last-minute courtesy list. And I do hope he has the good manners to turn it down . . . Be a darling and mail those for me. They are for the press, the fashion people and the VIPs. These are crucial! I want you to *personally* deposit every one of them into the box. Here's a checklist, so you can cross them off as they go in."

"All you ever talk about these days is *Chez Francesca*. Boutique this, boutique that. Don't you ever think of anything else?"

"*Really*, Igor."

"I mean it, Francesca. You're like a woman possessed. I didn't—"

"Lauren! I forgot all about Lauren Conrad. You know that she and Dr. T were . . . like that." She wrapped two fingers around each other and nodded portentously.

"You mean she was laying him?"

"Don't be vulgar. I just hope that she isn't implicated. That would be *too* horrible. But send out the invitation anyway. I want her to know that I have faith in her."

Igor stormed out of the room and into his office, slamming the door angrily behind him. "I've created a monster," he mumbled, staring at the large stack of invitations. "I give her this boutique to amuse her. And what does she do? Thank me? *No*. Repay me by devoting more time to me and to the house? *No.* Now she has no time for Igor. It's *Chez Francesca* this, *Chez Francesca that*. We run out of vodka and she barely even *notices.* And that goddamn Doctor Rothmore's diet—speed in the morning, Valium in the afternoon, sleeping pills at night. At least now she has to find a new one. This time I lay down the law: no more American drugs. Even if I have to drag her back to Zurich."

He leafed through the invitations and lifted his nose in disgust. Such friends. The *crème de la crème,* she called them. *Nouveau riche,* down to the last pseudo-copper penny.

Picking up Lauren's invitation, he studied the embossed rag envelope and frowned. *Three dollars apiece.* And what did it get him? After he went out on a limb to personally identify that Swiss account holder for her the least she could do was to show a little appreciation. Instead, she gave him the cold shoulder when his hand dropped down onto her knee. Had the audacity to jerk it away as he reached for her inner thigh. As if *she* had not come to him, crying and pleading in the first place.

Was it possible that she was too stupid to understand that his time was money. And that he would want a little return—or at least a premium—for his investment? "That ungrateful bitch," he stormed, "she gets not a cent more of my money. No caviar, no champagne, no three-hundred-dollar-a-head dinner. Not even a postage stamp!"

He grasped the envelope between his stubby fingers and deliberately tore it in half. He stared at the ragged edge and nodded, knowing that Francesca would aesthetically approve. Commercial papers with their mechanically cropped edges were just so trite.

He shredded it slowly into confetti, then watched

the shreds settle lazily into the bottom of his wastebasket.

Grinning with satisfaction, he crossed her name off the list, then proceeded to meticulously shred the rest of the stack. Knowing that the wise industrialist was the one who knew when to cut his losses.

"Lauren darling," Sloan gushed into the phone, "you don't *happen* to be watching the eleven o'clock news, do you?"

"Yes." She opened her mouth to say more, but the words froze in her throat.

"Wonderful. In that case I won't keep you. I just have one thing to say to you: You're fired. Effective immediately."

"Wait a minute. Sloan . . . let me explain. I was working on the Rothmore case myself. Just this morning . . ."

"Darling, you don't need an explanation. And I'm sure mine will be plastered all over the papers tomorrow morning. Although as president of the network, I also need no explanation. Don't bother coming in, tomorrow. The registered letter will be in your hands first thing."

Bob Radin lowered himself wearily into the marble tub. Leaning back against the padded headrest, he waited for the feeling of paralyzing exhaustion to fade.

The image of Lauren's lush body shifting in the black water continued to haunt him. Sending her away had taken every ounce of his willpower. Afterwards, he had spent the night staring at the shimmering cityscape, emptying a bottle of brandy while the lights blinked out one by one.

He stared at the place where her head should have

rested, hair spead out over the marble ledge like an odalisque. "You're weakening," he said, feeling the last of his iron-clad resolve being sapped from his limbs and slowly washed away.

He had never felt this way about a woman. His marriage to Kim was O.K. in the beginning. Her father was the head of Starcrest Productions, and he needed that first big break. Soon she began to go her merry way—actors, producers, directors, junior execs—while he spent his evenings alone, working. The joke was on him, because when the first big picture came, it came from MGM, not from Starcrest. He hadn't needed Harry after all—but he already had Kim. By the time they terminated the six-year marriage, no one was laughing.

"Once is enough," he thought. He picked up the remote control and spun through the channels, settling on a movie. "I can't trust her. No matter how perfectly we seemed to fit together. There's always going to be that one little friction. Sooner or later it will wear through the rest. That's the bottom line."

Vivien Leigh lifted her hoop skirt and tore across the room, her corseted breast heaving with passion. "Oh, Rhett," she breathed imploringly. ". . . Rhett . . ."

Gone with The Wind. The antique English grandfather clock struck a sonorous chime eleven times. After twenty years of unbroken bachelorhood, Radin knew the ins and outs of that lifestyle. He also knew that once he went back to active status, there would be no shortage of desirable women clamoring after him.

"Quite frankly Scarlett . . ."

Clark Gable twitched his trim moustache, dimpled his cheeks, and it was over. It was always so simple in the movies. Just *I don't give a damn,* and that sealed it.

Vivien swept her eyes over the battle-ravaged estate.

For a moment, he thought he was looking at Lauren.

Avoiding the final heart-rending seconds, he flipped the control once more. Five minutes into the broadcast, Channel 3 flashed on the footage of Rothmore being brought in to the precinct.

Without a moment's hesitation, he was on the phone.

"Answer it, dammit," he cursed, throwing on his crumpled shirt and slipping into his trousers. "I know you're . . ."

"Hello." Her voice was muted. Expressionless.

"I saw the broadcast, Lauren. Are you okay?"

"I'm fine, Bob. Thank you for calling. After last night, I hadn't really . . ."

"Forget last night. I'm talking about right now. You can't just tell me that . . ."

"Okay, so I'm lying. Last night I lost the only man who's ever meant anything to me. Then I broke it off with Ted. Five minutes ago Sloan called to tell me I was fired. I feel like slitting my wrists. Do you feel better knowing that?"

"I'm coming over."

"No, you're not. I appreciate your call. That's all you need to do for me. And don't worry. I told you that Conrads always come out on top . . . Maybe that was an exaggeration, too. But I am a survivor."

"*Don't cut me off,*" he pleaded, slicing through her carefully constructed equanimity. "I want to see you Lauren. No matter what happened. Don't you understand that? I'm coming over right now."

She shrugged uselessly, hearing the tinny echo of her sobs in the phone.

"I love you, Lauren,"

She hung up and stared into her reflection in the bathroom mirror. Her hair was matted and limp, and the mascara had flowed down her cheeks. She looked pale, drained. Like a corpse.

"You wouldn't really have done it, would you?"

Her reflection shrugged with an enigmatic smile, dropping the razor blade and growing smaller as she slowly walked out of the room.

Lauren snuggled close to Bob as he slept soundly in her big canopied bed. She recalled the events of the previous evening when he had rushed to be with her after the fatal newscast. She had opened up to Bob more than to anyone in her life—telling him about her fears—about the self destructive actions that she seemed to have no control over. She even admitted being drawn to Ted in some inexplicable way—but how shallow and empty it was compared to her feelings for Bob.

She had poured her heart out for hours trying to make him understand that she needed his kind of love desperately—that it was her only salvation. She had even said that losing him would be the worst thing that could happen to her—even worse than losing her job. She had sobbed out all of her frustrations until her beautiful face was swollen out of shape and his shirt was soaked with her tears.

Bob had listened to everything with little response except to hold her gently.

When she had finished, exhausted, he took her tear-blotched face in his hands. His own eyes were glistening.

"Lauren, I want you to be my wife," he had said huskily. "I love you too much to let anything—especially pride—keep us apart."

She had been too stunned to answer—so overcome by relief that she could only burst into a fresh spasm of sobs as she clung fiercely to him.

No answer was necessary. He had picked her up and carried her to the bedroom where he tenderly slipped the creamy silk Dior robe from her shoulders.

They had fallen onto the bed in each other's arms. Then he had gently caressed and kissed every inch of her body—very slowly, almost reverentially. The light from a full moon filtered in through the sheer curtains, silhouetting their bodies. She accepted his caresses silently, tears still flowing from her eyes. When he had at last reached her lips, they kissed with a passion that was almost agonizing. Then she began her exploration of his body. Beginning at his toes, she flicked her tongue and lips up his strong legs, lingering at his thighs, then softly encircling his already rock hard penis. He had moaned with pleasure, thrusting his hands into her thick mane of hair.

Just as his control was beginning to dissolve, she released the throbbing organ and proceeding to his nipples, encircling each of them tantalizingly with the tip of her tongue, then on to his neck where she nuzzled into the hollow of his throat. Her lips nibbled his ear, his forehead, his cheeks, finally coming to rest again on his trembling lips.

An animal cry tore from his throat as he slid on top of her. Their lips met again as he entered her. For a long moment they didn't move, locked together from head to toe, almost one entity. Then it had begun to overwhelm them and their lovemaking had taken on a frantic pace.

Hours later, when they had finally spent themselves, they had fallen into an exhausted sleep, locked in each other's arms, with Bob still inside of her.

Lauren felt Bob stir besides her. She realized in astonishment that just remembering last night's lovemaking had caused her aching loins to throb with fresh desire.

Reaching for her husband-to-be she found that he had the same idea.

"We're home, Madame," drawled the chauffeur.

Francesca nodded and slipped the bottle of scotch from the portable bar into the pocket of her chinchilla coat. Leaning against the car door, she fell against his arm and was led in a stupor across the driveway. "That will be all, James," she slurred. "You may go now."

"Perhaps I should help you . . ."

"*I said, that is all.*" She swayed against the door and pushed herself inside, determined not to break down in front of a servant.

Sinking down onto the Aubusson rug, she stared up at the haunting Modigliani portrait above the mantle. "Stop sneering, you bitch," she mumbled. A moment later she took off her spiked heels, and launched them one after another toward the painting, jerking away as she heard the thump, and then the rip of the canvas. "You mean nothing," she cried.

"All of you. You mean nothing. You are tasteless vulgar trash. Here I offer you the most exclusive boutique Rodeo has ever seen. And what do you do? You don't even attend the opening. You're *peasants. Do you hear me? Riff raff.*"

She pulled on the cord to summon a servant, and wrestled out of the coat, heedless of the liquor spilling onto the priceless spun-gold and red silk Bokhara. "And I thought you were my friends," she moaned. "You thoughtless slobs. I can understand those tasteless editors missing it. But the rest of you? It just makes no sense. Don't you understand the accomplishment? The *triumph* of *Chez Francesca?* Not one of you from the entire 'A' list? *Unthinkable!*"

And yet it had happened. The Chandlers, the

Mayers, the Pecks. Lauren Conrad and Crystal Cooper. Even Bob Radin had somehow failed to arrive at the exclusive opening. Instead, the only attendants were assistant editors and second-rate Ladies-Who-Lunch, all of whom had received last minute invitations. An entire room filled with the boring women she had been cajoled into inviting. Not another person of quality in the entire second string group.

"Maybe I should have chosen a wider selection of designers," she wondered. But a moment later she shook her head bitterly, as she ran down the scrupulously deliberated roster. The House of Chanel, Andre Laug, Galanos, Valentino, Armani, Kenzo. And the *ambience*. Findlay for flowers, catering by Milton Williams. It was all for nothing. All her compromises. She had nothing but possessions and a demanding husband. Not even any real friends. Not the one thing that might have mattered—a child. Nothing but emptiness in her life. No one to appreciate her talent.

Yes, Francesca nodded. *It is all too obvious that in this town there is no one with a true appreciation of quality.*

"Madame called?" Marta appeared, rubbing her eyes.

"I will have my bath now," she commanded.

"Thank God Igor had a headache tonight," she sniffed, slowly rising out of the perfumed bubbles. "He will never know of tonight's humiliation. And Violet. As soon as she's out of the clinic, I will bring her to Paris."

She slipped into the pale silk negligee she had flown in for her private collection from Rome, then padded quietly into Igor's chamber. "Darling," she sighed, slipping in between the soothing Porthault sheets, "your Francesca is home."

He snorted briefly in his sleep, then rolled onto his back.

"Wake up darling," she cooed, running her fingers all over his broad chest as she covered his face with gentle kisses. "I want to make love to you." Her hand travelled down to his flaccid cock, urging it into fullness. "Darling, I need you so much tonight."

He stirred and she felt his warmth flowing into her urging palm. His cock rose to half-mast. "I'll be so good for you tonight," she purred.

"Not tonight . . ." he groaned in his sleep, ". . . I'm so . . . tired . . ."

"Oh *yes* tonight," she giggled, sucking tantalizingly on his nipples. He was so inviting, so peaceful. Just like a little boy. "Take my breast into your lips. I want you to suck them. Very tenderly. I know how much you like that. Well, you can do it, darling . . . Go ahead. Every inch of me is yours tonight." She ran his hands over the Rubenesque ripples of her body, slowly increasing the pressure of her fingers on his cock.

With sleepy irritation he yanked away his arm, lodging an elbow in her rib. "You're such a brute," she sighed. "You may take me hard and fast tonight . . . But first, I want to be wooed."

Beneath the sheets his penis faltered and began slipping through her fingers.

"Any way you want," she nodded, tossing back the covers. Hiking up her negligee, she straddled him. Her body sank lower as she began to sigh with delight, rubbing his shrivelled member against her throbbing clitoris. "*Anything.* I am yours, Igor. You may even make love to me *à posteriore.*"

"Please," she begged, rotating her hips. "Take me, my darling." Bouncing up and down against him, Francesca seized his flabby cock more tightly, and tried to force it inside her trembling labia. Tears streaming, she looked at his stubbornly dreaming face and tore apart the precious silk. *"See what I'm doing for you?"* Her hand squeezed harder around him. He opened his eyes and she nodded gratefully, lowering her pendulous breasts down to his lips.

"Mmmmmmphhhhh," he spat, crashing his head violently into her cleavage.

"Yes, my darling . . . *yes* . . . I'm burning for you . . ."

"You horny bitch," he erupted, throwing her aside. "Get your *flabby boobs out of here and let me get some sleep."*

She raised the Waterford decanter filled with Chevas Regal up to her lips and surveyed the magnificent dressing room with cool approval.

The accomplishment of a lifetime, she nodded. The endless racks of designer fashions loomed before her. She ripped open the drawers and stared at the piles of briefs and panties knowing what they looked like by heart. Sweaters in a hundred subtle cuts and hues. Silky imported chemises, and devastatingly sexy lace camisoles. The textures soothed her fingers. Supple to the touch. Every ounce an exquisite original, created just for her.

She sank into the petit point chair before the inlaid ebony vanity. "First the perfume," she sobbed, rubbing First Joy, then Bal de Versailles, then Opium onto her trembling skin, covering every inch of her body. "A lady must always have perfume."

"Powder." She picked up the puff and patted it all over her face, then down her neck and breasts. Now the eyeshadow. Her fingers followed the path they had traced a million times. "And mascara. Musn't forget the dramatic touch."

Rouge . . . lashes . . . "Lipstick," she cried, applying the thin pencil with an exaggerating bow motion, then letting it fall onto her chin, tracing a line down her neck as it fell to the ground. She groped for the decanter of scotch, then brought it hungrily to her lips.

"Now shall I wear a Dior? Or maybe a Valentino?"

"*Both,*" she giggled, wriggling into two pairs of silk panties. "A bit of lace." She threw a camisole over her head and slid into it.

"Now for the dress. An evening gown? I can't decide," she grabbed dress after dress, Galanos, Norell, Halston. "No—it's much too early in the morning. And I'm cold, so cold." She stumbled to the closet of furs and ran her trembling hands over them, then began ripping them off of their hangers. One by one she slid them over her shoulders, minks, foxes, sables.

Crawling to the jewelry vault, she threw open the door and grabbed wildly at the rings and necklaces. One by one, the ruby chokers, sapphire pendants, the emerald and diamond bracelets rained down on her. She put them on greedily—her possessions . . .

Pulling herself to her feet, she staggered back to the dressing table, and stared into the lighted mirror, nodding appreciatively. Her hands groped through the top drawer and removed the prescription vials. Seconal, valium, thorazine . . .

She washed the contents down with the remaining scotch.

And now I'm so tired, she yawned groggily. *So tired, and nowhere left to go. Nowhere worthy of Francesca Van Rensalaer.*

She fell back against a clothes rack, clawing desperately to keep her footing. The fabrics sailed off into space, spreading out in a pallet of unseen hues. *Yes,* she nodded, tearing down another handful of clothing, then another. Piling it all in a heap on the floor.

You are my friends, she nodded smiling. *My beautiful, stunning companions. The only true friends I can count on.*

She dropped softly onto the heap of filmy chiffons, silks, velvets, brocades, cashmeres and furs.

And then Francesca slept.

Igor snapped open his eyes as the dawn sunlight flooded his bedroom.

"Francesca," he called into the adjoining room. "Francesca, where is my coffee?" He slipped into his black Gucci dressing gown. "Damn that bitch. Ever since I bought her that Rodeo property, it's been the same story. She knows I like my coffee the moment I wake up."

He headed into the study and briefly scanned the ticker tape. Then he placed a call to the Zurich office, growing more and more impatient. "You heard me," he bellowed at the trembling account clerk on the other side of the Atlantic, "I return tomorrow, and I will have those papers ready."

"Francesca," he roared one last time, then burst out of the office and into her dressing room. "Francesca—what is the meaning of . . ."

He stared at the jumble of clothing and jewelry uncomprehending. Then he saw Francesca—the streaks of lipstick and mascara shooting across her bluish cheeks.

"Darling?" he whispered, staring at the lifeless features. "Answer me. *I'm speaking to you, dammit!*" He leapt to her side and began tossing aside the designer clothes. He shook her shoulders violently, then clutched her cold throat in his hands.

"How could you do this to me? Francesca," he sobbed, "how *could you?*"

His fingers tore at the last layers, until she lay before him naked and still.

"You bitch you bitch you bitch," he screamed, plunging his rigid cock inside her. "Didn't you know that I needed you?" With an anguished groan, he came in a torrent.

Fifty-five

Crystal yanked down the rearview mirror, tired of looking at the clouds of black oily smoke pouring out of her exhaust pipe. And only twenty-four thousand miles on it.

"Just don't make them like they used to," she grimaced, staring at the mangled fenders. "Next time, I go for something a little more practical—and fun, like that sexy Lotus Europa." Considering the fact that she had enough clothes and jewels for now—and the fact that there seemed to be no reason yet to buy an expensive house—maybe it wouldn't be a bad investment. If only there were a way to cut the fender benders down to two or three a year.

She thought of Lauren's expression yesterday as they were driving on the Hollywood Freeway. Crystal wondered if her erratic driving was the reason Lauren had so abruptly dismissed the notion of catching a ride to the station this morning.

Come to think of it, she seemed to have missed the 7 a.m. jogging call as well. No matter. If Killer Conrad was pouting about calling it off with Dr. T, she would bounce back soon enough.

In all probability, Lauren already had the next one lined up, and at the starting gate. Probably that charming Bob Radin—although he had been conspicuously absent in recent days.

"Some people have all the luck," she thought, turning up the RedRock drive and screeching to a halt inches behind CJ's limo.

She walked through the entryway and into the newsroom, for once hours early. A silence blanketed the cavernous room, broken only by the gentle murmur of the wall monitors. Ever since the death of Dale, things had been morosely quiet. Today it was practically a tomb.

She unconsciously slowed her pace, sensing the eyes following her as she moved toward her cubicle beyond the far side of the room.

The thought of a tag dangling conspicuously from her sleeve, or eye shadow smudged on her cheek, flashed briefly into her mind, then vanished. As she rounded the corner and came face-to-face with Winston, she took one glance and knew.

"I tell you we were *working* on the story," Crystal repeated, feeling the mortar of the brick wall before her growing thicker.

"So did Lauren," Sloan shrugged. "I'm sorry. But as things turned out, Channel 3 broke the story first. Put yourself in my position and tell me what *you* would do. I simply cannot jeopardize our ratings . . . This station cannot afford a scandal. Whether it's true or not, everyone will assume that Lauren was covering for Rothmore."

"You can't do this to Lauren!"

"Crystal, I don't know when you became that imperious bitch's Number One fan. Nor do I give a shit. Let me make something plain to you: *I* am the president of this network. My job is not to see that every employee who gets herself involved in a scandal is given a fair public trial. My sole responsibility is to our image. You and I have had our little disagreements in the past. I am willing to let sleeping dogs lie as far as you're concerned. But the fact is my only loyalty is to SBN."

"I simply will not sit idly by while you fire Lauren for your own vindictive reasons."

"Darling, if I were in your position, I wouldn't make threats that have no basis in reality. I may not be able to fill your overflowing 38C cups with Jewel Beale. But let me assure you that she would step into your shoes quite nicely. And there are always a thousand other tall stacked blonds waiting in the wings as well. I have already begun negotiations with Sid Gold concerning a very suitable replacement for Lauren. By next week, we are hoping to launch a new, subtler format, with the team of Brad Canton and Crystal Cooper. Either you start toeing the company line, or we reformat your role right after the transition."

"You may not have to wait that long," Crystal spat out, shaking with rage as she fled from the office.

CJ Redfield stood facing the window wall, bleakly surveying the Hollywood Hills. His direction was clear now.

If Sloan had inherited the blackmail information, preparing to use it, he really had no other option. This afternoon he would tender his resignation to the board, citing "personal reasons"—the health of his wife.

Sloan knew as well as he that Peggy's ailing heart would never survive the traumatic outpouring of the facts. Even if she suspected that Conrad and Cooper had supplied him with the raw data outlining her little profit-sharing scheme, it made little difference. Given a few weeks, she could find a way to clean up the memory files of the computer, obliterating any past descrepancies. Just as he had to do in the first critical months of the Network, when the money for a desperately-needed infusion had to be piped in invisibly, and continually transferred from computer-to-computer. A calculated risk.

But as long as Kikki or his wife remained alive, CJ Redfield would remain vulnerable. Even if they worked out an arrangement now, Sloan could always attack again. In a month, a year—the timing was irrelevant.

If Sloan were smart, then she would realize just how defenseless he was. Because at the moment, with top management tottering for the second time in a year, even firing her was risky. The Satellite Broadcasting Network's image was still shaky. One more changing of the guard might entirely erode investor confidence. Jeopardizing RedRock, by lashing back in retaliation, had always remained out of the question.

"Curious," he mused, "how damned *emotional* the investors get in any operation." The crucial profit operations—buying and selling—always echoed the same irrationality. "Changes in the wind" always brought a dramatic flurry of trading. But with varying results. Even FCC allegations of corruption could trigger a backlash which brought public stock skydiving. If the investors somehow or another *felt* confident about the outcome. Because of an intuition, a gut feeling, company loyalty. So irrational.

He had spent a lifetime studying people. The calm technicians who built up a bulwark of logic based on improbable assumptions. The emotional ones who secretly plotted every breath they took with the precision of a chess grandmaster, labeling it "instinct" or "hunch." After watching Sloan rise to the top through half a dozen years, classification of her category had somehow eluded him.

He felt rather than heard her footsteps as she entered the office. Broad efficent strides, with a touch of jauntiness. Her eyes were boring into his back. Angered by his indifferent authority, but too cautious to launch into an immediate attack.

He shook his head in approval. A wise approach. He probed the silence with his back turned to her, feeling strangely calm. Almost aloof. Was it resignation seeping into his marrow?

She shifted impatently behind him, drawing an anxious breath.

How to begin? He stared at the good luck ten-dollar gold piece his father had charged him to keep always in the office. Silly superstition. Heads we play it safe. A quiet, orderly agreement, with a letter of intent. Tails we try one last ditch effort, then prepare to retreat if it fails.

He grinned boyishly as the coin sailed end over end in a two foot arc, falling neatly into his left palm. Tails up.

Sloan opened her mouth to suck in air once more, then cleared her throat and began to speak.

"What the hell have you done?" he roared, spinning with startling ferocity, and knocking her off guard.

Her face fell briefly, then regained its composure. "Let's not get into an emotional shouting match," she parried. "It was a regrettable decision. But as president of the network, it was mine to make. I felt it was necessary to remove Lauren before the publicity dragged down the entire news show. Her connection with Rothmore is all too well known. I thought I made that perfectly clear in my memo."

"Unfortunately, it has not been borne out by the facts. Take a look at this morning's papers, or videotapes of the news on any of the local stations or national networks. I don't see any mention of her name. And if the allegations you make are so well known, I find their omission astounding. In a town where every peck on the cheek is grist for the rumor mill, I can hardly believe that they could ignore a connection like this. Particularly if it were half as juicy as you seem to think. You know that I find cheap sexual innuendo personally offensive. But when an executive of my network acts on such hearsay and fires a valuable asset, it is totally inexcusable."

"So you fixed it? *Didn't* you? How much did it cost the network this time?"

"I will not stand for such accusations, Sloan. Especially not from you."

"Oh yes you will, CJ. And I've got a lot more to say—to the Board. Starting with the fact that you never really intended to broadcast the media probe. You wasted millions of dollars and a chance to break into the heights of the Big Three. And not just to save that adolescent princess of Crystal."

"That's absurd!"

"No it isn't. You executed every possible maneuver to stall it. Pushing back the broadcast date time and again. Tearing up each successive promo campaign and changing the focus five different times. Just to keep the *Tribune* from publishing the material. All the while buying time, while you tried to figure out how to defuse Rob. It was all useless."

"So you've found me out, have you?" His tone was belligerent. Mocking. He saw the anger mounting behind her eyes, and smiled.

"Don't force me to do it, CJ."

"You wouldn't dare," he challenged. Prodding her more.

"You know I would." She laughed nervously. "And I'm *sure* this is one story they *won't* sell. Not at any price. It's got so much *human interest.*"

He sank gently into the chair behind his desk, eyes locked with hers. The burnished leather creaked softly. Behind Sloan, Calvin Jennings Redfield waited stoically, his face drawn and unearthly pale.

Her eyes shone more fiercely, pinning him to the chair, as a victorious smile crossed her lips. He felt the power slowly being drained out of him. "Retreat," Calvin ordered, his voice touched with pleading. "Don't sacrifice the family for a stupid suicide plunge. Think of Margaret."

He nodded. He had always intended to bring Kikki home someday. Once Margaret had finally succumbed. With all danger past, she could move quietly back to the seclusion of the Pacific Palisades. He could maintain his seat on the board. And maybe five years down the road—or ten—he could try it once again. He tossed aside the Schwartz dossier and smiled resignedly.

Then he saw Sloan's eyes drop as a flicker of doubt crossed her features. He knew then that she was bluffing, and he had won.

"Then do it," he hissed, pressing a button hidden underneath his desk. Taped voices began bombarding the room and bouncing off the walls.

"Of course I'm sure of it, CJ. We've got the evidence right here. Dates, times, computer entries and exits. Signed documents from bank officials in Bermuda and Zurich, attesting to the fact that the account belongs to Sloan Schwartz. Joint holding with Rob . . ."

". . . Of course, I would," Jewel's syrupy voice echoed, *"if you really think that it's necessary. If it'll help, I'll even go into explicit detail. How Sloan sexually assulted me in her Rolls in the parking lot of the Beverly Hills Hotel. How she and her live-in secretary deal in cocaine parties, to feed her hundred-dollar-a-day habit . . ."*

"Yes, it's true, Miss Schwartz has been paying me to keep my mouth shut about Steinholtz's death."

"As Sloan's psychiatrist of twenty years, I can attest to what you're saying. Not just the heavy drug dependency, but the periods of tremendous emotional

depression. The institutionalizations throughout her adolescence . . ."

"That's . . . crazy. They're all lies, CJ." She stared terrified at the now silent walls. "You're accusing me of drug dealing and murder . . . Everyone knows that . . ."

"Just like they know about Lauren?" He buzzed the intercom and stared right through her. "It's funny, Sloan. You know, I just signed your fifteen per cent merit raise yesterday afternoon. Not only that, but I happen to be holding a bonus check for you: $50,000. And I know just how much you need it. I'll tell you something else amusing: you disgust me. I hold you in personal contempt, I think of you as the scum of the earth, a pervert.

"You're finished, Sloan, not just here, but in the entire industry. If you know what's good for you, you'll get out of the country—for good. Your office locks have already been changed. In fact, as far as I'm concerned, you've never even existed.

"But there's one last thing you had better understand before you go. Power. You see, my dear. I can put a bullet through your head on Sunset Boulevard in the middle of the afternoon, and no one will ever admit to seeing it. Within a half an hour, a dozen unimpeachable sources will say they've seen me in Palm Springs, or Pacific Palisades. Or even the moon. And no one will ever question it.

"Questions are counter-productive, Sloan. I want you to keep that in mind." The outer door hissed open and his personal chauffeur stepped in, eyes burning with bloodlust and his massive body ready to attack.

"If you have any additional questions, you may discuss them with Thomas on the way out."

She stared blankly at the network head, her face a death-like mask.

Sloan Schwartz slowly walked through the

zebrawood doors for the last time.

Crystal rode up the elevator, casually noting the scratches which had appeared on the glass doors over the months. In time, they would have to be replaced, just like everything and everyone else at RedRock.

For Conrad and Cooper, the end had come just a little bit sooner. Somehow, the thought of mortality wasn't as comforting as she had hoped.

The decision had taken only fifteen minutes. But the question of *how* to quit had taken two hours. Eventually, she had decided to do it immediately, giving the month's notice required before her year's contract ended. Four weeks in which to give the tightest, straightest reporting the nation had ever seen. Or at least her viewers. Ironically, just this morning their Q recognition ratings had hopped up another point and Deena was negotiating for a five-year renewal starting at $300,000 a year with options. At least this time, she would have no trouble landing another anchor job. If there were any real ones left to be had.

Whatever loyalty she felt toward Lauren, it was only the straw that had broken the camel's back. The final, unavoidable sign that the RedRock management had totally abandoned any pretense of responsibility to their audience. With Dale and Lauren gone, there was no one left to fight for the "Now News" concept. As soon as her replacement was signed on, they would be free to run the news like one more sit-com, lots of smiles with nothing behind them.

Maybe Sloan was right, and the audience just ogled her bosom and ignored the rest. Maybe they even thought of her as a dizzy blond. It made her Last Stand seem pretty lame and self-destructive.

Somehow, her image no longer seemed to matter. That was something for the Imagus experts to worry about. Even more than the recognition, money and the perqs, Crystal thrived on the feeling of contributing something. Giving her all and feeling that it somehow made a difference.

Maybe it didn't matter in Hollywood. There were a million Dr. Clark Fieldings out here, convinced that the old values were just one more computer program, waiting to be updated. But maybe somewhere, on PBS or even a small local station, there was an audience who cared about getting the straight, undiluted stuff. Viewers who would look beyond her appearance, and discern between filler and facts.

The double doors opened and she nodded briskly to Barbara, noting that the dread Front Desk had for once made no move to intercept her. Ironic.

Bursting through the inner door, she held out the signed letter and quietly announced, "CJ, I quit." Then she noticed Lauren sitting on the couch looking as radiant and confident as ever. Before Crystal had a chance to react, her partner sprang up from her seat laughing. She threw her arms around the bewildered Crystal, "Honey, I'll never forget your marching in here like a sacrificial lamb for me. You may not believe it, but I would have done the same for you. Everything's o.k., we're a team again! Tell her, CJ." The two women collapsed on the couch together, laughing, crying and hugging, while CJ Redfield looked on paternally.

Fifty-six

Joel and Crystal walked arm-in-arm across the sand looking at the brilliant stars so close they could almost touch them.

"Christmas in California," she mused. "I'd like to reach up and grab a handful of those stars to hang on my tree and then put them away to take out next year."

"Did you reach Marcie?" Joel's voice was unusually concerned.

"Left a message with the butler. She was attending someone's coming out party." She shrugged and tried to focus on the perfect night. The kind which kept people flocking to Southern California. And staying there in spite of lost dreams or faded hopes.

Tonight, Joel was quiet, almost reflective. His smooth bantering charm and cocky arrogance had been swept aside, revealing a kind of gentle warmth she had never seen in him.

A chill suddenly crept up her legs even though the air was balmy. As if trying to ward off some premonition, she pulled him closer to her. He opened his jacket and threw it around her shoulders. Sliding her arms around his waist, she raised her lips to his.

He pressed into her and ran his fingers through her tangled curls, then gently brought her down beside him on the damp sand.

"I love you." He kissed her again, letting his tongue probe the warm depth of her mouth. Abruptly he turned away, and stared at the black ocean.

". . . But it's just not enough to keep me here, not any more. I spoke to United Artists today. The picture is dead. So is the pilot script I did for Radin. I can keep writing lifestyle articles and reviews for second-rate magazines. It's easy enough to get by. I know you've been looking at houses in Beverly Hills and Bel Air. And I guess that's great, if it's really what you want. It's just not for me. I hate the phoniness, the smiles turned on like switches. I guess I'm just sick of glitter. The cost is too high."

She felt the chill slowly seeping into her bones. "I wouldn't want to live in Malibu Colony year round. But between your place and a house in town, I really think we could manage okay. I've done some cold-eyed figuring, and I can easily swing it. I'm liberated, you know. I don't care who earns the money. I love you Joel, not your pocketbook, and my raise is going to help assure us a comfortable life. I know it's just a matter of time before your novel hits the right editor. In the meantime you could devote your full-time to finishing it."

"I can't, Crystal."

"Joel, I need you! Honey, I can afford it. The Lotus can wait a year."

"It's not just money. I feel stifled by your lifestyle. I've got to be free."

He stared down at nothingness and shook his head. "I rented the beach house today to a New Yorker. For a year. It was time for a change."

She felt the blow coming and braced for it. "How much of a change?"

"I took that teaching job in London. I start in two weeks." He suddenly brightened. "You told me you always wanted to tour the Continent . . . I want you to come with me."

"I'm a lousy cook," she sighed. "Mom always told me I was a lousy cook."

"We'll eat out then. Mixed grill, steak and kidney pies. Broiled bacon and soggy chips with vinegar . . ."

". . . But I do make a mean pot of tea. I had a recipe for scones somewhere . . . Once . . ."

"We'll have three weeks between terms. Just think of it: Copenhagen, Paris, Rome, Aachen, where Charlemagne was crowned Holy Roman Emperor. Amsterdam, Spain . . ."

". . . the Riviera. I always dreamed of going to the Riviera . . ."

". . . Don't forget the bullfights in Madrid . . ."

"How could I?" She rolled onto him giggling and took his face into her hands. "We'll rent a cold-water flat and buy a Cheshire cat. I'll knit sweaters and type your manuscript . . ."

Her tears flowed down onto his cheeks, mingling with the slow steady stream from his eyes. "Joel, my poor darling Joel who won't grow up. Don't you realize that we're not two love-struck kids in our twenties, just starting up on life's big adventure? I'm thirty-five-years old. And you're nearly forty. We can't just fly out the window like Peter Pan and Wendy, and play at life like it's one big fairy tale . . . At least, I can't."

"I may be impractical and a dreamer. But I never pretended to be anything else. I can't live your life. I've got to find my own way." He buried his head in the warmth of her breasts and sobbed. "You're the most wonderful, exciting woman I'll ever find. And I love you, Crystal Cooper, at least you know that."

Nodding, she pulled him tighter, feeling the damp night chill bite into her flesh, while she clung to his warmth like a swimmer enveloped by the sea, going down for the last time. "Joel, I need you so much."

The wind lashed into them, whistling above the pounding surf. In the distance, Christmas carols and the clink of glasses and laughter wafted above the waves.

They made love passionately on the beach, their tears mingling with the stinging sand.

Fifty-seven

"Crystal Cooper here," she mumbled groggily.

"I'd never know it from the frog in your throat. You never use the throaty growl on the broadcast. I kind of like it. Anyway, it's time to get your middleaged ass out of bed. I've already made our reservation at the Polo Lounge. And Elizabeth Arden or not, you're going to meet me at twelve o'clock. Sharp. I've got some *incredible* news."

Lauren plopped back into Bob Radin's king-sized four-poster and stretched languorously. "The hell with jogging," she giggled, wrapping her arms around the sleeping giant. "We've gotten enough exercise in the last few nights to last me a month. Or at least until tonight."

Crystal's baby blue BMW sputtered to a halt beneath the concrete porte cochere.

Beside Smitty, Lauren stood with her arms folded across her chest.

Crystal launched out of her car and into an apology. "I'm sorry. I really tried to be on time. But I ran into . . ."

Lauren's eyes flashed down to her new wafer-thin Piaget. "Don't even attempt an apology," she laughed. "I'd faint if you were ever on time."

Taking Crystal's arm she turned and walked up the

runway carpet, nodding at the familiar faces as she spun through the revolving door.

In spite of the Arden beauty analyst's assurances, Crystal felt as though her tear-saturated cheeks were puffed an inch beyond her face. Her shoulders refused to stop sagging. She ordered her legs to keep moving, with confident sparkling steps. Effortlessly, just as Lauren had. But each motion seemed to cut into her.

Instead of feeling like a sensuous siren of the airwaves, Crystal felt like the little mermaid in the Danish fairytale. The one doomed to spend her days on the land with each step stinging like a thousand knife slashes.

With well-practiced indifference, the two women ignored the fawning stares of the papparazzi, and the hostile glances of the young starlets stranded outside the doorway of the Polo Lounge, waiting for a table.

"Ah. *There* you are," Walter beamed with outstretched arms. He ushered them in to the center of the room, and hovered long enough to light Lauren's Sobranie. "For a moment, I thought you might stand me up. And when I've been saving you the *numero uno table,* too."

Rushing over, the waiter plunked two glasses of Perrier with a twist of lime onto the table. "Ze usual, mesdames?"

"Mais naturellement," Lauren responded. "Crys?"

"Sure. That's great."

All around them was the familiar easy hype and chatter, the knowing nods and telling smiles. Even after coming here a hundred times, Crystal still couldn't quite shake the feeling that it really was what it appeared to be. And that the lives of the Polo Lounge crowd were also what they advertised: luxuriant, successful, filled with blase acceptance and unshakable power. Although she was friendly with a quarter of the gathered elite, and sitting beside Lauren, Crystal had never felt more alone in her life.

"Your Perrier can't be that interesting," Lauren gently prodded. "I've never seen you like this before. Two minutes, and you haven't even really checked out the crowd. Even *I* noticed Redford holding court back there in the corner. And I think I just caught a glimpse of Meryl Streep out on the Loggia."

"Sorry," Crystal murmured, feeling her stomach still tied up in knots. Her head was pounding, and she felt the nausea starting again. "Maybe it's the flu," she thought, almost hopefully. She could go to bed and pull the covers over her head. Take a few aspirin and wake up in a day or two, refreshed and painless.

"Haven't you even been listening?" Lauren prodded gently, "I was asking about that shrink you went to see?"

"Who could ever forget."

"He was right. Isn't there *anyone* you don't worry about? Francesca's suicide, Winston's identity crisis. When CJ is going to turn the information about Sloan over to the cops . . ."

"You know, that still doesn't sit right on me. I mean, protecting the network's public image is fine. And he explained the whole thing. About how much the investors would be hurt by a major scandal. Jeopardizing the ratings. But to let her just walk off scot-free with over a hundred thousand dollars—even if she does leave the country."

"Don't change the topic. We're talking about Crystal Cooper, and the Mother Hen Complex. Don't you think it's time for you to start thinking of Number One? Joel's a perfect example. I'll bet you spend an hour a day worrying about *his* feelings, *his* ego. *His* . . ."

"Not anymore, Lauren. We broke up last night."

"Don't tell me he pulled that number again. Crystal,

don't get sucked in. That's the third time he's . . ."

Crystal's face fell. She felt the icy air clawing at her. The sound of the surf pounding in her temples. "He's moving to England. In a week."

"I'm sorry honey. Guess I really put my foot in my mouth this time. Do you want to . . . talk about it? I mean, I may not be the best listener in the world, but . . . but I really want to help," Lauren responded gently as she reached for Crystal's hand.

"Thanks anyway," Crystal shook her head, burying her gaze in the platter of Eggs Benedict as she waited for the teariness to subside.

Funny how things have turned out, Lauren thought, nodding to Ed MacMahon as he swept through the ritual round of table-hopping. *Sitting in the Polo Lounge across from Crystal, and actually caring. You never* really *hated her in the first place. But who would have thought she'd turn out to be the closest thing to a friend I ever had?*

Across the table, Crystal was still staring blankly into her plate, as her fork occasionally dipped and pretended to chase a bit of Hollandaise. Lauren watched her friend with a feeling of helplessness. "Damn that bastard," she fumed to herself. "He's not worth one of her gold chains." She looked at the curly blond head wondering how to snap Crystal out of this depression. Try as she had as of late, she still wasn't great at communicating at an emotional level. Years of repression were hard to overcome, though the genuine sympathy she felt for her partner was a sign that the layers of armour were peeling away.

"Well, we're certainly scintillating this afternoon," Lauren finally laughed. "Maybe we should talk about the weather. Or how about this evening's broadcast? I haven't seen the footage of CJ's address to the NAB, but

Holly says it's terrific. She'll never measure up to Dale, but so far I *am* impressed. In the meantime, there's the space shuttle fiasco, the assassination of . . ."

"I could've sworn that there was some burning reason for this lunch. This morning when I spoke to you on the phone, you sounded like . . ."

"We'll talk about it later." After Crystal's announcement, it was hardly the time for a celebration. "Nothing pressing."

"Except for my reporter's intuition. I may be feeling a little under the weather this afternoon, but I am not blind. Something big is going on beneath those aggravatingly nonchalant eyes of yours. Now either you come clean of your own volition, or else I *pry* it out of you."

"I just didn't want to mention it now. Just when you told me about Joel."

"More bad news?"

"Hardly. It's about Bob. We're getting married."

"That's fantastic." She leapt across the table and hugged Lauren, almost knocking over her glass. "The best news I've heard you report in weeks."

"When's the wedding? Where's it going to be held? . . . *Waiter, may we please have a bottle of Dom Perignon?* . . . I'm so excited I can't believe it! Lauren Conrad getting married! How in hell did you get that hunk to pop the question? What did he say? . . ."

"Slow down, partner. I told you we only decided a few days ago. We haven't even thought about the details."

"Well then, you better make something up, and fast. *I* am not about to be scooped by *anyone* on this story. It's going on tonight, whether you like it or not."

"Sorry. Hope you'll forgive me for being so forward . . ." called a distinctively British voice over Lauren's shoulder. "But my name is Sir Collin Booth. Perhaps you're familiar with . . ."

"The Collin Booth?" Crystal squealed. "I've been a

fan of yours for years. By all means *do* sit down. We were just about to celebrate . . ." Her words evaporated as she saw him lock eyes with Lauren.

"I've always found your work so *haunting*," Lauren murmured, leaning forward as she turned on the charm. *Maybe his clothes were a bit old-fashioned, but those eyes . . . Sir Collin Booth. It was a name she had been fascinated with for years. . . .*

"Aren't you forgetting something, Lauren," Crystal said pointedly.

"Perhaps you're not aware of it," Lauren purred on, "but there are a lot of devoted fans of yours here. I've always found something so . . . *provocative* about your films. A certain undefinable sensuousness." She flashed him a seductive smile and tossed her mane back haughtily, feeling a rush of excitement as he snapped at the lure. She reeled him in slowly, allowing him to lean closer as she dropped her voice.

Crystal was amused at Lauren's usual reaction. *Well, from now on there'll be no more of that competition,* she thought. *As of today, the field is wide open. And you, Ms. Lauren Conrad of Now News, are out of commission in the man chasing department.*

Beaming her radiant smile, Crystal shot her leg under the table and allowed her toe to sink into Lauren's knee. Gently enough to let the point sink in. "Didn't I just hear you paged?"

Lauren's eyes registered amused understanding. "What are you *talking* about? Walter would have brought the phone over to the . . ."

Crystal shook her head determinedly. "I distinctly heard him mention a call for you. From *Bob Radin.*"

"Oh." Lauren nodded giggling. "In that case, maybe I'd better go see . . ." She shot Crystal a broad wink as she headed for the exit.

"Give him my love, will you darling?" . . . Crystal

turned back to the British director and continued. "I've always thought it would be wonderful to do a story on British films. You know in Hollywood, there's a very one-sided view of what the movies are all about . . . But judging from your work . . ."

"It's such an enormous difference, I shouldn't know where to begin. Perhaps if you're free for dinner some night this week?"

"I always make time for my work."

"Then perhaps I'll have to try to focus on . . ."

But don't try too hard, she thought, as his eyes melted into hers.

Redfield mounted the stage and headed for the podium, feeling his elation soar as the audience roared with applause.

A year-and-a-half earlier, the National Association of Broadcasters had rippled with laughter when a speaker mentioned the name RedRock. The Big Three had fought the FCC application tooth-and-nail, leaned on his advertisers, tried to lure the Satellite Broadcasting Network's affilate UHF stations out from under him.

Even the Writer's Guild had done their share, suing for inadequate copyright compensation from the superstation. Tonight, even the strikes and boardroom battles were a million light years away. At long last, they had all accepted the inevitable and reluctantly agreed to his terms for peaceful coexistence. Sealing it with the invitation to be a keynote speaker at the NAB convention.

He looked out into the audience and smiled as the house lights dimmed.

"Ladies and gentleman, first of all let us congratulate ourselves on the finest television programming in the history of our industry this year. On behalf of the Satellite Broadcasting Network, I would like to thank the . . . 'Other Three' . . ."

tured, I always felt I had to finish him, it helps you
know how much your friends love more to me — even
though I don't let it show nearly often enough.
Crystal started to wander over to a window.

Fifty-eight

Lauren and Crystal stood before the glass bedroom wall in Bob Radin's hilltop house. The sun cast a golden haze over the spectacular view as it slowly lowered beyond the hills.

"The guests will be arriving any minute," Crystal announced nervously as she fumbled with the tiny pearl buttons on Lauren's pale peach *crêpe de chine* Halston.

"Take it easy, Crys," teased Lauren. "I'm the one who should be nervous — I'm the bride."

Crystal looked at her former rival with genuine warmth and more than a little awe. Lauren had never looked more beautiful. Her blond hair was pulled back and caught with a garland of peach colored tea roses and white baby's breath. Her handkerchief-hemmed long-sleeved dress skimmed the slender body in understated elegance. Her only accessories were delicate peach satin sandals and the exquisite diamond necklace which had been a gift from Bob.

"Jesus, Lauren," Crystal sighed as she smoothed her Holly Harp chiffon print. "Don't you ever lose your cool?" Lauren hugged her affectionately.

"You of all people should know the answer to that, Crystal. I really don't know how I would have gotten through the last year without you. Thank God you had enough insight to see beneath that armoured front I always felt I had to hide behind. I hope you know how much your friendship means to me—even though I don't let it show nearly often enough."

Crystal noticed in amazement the tears welling in her partner's amber eyes—and struggled to contain her own brimming lids. "I'll be damned if I'll ruin my eye makeup even for you, Lauren Conrad!" she parried tearily.

Walking into the mirror-lined dressing room she studied her reflection with approval. "Still got a few good years left, old girl," she chuckled to herself. Her eyes focused on the delicate emerald earrings Joel had given her before he left. "Even emeralds can't outshine your eyes," he had told her. Annoyed with herself, she brushed all thoughts of Joel out of her mind and proceeded to repair her tear-stained makeup.

Lauren continued to watch the approaching sunset. Her mind wandered back to that day so many years ago when they told her that her mother was dead. She remembered the hopeless feeling of knowing there was no one left who really loved her and how she had vowed, even as a little girl, never to let anyone know that it mattered. "Thank you, Crystal and Bob, for helping me break through that self-destructive facade," she whispered.

The continual sound of the door chimes reminded her that it was almost time. In a few minutes her entire life would change. Oh sure, she would still be the imperious Lauren Conrad, one half of the famous Conrad and Cooper newsteam. But now she would have someone to share her life with, forever—

The sun glowed crimson against a darkening sky. "I think at thirty-three I've finally grown up," she thought as the strains of Mendelssohn's wedding music floated through the room. The image of Ted flashed briefly her mind—and out just as quickly. "I've never been so sure of anything in my life," she marveled silently. "This is where I belong."

"Lauren, you're going to miss your own wedding," Crystal exclaimed as she bounded back into the bedroom.

The two women looked at each other, both remembering the traumas and craziness of the past year.

"I'm so happy for you, Lauren," Crystal whispered. "I can't say I don't wish I had someone like Bob to whisk me away on a white horse—or at least in a silver Mercedes—but it took me a long time to find—"

"You will also have the famous Lauren Conrad Radin as your best friend and co-conspirator against the world," Lauren grinned as she pulled Crystal towards the door.

At that moment a buoyant Bob Radin entered with Lauren's bouquet of roses and lilacs. He gathered the two women in a bear hug. "Now which one of you is the bride," he teased. "I can't seem to remember so maybe I'll just marry you both!"

"Oh no you won't," Lauren laughed. "I'll share the spotlight on camera with this blond bombshell—but I'll be damned if I'll share it under the covers."

They giggled hilariously and walked down the hall towards the waiting guests.

"My dear, dear friends," the Reverend Gearheart's voice boomed to the gathered throng, "we are gathered here today to celebrate . . ."

"Isn't it just too beautiful," Violet gushed, staring up at her new protege, a darkly handsome young Latin model. Her face was smooth and unlined, thanks to the face lift and peel she managed to include in the plastic surgery needed for repairs after her scene with Rick. "Breathtaking," he agreed, eyeing Crystal's bosom swelling over the decolleté Holly Harp.

Winston gazed enviously at the glowing bride and groom; knowing if he ever found someone to share his life with it would be a very different kind of ceremony. At least he had come to terms with his homosexuality and gotten out of the drug scene—and away from Elliot.

Since Francesca's death several months before, Igor had kept pretty much to himself. This was his first appearance at a social gathering. To everyone's surprise he had arrived with a beautiful Italian contessa, almost a double for a young Francesca. Crystal's stomach lurched as she noticed the girl was wearing Francesca's prized sable cape and the diamond and ruby tiara that had been Igor's wedding gift to Francesca, so long ago.

". . . By the authority vested in me by the state of California," Gearhardt intoned, "I now pronounce you husband and wife."

Eyes overflowing, Crystal handed the wide pavé diamond wedding band to Bob and he slipped it on Lauren's waiting finger.

For one long moment they gazed into each other's eyes—then they embraced and kissed passionately as if there were no one else in the room.

The crowd began moving out to the tented pool area where masses of peach-colored roses and white lilacs filled the air with fragrance. A dance floor covered the pool and the clear skylight of the tenting allowed the guests to dance under a sparkling clear star-filled sky.

CJ Redfield watched the bridal couple as they recited their vows. How he would have loved seeing his Kikki radiant and happy. Standing beside a man who would cherish and care for her the way he had Margaret for all these years. But that wasn't in the cards. He had gambled and won in more contests than he could remember. The toughest challenge had been

Sloan. Even her shrewd back-handed maneuverings had been no match for CJ's steely resolve. He had always been lucky in calling the roll of the dice—but had his luck run out with his precious Kikki?

His gaze moved to include Crystal who stood to Lauren's left, her eyes brimming with tears as she listened to the ceremony. "Another gamble," he silently acknowledged. "The industry would have laughed me out of town if my female anchor team hadn't clicked. It would have taken Now News years to recover in the ratings." As usual, the Redfield instinct had been sound.

"I knew from the minute I laid eyes on those two that they were winners," he breathed with a self-satisfied sigh. "Not only did they set the industry on its ear professionally, but then Conrad manages to land the town's most sought-after bachelor. Radin's got himself a handful there—but I have a feeling he can handle it. Matter-of-fact, it could be a hell of a good thing to have him in the SBN family. Maybe it's time for us to branch out into film production—who knows, after that maybe a heavy block of stock in the *Tribune.*"

A flush of color seeped into CJ's face. His eyes, reflecting a haunted sadness, sparkled with the challenge of a new conquest.

Thousands of tapered candles shimmered in flower-wrapped candelabras.

A fifteen-foot table draped in peach damask overflowed with fresh lobster and shrimp, mounds of the best Beluga caviar, exotic fruits, imported patés, delicately glazed baby smoked turkeys and chafing dishes filled with assorted hot hors d'oeuvres. In one corner, a white gloved chef carved char broiled fillets and imported ham. A bevy of impeccably uniformed waiters circulated taking drink orders, pouring Dom Perginon and passing silver trays.

Dance music flowed from an eight piece band on a side lawn.

Shortly after the ceremony the wedding party was joined by the large group invited for the reception. Truly the "A" group of Hollywood's television and movie crowd turning out to celebrate with two of their own.

Lauren surveyed the glittering celebrities from her place beside Bob in the informal receiving line.

"You've finally made it to the top, old girl," she thought to herself wryly. "For so many years of chasing one rainbow after another you finally found the pot of gold. You're one of them now—at the top of the heap. You reached for the stars and caught them." For a moment the old defiant hauteur flashed in Lauren's eyes as she wondered, "but could there be even more beyond the stars?" The idea vanished as Bob encircled her warmly in his arms.

"The limo is waiting," Crystal called from across the patio.

Lauren had just finished changing into her traveling outfit. It may not have been practical for a long flight to Paris but she looked smashing. She had removed the floral garland and allowed her hair to fall softly to her shoulders, held on each side by an eighteen karat gold Cartier clip. Her light weight wool crêpe suit was the same tawny shade as her hair. The matching blouse was shot through with bronze and softly bowed at the neck. Diamond earrings sparkled at her ears. The two-hundred-fifty dollar bronze stacked heel pumps that Crystal had insisted she buy complemented the outfit perfectly. A matching cape edged with sable draped casually over her shoulder.

"Lauren," Crystal bellowed, "everyone's waiting!"

She grabbed her bouquet and hurried to the gate

where Bob and the remaining guests were assembled.

Suddenly rice was showering them and everyone was blowing kisses and waving.

She saw Crystal at the edge of the group, smiling pensively. "Crys," she called before getting into the gaily decorated limousine. Their eyes met across the crowd as Lauren tossed the bouquet into her partner's waiting hands. With a wink, they blew each other a kiss.

It was cold driving to the ocean at night. Crystal maneuvered the sleek silver Lotus to a stop and stepped out on a cliff overlooking the beach. She watched the sunset glow red and swirl in the mist above the endless roof of the string of Malibu Beach cottages.

An eternity ago, she had huddled in one of those at dawn, with a struggling writer's arms surrounding her. The memory of Joel flickered briefly through her mind, then gave way to the multitude of emotions flooding through her.

She smiled with bittersweet nostalgia as she reminisced over the past hectic year.

Who would have thought it was Lauren who would wind up with garlands in her hair! And with a fabulous man holding her lovingly, reciting his wedding vows, ready to share his life with her.

"Where did it all go wrong with me?" she asked the lone seagull who had perched on the rock above her. First Stephen Benjamin, then Adam Ward, then Joel. Maybe Dr. Fielding was right. She was looking for the father who had deserted her, and she unconsciously always picked the wrong men. It was time to erase the old tapes and make new ones.

She was stronger now. She smiled and threw a pebble into the inky water, watching the circles it made spread out and out until they disappeared. Life was like those circles, she reflected. It expanded and flowed and kept moving in ever wider circles until it ended. What would her life be like a year from now? she wondered. As soon as Marcie finished her therapy, she would come to stay. They would buy a beautiful house in Beverly Hills. Crystal was caught in her reverie.

Maybe somewhere out there beyond the hills, behind the canyons, under the blanket of stars, one man was waiting for her. A man with old-fashioned values. A strong steady man who could see behind her glamorous facade to the lonely woman underneath.

Crystal shook her head, frightening the gull away, "It doesn't matter," she exulted to the night. She jumped up and stretched her arms to the beckoning stars, filling her lungs with the clean ocean air. She felt renewed, refreshed, infused with new life.

All the uncertainty and yearning of the past year was behind. She felt strong, sure. "I have my career, my family, my friends, my dreams. But best of all, I have myself."

Crystal sank back into her Lotus, reveling in the sleek luxury surrounding her. She felt protected and warm. The car was a symbol of her achievement and she savored this moment in it.

Then she turned on the ignition, put the Lotus in gear and eagerly raced back towards the city, ready to seize the new day.

Teddi Sanford and Mickie Silverstein are a Peabody Award-winning broadcast team and have co-hosted their own radio and television programs in Atlanta, Philadelphia, and Los Angeles.

As the first female broadcasting team, Mickie and Teddi have been featured in leading publications such as *Time* and *Cosmopolitan*. They have made numerous television appearances as guests on *The Today Show*, Johnny Carson's *Tonight Show*, *Phil Donahue*, and *The Tomorrow Show*. Their journalistic credits include monthly columns for *New Woman* magazine and *Coronet* magazine in addition to many articles for west-coast publications such as *Los Angeles* magazine. NUMBER ONE SUNSET BLVD. is their second book.

Teddi and Micki reside with their families in Los Angeles.